Dog
Eat
Dog

The Lycan Files: Book 9

JP Cameron

A fitting book to be dedicated
To my three older brothers.
Mark, Matthew (sometimes known as Jamie)
And Simon.

Closer than pack at times,
But more often further apart
Than this Realm and the Real.

I could not ask for more fitting sources for
three troublesome troll brethren.

Thanks.
You know what for.

Copyright © 2021 JP Cameron

All rights reserved

ISBN: 9798387557309

Imprint: Independently published

Books in the Series:

Dog Days

Puppy Love

The Furry and the Furious

Barking Mad

Let Sleeping ~~Dogs~~ Gods Lie

Old Dog, New Tricks

Dogs of War

Double Dog Dare

Dog Eat Dog

Gone To The Dogs

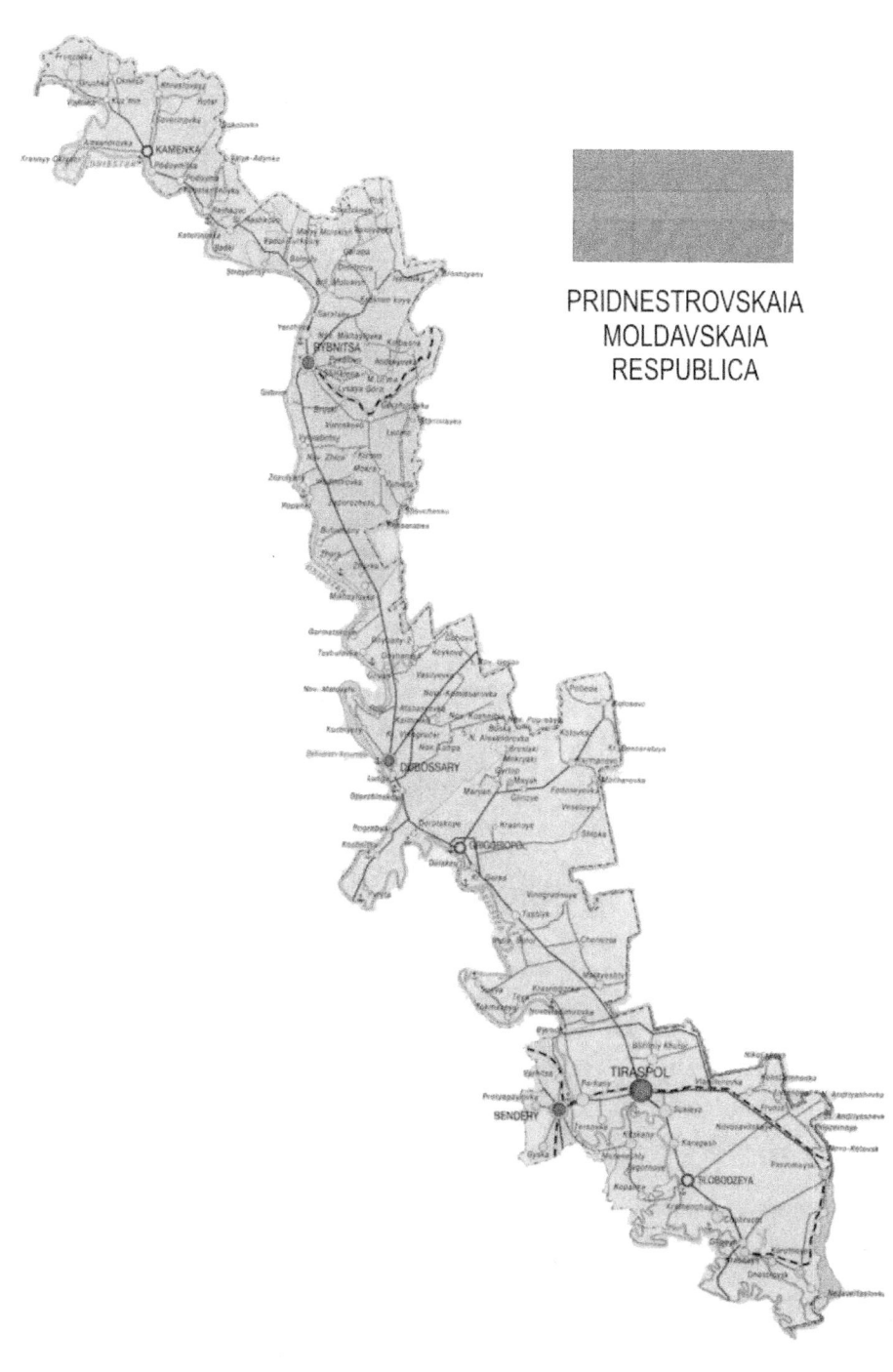

PRIDNESTROVSKAIA
MOLDAVSKAIA
RESPUBLICA

Sites you might find of Interest

Bendery Fortress

This is an over 600 year old fortification overlooking the river on the main road between Tiraspol and Chisinau. The land around the west of the fortress is still used by the army however currently mostly as a store for vehicles. You can enter the fortress now from the south, where a nice looking entry and huge park have recently been constructed. In the park, you will find the new Alexender Nevsky church and a small museum with different kinds of military equipment found in the region).

Inside the fortress are many real historical cannons, trebuchet replicas, and a museum to the Swedish-Ottoman conflict over the fort. There is also a souvenir shop, a museum of medieval torture instruments, shooting range (for crossbows), historical dress-up and a small cafe with toilet facilities. The fortress is currently being renovated, however it is safe to access most parts of the walls and at the entrance of the fortress you can climb the tower providing nice views over the surrounding area, the Dniester river and the newly built park around the Alexender Nevsky church.

Chitcani Monastery

Noul Neamț Monastery is an all-male Moldovan Orthodox monastery located in Chițcani, near Bender and Tiraspol. The name (which means "New Neamț" in English) signifies that the monastery is a successor of the Neamț Monastery in medieval Moldavia.

The monastery was founded in 1861, when several monks from the Neamț monastery left and founded Noul-Neamț in Chițcani. The founding of the new monastery was a protest against the measures taken in United Principalities of Romania to confiscate monastery estates and forbid the usage of Slavonic language in worship. At the time, Chițcani, like all of Bessarabia, was part of the Russian Empire since 1812.

On 16 May 1962 Soviet authorities closed the monastery; the buildings became a hospital.

The monastery church was reopened in 1989, followed in 1991 by the Romanian-language school for Orthodox priests, under the leadership of Wincenty Morari, bishop of Bender.

Suvorov Square and Monument

The square as it is understood was formed at the end of the 18th century, almost immediately after Tiraspol gained the status of a city and a district center. In 1798, in the area of the current City Palace of Culture, a wooden Pokrovskaya single-faith church was built. At the beginning of the 19th century, a stone church was built in a new place (GDK square). In place of the central part of Suvorov Square, a bridge was built across the river that flows into the Dniester. The bridge connected the western and eastern parts of the city and existed until the reconstruction of the center of Tiraspol in the 1970s.

In 1912, at the entrance to the bridge, on the west side, a Arc de Triomphe was installed in honor of the 100th anniversary of the victory in the Patriotic War. A chapel-monument to Tsar Alexander II was erected n Pokrovskaya Square. In Soviet times, Pokrovskaya Square was renamed the Stalin Constitution Square, and later the Square of the Soviet Constitution. Since the 1970s, the square began to take on recognizable features: the majestic Memorial of Glory was built and in 1979 an equestrian monument to Suvorov was erected, which became the symbol of the city. In 1992, in connection with the celebration of the 200th anniversary of Tiraspol and to commemorate the special role commander Alexander Suvorov had in the founding of the city, the square acquired its current name.

In the 2000s, the appearance of Suvorov Square was significantly updated. In 2010, the Glory Memorial located in the southwestern part of the square was reconstructed.

Kvint

KVINT ("cognacs, wines, and beverages of Tiraspol") is a winery and distillery based in Tiraspol, the administrative centre of Transnistria. Kvint products are certified 'Made in Moldova'. Founded in 1897, the company produced only vodka until 1938, when it began producing brandies. It is the oldest still-operating commercial enterprise in the region. Locals consider KVINT a national treasure and a symbol of their country. Its factory is shown on the 5 Transnistrian ruble banknote.

KVINT is one of Transnistria's largest exporters, to Italy and China as well as Russia and Ukraine; its brandy has gone to the Vatican and into space.

Transnistria lies east of the Dniester River. The grapes grown here are Cognac variety. KVINT's award-winning Prince Wittgenstein brandy incorporates Bianca, Aligoté, Pervenets of Magarach [Pervenet Magaracea], Riesling, Riton, Suruchensky White, Ugni Blanc, and Colombard grapes.

The company also grows traditionally European red grapes, such as Malbec, Ancelotti, Saperavi, Viognier, and Syrah (Shiraz).

Sites of Interest

Contents

Prologue

Chapter 1

Chapter 2

Chapter 3

Chapter 4

Chapter 5

Chapter 6

Chapter 7

Chapter 8

Chapter 9

Chapter 10

Chapter 11

Chapter 12

Chapter 13

Chapter 14

Chapter 15

Chapter 16

Chapter 17

Chapter 18

Chapter 19

Chapter 20

Chapter 21

Chapter 22

Chapter 23

Chapter 24

Chapter 25

Chapter 26

Chapter 27

Chapter 28

Chapter 29

Chapter 30

Chapter 31

Chapter 32

Chapter 33

Chapter 34

Chapter 35

Chapter 36

Chapter 37

Chapter 38

Chapter 39

Chapter 40

Chapter 41

Chapter 42

Chapter 43

Chapter 44

Chapter 45

Chapter 46

Chapter 47

Chapter 48

Chapter 49

Chapter 50

Chapter 51

About the Author

Prologue

Where do fairy tales come from?

I mean, we all know that the stories told children by their parents, whispered as tales by old wives to any ear that might listen, the yarns spun around the crackling fire on the darkest of evenings when the cold wind bit hard and the shadows seemed thicker than ever ... all these were meant to give fair warning to the young or foolhardy. To ward them away from the dangers every mortal faced, whether they believed in them or not.

But why fairy tales? Why stories?

Wouldn't it be better to simply warn the listener not to lean over the deep pools or tread the treacherous lagoons where monsters lurk with long fingers ready to snag and catch? Or to tell the traveller of the creatures lurking in the deep forests where they seek to explore, with sharp teeth and long claws and a hunger for blood and flesh?

Why, instead, spin a tale of some child or hero, spinning a creative narrative to beguile the listener and oft times mask the true horror of what the story is *really* about?

It's really quite simple.

Mortals do not like being told something, especially if it's *not* to do a thing.

Tell a mortal that they cannot jump off a cliff, as a monster is lurking below that will eat them alive ... and they'll already be diving headlong off the edge as you finish the sentence. Inform a mortal that the forest they wish to explore is filled with ravenous creatures that will drink their blood and feast on their flesh ... and they will call you mad, and tell you you are exaggerating. That they have read up on the local wildlife and nothing harmful exists there.

Many tribes folk of far-off and as yet undiscovered (meaning not on *civilised* peoples' maps) places are struck by the utter insanity and stupidity of explorers the first time they try to warn them of the dangers and horrors of a place *they* know not to go, that countless generations who have come before have taught them never to *go there* … only to see the men and women 'who know better' blithely wander to their doom, laughing over the ignorant savages as they go.

So instead, mortals learned that stories were the best medium for passing on a warning, of telling the next generation the things they should know to help them survive the trials and dangers of their world, their home. And the creatures who exist beside them, the horrors that are real and very, very deadly.

And yet even here mortals fall afoul of their own nature. The fairy tales and old wives tales become childish interpretations of the original instruction. The purpose of the warning lost as generation after generation weaken and water down the elements *not suitable for their children*. The big bad wolf that threatens to eat Red Riding Hood, having devoured her grandmother, becomes more puppy-like, with floppy ears and big soulful eyes instead of serrated teeth perfect for removing flesh from bone. Talons capable of rending life become stumpy paws, and the creature that once inspired terror now delights the child, inciting giggles instead of fear.

Until they meet the wolf in real life, and understand … before they are eaten … that the story had a lesson. One they failed to learn.

The moral here is that there is always a kernel of truth in just about every story, a warning that existed *for a very good reason* and was thought important enough to hand down, generation upon generation, to help those that came after.

To make sure the next generation didn't end up being *the last one*.

The trick is to find that truth, buried as it is now in *Disney* song and dance, with prettified monsters that would scare no one. Not even themselves. And woe betide those who think there is nothing to learn from those that many great explorers have called *ignorant savages,* the men, women and children indeed who hold to the old truths, who know the secret of the dark.

That it has teeth.

Chapter 1

Herne had been kidnapped. By mortals.

The fucking idiots.

But '*kidnap*' didn't quite fit what had happened. Firstly, Herne was no kid. He was an elder immortal, an elemental being who ruled the Wyld Court and had caused the mortals countless centuries of terror with his Wyld Hunt and savage ways … before the Accords put paid to that sort of behaviour. The actual phrase *to kidnap*, I'd found out one evening whilst horribly bored, dated from the late seventeenth century and meant '*to steal children to provide servants to the American colonies,*'.

From *kid - child*, and *nap - snatch away.*

He hadn't been snatched to become a slave in the United States of America's colonies, if you could even call the sprawling mass of mortal insanity that anymore. In fact, some sketchy evidence my newly found mother shared with me just before I left the Wyld this last time led me to believe his captors were *much* closer to home.

DOPA.

The *Department for Occult Practices and Arcanology*. A division of the same secret service that my mortal … well, ally more than friend Cormac Wessen Smith belonged to, though he was a member of OPS instead. The *Office of Preternatural Security*. The guard dogs to their researcher colleagues. The same mortal shadow-organisation that my mother, Margaret May Black, had been employed by, I'd found out. She had been involved in a truly insane project based on old world thinking, Cold War stuff of nightmares, with the intent to summon and enslave Herne years ago to ensure Great Britain's safety against any and all threats.

Leading to a *lot* of dead governmental staff as well as her going missing, presumed thoroughly terminated.

Instead, Margaret May Black had defected to the Wyld, becoming Black May. To be with the creature she chose to love, and in time bear him a son. Me. Only to then be poisoned by a vicious little rotling called Baba Bohdana, and eventually dying without me ever knowing her.

Now I'd stumbled on evidence that DOPA had had dealings with the traitorous Wyld crone, for how long I had no fucking clue. Arranging for creatures of the Real to be handed over to them in return for knowledge, power … whatever the rotling had demanded. I was pretty sure they'd been up to the same sort of shit in the Mortal Realm but currently had no definitive proof to confirm that. However, DOPA definitely had helped Baba Bohdana subdue and then remove from power the Lord of the Wyld.

Stealing him away to fuck knows where. For fuck knows why.

And not just him. Into the bargain, they'd also grabbed the Harrowed Queen. That fucked up merging of the *death of immortals* and hate-filled Morgana, which the Lord and Ladies of Ivory and Shadow were actively hunting to terminate with *very* extreme prejudice.

This was *so* fucked up, it wasn't even funny. Even to me.

The trafficking of either mortals or immortals against their will was strictly prohibited by the Accords, implemented to keep the peace between the Realms and stop Armageddon from landing in all our laps. Gone were the days when faeries stole children from their beds, replacing them with changelings whilst the poor mortal kids spent a confusing and totally fucked up time in the Real. Or when mortals imprisoned creatures of the Real and tortured them for 'research', draining them of their vital fluids to produce questionable anti-aging tonics or life-saving serums that might or might not work.

Both sides had been guilty of some truly gods-awful acts of torture and torment, and the Accords were *very* clear on how mortals and immortals were to be treated in the future. And the penalties perpetrators should expect if they were stupid enough to try that crap again.

Yet here we were. Again. The mortals stepping over the line and breaking rules as they went. Again.

It probably helped that the Furies seemed to be no more, those monstrous law keepers who previously acted as judge, jury and nasty as fuck executioner for any Accord breaker. By all accounts, Morgana had done away with them. Erased them utterly, given there had been no sight or sound of the cruel sisters since she had sent one of them back broken and infected with a lethal virus. Crafted, by the way, by another complete idiot who now worked in Twilight under the tutelage of the Norns to make amends for her truly fucked up behaviour over the centuries.

No greater threat to enforce the laws in the Mortal Realm, or the Real. Nothing to make any creature, be they High Court fae or lowly idiotic mortal, dread the very thought of fucking with the rules and suffering the consequences.

DOPA, with their links to the Real and the intelligence network OPS provided, would be ideally placed to know of the Furies' absence. And it wasn't a stretch of the imagination to foresee someone thinking this might be the perfect time to play silly buggers. Mortals, as we all know, are past masters of doing the most idiotic thing at the very worst moment. It's like their superpower.

I growled out a sigh, reaching for my third mug of coffee and draining down the dregs as I looked across at my Alpha, who had sat through my wearied and pained debrief with a thoughtful, calm expression hiding anything she was actually thinking. Whilst all I could do was tell her the facts, and dream of my big comfortable bed back at home waiting for me.

Felix remained outside, in the main office of *Good Deeds*. Catching up with Ellie on her version of the clusterfuck we'd encountered in the Wyld, and being walked through each and every use of magic with notes on what she needed to focus on to improve her newfound craft. Most importantly, I guessed, how she should avoid agreeing to go along with any more half-arsed ideas of mine in the future, which could lead to their Goddess being drained of a whole bucketload of life energy. Even if She could spare it.

"Ah have tae admit, Morgan." Jessica Walker finally spoke, a small smile touching her lips. "If it were any other person bringing me this convoluted tale of betrayal and deceit, ah would be less than inclined tae believe them, and instead question the sanity of the teller. Ah mean, the sheer level of stupidity you tell me the crones and un-Lords showed …"

I started to growl out a reply but bit down on the words as Jess just shook her head, waving one hand to reassure me.

"Dinnae worry. Remember, ah am familiar enough with the idiocies of the Courts tae know the truth of things. Ah dinnae doubt yer words, and ah am certain you are nae deluded nor mistaken in what you have discovered." She reassured me, that smile genuine and warm. "As well as being certain ah will receive a full, *written* debriefing of the Wyld Court's troubles at yer earliest convenience."

Damn. More bloody admin. Despite me having given my Alpha a complete rundown of events verbally, she was a stickler for making sure all such matters were recorded in Oracle. Not just so that the rest of the pack would be kept up to speed on all things Real related, but also to appease Jessica's desire to have things neat and squared away.

She *abhorred* chaos.

"Now, tae the crux of our problems. This matter of mortal involvement in Herne's disappearance is, frankly, disturbing." She continued, her smile thinning to a hard line as she frowned. I caught the mixed scents from her, frustration battling with a thin veneer of dismay, even fear. And that shook me. I mean, it takes a lot to scare a lycan Alpha, but breaches of the Accord on this scale were no laughing matter.

Wars had started for far, far less.

I drew a breath, wincing as my body chose that moment to loudly complain about the recent ill-treatment I'd put it through. Fighting five of the lesser Courts' favourite champions, including a fucking dragon, and then having to throw down with the Bayun Cat to end his suffering. All that, after tangling with wendigos and ling-worms. It had been a fun few days, and I was feeling more than a little ill-used.

"Good to know your powers of understatement are as strong as ever," I forced a grin, shaking my head. "Frankly, I was more leaning towards this being a complete and utter cluster-fuck of epic proportions."

"Dinnae think ah am taking this matter lightly, Morgan. Of all the pack, you know me better than that." My Alpha reprimanded me lightly, as she tapped a few notes into her ever-present e-pad. "But ah have tae ask. Is there any chance this evidence could have been faked? Or yer mother mistaken? She *had* just been transformed in tae a creature of dark Wyld magic, as well as recently returning from the dead. That introduces a certain level of confusion in tae her testimony, ah have tae tell you."

Truth is, I'd asked myself the same thing. Firstly as Felix and I travelled back to the Mortal Realm from the Wyld, then again in the taxi from the Way I'd called us since I was too bloody tired to walk. I'd known that despite my powerful desire to bundle Bear and myself back home to go hide until all the bad shit went away, I had to report to Jessica. She had to know what had happened, what sort of shitshow we now faced.

I *had* planned on sending Felix home though, given she had been through the ringer in the Wyld. But the young witch stubbornly refused to do the sensible thing and go rest. Instead she figured she needed to speak to Ellie urgently, and between them crack on with checking my mother's grimoire. There was a slim chance it had important stuff to tell us, alongside her journal which I'd kept a firm hold of.

I was pretty sure it was the journal that had the clues as to what the furry fuck the mortals were up to, and where my father might have been taken. Maybe even why. The grimoire, her Book of Shadows or whatever you wanted to call it, would probably just show the sort of witchcraft she had practiced. How close to the line of right and wrong my mother had danced, since with magic there is no Good, no Evil. Just intent and purpose.

Having finally met her, and seen Black May in action, I was under no illusion that my mother had done bad things, and acted in a manner to inspire fear as well as respect in creatures of the Wyld. And that took some doing, especially for a mortal.

I shook my head, knowing Jess had to ask but that there was no doubt in my mind.

"It's them. DOPA's behind this shit." I patted the journal that was sitting on the table, lying open at the photograph page-marker my mother had shown me in the Wyld. "I've got no idea why they showed up kitted out in gear from thirty or forty years ago, but these are who Briar saw in the glade with Bohdana. Who ambushed Herne and Harry."

"Ah am unfamiliar with this Harry?" Jess quirked an eyebrow, so I shrugged.

"We can't keep calling her the *Harrowed Queen* since she's technically not a Queen, she doesn't have a Court and I'm not even sure she's even a *she*. Not in the biological sense." I explained my reasoning, seeing my Alpha roll her eyes. "And it helps make her less threatening. Harry *could* be short for Harriet, but then you've got the whole *Dirty Harry* or *When Harry Met Sally* thing too that makes her way less shit-scary, and more darkly humorous. So … Harry."

"Ah keep forgetting tae stop questioning yer specific brand of logic, Morgan." She replied with a wry smile, tapping a correction into her pad. "But until we agree some better name, Harry will have tae do. Fer now."

My Alpha set aside her pad, looking across at me as her expression settled back into a serious frown.

"If that is all, we are left with the undisputable problem of what tae do next?" She told me, ticking off her thinking on one hand. "What you have told me is nae proof enough of the mortals breaching the Accords, tae stand up in any tribunal or hearing. Ah cannae take an old photograph and the recollections of a grieving, mute youngling kami tae the other Alphas or tae anyone else fer that matter. Nae matter that she is your half-sister, ah would appreciate speaking tae her mahself tae confirm what she saw. Or didn't."

I probably should have felt some brotherly instinct to defend my sibling to my Alpha at that point. But Jess was just saying we didn't know enough yet, and how weak our position was to take any sort of action. She had my back, but this was way bigger than just a case of disappearing Real denizens. I wouldn't be able to half-arse my way on this problem, no matter how much experience I had doing exactly that.

"Before ah'm comfortable convening the Courts and mortal tribunal on this matter, ah'll need tae corroborate yer findings with yer sibling, and speak tae the remaining Crones about what their sister spoke of …" She began, and I winced at the thought of having to return to the Wyld so soon after the mess I'd caused there. The sort of antagonism I'd stirred up, for not just me but all Redcloaks. The un-Lords and un-Lady, as well as the Crones, had been crystal clear on the sort of welcome we might expect if I returned to cause any further trouble.

And all so soon after getting Herne to promise to stop turning us into his Hounds as and when he liked. Way to go, Morgan!

At that moment, someone knocked on the meeting room door. From their scent I knew it was Scott, one of the junior members of the pack. He had been manning *Good Deeds'* front desk when Felix and I showed up, and had helped cart my Redcloak gear and a grumbling Bear inside whilst I'd limped along behind. I must have looked how I felt, since he hadn't even tried a single sarcastic quip at me needing so much help, and we in the pack *never* miss a chance to shit-talk each other.

Now he was sending out seriously worried vibes, like he'd just found out the Tax Office was coming to audit our books again. Plus, Jess had asked for us not to be disturbed after I'd stumbled in, still carrying Herne's gore-soaked spear and stained with the blood of the champions I'd defeated. Dragon blood *really* stinks, just so you know.

"What's amiss, Scott?" Jess asked, loud enough for him to know he could come in.

The lycan cracked open the door and popped his head through, and I read just how worried he was from his expression.

"Uh, sorry. Jessica. Morgan." He apologised, running fingers through his shoulder length mane of hair. Scott Wyndham had the sort of natural looks that should have seen him on television or in the movies, swashbuckling against dastardly villains, carousing with fellow piratical shipmates or having his arse saved by the beautiful female lead character against all odds. We'd jokingly nicknamed him Jack for the Johnny Depp character he resembled, which he only ever half-heartedly complained about.

"Nae apology needed. What has happened?" Jess asked with no recrimination. She too had caught his scent, and knew this had to be important for him to ignore her request.

"Uh, it's the pups." He looked across at me, and I remembered I'd handed my case load over to the fresh batch of lycans we were looking to bring into the pack. To replace those we'd lost in all the horrific shit we'd weathered these past few months, what with Morgana's escape and her reincarnation involving the Harrowing of all bloody things.

"Fuck, seriously?" I groaned, knowing this was probably coming back to bite me somehow. "What've they done? I just asked them to walk the streets, talk to my contacts and check the details of the latest disappearances. Nothing crazy, honest!"

"Ah am fully aware of what you tasked them with, Morgan. Ah asked Emma tae speak tae them after you left, just tae make sure you hadn't given them any … ideas, tae act as unwisely as you yourself do on occasion." Jess told me, before looking back at Scott. "What about them?"

Scott looked from me to her, and I caught the sudden spike in his scent as he grimaced.

"Uh, well. They were out looking into two new cases. You remember that family of trolls brothers we had living in the cells under our old office? One of them turned up yesterday, saying his brothers had been taken." He finally admitted, shaking his head. "Emma didn't see any reason not to let the pups go check out the trolls' last location, scout out any clues. But something must have gone really wrong, coz I just got a call from one of our contacts."

"They've been arrested. By OPS."

I mean … what the actual fuck?

Chapter 2

So, back to the Tower of London I trit-trat-trotted like the Billy Goats Gruff in the stories. Except with less goats or trolls involved, but with more swearing. Kind of like the 18+ version.

I was beginning to think if I had to keep showing up at this place, I might as well buy a season pass. Or at least get a photo ID so the bloody Tower Yeomans didn't keep putting me through the ringer whenever I showed up for a chat with Cormac bloody Wessen Smith.

Thankfully, this time I had Jessica along with me, since she'd decided the imprisoning of more members of her pack required her direct involvement to rectify. I knew she and the other Alphas had been recognised officially by OPS, identified as assets to provide assistance as and when required, which meant instructions had probably been issued to any and all about the level of respect due them and the simple truth that you didn't fuck them around like they seemed to think they could me.

The other reassuring fact I had in my head was that at least this time it wasn't *me* who had been picked up by the mortals' secret Security Service. Once was enough, thanks all the same.

As it was, I spotted a familiar face after we exited our taxi and approached the main entrance to the Tower. The red and black suited Yeoman who had twice given me the complete run-around when I showed up to seek entry, his bearded whiskers almost twitching with joyous anticipation of pissing me off all over again.

But then he spotted my companion, and I swear I saw every bone in his spine stiffen to almost ram-rod straightness. Whatever devilry he'd planned was shoved back in its box, and I had to fight hard not to slap a smug smile all over my face.

Ignoring the milling crowds all around us, and the queue of mortals lining up patiently to gain entrance to the old castle and all its finery, Jessica strode up to the man guarding the gate. Now normally our Alpha was the soul of politeness around mortals, playing by their ridiculous rules and generally avoiding drawing any attention to the simple fact of what we were, and what we were not. Perfectly camouflaged, not causing any panic or trouble.

Not so much today.

"Ah believe you know who ah am, and who mah companion is." She told the guard bluntly, her tone sharp and just a little bit of tooth added for bite. "You will tell Cormac Smith tae let us pass, and fer him tae meet us without delay. Am ah clear?"

"Uh, excuse me. Miss?" A man in the queue piped up, looking haggard from trying to keep three loud and energetic children in check whilst who I had to assume was his wife looked thunderously across at us. "There is a line, in case you didn't know? If you don't mind waiting your turn …"

"Sir, ah mean nae disrespect tae you or any other of you waiting tae waste the day wandering around the Tower." Jess looked back at him, and the man visibly flinched from the hard edge to her normally calm eyes. "But this is a private matter, and frankly none of yer damn business. So shut up, step back and wait yer turn. Otherwise ah cannot in good conscious say you will like what yer children are made tae witness this day."

I shook my head at him as well, giving him the *this is way out of your league and nothing you want to get involved with* look that I often used on curious mortals who stepped into our world and lives accidently, and who had to be moved on before they witnessed something that would haunt them for the very short time that they had left to live.

Of course, this *being* a mortal, he chose the path of idiocy.

"Madam, I don't care who you think you are!" He blustered, red blotches showing on his cheeks from either anger or embarrassment. His wife was practically spitting with self-righteous indignation, but the three children had frozen as they stared at Jessica. Young mortals often still have the instincts they were born with, the fear that tells them something bad is waiting in the shadows, or something dangerous is lurking under the bed. It takes time for those senses to be blunted, turning them into disbelieving adults who blithely walk into danger wide eyed and uncaring. Like their father, talking back to what they sensed was a dangerous wolf in a different form. "You can't speak to me like …"

Jessica snarled.

Now, anyone can make what they think is a proper growl or snarl. Mortals do it all the time, for fun, mock fighting or actually when angry. I think the problem with that is they base the noise off the sounds made by their domesticated dogs, the poor buggers that were once wolves, savage predators that roamed the wilds … but now only faithful companions to be cuddled on the sofa and fed treats for doing tricks. Those sort of sounds are on the same level as the gurgling blubbers of a newborn pup compared to the real deal.

Jessica's snarl was something else. A thing from primeval times, filled with the promise of blood and violence. It wasn't loud, she didn't bay out her fury, but the timbre of it travelled through the air and punched the mortal and his family squarely in the deeply buried instincts that all living creatures have … for flight or fight. Neolithic mortals, hearing that sound, had cowered in their caves with spears held in shaking hands, awaiting certain death stalking towards them.

The father of the children staggered back, even as the mother grabbed hold of the youngsters as they immediately started bawling. Her face went from righteous fury to abject terror in a heartbeat, eyes draining of all rage and filling instead with panic. Several others in the queue nearest them also stumbled away, eyes widening as they felt an unknown terror gripping them. I could hear their hearts begin to thump in their chests, and their breaths stutter as panic blossomed and grew.

"Unless Cormac Smith wants an *incident* on his bloody doorstep, I suggest you get him down here. Right *now*." I told the Yeoman sharply, as

Jess eyed the cowering mortals with eyes that had begun to burn with yellow fury. The guard grabbed out his handheld radio and spoke quickly into it, even as I caught unsubtle movement in the guardhouse behind him. Probably more fancy-dressed soldiers readying weapons in case this all went south horribly.

"Uh, Ms Walker. Mr Black. The gentleman is on his way up, and says he'll meet you inside." The guard told us as his radio squawked out the good news, and another Yeoman stepped quickly from the guardhouse. This one wasn't pointing a gun at us, which was a good sign, and he beckoned for us to pass through the barrier and head on in without even trying to make me pay.

"Mah thanks, sir." Jessica told the guard, then looked back at the cowering mortals behind her. "Ah also thank you fer your patience. Ah hope you enjoy all the Tower has tae offer. It is quite something, if you take the time tae enjoy it."

With that, she stepped past the guard and barrier, with me following behind. I shot the soldier a sharp grin, knowing that from this moment on I'd most likely encounter a *lot* less hassle and mick-take if I ever visited the place again on official business.

Yeah, I know I should have had some sympathy for the guy, knowing he had to deal with mortals every single day with all of their idiocy and frustrating habits. But still, I'm self-aware enough to admit I enjoyed watching him squirm *just* a little.

The Yeoman guided us through the warren of passages that made up a section of the Tower's ground floor which civilians were never allowed to see. Ostensibly because they were the kitchens, quarters and private places for the soldiers stationed to guard the aging complex and royalty if ever they were visiting, but mostly because they led to OPS's front door.

"Ms Walker. Mr Black. I had a feeling I would be hearing from you today." Cormac greeted us as we turned a corner and found ourselves facing a second guardpost, taking up both sides of the corridor. It forced whomever approached to pass between the two solid looking defences, in which I could see a pair of heavily armoured and armed guards waiting patiently to deter intruders. These were no brightly dressed Yeoman that traditionally warded the Tower and told its long and dark history to visitors, though I knew even those men and women were ex special forces and highly trained military personnel.

No, the pair who guarded the corridor put me in mind of highly trained Doberman security dogs, trained to inhuman levels of endurance and lethalness. I smelt cold-iron and silver on the soldiers, meaning they were armed and armoured to face off against Real as well as mortal foes, and I assumed they would have a nasty mix of weapons to ruin anyone's day who thought it wise to try to get past them.

Cormac Smith was wearing his standard well-tailored grey suit that matched his greying hair and flat grey eyes. It was as close to a uniform as I could imagine him ever wearing, a typically British version of the Men In Black that fill every dialogue on alien conspiracies and theories of cover ups by the US Government on matters of extra-terrestrial life. His armour against the reality of what he faced daily, the madness of the Real intruding on the Mortal Realm.

But beyond that, I straightaway clocked changes in the agent whom I'd had quite a few dealings with recently. None of them good. Dark circles lurked under his eyelids, and stubble covered his chin and lower cheeks, giving him a rough and rumpled look. But what was more of a give-away was what my lycan senses picked up … this from a mortal who had gone toe-to-toe with the crazed and murderously insane Lykaois without flinching, and had voluntarily stepped into a full lycan Blooding to arrest me without breaking a sweat.

Now? Now I could tell he was stressed, tired and more than a little troubled. I figured not of all it was about our sudden visit, but I had to assume we were in no way making his day any easier.

Aw, shucks.

The OPS agent whispered something to the armed soldiers, too low even for me to make out, before nodding to the guard who had escorted us.

"It's ok, George. I'll take it from here." He reassured the Yeoman, who gave a sharp salute and turned on his heel, retreating back the way we'd come without a single glance back. Ex-military, definitely.

"If you would follow me, I'll find us a room where we can talk." He told Jessica, according her his attention given her status as Alpha. For her part, she had reigned in her momentary snap of anger, and was as calm and implacable as ever. Just two professionals meeting for a simple chat. And of course, me tagging along like the random mutt off the street.

Beyond the guard post, the corridor made several turns before heading off into the Tower, even though my brain was telling me we'd travelled further than the footprint of the building. But Cormac stopped and instead faced what looked like a solid old-stone wall, tapping his fingers with seemingly random purpose on several dusty stone bricks.

There should have been a grinding or groaning noise, the rasp of stone on stone. Maybe even the clunk of gears, mechanical and oiled. Instead, the stone wall simply split silently and shifted to either side, revealing a much more recent and twenty-first century looking set of elevator doors.

Cormac tapped a code into a small, discreet pad and then pressed his hand against a reader. This blinked twice, accepting his code and print before the doors slid open.

"If you wouldn't mind?" He motioned for us to enter first, which I was loath to do on sheer principle. Not because I'm a gentleman, but I'm a highly distrustful lycan who expects the worst of situations because invariably that was what hit me in the face. Walking first into a metal box, without knowing what waited for me … yeah, that wasn't going to happen. But Jessica stepped forward, turning on her heel once she was in the lift. Unharmed, and nodding for me to follow her.

I grumbled a growl under my breath and stepped inside. My muscles clenched, fearing the sudden snap of a trap but I should probably learn to trust OPS since nothing bad happened. Instead, Cormac waited a moment outside before joining us.

The doors slid smoothly shut after a long moment, then made an ominous clunking noise that told me some sort of locking mechanism had engaged. Jessica and I exchanged looks, and I coughed meaningfully at the agent.

"It's just a precaution against infiltration." Cormac told me, as he placed his hand against a panel on the lift wall that looked no different than any other. A light blinked twice, and the metal slipped aside to reveal another keypad, into which he tapped a second code. Not that I was looking, but I already had both memorised. Just in case.

"Now, if you would stand still for a moment, this should cause only a little discomfort." He told us both, before a faint hissing filled the air. Sparkles flickered all around us like miniature fireworks and I tasted a metallic tang on my lips and tongue as I took a wary breath.

"Silver laced vapour, with minute iron traces. To dispel any magical influences or reveal anything that might be hiding from sight." Cormac admitted, a wry smile lighting his tired face. "Like a young witch, maybe, who is very good at cloaking herself."

"Hello, Miss Price."

Chapter 3

I swore as Felix's crafting splintered and broke apart, revealing the young woman crouching down in the corner of the lift with a guilty look plastered all over her face. I hadn't sensed a bloody thing, not even a twitch of my reliable lycan senses to tell me she had come along for the ride.

For fuck's sake.

"Uh, hi guys." Felix straightened up, pressing down on her clothes to smooth out the rumples caused by her crouching low. "I just … well, you both ran out of the office so quickly, I thought something was up and you might need a hand. And I'd finished talking to Elspeth so I …"

"Just tagged along, thinking it would be clever to show off and walk into a top-secret facility unnoticed?" I growled, shaking my head. "This isn't a bloody game, kid. What were you thinking? They could have *shot* you if they'd wanted to, for fuck's sake!"

"Quite true." Cormac interjected smoothly. "But in this case, I think we can put this one time down to youthful exuberance, and just this once ignore the usual penalty for attempting to break into Her Majesty's property, let alone an OPS secure facility. This once."

Jessica gave short nod even as she sighed, pinning Felix with a hard stare that told me the young witch had managed to fool her as well. Despite Cormac's assurance, I figured someone was going to have the book thrown at them when this little catch up was done with. No matter how smug my friend might be feeling for fooling us, she would soon learn to regret her actions after suffering one of our Alpha's dressing downs.

"Ah agree. Since she is here, ah suggest we let her stay fer now as ah dinnae wish tae waste any further time having her returned tae the office." The Alpha reasoned, then nodded to me. "Ah expect you will want her tae be bound by the same oath that Morgan unwittingly took tae his misfortune?"

Cormac nodded, smiling slightly.

"I requested a copy to be drafted as soon as we detected her presence accompanying you both. Miss Price can sign her acceptance momentarily." He agreed whilst also managing to control any sign of smugness to show that he and OPS had not been fooled, only us. I placed a heavy hand on Felix's shoulder, firmly forestalling any attempt of hers to disagree. "Now that we are all present and correct, we can proceed."

Whether that was just a statement or a command to whomever was listening, the lift hummed into motion, my stomach telling me we were descending quickly. I shot a hard look at Felix, who mouthed *sorry* to me, and had the decency to look thoroughly embarrassed. Yeah, right. Like that was for real.

Guards met us as the doors slid open, wearing the more familiar OPS uniforms and carrying the well-used weapons that I had come to expect rather than the frippery of the Yeoman. But I still couldn't work out why the bastards who had kidnapped Herne and Harry had been kitted in such archaic gear, if they had access to the same stores like every other division of the Government's shadow organisation. Maybe DOPA had a different dress code, hell if I knew.

True to Cormac's word, there was also one of the agents waiting with the armed escort, with parchment and quill pen held ready. I smiled grimly as I recognised the young woman who had been present at my own binding, guessing she got the fun job of stabbing people with sharp objects all day long. She gave me a look over her glasses, clearly remembering me as well, but forbore to return any other sign of recognition.

I knew what to expect, so kept a firm grip on Felix when the woman quickly took her hand and pricked her skin to draw blood before wetting the quill's nib.

"Fuck, that hurt!" Felix swore, sucking on her palm and glaring first at the agent and then at me.

"Pain teaches us a lesson, young padawan. This one being not to be such a smart-arse." I told her, and motioned for her to sign the document. "Do it, or Cormac will find a nice cosy cell to lock you in until we're done."

Swearing under her breath, the young witch scribbled her signature with the bloodied pen. She hissed at the burning sensation as the binding took hold, but I just nodded to tell her it was ok and expected.

With that task done, the quill woman and guards departed, and Cormac led us along the spacious corridor until he chose a random door and headed inside.

The meeting room was far more comfortable than the interview room I'd woken to find myself in when OPS detained me last time. The seats looked more expensive than the simple metal torture instruments in that other room, and turned out to be quite comfortable when I sank my arse down on the nearest one, making sure I kept close to the door. In case of trouble either coming in, or trying to leave. You just never know.

Jessica settled down opposite Cormac, whilst Felix sulkily threw herself down into the farthest chair from us all. The agent had somehow arranged for refreshments to be waiting for us too, and he poured out four cups of coffee that he passed out before anyone even asked.

Four. Like the bastard had known Felix would sneak along. I had to assume this was High King Bran's doing, though I thought the magically alive head of the last giant of England only saw visions of threats to the island's safety. Even on her worst day, Felix didn't rate that sort of notoriety. Whatever, it did little to improve my mood.

With coffee dispensed, Cormac settled back, looking across at Jessica and myself. Ignoring Felix for now.

"Why have you arrested members of mah pack, Agent Smith?" My Alpha cut straight to the point, gazing at him coolly over the rim of her cup. I didn't bother worrying about the drinks being laced with anything, as they had done with me previously, since to do so to Jess would be tantamount to announcing war on us lycans, and no-one wanted that sort of trouble.

"*Detained*, Ms Walker. Not arrested." He corrected, smiling again slightly as he opened a manilla folder, much like the one he had had of me when we sat in a very different room, discussing my immediate future. "Your new ... recruits crossed into an active OPS investigation and were seeking details from key witnesses that we have under surveillance. As I am sure you remember, we agreed to notify each other if ever there was a chance we might ... *butt heads* I think was the term you used, over any hunts or investigations we found ourselves both involved in. Has that changed?"

"Nae, nothing has changed. Fer me, at least." Jessica answered, taking a sip of coffee and thinking before she continued. "So, yer organisation is investigating ...?"

"It has come to our attention that a small number of citizens of this Realm, though not *originally* of this Realm, have become ... *difficult* to locate. Most recently from the time of Twilight's return, and Morgana's attempted invasion. But possibly from before then as well." Cormac admitted, using the typical non-committal speak I guessed was taught to all secret service agents when they graduated into a position of trust. "The numbers of missing individuals, as well as their unconnected nature, did not lead our analysts to believe we would require the services of any third party to investigate this matter. Yet here we are."

My Alpha exchanged a look with me, and I shrugged an acceptance at her unspoken question. There was no need to keep what we knew from the agent, and it might grease the wheels of their freedom if we shared, let alone maybe get some much needed answers as well.

I reached into my pocket and drew out my mother's journal, seeing Cormac cock an eyebrow but making no other comment.

"Ah believe, in the spirit of our agreement tae work together, ah can greatly aid you in yer investigation." Jessica told him with a cool, calm smile. "By fickle chance, it seems we have indeed *butted heads* on this case of Real citizens disappearing. Morgan here was involved in an entirely separate hunt involving the Wyld Court, and has come across some information ah believe sheds light on what … maybe who is tae blame."

Cormac looked at me with the question plain on his face, but I just shrugged as I slipped open the journal and slid the photograph out from between its pages. I slid it across the table towards him.

"I'll be needing that back. Family property, you understand." I told him, as he carefully reached over and picked up the print. "But I have it from a reliable witness that those men and women are behind the disappearances. They've been working with a Crone of the Wyld Court, kidnapping creatures from the Real in exchange for enough power for her to try a coup. She failed, and I reckon Wyld's safe now. But not before the bastards nabbed Herne as well."

The OPS agent studied the picture, before taking a breath and setting it down once more.

"This reliable witness you say gave you this, and named these as the perpetrators of the disappearances?" He spoke slowly, thinking through his words. "Would you mind revealing their name at the very least?"

"Sure, I figured you'd need to know if you were going to trust what we've learned." I shrugged, given how my parentage these days was less than a closely guarded secret. At least it wasn't a complete mystery to me now, whilst until recently it seemed every bugger I stumbled across had had the scoop on my missing family. "She worked for you. Well, DOPA back in the day. Margaret Black, professor of something to do with rituals and shit. Witch by trade. Before she skipped over to the Wyld to be with my father. Herne, the horny ruler of the Court. Who'se been nabbed, like I just said."

Cormac thought for a moment, before reaching inside his pocket and pulling out a slim tablet that looked a lot like the one Jess used, just smaller. He tapped at the keyboard for a moment and read whatever came up from his query before looking across at me, expression closed.

"It is our understanding, and recorded that Ms Black is considered a casualty of a rather unfortunate and ill-advised project that took place whilst I was still a junior field agent of OPS. There is no record that she had survived the failed ritual, nor any suppositions of how she might have escaped unscathed from the stupidity that cost so many lives. Only possible theories as to the cause of the accident … *intentional sabotage* being one." He told me, and reached over to tap the faded picture. "If your mother *has* been in the Wyld Court all this time, I would struggle to consider her a *reliable* source of information, given the effects of the Real on any living mortal. Let alone the fact there will be those who might think she is simply seeking to point fingers elsewhere, shift blame for her possible involvement in the disaster I mentioned. Family, you did say. If she might be looking to return to this Realm, say, to be with her son …"

I growled but bit back on my anger. The agent wasn't being personal, just voicing his doubts and what others might think, might suspect. I'd prepared for them on the journey over to the Tower.

"Normally I'd agree with you, but the truth is, she hasn't hiding from prosecution in the Wyld Court and now wants to come make happy families with me back here." I replied, the truth still painful to voice but not as much now I knew what had happened. Why we'd been forced apart. "Margaret Black … Black May as they knew her was killed by Baba Bohdana of the Wyld Court shortly after giving birth to me, but then that twisted mushroom fucker used my mother's spirit to create a fetch to try to kill me. We messed up that plan, and Black May will be taking her place as a Crone just as soon as she puts herself back together again. So there's nothing here she's trying to hide, no reason for her to point a finger at anyone innocent. This lot, or at least some of them were witnessed kidnapping Herne by my stepsister, the kami now sitting on the Wyld Throne as Lady, and my mother corroborated the evidence she gave. It's them."

I growled out, reaching over to reclaim the picture and holding it up for him to look at again.

"DOPA. The same people she worked with to try and trap Herne the first time." I looked for any sort of deceit in Cormac's eyes, any hint from him that he knew of what had been going on and was covering this shitstorm up. "They've been kidnapping, stealing … whatever the fuck you want to call it, they've been doing it to Real creatures here and in the Wyld. Maybe in the other Courts too. And you are going to tell us why, or the shit is really going to hit the fan."

Cormac studied the picture for a moment longer, then shook his own head.

"You say your mother died, but has returned to life once more?" He queried, and I nodded once, waiting for the punchline. "Then I can only assume there is some sudden and strange spate going around, undoing the finality of what we call mortality. I know of the events around Gregory Allen's return, and now your mother's. But I have to assume your colleague, Elspeth MacElvy has not been up to her tricks again and breaking fundamental laws?"

Both Jessica and I looked at each other, confused but shaking our heads to confirm the truth. Cormac smiled.

"I thought not." He pointed at the picture I was still holding. "This then presents us with a quandary. A dilemma, even. Because, to my knowledge and according to the records I just reviewed in our archives, the men and women your mother thinks are behind these disappearances are very much deceased. Dead. Having lost their lives in that tragedy, or shortly after. In fact it is noted they one and all suffered a possible curse on all those involved in that ill-fated event. A death hex from the Wyld itself."

I went to speak, but Cormac stopped me.

"No, Mr Black … Morgan. This is not some simple administrative mix up, nor is it anything like the matter of Dr Robert Knox and his twisted genius." I'd been about to remind the OPS agent of their wayward colleague who had managed to cover up his extended life numerous times over, having *'died'* enough times to probably earn a Guinness World record. "If you cast your mind back to events not so long passed, I raised with you the matter of a missing folder which pertained to Margaret Black's employment at DOPA, specifically the project which my organisation believed led to her untimely death alongside so many others. Being unable to source its location, I made sure I was briefed and fully versed on the circumstance of her disappearance and all those involved in case whomever took the folder was looking for something to use against us. And I can promise you, whatever your step-sister and mother think, this is not some DOPA Black Op that we have been covering up. I know *intimately* the fates of all those involved, from first hand records and eyewitness testimonies."

"If what they saw is true, then I can only think of one way of describing what we face." He smiled suddenly, momentarily erasing the tired lines shadowing his face. "*You best start believin' in ghost stories, Mr Black. Yer in one.*"

The sod even got Geoffrey Rush's voice perfect.

Chapter 4

Bugger.

Not the answer I'd been expecting. I mean, ghosts?

"If you will bear with me a moment, I will allay your concerns on this matter so we can begin pooling our resources to identify the *real* culprits." Cormac told us, and Jessica nodded her agreement.

The agent picked up a handset that was sat on the table near him, and spoke quietly into the receiver. I quashed the urge to listen in, instead focusing on what this latest revelation meant.

I'd been positive this was DOPA, OPS or whatever. The shadowy mortal organisation playing silly buggers and breaking the rules. Thinking themselves above or not bound by the Accords everyone else had to live by. Well, most people … given how often we lycans skirted the letter of the law. And Elspeth, given she'd broken her oaths to her Goddess, let alone had the Furies after her after bringing Gregory back from the dead.

Ok, so it is never completely black or white. But for fuck's sake, it had all lined up so nicely.

Cormac reset the receiver, and settled in his chair, obviously waiting for whatever he had spoken to his colleague about. I caught Felix's unashamed yawn and stretch in her chair, the events of the Wyld starting to catch up on the young witch. Hopefully we'd get to the bottom of this shitshow and be on our way out with our young packmates before she started to snore in her seat.

Moments later, a knock on the door had Cormac rising to his feet before any of us reacted, as he walked briskly across the room and opened it to show Miss 'Let Me Stab Your Hand' waiting outside, holding a second folder. He took this, thanking the agent who simply turned on her heel and left without even trying to peer into the room, showing any normal curiosity as to what this was all about. No obvious interest whatsoever, which was almost inhuman for a mortal.

The agent returned to his seat, flipping open the folder and running his finger down the papers held within.

"As I thought, those individuals from your photo are, one and all no longer employed by DOPA, OPS or any other division. Nor are they still card-carrying members of the living human race, and have as Monty Python put it, *kicked the bucket. Shuffled off this mortal coil. Run down the curtain and joined the choir invisible.* They are, in a few words, ex-living people." He drew out a sheet of paper, and passed it across for Jessica and I to read. It was a list of names, with ID photos to match, and by them were listed specific dates and locations which I had to assume marked their deaths.

"Work getting a bit much?" I asked, since until recently, Cormac Wessen Smith had displayed only clinical and cool turns of phrase, an unruffled demeanour despite the situation he found himself in and generally the sort of poise that old Colonial types used when invading new countries and planting their flags imperiously on someone else's grass lawn. Not the sort to be quoting Monty Python at us.

"That is a fair assessment." He admitted, running fingers through his hair before taking another sip of coffee. "We are still running down all the possible double agents and provocateurs that Morgana planted both in our own organisation and the ruling government, as well as handling the fallout of a Realm invasion on multiple fronts. Despite the impressive work done by the Courts and our own Power, leaks still occur. Knowledge seeps out. Until we can screen suitable replacements, I am covering the United Kingdom's operations for OPS and DOPA, and am part of a restructured task force overseeing our European operations as well. There are, literally, not enough hours in the day without us now having to deal with ghosts as well."

"I'd say congrats on the promotion, but … well …" I replied blithely, and he smiled wearily and raised his cup once more.

"Indeed. Well." The agent nodded for me to look at the list, and get on with things.

The list was short, detailing a dozen individuals, including my mother. Margaret May Black. They had her and five others listed as having died at Arbor Low on the 1st May 1963, so I had to assume these were the top level scientists and researchers involved. Not the admins, the technicians, the flunkies whose job it was to arrange all the little details and make sure everything worked for the smarter, higher paid idiots running the show. No one bothered noting how many of them had died, or at least not in this folder.

Dr Gerald Heffer. Dr Susan Wallace. Dr Paulo Perez. Chief Technician Jeroen Esters. Snr Consultant Margaret Black.

Five dead, killed in the chaos when my mother disrupted the ritual they planned to trap Herne with. Instead, she had released him and his Hounds to punish the foolish mortals seeking to put reins on elemental lightning, and then vanished with him back to the Court. Presumed dead in the bloodshed.

Their deaths were hers to own, and just another indicator that my mother was a complicated woman with a moral compass pointing in the direction she desired. No wonder she had survived in the Wyld Court for as long as she had, and made the sort of the enemies she did.

The remaining six names drew my eye.

Division Director – Dr Zarkof Bremmer

Head of Security – Jurgen Blass

Biomedical Expert - Dr Petra Ingless

Research Lead - Dr Corin Blasé

Lead Liaison - Eselle Monrose

Paranormal Physicist – Dr Erunt Von Wyndham

All had survived the May Day slaughter, but none had lasted longer than a year after that date. Dr Bremmer was the last one standing from the list, with his date of death being the anniversary of the fucked-up ritual in 1964.

"Was there anything, I don't know, suspicious with all these people dying so close together?" I queried, trying to think what could have been the cause. "You said some people thought they were cursed?"

Cormac checked through several more pages of the folder, shaking his head before replying.

"Full and detailed autopsies were performed, with broad spectrum forensic and preternatural screenings, to identify any malicious intent behind their deaths." He told us, shrugging slightly. "Three of the surviving six took their own lives, leaving detailed notes explaining their reasoning. The other three, including Dr Bremmer, seem to have had natural deaths. They went to sleep, and did not wake up again. No poison or enchantment found on their bodies. But given the lack of evidence, yes, there was a note made on their files pertaining to malignant curses. Just no proof of any such thing."

"What happened to them after the ritual?" I was hunting for anything to link them beyond that one event, anything abnormal that might explain why my mother had shown me that photograph. We still hadn't explained the beetle-suits, whatever they were used for.

"There *was* an internal investigation into the operation, based on some doubt over the proper protocols followed for authorising its green light." Cormac spoke slowly as he re-read through the detailed notes from the folder. "Dr Bremmer and his team returned to the DOPA site they had been working from whilst the review began, but it seems every one of the surviving senior team passed away before any were called to task for their actions. Frankly, this whole thing would never have been given a green light today and shouldn't have been back then if someone with common sense had been involved. It's a debacle from start to finish with personnel ignoring strict protocol and procedure, instead letting their egos run riot. In your mother's case, included."

I wasn't going to argue that point, knowing I had *no* leg to stand on trying to defend her. She had known what she was doing, and the consequences of her actions, and had still gone ahead and fucked things up royally. Costing too many lives.

"Ah, and now I remember. Another symptom of old school thinking and backwards logic." Cormac sighed heavily as he continued reading, and I got that *oh oh* feeling that usually heralded bad news.

"What's wrong?" I asked stupidly, since I had no doubt the agent was about to explain his frustration, otherwise he wouldn't have spoken out loud.

"Parts of this project have been redacted. Even from the original source file and OPS reports, all clearly marked *Eyes Only* clearance which means everything should be there to view. The site Dr Bremmer and his team returned to, for example. As well as some of the findings made by the coroners who investigated the individual deaths. Bits taken from statements made by Dr Bremmer shortly after the ritual's failure." Cormac flipped through more pages, shaking his head. "It's the sort of paranoid idiocy that makes my life so much harder, when all it is, is plain stupidity. Hiding our own information from ourselves. Always ends up being nothing important after we spend valuable resource tracking down the redacted information."

"And yet …" I couldn't helpful, earning me a sharp look from him.

"Yes, Morgan. And *yet*." He sighed, thumbing his forehead and sitting back in his chair. "You have brought me evidence of ghosts, of dead men committing Accord breaches and the very file that disproves your accusations is missing information, Something does not feel completely right but I won't have any more answers for you right now. I'll have to speak to some people, access our archives and cross reference some details before this makes more sense."

"What about the beetle suits?" Felix spoke up, giving up on her sulk finally and engaging in the conversation. Granted she wasn't even supposed to be in the meeting with us, but I figured she was allowed one question. One only.

Cormac flipped through several more pages, frowning.

"Those are definitely of old DOPA design, but again, there is little information about them in this file, and even some of that has been redacted too." He admitted, sighing before looking across at the picture. "Details of our R&D capabilities are strictly *Need To* Know, and frankly, you don't. But I break no rules by admitting we have investigated the use of suits designed to minimise or neutralise the effects of the Real upon mortals. Purely for use in accordance with our agreement with the Courts and how we may or may not act in the Real, of course. But if the individuals involved in Herne's capture wore suits from this picture, they must only have access to hardware many variations out of date. I'm honestly surprised they were of any functional use, given their age."

"Is it nae possible such items were acquired through the black market? Ah am not casting aspersions on yer organisation but these thing do happen." Jessica asked, her knowledge of such matters based on many years of experience, having to find *alternative* sources for the equipment we lycans needed when mortal law strictly precluded the purchase of such things. You'd be surprised how many ingredients we use against creatures of the Real that show up 'red-flagged' on websites as they also happen to make explosives or poisons used by mortals against themselves. Further idiocy, but what can you do?

"I will not say it is entirely impossible, since I am too long in the tooth to think in absolutes." Cormac replied with a dry smile. "But OPS and DOPA equipment is stored at secure sites under strict security, and we catalogue each and every item we develop or produce no matter its age or function. There are severe penalties we apply to any employee looking to profit from the sale of old stock, and almost all markets, be they black, white or rainbow coloured, know that to handle such goods will eventually land them in *very* hot water. With OPS happily cranking up the heat."

A knock on the door interrupted any further conversation, with Cormac again rising to see who it was. It turned out to be the young woman of the quills again, and I had to wonder if everyone else had gone home for the day and she had been stuck with on-call duties for maybe stabbing the wrong person. But this time she was accompanied by one of the armed OPS guards, and even with their hushed tones I caught enough of the exchange to know something was up.

Ok, so I can only resist listening in on conversations for *so* long. Blame my wolfie ears.

Jessica obviously had no shame in listening in either, as we looked across at each other. She nodded, the only sign of her readiness for any sort of trouble being a slight tightening of her jaw and a shift of her shoulders in her immaculate and tailored suit. I cracked my neck, giving Felix a quick head jerk toward the door to give the young witch warning.

Cormac turned back in time to catch my gesture, rolling his eyes but biting down on the automatic sigh to show he knew we'd heard.

"It would seem I am wanted elsewhere urgently. If you would wait here until I return, I will arrange for your colleagues to be released into your custody and they can meet us outside the Tower after they have been debriefed. There are no formal charges being brought for any of them." He told us calmly, but I caught a sudden spike in his whole demeanour. Before, he'd been weary enough that anyone else would have been slumped over their desk, sleeping like Rip-Van-Winkle. But now he smelt of annoyance, bordering on angered frustration. Something he'd been told did not sit well with him. "I won't keep you longer than necessary."

With that he left the room in the company of the woman and guard, closing the door quietly but firmly behind them.

Jessica immediately turned to me, the question writ clear on her face.

"What did you do, Morgan?" She asked quietly, but I shook my head, certain of one thing. This wasn't my fault.

Then we both looked across at Felix, and I coughed meaningfully.

"Hey! No fair!" She almost squawked. "Fine, I snuck in when I shouldn't have, but that's it! This is nothing to do with me."

Jessica took out her mobile phone, finding that against all odds, she had a signal. She dialled a number quickly and waited until it connected.

"Elspeth? Ah would appreciate it if you could drop whatever it is you are doing, and come over tae the Tower of London." The Alpha spoke softly into the phone, no trace of ire or annoyance in her voice. Just instructing a colleague on what needed to happen. "Yer student decided tae tag along, and ah'd appreciate you coming tae collect her whilst we deal with our detained colleagues."

I caught the sharp, exasperated retort from the other end of the conversation, and knew that Felix was in for a serious talking to when her teacher in all things witchy-woo showed up. The young woman seemed to guess that as well, as she curled up a little more in her seat, looking thoroughly dejected.

Cormac was gone for long enough that I was almost ready to start singing again … a fact I knew would drive whomever was listening in on our conversations to distraction. Neither Jess nor I were under any illusion that there *wasn't* someone attentively taking down everything we said, to be reviewed and analysed later. This *was* OPS after all.

Just as I was about to crack on with my version of Kate Bush's *Time after time* as a subtle hint, the door opened and Cormac reappeared.

And neither Jess nor I could miss the fact that something had him *very* upset. Pissed, even.

"Ms Walker." He spoke with clipped tones, the anger visible in his eyes, and making the dark rings under them all the more obvious as he focused on my Alpha. "I have just been instructed that any further investigation into these disappearances by your pack is to halt. Cease. No longer take place. The case is deemed closed, the individuals involved most likely having returned to their Courts without informing friends or family still remaining in this Realm or the Real."

"What the fuck?" I growled, not believing what I was hearing. "After what we just fucking brought you? The photo. What my half-sister witnessed. Herne being bloody kidnapped. We're just supposed to think he fucked off on a jolly and didn't bother to tell anyone including his own Court? And he went off with a bunch of fuckers dressed in beetle suits. *Really?!*"

"Mr Black, the viewpoint I have been presented with is that our organisation is stretched incredibly thin after the recent traumatic events that you yourself were actively involved in, and continues to face numerous challenges that frankly are above your clearance to discuss with, and beyond your ability to understand." He replied to me, dead pan. The anger a snarl in his eyes only. "I have been reminded that we need to carefully manage our resources, and that chasing down miscreants who already spend their energies toeing the line of mortal law with ageless disregard to those same laws is not high on our priority list. As such, we will *not* be pursuing any further enquiries into this matter, nor would we advise you or any member of the lycan committee expend energies there also. That might be seen as a disregard of the law by yourselves too."

"As to the matter of the Lord of the Wyld's supposed disappearance," He carried on, a muscle clenched along his jaw. "I will remind you no formal invitation has been received by us from that Court to involve ourselves in what I have been told is a matter that did not take place on mortal soil and as such, *not our business*. Your Alpha should also be wary of any involvement in Court matters that she or any of your other pack leaders have not been formally invited to hunt on."

I snarled, ready to tell Cormac just where he could shove his rules and law, but Jessica laid a hand on my arm, stopping me without even saying a word. She locked eyes with Cormac, reading his face for a moment, before nodding.

"Ah understand yer organisation's position, Agent Smith. After all, we *all* have someone we have tae answer tae." She told him with no trace of sarcasm or anger in her voice. Just acceptance. "If that is all, then ah believe we should collect our colleagues and leave you and your organisation tae focus on those higher priority items. Ah would hate tae waste any more of yer time, and am sorry fer arriving without prior notice."

"Not at all." He replied blandly, face just as poker-straight. "I recall one time I called at your offices quite late, before Mr Black and I went to meet one of the Sisters of the Arch. We should never feel we cannot call on one another at such times, if we feel the reason merits it and the other party may benefit from what we have learned."

I knew they were talking in code, making sure whomever was listening was confused as fuck and missing the point. But unfortunately, I also had no bloody clue what they were agreeing to. Instead, I just kept an angry snarl on my face, playing the pissed off mutt.

To be fair, it wasn't too hard a part to play. *Beyond your ability to understand?* What the fuck?

"I will see you three out then." Cormac told us as Jessica nodded once. "It's the least I can do."

Felix obviously wanted to ask what the hell was going on, so I stepped close to her and wrapped my arm unsubtly around her shoulders.

"No unscheduled sightseeing tours today," I told her gruffly, feeling her tense under my grip. "You're in enough trouble as it is, so I'm just making sure I know where you are until we're out of here. Don't make this worse than it is by pissing off this lot with more lip or attitude."

That seemed to do the trick, as she let out a heavy breath but bit down on her questions. I gave her a quick nod, hoping she'd understand, and steered her after Jessica and Cormac.

Thankfully the queue had vanished by the time we made it to street level, the sun dipping towards the horizon to herald evening's approach. The Tower was closing down, and the mortals filling the open space before the castle's entrance were now mostly city workers heading home or heading out of a well-deserved drink. We'd been down in OPS's headquarters far longer than I'd realised, getting absolutely bloody nowhere. But then again I was still catching up on mortal time, having bounced around the Wyld and lost track of a mortal-based *day* system given how time passes so randomly in the Real. One moment could drag on for a day, one day could burn through an entire month in the blink of an eye. Plays hell with me, and I usually get to crash out and sleep off the unnatural jet-lag it causes.

Not this time though.

Cormac stepped up to the barrier as we crossed through, the moustache-bearing Yeoman standing at his side and trying not to glower at us as we walked across the square.

"What …?" Felix started to say, but Jessica just shook her head.

"Not here." She cut her off, confirming my suspicion the pair had agreed something in the room. "Look, there's Elspeth."

I checked, seeing the witch walking towards us at a fast pace, stride long. Full of purpose, which I reckoned meant she was about to deliver a blistering dressing down to Felix, just as soon as we were out of the public eye and beyond hearing of anyone normal. My ear still ached from the last time she'd blasted me for over-use of a particularly offensive word to women-kind, and I felt a flash of sympathy for the young witch … before remembering she had dropped herself in the shit by hiding behind a veil and tagging along.

From behind us, coming out of the Tower and moving to join us with their own escort of Yeoman guards, our newest packmembers caught sight of Jessica and I with looks of chagrin, humour and annoyance mixed amongst them. None of the newbies, the pups, seemed to have been hurt in any way, which meant they had gone peacefully enough when OPS detained them. One good thing, I guess.

I lifted my arm from Felix's shoulders, sure in the knowledge she wouldn't do a runner but instead face the music for her actions, and waved to Ellie.

The witch smiled, raising her hand as well ... but suddenly her expression froze and her step faltered. At the same time, I felt Felix jerk beside me, slamming into me as she suddenly stopped. I tasted surprise, and fear, spiking in the cool late afternoon air.

And my senses lit with savage lightning, a ripping and tearing of the very air around us that stank of Veil-taint but of massive power unleashed as well. Pressure hammered down on me, like we'd suddenly dropped from on high, even though my feet were firmly planted on the ground.

"Morgan, there's something ..." The young witch started to say.

Then all fucking hell broke loose.

Chapter 5

Explosions ripped through the quiet bustle of the Tower Square, shattering the background hum of mortal life like a boulder tossed into a lake. Savage thunder boomed like a roaring cascade of cannon fire, and the very air split all around us in a maelstrom of destruction.

I've said before that lycan are proof against magical attacks. Lob a fireball at us and it'll bounce off our furry hide, try to drown us in a watery bubble and it will pop like a pricked balloon. Anything *directly* set against us will ground out and fail. However, rig an explosion to occur as we step through a mystical trip wire or step on an activation rune, and we're as vulnerable as mortals to the indirect threat and danger.

Both Jess and I were caught completely unawares, our lycan senses failing to warn us as the ground heaved upwards and stones splintered all around us. Smoke roiled in to cloak the whole square, as flames erupted on all sides, tainting the air with burning flakes and the acrid stench of chemicals. We were tossed from our feet, as I desperately grabbed Felix and tucked her inside my reach, rolling and bouncing across the shattered stone. Off to my left, I heard Jessica snarling out very unladylike curses, as she tumbled in the wake of the blast.

Secondary explosions rang out, making my ears throb, as fire erupted all around us. Smoke filled the air, thick and cloying, so that the entire square was shrouded in semi shadow, apart from the flickering bursts from whatever was on fire. And an odd, off-key whine filled the air, shrill to my sharp ears. Like a drill, digging into my skull.

Wrongness assaulted me, my sense stunted and dulled. I couldn't taste anything but the smoke and something like acid that fouled my tongue, so much so that I gagged and spat to rid myself of the taste. But my eyes teared, unable to part the gloom, and I realised this was no normal attack. Whomever was behind it had planned to deal with something other than run of the mill mortals.

Movement blurred in the smoke, and I scrabbled to my feet even as I pushed Felix behind me. I lashed out with my fists, a voice inside me telling me I didn't dare Change. Not here, not where we stood. We were too exposed, there had been mortals all around us when the explosions went off. Jessica would skin me if I swapped suits and then appeared in front of civilians, or was caught on camera which was more likely given how much mortals loved to film horrible events like this.

I caught the smooth clack of machined parts even as the air swirled before me. I tried to duck, but Felix was leaning against me with one arm wrapped around my waist so I was caught, unable to dodge as four impacts lit against my shoulder and lower abdomen.

Pain fired up from the strikes, needle-sharp, but even as I reached for the wounds I felt a different wrongness sinking into my veins, swirling in my blood. Fucking *wolfsbane*. My questing fingers found darts embedded in my body, hypodermic fucking injectors that had pumped their load into me.

Ah, shit on a stick.

Wraiths swirled in the smoke, and I heard more shots fired like dull impacts in my bones. That had to be Jessica, the bastards pumping her full of poison as well. Whoever these fuckers were, they had come prepared, somehow rigging the explosion without triggering our lycan-born sense of danger and then weakening us before moving in for the kill.

Bastards.

I staggered, fighting nausea and weakness surging inside me. I'd only just gotten over being poisoned by Baba Bohdana in the Wyld and my body was feeling sorely abused, but fuck me if I was going to lie down and get deaded right now.

"Felix, can you do anything about this fucking smoke?" I snarled, plucking the darts free and reversing them so I held long needles in both fists. I might not have my claws, but these were long enough to do damage if I hit the bastards hard enough. And despite the wolfsbane coursing through me, I was pissed and full of fury.

"Can't. Feel … weird …" Felix half whispered, then collapsed to the broken ground. She hit with a dull thud, boneless, and I snarled a curse. The bastards had done something to her too. Something in the smoke maybe. Whatever it was, she was out of the fight before it had even started.

I knew I couldn't leave Felix defenceless, but I had to find Jessica and Elspeth in all this shit. So, fighting back a groan from my abused muscles, I hefted the young woman up and over my shoulder. Normally, I wouldn't have even noticed her weight, but whatever the bastards had used to deaden my senses was also sapping my lycan strength. I felt as weak as a mortal, bringing back horrible memories of facing Gregory Allen in Morgana's arena. Shit, could this be something similar? Was this more of her shit, coming at me even after the fae lunatic was dead … well, sort of?

I staggered in the general direction I'd seen my Alpha hurled, breath hissing through my teeth. I passed several still bodies on the ground, torn apart by the explosion, but thankfully none of them were my friends or our new packmates. Mortals, innocents caught up in whatever the fuck this was, their blood spilled all over the ground and the horror of their last moments writ clear on smoke-stained faces.

Snarls and growls drew me as I staggered over the broken concrete, to find Jessica on her hands and knees. She had pulled a dozen darts out of her body, but several were still stuck in her back, out of reach. Letting Felix slip gently to the ground, well as gently as I could manage given how shit I felt, I crouched down and gripped her shoulder.

"You ok?" I asked stupidly, earning a grunting laugh that was half pain, half humour-filled.

"Ah would say … nae. But that much should be … obvious." She hissed out, as I plucked out the darts still lodged in her. "We cannae Change here, nae matter what we face. The risk …"

"Yeah, I know." I growled. Whoever these fuckers were, they'd planned the location of the attack to keep us locked to one shape only. Too much chance of exposure, especially on the back of just how much hard work OPS and the Courts had put in place, to blanket Morgana's ruination of London. "Any idea who these fuckers are?"

"Nae clue. But they … left … me this memento." Jess told me as she pushed herself up, wincing.

Looking down, I saw the hilt of a combat knife buried in her side, just below the ribs. The design was odd, making me think back to the types of weapons my old friend Terrigyle Munstrum would have had in stock, before he was killed saving my skin. Whatever, it looked well used, not the sort of toy you see idiot mortals stabbing each other with in gang fights over turf or some other stupid reason these days. This was a professional's weapon. A soldier's blade.

"Who the fuck are these people?" I spat out a mouthful of poison, already pulling the shit from my veins like I had in the Wyld. It hurt to do so, but until I learned Lykaois's trick of burning it off, I had to get rid of it the old-fashioned way.

"Your worst nightmare, wolf." A voice grated far too close, not having pinged on any of my senses.

A boot slammed into me, and I rolled across broken ground, cursing as a form shifted in the thick smoke. Manlike, it looked odd, wrong to me somehow. Far too massively built in the shoulders and arms, like a child's drawing of a superhero or monster. But what was far more telling was the fact the fucker was clad in a close-fitting set of full body armour, fitted with antenna over its head and arcing around its broad back. And its helmet was set with bulbous curving lenses, everything about the thing shouting one word to me in Briar's voice.

'Beetle'.

These were the fuckers who had taken Herne.

Waves of weakness rolled over me as the bastard closed with me. Something about the figure was sapping my strength, ruining my desire to rip the fucker's head off or smash it through the ground. But I still had my anger, and I spat out another mouthful of wolfsbane, feeling its effects lessen inside me.

"If you knew my nightmares, you'd know how fucking low on that scale you and your weird-arse armour rate. Why don't you take off that stupid helmet so I can see what sort of idiot I'm about to spread all over this bloody square?" I growled back at it, as I reached for my Wyld-strength, to bolster me, keep me in the fight.

And found nothing.

Ah, shit.

I tried to summon my Ivory armour to sheath me, or my Shadow brand to freeze the bastard where it stood, but nothing answered me. I was cut off, any talents I'd been granted taken from me somehow. Again. Fuckity-fuck fuck!

"I'm going to enjoy taking your head." The bastard grated, its voice altered by the helmet it was wearing. But I thought I could pick up some sort of accent, South African maybe. Harsh, Germanic possibly. But definitely not run of the mill local. "But firstly, I think I'll gut your lady-friends here. Well, one lady. One bitch, but beggars can't be choosers."

The figure came at Jessica even as she staggered to her feet, the lycan Alpha fighting to keep upright against the multiple doses of poison running through her. Normally she'd be ripping this joker apart without breaking sweat but I could tell she was just as weakened as me, if not more so as I'd managed to rid myself of most of the wolfsbane. But the weakening effect the attacker was causing still had me feeling as feeble as a new-born pup.

The attacker's monstrous arms lashed out, one hand punching Jessica across the face even as she tried to block. She spun, but the figure snagged the knife hilt buried in her side and with no effort, yanked it free in a spray of gore.

"The question is, wolf, which one should I cut first?" The figure asked almost jovially, waving that big combat knife in the air as Jess's bloody dripped from its edge. "Do I start with the she-wolf, or the little witch? Who's going to hurt more for you?"

I came at him, staggering across the broken floor and snarling my fury. I didn't care that I had no special Court talents, not even that I didn't have my lycan strength. Whatever it took, I was going to throw everything I had at stopping the bastard from hurting either Jess or Felix.

I might as well have taken off my boot and thrown it at the attacker, the little good I did. With no strength and my co-ordination shot to shit, my target had all the time in the world to casually slap my fists aside, and lash out.

Bright pain erupted in my stomach as the bastard buried the long knife deep inside me. I felt it rip through things I'd prefer were left intact, and spat out a mouthful of blood as the fucker ripped the blade free. Even as I buckled, the stranger hammered the sharp tip into my left shoulder, ripping through muscle and making my arm suddenly numb before casually kicking me in the stomach, splashing blood everywhere as I tumbled back onto my arse.

"Sit the fuck down. I'm gonna make you watch as I bleed your friends." The figure laughed harshly, swiping the knife on its armoured leg to clean off some of my blood. "Then, when I'm done with them and only then, I'm gonna take your head."

Sick fury filled my head, as I grabbed the wound in my stomach with my working hand to try and keep things inside me that threatened to leak out. I couldn't feel myself healing, it was just wet and hot and slippery, and I had the horrified realisation that whatever this thing was, it had switched off everything supernatural about me. I was bleeding out, and I couldn't fight the fucker.

I couldn't stop it killing Jess. Killing Felix.

Killing me.

Chapter 6

Something spun out of the smoke, slamming into the figure and making it stumble away from the prone figures of my Alpha and my friend even as it raised its bloody knife.

I recognised Elspeth's bag, the one she always carried crammed full of tomes, vials and other items useful to her craft. In darker times, mortal women used to carry bricks in their small handbags to defend themselves against arrogant, chauvinistic men ... but they had nothing on the punch that Ellie could throw with her carry-all.

She staggered out of the smoke behind it, red hair in disarray and clothing burned.

"Get away from my friends!" She snarled, as the air around us sang with electrical charge. Green fire surged in her eyes, and I caught sight of her familiar forming above her. The phoenix, a creature of flame and fury that she could summon when threatened to defend her. The last time I knew she'd called on it, we'd been facing a shape changer that had taken the form of an ogre whilst we were trying to free Artur Pendragon. The phoenix had cut out the bastard's eyes and slashed it to shreds before we'd done a runner, eager to escape the sewer roof falling on us.

The attacker snarled a curse, reaching up to its shoulder and adjusting some device that was fitted there. I immediately felt the waves of weakness slam into me, stronger than before, like a storm crashing against the shoreline. It was all I could do not to throw up as my vision swam but I forced my hand against my wound, pain flaring inside and keeping me conscious.

Ellie spat out a curse, her skin paling and the fire shivering in her eyes. Her familiar gave a shriek as it flickered, fire dimming under the onslaught of whatever negating effect the attacker was throwing out.

Desperately, the witch lashed out … not at the attacker, but upwards, into the smoke.

Emerald fire blazed, shattering upward and shredding the smoke so that the shroud covering us began to tear, break apart and disappear. I sucked in a breath, tasting fresh air finally, and dragged myself upright to stand, one hand jammed in my stomach but finding some life in my other arm again … enough to raise my fist weakly. Fuck it if I wasn't going to go out this way. Not like this.

Another figure appeared in the thinning smoke, clad in the same outfit as our attacker. This one bore a gun much like the ones we used when we needed to hit our targets from a distance or to deal with large numbers of targets, fitted to fire the darts that had poisoned both Jess and me. Even as Ellie turned to face the newcomer, it bashed the end of its gun into her face, dropping her to the floor in a splash of bright blood.

"Cover's blown. Hostiles inbound. We're moving to the secondary objective." The newcomer instructed with clipped tones, pointing with the gun. "The Doctor will want to deal with the two witches personally. Take them, and let's go. Leave the wolves."

Our attacker snarled a curse, those featureless orbs comprising its face plate shifting between Jessica lying bleeding on the ground to me, and then over to Felix and Elspeth. Finally, it slammed its knife into a sheath angrily and grabbed up the young witch's unconscious body.

"We ain't finished, wolf." The figure snarled at me, even as I caught the sound of gunfire and shouting somewhere off in the thinning smoke. I might have heard my name called, but I was fighting to stay upright and conscious from blood-loss and being poisoned. Things weren't working as they normally did. "We'll be in touch, and we can pick things back up again. Till then …"

I knew it was coming, but I couldn't stop the huge fist that slammed into my stomach, splashing gore from my wound and sending me crumpling to the floor, writhing in pain. Blood gushed from my mouth, and I howled out my agony as I saw Elspeth gathered up and slung over the attacker's second shoulder with negligent ease.

Then the attackers faded back into the smoke, leaving Jessica and me bleeding out on the broken concrete. Greyness gathered over my eyes, but I snarled in fury and forced myself onto my hands and knees even as pure poison sang from the wound in my stomach and the one in my shoulder. Bleeding heavily, gasping like a dying bull, I dragged myself across the six feet separating me from my Alpha, slumping down beside her in a puddle of gore.

Fingers slick with my own blood reached out to check her neck for a pulse, finding it slow and horribly erratic. The wolfsbane was coursing through her, fouling her entire system, and unless I countered it, she'd suffer permanent damage from the sheer amount of the fucking stuff they'd pumped her full of.

Luckily, though I hadn't thought to bring any weapons with me on our trip to see OPS, I was still wearing the stained clothing I'd had on me for my trek in the Wyld. And that meant I had Redcloak supplies stashed. It took me far too long to rip open my pockets and spill out the contents, but I finally found the container holding my garlic and popped the lid.

Mashing the bulbs, I groaned as I freed my other hand from where it was held, holding me together. With blood pumping out of the wound into my lap, I gripped Jess's jaw and forced her mouth open. Then I jammed in shredded garlic, rubbing her throat to stop her choking as she involuntarily swallowed.

She jerked, coughing and writhing but I held on, forcing another mouthful of the potent antidote down her neck. I used up all my supplies, knowing she needed as much of the stuff inside her as I could get, to start stemming the wolfsbane's effects.

Her pulse began to slowly settle, and I felt the weakness that had afflicted me start to drain away like fog burning off under the sun. My pain addled thoughts were slow to make sense of that fact, but I finally realised it must mean the attackers had gone. Taking Felix and Elspeth with them. To fuck knows where, and we didn't even know who the fuckers were or why we'd been targeted.

Sirens screamed in the distance, growing steadily louder, and I heard the stomp of booted feet on the ground, nearing our position. Someone was shouting my name, Jessica's too. Despite the weakening effect vanishing, I was in no state to fight if this was more trouble coming at us, so I just curled myself around Jessica. Protecting her with the only thing I had left, which was my bloodied and broken body.

Then I let myself fall into the greyness and pain.

Chapter 7

Waking up hurt.

A lot.

I've started rating the times I've woken up to pain, to try to get a grip on what was normal for me, and what resulted from the sort of scary shit I found myself in all too often these days. Up until recently, I had had Morgana flaying the skin from me and breaking a good number of my bones as a contender for the worst morning after experience. But then I'd had to channel my life energies into my mother to help return her to life, freeing her from servitude as a fetch to Baba Bohdana. I *technically* hadn't had the morning after from that experience to compare yet, but at the time, I think I would say it beat Morgana hands down.

Both paled to mild irritation compared to how I felt right now.

I was lying on a bed, butt naked apart from a sheet stretched over my frame. I could feel bandages wrapped around my stomach and my shoulder, the wounds underneath finally knitting together again. But even with my lycan nature working again, I was horribly weakened. Blood loss, trauma, poisoning and the earlier events from the Wyld all had written their bills for me to pay, and they weren't leaving until things were settled.

I was also hooked up to what I had to guess was a wheeled fluids and blood rig, with IVs running into my arm. Whomever had done the treatment seemed to have been thorough … normally I wake up no matter what when someone tries to stick needles in me.

Knowing I needed something to help me get back on my feet, I reached for that touch of the Wyld inside me … and almost crowed with sheer joy as I felt strength flood through my body. Not enough to sort me out completely, but definitely enough so I might find out where I was, and how I'd gotten here.

And then start asking more pointed questions. Like who the fuck had attacked us. Why they'd done so. Was my Alpha ok. And where the fuckers had gone, taking Elspeth and Felix with them. Simple, easy stuff like that.

"Where the fuck am I?" I asked, not expecting anyone to answer. But I felt it needed asking.

So I was surprised when someone did.

"*In the House of Elrond,*" A damn good impression of Ian McKellen as Gandalf replied. "*But it is not ten o'clock in the morning. Nor is it the morning of October, the twenty fourth. But you have been doing absurd things like Frodo since you left home.*"

I rolled my head over, feeling the muscles in my neck protest, to find a surprising but familiar figure settled in a comfortable chair, eyes of amber fixed on me.

"Manisha? What the fuck are you doing here?" I rasped, finding my voice still hoarse from the smoke and shit the bastards who'd attacked us had used on me.

The Ivory Champion, personal guard captain to Titania and general bad-ass smiled sharply as she closed a book she had been reading, and pushed herself up from the seat to join me at my bedside. She was dressed in simple clothing, linen and cloth under a tabard emblazoned with the Ivory crest. No armour, and she wasn't even carrying a weapon that I could see. But since I knew I could summon armour through my Ivory brand, I had to guess she had the same talent. And with a weapon in hand or no, she was an Ivory fae of deadly prowess, even standing there in what looked like fancy pyjamas.

She eyed me critically, making me conscious of the thin sheet covering my otherwise naked body. Usually I'm not worried about the whole butt naked thing, but right now I was feeling vulnerable and broken almost beyond repair.

"An Errant of the Court needs to take better care of himself." She told me, her stern expression slipping into an easy smile. "And know his limits. You taxed Lancelot's talents greatly to fully purge the foul poisons and undo the damage wrought atop one another. She wanted you to have her thanks for providing such a challenge, but asks you do not damage yourself so badly again any time soon."

"It's not like I was *trying* to get killed!" I growled, even as I tugged the IVs out of my skin, hissing as that added a fresh complaint to the long list I was dealing with. "And you haven't answered my question. Apart from an obscure *Lord of the Rings* reference, I still don't know where the fuck I am or what you are doing here."

"You reside in a place of safety," She replied with a shrug, reaching to the side and pouring me a glass of water. I downed the chill liquid gratefully, motioning for a second. "As for what I am doing here? My Lady has made it clear she has vested interest in your continued wellbeing, and that her Knights are to offer aid whenever we feel it is needed. Asked for, or not."

So Titania had her Knights keeping tabs on me, watching my back and with a 'carte blanche' to intrude whenever they saw fit, if they felt it was in my best interest? Part of me was pleasantly surprised and grateful, given the number of times my arse ended up in the fire. Another part however wondered just what sort of trouble the Knights might cause, given their immortal definition of 'offering aid'. The last thing I needed was a bunch of sword wielding lunatics gate-crashing my personal or professional life in the Mortal Realm on a whim.

"Besides, there is a matter my Lady wishes to discuss with you, Errant." Manisha added as she reached over and poured more water. "But I think that can wait, given the current predicament you and your Alpha find yourselves in."

"Jessica. How is she?" I felt my stomach lurch, the fear running cold fingers down my spine I remembered her heartbeat under my bloodied fingers, the feeling of her life gushing out from the wounds inflicted on her. "Where is she? I need to see her."

At that moment, the door to my room opened and I found myself wholly unsurprised to see Cormac Smith step inside. His grey suit was blackened and bloodied in places, his tie undone and loose under his collar. Whatever he'd been through, it had left its mark on him.

"To answer your immediate questions, you are in a safe house, a location both Manisha and I agreed offered you both the best chance of recovery whilst removing you from immediate danger. Those individuals who ambushed you will be seeking you in all your usual haunts and regular locations, and have at their disposal the means to circumvent anything but the most heavily armoured defences to reach you."

"There is also the matter of … collateral damage, to civilians … mortals … around you to take into account." He continued, and I remembered the bodies I'd stumbled over in my haste to find my Alpha and my friends. "The perpetrators have shown they do not care about inflicting casualties on bystanders if it means achieving their mission's goals. Thus, removing you from the Mortal Realm and relocating you to a place of safety that Manisha assures me is proof against intrusion removes the chance for further injury or death to anyone unfortunate to be near you."

It made sense, and it answered my question. I was back in the Real, stashed under Ivory protection. That dealt with the immediate issue, and meant I could focus on the other burning need I had.

"Where's Jessica?" I repeated, squirrelling away the knowledge that Cormac must have reached out to Ivory himself and requested sanctuary. Why he hadn't chosen Shadow, given my direct affiliation and also personal link, was either an indicator he knew nothing of my bloodlink to the Morrigan, or he did not trust them as much as their brighter cousins. Personally, I reckoned neither Oberon or Madb were safe bets in terms trustworthiness, but Manisha I could rely on.

"Your Alpha is resting as best she can." The Ivory Knight told me, and despite fae usually being as readable as a block of stone, I picked up on the nuances in her voice, telling me things were simply not right with Jess. "The substance used to poison both you and her seems to be some sort of wolfbane-based chimera. The use of garlic blunted the initial symptoms, however the damage it has wrought taxed both Lancelot and our healers greatly. And …"

"Go on, hit me." I grimaced, bracing myself.

"Not when you are still so sorely wounded. It would not be fair." She shot back at me before shaking her head. "Morgan, the substance used on you is some sort of engineered product, that defies all the normal cures. It is almost like it is *sentient*, has a life of its own, and defeats any attempts to simply remove it from your Alpha. It is obviously tailored to target full-blooded lycanthropes, and we were only able to halt its progress towards its intended conclusion. Not remove it from her."

"Your Alpha … well, the truth is she is dying. The wounds inflicted on her remain unhealed, and the poison continues to weaken her. Unless we are provided with an antidote or more information on what this foul creation is, we can only delay it from ending her existence." Manisha reached over and clasped my unwounded shoulder in sympathy. "I am sorry, Morgan. I wish we could do more, but whomever crafted this made sure it was effectively resistant to our craft and skills as well."

Fuck.

I pulled the sheet off me, not caring that I exposed my nakedness to the room. Cormac glanced upwards to the ceiling whilst Manisha simply ran her eyes down my lean, scarred body. Taking me in from head to foot with a casual glance, and that sharp smile of hers.

Seeing light linen pants and a loose t-shirt folded neatly on a chair beside the bed, I hobbled over to them and carefully started dragging things on. My stomach wound pulled, and my shoulder protested resoundly with all the movement but I didn't give a flying fuck.

"I need to see her." I told them both, before focusing on the Ivory Knight. "Then we can talk about what the hell happened at the Tower and who the fuck tried to kill us. Not before."

My voice made it clear the order of priorities, as did the set of my jaw and my squared shoulders. Even as I bit down on the stab of pain. The fae simply nodded and offered her arm as if to support me. I mock growled, shaking my head and limping to where Cormac held the door open.

They'd stashed Jessica in a room much like mine, down the hall and to the right of where I'd lain unconscious. Both rooms had been crafted with no windows on any wall, instead charmed to give the illusion of sunlight warming them. Perfect to stash people away from sight, making sure no-one got a peek in to confirm the occupants or a possible clear shot from outside with a decent sniper rifle, long bow or the like. In the Real, anything was technically possible.

She lay in a comfortable bed, hooked up to more IVs and fluid bags, though that was the extent of the 'mortal' science allowed in the room. Instead, glowing rune stones had been set around her bedside, each one pulsing with the beat of her heart, whilst behind her a tall glass-like column stood, filled with swirling glittering fireflies that spun and weaved in some strange pattern. Threads of fire wove out of the construct, entwined and interlaced over the lycan Alpha's body as she lay under a sheet of white cloth.

Thankfully my Alpha was awake, but I could see just how ill she was. Sweat soaked her skin, which was an unhealthy grey, and her eyes were narrowed in obvious pain. But she still managed to smile as I stumped in, followed by Manisha and Cormac.

I also noted the two Ivory Knights standing guard, each to the side of her bed. Neither were fae I recognised, but both, unlike Manisha, were fully armoured and had their swords unsheathed. Though their points rested on the simple wood floors underfoot. Their gaze settled on me, judging, then moving on as they obviously found me in no state to present a threat. I caught the minute stiffening of their stances as they caught site of their Knight Captain enter with me, and had to fight to stop a hard chuckle at their need to appear alert. Guards were the same the Realms over, always ready to shit themselves over being found relaxing when on duty, not taking their duties seriously.

"Morgan. Ah cannae tell you how good it is tae see you up and on yer feet." She told me with a weak smile, coughing at the end and drawing a hard breath that rattled in her chest. "You had me worried there fer a moment or two."

I forced a croak of a laugh, pushing down the fear at seeing just how bad a shape our Alpha was in. Jessica had always been a rock against which everything else broke, even when Lykaois had laid her out whilst possessing Jacob. Her strength so much more than any of the rest of us mutts, her endurance carrying her through the loss of her mate and partner, keeping her focused on the tasks ahead of us. If anyone could claim to be the unspoken leader of the Alphas, the top dog, it was Jessica even though she never once acted in that way.

To hear that she was dying … to see her like this? It broke things inside me. Lots of things.

"It'll take more than a couple of weird-arse psychopaths in stupid looking insect armour to put me down. Or you." I told her with false sincerity. "We'll be up and after the bastards who took Felix and Elspeth before they know we're coming. And we'll make them pay."

Jessica smiled but shook her head.

"Nae, Morgan. Ah'm of the opinion ah will be staying here fer a while yet. It'll be down tae you tae lead this hunt." She told me, coughing again. When she recovered, she motioned to Cormac, standing silent behind me. "Agent Smith. Morgan will act in mah name and that of mah pack, and ah would appreciate you according him the same support and aid you if ah asked it of you. We have our people tae find and get home safely."

Cormac smiled warmly, shrugging in an easy manner.

"Ms Walker, as you know, Morgan and I are well acquainted with working together already. Nothing in my eyes has changed to prevent us from causing the sort of chaos and destruction that you would expect from a Hollywood movie, as seems to happen naturally when we work together." He commented with dry humour. "So please do not expend energies worrying which are best used for healing. We should let you rest."

She nodded gratefully, shooting me a final look.

"Cormac has assured me our new packmates were nae harmed in the attack, and have returned tae the office with nae further incident. They will inform Emma and the others of what has happened." She told me, gritting her teeth against a wave of pain. "Emma will get word tae the other Alphas, and they'll make sure everyone else is safe. You need tae find our lost friends, Morgan."

With that, she settled back with a groan, closing her eyes and shivering with fevered shakes. I felt Manisha's hand on my shoulder, steering back towards the door and this time I had no strength to argue or fight.

The fae escorted me to another room, this fitted with a large table and ornate chairs, and with large windows that normally would have let in the daylight from outside. However, these were heavily shuttered, and illumination provided by crystalline torches sat in sconces fitted to the walls. Fruit filled bowls on the large wooden table, and fine crystalline carafes held an array of what I guessed were the strong Real alcoholic beverages that were not sold the mortal side of the Veil.

I slumped down in one of the plush chairs, shaking my head when Manisha offered me a glass of something purple in colour and giving off the vapours normally associated with paint stripper. She shrugged, taking one herself while Cormac poured himself a large mug of coffee from another table and sat another in front of me without bothering to ask.

OK, so the guy gets me. Sometimes.

"I am sorry that we have been unable to cure your Alpha so far." Manisha told me with true sincerity in her voice as she settled in a chair opposite me. "But I can promise you we have not given up hope, nor will our healers stop attempting to push the poisons from her body and heal her wounds. Lancelot herself will do what she can, once her energies are restored from working on you."

"How long do you think she can last?" I asked, taking a pull from my mug. The coffee was, as expected, excellent quality and flavoured with a selection of nuts to give it a pleasant tang. I let the warmth of it seep inside of me, soothing a little the aches as my body slowly rebuilt itself.

"Your Alpha is a fighter of considerable strength, and I cannot imagine she will simply lie back and accept her fate." The Knight Captain said with a smile, before her expression turned serious. "But there is only so much energy she can throw at this thing before she is without the will left to keep breathing, keep living. Our healers do what they can, and if matters take a turn for the worse, they will place her in the *sleep of death*, which should slow her weakening somewhat. But if there is an antidote to be found, I would hazard you need to find it soon."

"We call it a 'coma'," I told her, nodding since that was all I'd really expected. "Makes it sound a whole lot better and less bloody ominous than *sleep of death*. Just a hint for future conversations."

She shrugged, and I shook my head. That was the way with immortals. They'd been doing and saying things for thousands of years, so why change?

"Ok, how about we try an easier one then? What's so important that Titania needs to talk to me about, when I *should* be back in the Mortal Realm, finding Ellie and Felix, and putting those fuckers who attacked us in the ground." I growled, gripping my coffee cup tightly. "Coz I'm pretty bloody sure they're the same bastards who took Herne *and* the Harrowed Queen as well. Just saying, if it helps speed things up."

Manisha and Cormac exchanged looks, and I braced myself for whatever bad news was headed my way. I could feel it coming, like the boulder bouncing down the mountain side that you just *knew* you couldn't dodge in time. They should probably call it the *Wiley Coyote* instinct.

Finally, the Ivory fae set aside her glass and looked across the table at me, intently.

"Morgan Black. Errant of Ivory." She began, which was never a good sign when people started throwing titles at me. "Our Lady, Queen Titania … she wishes to ask. What do you know of the Court of Shadow placing hidden agents in our very heart? And their purpose?"

And the penny, that had been bouncing for months now, finally dropped.

Fuck.

Chapter 8

I *knew* this would come back to bite me one day.

Well, happy 'proving myself right' day!

My mind bounced back to when Ellie and I had stood in the sewers beneath London, in the Lady of the Lake's domain. With stinking grimalkins lurking nearby, faced with two very dead bodies entangled where they had supposedly fallen after fighting to the death.

A nice, simple trick played on a poor dumb lycan by an immortal. And I'd fallen for it, hook line and bloody sinker. Accepting things at face value whilst I let myself be distracted by bigger fish frying.

The truth was, Bodian Jones had been a lycan low level runner. A Redcloak with a reputation so blackened by dodgy dealings and criminal intent that none of the Accord-abiding packs would work with him. Only the Nighters, given their alpha didn't mind breaking laws himself as long as nothing ever led back to his door. And Bodian had proven a useful tool for not only the Lady of the Lake but that bastard alpha too. Even dead, the little shit had been used to run a game on me and Jessica by Talen Orben, when one of their own pack claimed to be the dead lycan's lover.

Talen and his lunatic mate had used the all too obvious lie to force me to fight in the Blooding, as a challenge to Jessica's authority over our whole pack. That had ended badly, with me beating the lying mutt to a pulp, but the entire Nighter's pack had paid the greater price, wholly eradicated when Talen made a stupid-ass claim to rule over all the packs. With a little help from Robert Knox and the tricks taught him by Morgana.

To say that evening still haunted me would be a serious understatement. I'd lost good friends that night. Packmates. And no matter what Jessica told me, I'd carry the blame inside me for as long as I drew breath.

The other body, I'd found out, belonged to one Sir Jasper Ne Cu Boireann. Who went by the moniker *the crying knight* with actual tears tattooed on his cheek. Supposedly for all the foes he had slain, showing his true knightly bearing as a honourable Ivory fae in the Court of Oberon and Titania.

Except he wasn't.

When I'd checked the fae's body, I'd accidently triggered a glamour he'd been under, reverting him back to the Shadow fae self that was his actual truth. A plant, a mole, a spy in the Ivory Court. I'd tried to find out what the fucker had been up to with the Morrigan one time and literally almost had my head bitten off, and been told never to mention my findings to anyone. Or else.

But yeah, I'd known.

Manisha sighed as she obviously read the truth from my silence, settling her hands on the table to obviously stop herself from doing something rash.

"Morgan Black. The role of the Errant is to work with *all* the Courts," She reminded me, as I tried to work out how not to be painted as the idiot here. "To help settle discord between them, not keep secrets from either one. Secrets that might *just* be found out and have the potential for causing untold harm and damage to the goodwill and trust that exists between them. Like, for example, my finding out that the Shadow Court have placed their own kin in our midst, and have been investigating matters of Ivory business themselves without our knowledge."

I held up my hands, shaking my head and trying to look as innocent as I possible could. Which was not much, given the facts.

"Hey, I don't know anything about there being *agents*, plural." I told her, knowing this was the simple truth. "And I don't know anything about what or why Shadow is up to. What Mabbie thinks she's doing. All that happened was I stumbled over a corpse of what I thought was an Ivory Knight when I was investigating Excalibur's theft. Sir Jasper. Your Crying Knight. But it turned out he was Shadow fae, under glamour. That's all I know. Seriously."

"Excalibur. As in the sword of King Arthur of legend. A portal key?" Cormac enquired, and I nodded, shooting a look at Manisha.

"Yeah, that's the one. We ended up finding Manisha's brother … *Artur* Pendragon … imprisoned in the Lady of the Lake's sewer getaway. He was mixed up in a whole shitstorm with that particular lunatic." I gave the agent the cribnotes, since I knew he was aware *something* had happened at the Natural History Museum, but not sure what my Alpha might have told him. "The Lady was pissed at Obie and Tit… um, the Queen for dumping her arse here in the Mortal Realm when the whole *King of England* ploy fell through, and she used Manisha's idiot brother to try to set off a bomb in Camelot's heart with the sword. That's all."

The agent nodded, and switched his attention to the Ivory fae.

"If it helps, I believe Morgan when he says that is all he knows." He said, and I was surprised to realise the agent was defending me. "And if the double agent was mixed up in the theft of *one* portal key, does it not stand to reason …?"

"Yes, yes. I see the logic of things." Manisha sighed, taking a drink from her glass to give her a moment to think. "I don't like it, but I cannot argue how it looks."

Me, I let my ears prick up at the mention of portal keys. They were a pain in the arse at the best of times, allowing their bearers to pop through the Veil unharmed from one Realm to another. And on top of that gifting the bearers with certain special abilities as well. Excalibur had enabled Artur to be an unbeatable warrior whilst he wielded it, and I knew of several other keys that had caused a lot of trouble in the hands of mortals over the years. King Solomon's ring being one, allowing the wearer to not only traverse the Realms but also enslave certain creatures to do their bidding. Genies, djinn, efreets … those fae of the air who filled Arabic fables. The sod had been like a hoover across the Real, enslaving every bugger he could to take back to the Mortal Realm to do his bidding.

The Knights Templar had also had a portal key actually made in the shape of a gate, which allowed them a place to hide their ill-gotten riches and access to armour and weapons that made them unstoppable against the pagan hordes they faced. Until they fucked up and pissed off the wrong people back at home, and had to do a runner into the Real to escape being burned at the stake for heresy and witchcraft.

Every time mortals got their hands on one of these powerful objects, they invariably fucked things up royally for themselves, but caused a shitload of pain to a whole load of random and unfortunate people along the way. Every time.

Portal keys were claimed and strictly controlled by the Courts, and to my knowledge, Ivory held the lion's share because, well, Oberon demanded it to be so. After Excalibur's theft, I had assumed the idiot had had his security protocols checked and had changes implemented so we didn't face that sort of fuck up all over again.

Maybe I'd given the immortal fuckwit too much credit.

"The matter my Lady wished us to discuss, Morgan," Manisha finally started to explain and I made sure I gave her my undivided attention. Or as much as I could spare, worrying about my friends, my Alpha and planning all manner of nasty shit to do to the bastards who'd hurt us. Probably at least ten percent then. "It is two-fold. Firstly, after I was granted the honour to serve my Lady and Lord as Knight Captain, I instituted a review of our security in the Court. I knew that Morgana had managed to infiltrate our defences on multiple occasions, and as you were there to witness, I also understood members of Madb's Court were able to attempt an ambush on the very Court of Bones. So I was expecting to find … *issues* that I would need to address."

"However, what I was not expecting to find were agents of Shadow in my very cohort." She admitted with an angry spark of fire flaring in her eyes. "Shield maidens. Swordswains, all sworn to ward my life as I have done theirs, sworn to serve our Lord and Lady. I had fought and feasted with them, yet they were not who they pretended to be. Their purpose and honour not bound to my own, nor that of Ivory."

She took a moment to drink, as I digested the fact that Sir Jasper had not been Madb's only spy. It made sense, why would she gamble on only having one asset in her cousin's Court if she could plant more? I guess it just sucked that Manisha had found out that supposed friends were something way less than that.

"The discovery was … troublesome, but we managed to avoid any unnecessary bloodshed." She finally continued, and I had to wonder just how *that* had happened, knowing how ready to fight she had been when I'd first met her, based on my sarcasm and mockery alone. She must have had to reign herself back in massively when faced with traitors and spies. "However, before these tricksters made their escape, one who was particularly close to me imparted one reason for their existence. Their purpose in my Court."

"A matter of portal keys."

"What, Madb wanted to steal some?" I hazarded a guess. It was entirely possible … Oberon hoarding them all *had* to piss his Shadow cousin off shitloads, and the way I knew Madb, she wouldn't be shy about answering that annoyance with actual deed. "I get it, embarrass Obie and get herself some of his riches in the bargain. Classic Mabbie."

But the Ivory fae shook her head.

"No, Errant. The Queen of Shadow was not seeking to gain portal keys." She replied, and I felt a twitch in my gut, telling me I wasn't going to like what she was about to say. "Instead, she had her agents investigating rumour that someone *else* was thieving from the Ivory Court. Had in fact been carefully removing portal keys from our vaults and leaving charmed replicas in their place."

"Not only keys, but also kin." She continued and my gut clenched again. "The Queen of Shadow had set her agents the task of investigating Ivory kin, those who had vanished over the many passing years. For she herself had found members of her Court lost, without adequate knowledge behind their location, or any truth of their demise. Just simply … vanished."

"Quietly, carefully and never in enough numbers to arouse suspicion," The Ivory fae announced with certainty. "Both Courts have lost members and we knew nothing of it."

Oh, this day was just getting better and better.

Chapter 9

I sighed a heavy sigh, reaching up to rub the ache I felt growing between my eyes, as the boulder from the avalanche was joined by several friends and they all started to party.

"Let me see if I'm getting this straight." I pushed aside my cup of coffee, counting things off on my hands. "One, despite the shitshow that was Excalibur's theft, no-one thought to keep an eye on the oh so precious portal keys or even bother to make sure they were all where they were supposed to be until you came along?"

"Two, I get that being immortal means you lot live a lot and go off doing many things to keep from getting bored, but no-one noticed people going missing and not showing back up again? In either Courts?"

"Three, whilst all this is happening, us mutts start hearing of Real creatures vanishing from the Mortal Realm. Possibly taken by Morgana, possibly killed but no-one knows for sure so we start to stick our noses out and ask questions … and get arrested by bloody OPS for tramping all over *their* investigation. Which no-one told us about."

"Four, I stumble into a total clusterfuck in the Wyld where Herne has vanished. Only to find that Baba Bohdana has been supplying weird arse mortals in silly insect armour actual Wyld creatures of the Court *and* then betrays Herne, packaging him off as well as the Harrowed Queen." I waggled that finger vigorously at the sheer stupidity of it. "All under the other Crones' noses. And these fuckers had a way of appearing in the Wyld, laying a trap for those two as if … oh I don't know … they had access to fucking portal keys!?"

"And finally, having put paid to Baba Bohdana and her little arrangement, I'm only back in this Realm a day, and *some fuckers in stupid insect armour* blow up my Alpha and me, try to kill us and then fuck off with two of our friends. Right outside the office of OPS, one of the most secure and safe locations we could possibly think of. As if they had, oh I don't know, portal keys to let them hop all over the fucking place?"

"Is that about it?" I waggled my whole hand at both Manisha and Cormac, my anger and frustration giving a bite to my words. "Or have I missed anything else fucking salient?!"

Manisha and Cormac both seemed to understand my feelings running a little wild right now, as neither tried to challenge my tone or swearing. Instead, they both looked across at each other before Cormac nodded, once.

I took that as a sign I could continue. So I did.

"Then, I might hazard a guess here. It's purely bloody hypothetical and based on no real evidence, but bear with me. Is it *possible* that the fuckers who were working with Baba Bohdana in the Wyld are the same fuckers who have been nicking portal keys from Ivory, and stealing away Real folk from *all three Courts*? And who attacked Jess and I just now, trying to blow us to fucking kingdom come?" I snarled, knowing that if I had been holding my cup right now it would have shattered. "Who the fuck are these people?"

"We call them the '*Grey Men*'." Manisha replied before Cormac could speak, her expression hardening. "I have crossed swords with them twice, a long time ago. They are an abomination, and something I and many others wish the mortals had never been allowed to create. For these creatures to be a part of this long conspiracy, it makes me wonder who would dare be so foolish?"

"Ah, if I might interject?" Cormac enquired politely, and the Ivory fae nodded, settling back in her chair and drinking from her glass. But for once the inscrutable fae demeanour of the Knight was definitely ruffled, her anger bleeding through.

I turned to face him, wincing as my wounds pulled, as I focused on the pertinent details of what I'd just heard.

"Mortals 'made' them?" I asked, having some horrid flash backs to recent fuckery involving mortals messing around and making things they shouldn't. "Don't tell me this is one of Knox's pet experiments? What the fuck did DOPA have the bastard working on?!"

The OPS agent slipped a file from inside his damaged jacket, laying in on the table like a magician spreading out the cards of his next trick.

"Robert Knox did indeed pioneer some of the skills required to craft what our Ivory companion calls a Grey Man, yes, but his contributions came at a later date, well after the initial test subjects were drafted, and the process initiated." He admitted, shrugging his shoulders. "The … ah creations we are talking about are based on a Second World War project overseen by the Allied Forces."

"Project *Chimera*."

The name was an ugly one, and if it had anything to do with the *chimera* of legend, then I wasn't going to like where this was headed, one single bit.

"Up until the day before yesterday … yes, Morgan, you have been unconscious almost two days … I only knew vague details of a deep-black project that had been shut down and the resources, well, discontinued." Cormac continued, opening the file and leafing through several pages contained within. Not many, and I could see they were from different sources, coloured and written or typed, but all definitely old. "All assets burned, as we say. There were rumours of course, as there always are, of continued interest in the mechanics of the project. Folders of the scientists' involved going missing and such. But it was a dead, closed project, and there are always whispers and conspiracies abounding. It is something we mortals simply *do*."

"However, details from the assault on you and Ms Walker could not be so easily ignored, and so I requisitioned the pertinent files as well as any details of who might have accessed the information stored in them." The agent tapped his fingers on the tabletop, irritation evident in the stray gesture. "Only to be told that any all details of Chimera were sealed, beyond *Eyes Only* and above even my clearance. No mention of it to be made in any report, and any attempt to obtain further information or investigate it further resulting in severe penalties. By the same office and individuals who so recently locked down the disappearing citizens we both have uncovered."

"Uh huh. That doesn't dodgy as fuck *at all*." I drawled, and Cormac nodded curtly once.

"I wholeheartedly concur. That is why I went against the directive, and sourced whatever I could about Chimera from the dark web and contacts within and outside OPS who owe me a favour or two." He replied with a cold smile. "If someone *is* involved in reviving closed, burned projects and making free people vanish, whether from this or any other Realm, then I am duty bound to stop them."

"This is what little I managed to uncover before you woke."

"Project *Chimera* was one of many wartime projects undertaken by the European Allies to create a super soldier, an advanced combat-ready individual able to tackle any obstacle, face any challenge without fear of failure." He began, and I had to fight back the urge to hum the *Captain America* theme tune. "This was never intended as a weapon for use against our counterparts in the Courts, instead only meant to face the horrors created and utilised by the Nazis and their allies. Your packmate, Jacob Moon? I believe he faced off against one of the Third Reich's shock units, the *Werwulfs*. Genetically modified lycanthropes, monsters straight out of any horror story. Well, there were countless others, bred in laboratories and unleashed on the countries Hitler and his cohort sought to conquer, and the soldiers fighting to prevent them from achieving their goal of global domination."

I nodded, knowing a little of what the agent was talking about. The mortal histories had been carefully cleansed of any reference to monsters, freaks, demons and the like that had appeared across Europe as war raged, but there were always sources from those dark times if you knew where to look or who to ask, and I'd heard more than a few stories and seen enough evidence to substantiate some of the weirder shlock-horror B movies of zombies Nazi soldiers, Allied forces fighting werewolves and other creatures of myth and fairy tale ... proving that when mortals go to war, there really is no line they won't cross, no depth they won't sink to if they think it would guarantee success.

Jacob had *not* been one of those sources, being as tight lipped about his past as, well, an incredibly tight-lipped bugger could be. He'd only shared one story with me, before things had gone to hell with Lykaois. But that had been bad enough.

"Well, the chimerian strike force or Scarecrows as they called themselves, or grey men as the fae knew them, were one answer." Cormac shook his head, his own feelings writ all over his face about what he'd learned. "An ill-conceived and baldly thought through answer, but one all the same."

"Allied command wanted soldiers who would follow orders no matter what, face horrors beyond anything any normal man or woman could handle, and keep fighting. Die even, but do so by negating Hitler's threat." He continued, grimacing with distaste. "That meant using men and women who believed, *really* believed in their purpose, their goal. Fanatics, borderline psychotics, individuals with certain personality flaws that would otherwise be deemed too extreme, too perverse for ordinary soldiers. The kind of soldier coming back from war but never truly leaving it behind. Or never coming back at all."

I grunted, my anger burning hot, the desire to growl at Cormac and get him to hurry the fuck up almost too much for me to push down. But I bit down hard on the beast inside, knowing I would give Cormac the time he needed to explain, to reveal who the fuckers were that had attacked us, and why.

Especially if these fuckers weren't from the Real, but locals. Mortals.

"DOPA specialists employed revolutionary and radical techniques to 'improve' these soldiers. Enhance them by surgical procedures, isolating certain characteristics key to success and binding one to the other." Cormac spoke slowly, distaste staining his otherwise normally neutral tones. "The records I gained access to were not complete, but the processes they used were, to say the least, ethically and morally questionable…"

"Ha!" Manisha had kept mostly quiet until then, but this crossed a line for her. Obviously. "Questionable?"

"Your mortal kin hunted unaffiliated Real creatures for their body parts, itemised them for their *skills* and then used barbaric techniques to graft mortal and immortal together." She hissed, eyes blazing with unholy fury. "My Lord Oberon, and Lady Madb, both became aware of this *project* and sent kin to uncover the truth of it. What we found? Ogre's limbs grafted to mortals to make them stronger. Troll-skin taken to be bound to your mortal soldiers to serve as armour. Goblin eyes plucked from their skulls to gift your mortal soldiers vision in blackest night. The gills and lungs from our mer-kin to grant breath under water like the fish in your oceans. They harvested parts from kin stolen from battlefield and from their beds, dismembered our people whilst they yet lived to ensure their barbaric *sciences* would succeed and created monsters of the mortals they worked on."

Cormac held up his hands in surrender, and I could tell he wasn't here to defend what had been done.

"I have read the justifications made, and I in no way agree with them." He admitted, seeing the fae nod once and the fire in her eyes turn done a notch, but only one. "But what Manisha Na Pendragon Cie says is only part of the truth. Whilst the primary aim of the surgeries was to increase the subject's strength, resistance to weapons of all kinds, able to survive in all manner of environments, there was a secondary element. Which I believe is why the fae know them as *grey men*, and why they so easily ambushed you and your Alpha."

"It is common knowledge in any surgeries where transplanting is required that the host body may reject the new organ or whatever it is they wish to bind one to the other. Grafting a new leg onto an amputee is not a simple task of sewing it to the stump, and that is just when the recipient and donor are of the same blood type, same basic species." He explained and I bit down on another growl, about not needing a lesson in medical procedure. "But for what the Allied forces and DOPA wished to produce, they were binding mortal and immortal … oil and water. Wholly different species, oft-times anathema one to the other and the reason for many, many failures until the scientists changed their direction, and stopped treating this as a simple mortal operation, and began thinking *metaphysically*."

"What I was able to obtain did not include the actual manner they succeeded, but they did describe part of what had to happen … and its consequence." He obviously caught my impatience, but in no way hurried his explanation, the sod. "The subjects underwent some manner of alteration at their core, which in effect fundamentally changed their *emotions*. The '*id*', the centre of what makes mortals so baffling to denizens of the Real, that part of the men and women that every religion calls a *soul* even. Something was removed in the process, the reports speak of failed test subjects driven mad, degenerating to extreme self-harm and suicide."

"But for those who endured this change, they became something more than they had been." Cormac shook his head, and I had to wonder at the sanity of the men and women who had volunteered for such an extreme alteration to their very self. I couldn't comprehend what would drive someone to risk so much. It was fucking nuts. "It was found that these men and women became emotional chameleons, so to speak. You could pass one on the street and not see them, not remember them. Speak to them, but lose any and all memory of them afterwards. They were able to simply enter where they wished, do what they wanted and leave without causing a single reaction from guards or individuals set to specifically watch for them."

A word sprang to mind, based on my knowledge of mortal history. They had had many faces and names for that sort of person … spies, ninjas, warriors who worked in shadow and whose aims were always to remain unseen.

"Assassins. You invented perfect fucking assassins." I snarled, and Cormac nodded slowly. "Fuck."

"When Allied command were appraised of this talent in the test subjects, they of course began sending the chimerians on ultra-black missions. They were used to strike fear into Hitler's High Command, slaying key targets in impossible ways, finding ways through the toughest security, the greatest defence." The agent explained. "I believe if thing had been different and the project not burned so thoroughly after its creation, they would have been sent after Hitler himself and possibly ended the World War in a far different manner than history tells."

"So what happened? What fucked up?" I growled out my impatience even as my brain ticked off the salient details. Assassins who wouldn't trigger a reaction from even our lycan supped up senses, who could get so close to any of us without us even realising? That was some messed up shit.

"They did. The chimerians." The OPS agent smiled sadly. "The reports I was able to access detailed barbaric occurrences on missions. Brutal torture of enemy soldiers, even cannibalism, though since these soldiers were no longer truly mortal that term might not have been wholly correct. But the truth seems to be, the surviving members of the Scarecrow regiment were less than stable, less than controllable and all too soon they became the monsters they were meant to be hunting. Turning on their own allies, their handlers and the scientists who had made them. Bloodily, painfully, and beyond any thing that those in command could cover up or ignore. So the project was shut down, those surviving chimerians either on mission or awaiting orders terminated with extreme prejudice. The mechanisms of their creation locked away and the success of the Allies' offensive placed back in mortal hands."

"The chimerians were locked back in Pandora's box. To be forgotten, lost and never ever to see the light of day again. Or so was the directive at the time."

I grunted a derisive snort.

"I thought you said you were only able to uncover a little information?" I snarked, shaking my head as I took in just how deep in the warm and stinky I'd landed. "That was a shitload you just *happened* to be able to get your hands on."

Cormac looked at me with his cool grey eyes.

"I have never forgotten the lessons I learned from my time serving Queen and Country in another capacity, nor my years as a field agent in OPS." He admitted with quiet confidence. "When we are at war, information is often the most effective tool and weapon any soldier can hope to hold, and can be pivotal as to who wins and who loses any engagement. And I have managed to acquire many sources, am owed many debts in my time spent protecting this Realm. All to ensure I can answer troubling questions quickly if the need is great. Like now."

"War?" I looked back at him, then at Manisha. "That escalated fucking quickly."

"This *is* war, do not doubt it for a moment, Morgan." The OPS agent replied, his tone sharpening. "A secure facility has been attacked, casualties inflicted. Blood has been spilled, even though the desired goal was not accomplished. Someone orchestrated these events, no matter how rash and ill-thought through they were. And that someone, or someones, are a part of the very organisation I work for, to protect against exactly these sort of things from ever happening."

Cormac looked across at me, clasping his hands together and pausing before continuing.

"The fact is, Morgan, I believe someone, or maybe a select few members of my very own organisation bear you, *specifically,* ill-will." He told me bluntly. "Whether due to the whole Morgana affair, or due to you blundering into their private operations, I do not know. But whoever they are, they are senior enough to attempt to place a gag order on me and my teams, and to have sufficient resources and drive to mount an offensive outside one of our most protected sites at short notice, in broad daylight, and utilising the services of ultra black-op soldiers of unnatural nature who *should no longer exist*."

"I deemed it wise to have you and your Alpha moved to a neutral location, as your homes and workplaces as well as those of your colleagues and loved ones will be under surveillance. Also the risk to civilian lives is too high to have allowed you to remain a target now that we now these assets, these grey men, have no conscience or code about killing innocents to achieve their goal." He continued laying out the whole shit-show. "The attack outside Tower Hill is being treated as a simple terrorist event, blamed on one of the more proficient cells we know operate in the city. At last count, forty-three civilians were harmed by the explosion, eight already dead from wounds sustained in the blast or by the actions of the chimerians."

"Your Alpha has been poisoned, and I can only believe the reason we are still speaking is that they lacked key knowledge of your … peculiar nature, otherwise you would be suffering as she is." He told me with the same bluntness, hammering home his points. "The attack, and any reference to you has been labelled with a *need to know* order from the office commanding core London OPS operations. Who I report to. They want to know where you are, and if you are alive still. And if they locate you, I believe another visit from the grey men is all but guaranteed."

"In short, Morgan Black, as of this minute, it seems OPS wish you dead."

Chapter 10

You know what, the only thing I could was ...

Laugh.

Cormac simply cocked an eyebrow, whilst Manisha cracked a sharp smile on her otherwise impassive fae features.

"Oh come on, you don't see the fucking funny side of this?" I almost spat out, shaking my head and grinning a dead man's smile. All teeth. "I've had a very pissed off ex-Lady of the Lake goddess want my head for pissing all over her carefully laid plans for revenge. A bunch of teenage hexenwolfen try to murder me and bury me in Greenwich park to cover up their stupidity. A vengeful Shadow fae puppet loose the *death of immortals* on me whilst she tried to trash the whole Court order and set herself up as a new Queen, along with her insane life stealing mortal. Traitor lycan alphas try to murder me, changed into truly fucked up Harrowed monsters, and even a lying, evil mushroom Crone who just wanted payback for being bullied by her sisters. Oh and let's not forget my murderous, infamous half brother Jack, also called The Ripper, and Baba Yaga, plus what might have been the god of lycan or just a Wyld immortal with delusions of grandeur wanting to use me as a puppet to take the Antlered Throne. All who wanted my skin, for one reason or another."

"With all that shit behind me, it makes a kind of twisted sense the fucking mortals would want their turn trying to kill me."

Manisha chuckled whilst Cormac just sighed and let my gallows humour pass without comment.

"Be that as it may, I think we can probably put aside the humorous commentary of this current situation and move to what our next steps should be." He commented instead, looking across at me with his calm grey eyes. "Would you not agree?"

"*Our* next steps, is it?" I asked sharply, knowing I was being petty but hell if I hadn't had enough reasons to let myself have one small, small tantrum. Just the one. "Seems to me I'm the only one at the table targeted by supposedly-non-existent super assassins, hired probably by *your* superiors to silence me and cover up the shit they've been pulling. You could just walk away, accept the gag order and get on with the rest of your life. No?"

Most mortals, when they get upset, vocalise loudly and gesture with vigour. Get all flushed as their anger take control, shout and generally act in a violent manner. It's something to do with how primates react, which David Attenborough has done quite an amazing job documenting through his life. So many documentaries available of them bouncing up and down on camera, flinging their own faeces in a rage.

Rarer are the types who grow quiet when angered. More focused. In some fundamental way enacting a polar opposite to their more vocal alternates. They tend to be way more dangerous, the ones to watch when they get upset as the resulting carnage can usually be seen on mortals' front-page newspapers, or picked out as chalk outlines on the ground.

Cormac was neither of these.

As I faced him across the table, he showed not a single flicker of emotion or change in temperament at my accusations. Neither hotter nor colder. Instead, he just looked back at me, expression calm and unruffled.

"Let me clarify two points, Morgan, which I think will speak to your question." He replied, lacing his fingers together. "Firstly, your Alpha herself requested that I work with you on the hunt for your attackers, and by defacto the missing individuals you and your pack have taken on the task of finding. I stated I saw no problem working with you towards that end, and I meant that wholeheartedly. And that was *knowing* there are members of my own organisation probably involved, and attempting to block anyone's attempts to aid you. Including my own."

I nodded, as I'd heard him say as much to Jessica. There had been no hesitation, no attempt to hedge or deceive her. Cormac had signed up straight away, willingly and of his own volition.

"Secondly, you should know what happened whilst you were recovering from your injuries and poisoning here." He continued, voice still level, unchanged. "As I said, the attack outside the Tower of London inflicted multiple casualties. Forty-three civilians wounded by the explosions which destroyed much of the forecourt that led to the Thames Clipper-service, the pathway around the Tower and granted tourists and locals access to various streets off the main thoroughfare. Eight who have died since then."

"I was part of the first response on the scene, and witnessed the chimerians before they retreated back through the Way they created, presumably utilising a stolen portal key. That is the only method I can think, the only explanation how they circumvented the security around the Tower." He continued, his eyes locked on mine. There was not even a twitch from his scent, nothing changing even though his words almost demanded an emotional outburst. "I witnessed their attack on you and Ms Walker, but also their casual and brutal treatment of the civilians who crossed their path. After they departed, whilst we assessed the situation, I provided first aid to those in most need and offered what little I could to those not hurt from the attack, but still with wounds inflicted. Physical or otherwise."

He raised up a hand, counting off fingers.

"Sarah Miller, age nine. I had to explain that her mother would want her to be brave and strong, to tell their father what had happened and how there was nothing he could have done to save his wife of twelve years."

Next finger.

"Jordan Assail, age seventy three. I tried my best to make him understand his family would not hate him for taking his three grandchildren out for a daytrip to the Tower, not knowing only he would survive."

Next one.

"Temperance Dahlia, age seventeen. She was terrified that the explosion was her fault, a judgement by God for her and her boyfriend sneaking off for a liaison despite her parents not liking their relationship. Matthew, age twenty-five, who she would never see again."

And another one.

"Gerald Hume, age thirty eight. On his first date with his new boyfriend, who he'd been chatting online with for the past seven months since joining a dating website in search of true love. Jeremy Isles, age forty one. They were planning to have champagne at the Shard, but Gerald wanted to see Tower Bridge lit up at night, and blamed himself for Jeremy's death."

He held up his fingers, looking across the table at me.

"You ask me if I wish to simply accept the orders given to me. To look the other way and allow this travesty to go unchallenged. When I have held Sharon Temple's hand as her life bled away. When I have bandaged Sean Christoff's eyes, knowing he will probably never see again. When I will probably be jeopardising my career, possibly my life and those others who I involve to see this thing done right?"

I went to speak but he stopped me, just with a shake of his head.

"No. That is my answer." He told me calmly, unruffled and yet with thunderous resolve drumming in every word. "I took my oath. To *protect Queen, country and all those who dwell here from enemies both foreign and of our own making.* And as God is my witness, I will hunt down the perpetrators, conspirators and anyone involved else in the madness that took place on *my* watch. And I will make them rue the day they were ever born, created or chose to enter this Realm. That, I can promise you."

There wasn't really anything I could say to that, even though I *did* have to bite down on a sarcastic quip or two that sprang to mind. The truth the agent had spoken quelled my jests, since he deserved some respect for sharing details he hadn't had to. Shown a part of himself that I guessed was private and carefully locked from everyday view.

No matter the lack of emotion in his voice, Cormac Wessen Smith *cared*. About his job, about the people he protected on a daily basis. He was more like Gregory Allen, the ex-detective and love of Ellie's life, than either probably guessed. Greg had just let the years of dealing with the rougher side of society wear his patience down until all he'd had left was his righteous anger to armour himself with. Whereas Cormac had let it polish his armour, hardening it around himself.

Gregory. Ellie's love.

Shit, I'd been so fucking stupid.

"Fuck, I've been so dumb." I struck my head with my palm, letting my wolf's grin slip free. "Your chimerian fuckwits have made one huge mistake."

"Care to elaborate on their foolishness?" Manisha asked politely, and I nodded.

"They took Ellie and Felix." I explained, seeing Cormac nod too as he caught on. "I don't know her exact title, but I'm pretty sure Ellie is chief witchy-woo of the coven devoted to Terra. And Felix just joined their circle, knitting group or whatever you call it. They're both protected by the Goddess of the Mortal Realm and those idiots just kidnapped them. They're fried."

In fact, I was surprised something cataclysmic hadn't happened already. If I'd been unconscious almost two days, that would have been plenty of time for Terra to enact her justifiable vengeance on the bastards who had my friends. A localised volcano venting magma all over the fuckers whilst allowing the pair to escape. Lightning strikes hitting one exact spot in the entire world to fry the fuckers in their gimpy insect suits. Anything.

So why hadn't it?

"I believe we probably should bring in an expert on that particular matter. He arrived not long after you woke but I thought it best to discuss … well, certain matters before he joined us." Cormac commented, and I felt my stomach again. This sounded like bad news, just when I was tapped out on my quota for the day.

By some unspoken command from the Ivory fae, the door to our room opened a moment later. I already knew who was about to join us, his scent uncannily specific. Probably had something to do with having been dead, and then having gotten over it.

Gregory Allen shot me an appraising look as he dragged out a chair and sat down, a frown marring his forehead. It still was weird to see the curving tattoos marking his face, a gift from Terra when Ellie had bound him back to himself using lifeforce that Robert Knox stole from his victims. Supposedly it told anyone in the know he was part of the Goddess's coven now, a protector rather than a practitioner. Someone not to mess with.

And as ever, there was that odd scent to him, that lingering *offness*. Not that I was saying he smelt bad, this was in no way a reference to him being a rotting zombie or anything. But something *had* come back with him when he returned from the dead, an ability to switch off whatever specialness it was that any creatures of the Real had. Rendering them vulnerable, mortal.

He'd used it on me once, making me just a simple mortal man in a fight we'd had. Almost killed me, the sod. But then again he'd been under the influence of one of Morgana / Harry's Harrowed slug-like worm children. I had begun the healing process of forgiving him … baby steps, but still.

"Good to see sleeping beauty's awake." He commented gruffly, and I smiled with my teeth. Yup, baby steps indeed. "Now is someone finally going to tell me what sort of trouble this mutt's gotten my Elspeth in *this* time?"

"Hey, you're supposed to be the big bad protector now." I shot back, shrugging. "Isn't it your whole *reason for being* to keep her safe at all times? What happened, you overslept or decided to slack off for a sandwich?"

"Boys, boys." Manish admonished us both, clapping her hands together sharply. "If you truly wish to compare the size of your manhoods to prove who has the mightier staff, then as we are in my Court's domain I claim the rights to judge. Unclothe, and we can begin the … *inspection*."

The way she uttered the last word was just plain wrong, as was the way she clenched her long, slender fingers. I knew fae had supernatural strength, and even the glimmer of a thought of what she was thinking of doing with her fingers made my brain stutter for a moment in rebellion.

"Um, that's ok Manisha." I reassured her, shooting Gregory a slightly wide-eyed look. One which he also seemed to share. "That's just how we greet each other. Nothing meant by it, right?"

"Yeah, just chewing the fat." The ex-detective agreed with a pained grin. "No inspecting needed here."

"Ahem, if we might get back to the matter at hand?" The OPS agent at the table interjected, earning a quirked eyebrow from Manisha, and even the suspicion of a smirk. "And yes, I understand my unavoidable comical quip. Ha, indeed."

"Morgan was just commenting on Miss MacElvy and Miss Price," He explained as we all settled back in our seats. "And the assertation that their captivity might be shortened by divine intervention, all our worries put to rest by a certain Goddess intervening in this matter. I believe you have something to add on this subject, Detective … sorry, Mr Allen."

"Don't worry. I still sometimes forget." Gregory commented with only a slight growl and pained tone to his voice, that I reckoned I only caught thanks to my heightened senses. "Sorry to rain on your parade, Morgan, but Terra's not coming to the rescue here."

"Why the fuck not?" I snarled, my momentary calm once more shredding back to anger and frustration. "She can't still be too weak from Morgana's attack, surely? And don't tell me my little trick in the Wyld took too much of her energies and I fucked things up coz I *really* don't want to hear it. She *is* the bloody Goddess of the Mortal Realm, right?!"

"She is." Gregory told me calmly, ignoring my outburst. "And that's the problem."

I stared at him, missing the elephant in the room, the cow in the car or whatever huge thing I couldn't see staring me in the face.

"It's one I actually get, it makes sense to me. I wish it didn't but it does." He decided to take pity on me and explained. "Laws, Morgan. Rules that everything and everyone in the Realm has to obey, follow and generally not break if we want things to continue as they should and not descend into anarchy, disorder and ruin."

"Terra might be the Goddess, the lifeblood of Earth and something so vast and eternal that I just can't wrap my head around it," He went on as I started to see where this was headed. Not anywhere I wanted, and with no happy ending like I'd hoped." But She is part of the Realm too, and so has to obey the rules too. It's not like the Disney cartoons of Greek gods and goddesses doing whatever the hell they wanted with no rules to follow. Terra is bound to ward life, to protect and nurture. She is the *shield* that stops anything bad from outside knocking down the door and ruining everything. Not a sword. A shield."

"If whoever has taken Elspeth and Felicity was from 'outside', not from the Realm, then Terra would have nothing stopping Her from acting." Gregory shook his head, as my hopes for an easy win guttered and died. "But Mr Smith has already explained to me that the individuals involved, whilst not what you might call *normal people*, are local. Men and women, people of the Mortal Realm. And as such, not for Terra to police, not for Her to judge and punish. Her hands are tied …a lot like how I used to feel, when I knew one little knock, one strong push, one shove in the right place and a very bad person would never be seen again, never trouble innocents again. But it wasn't for me to do."

I looked at Gregory, seeing the truth in his eyes, the acceptance despite the fact he was talking about a guaranteed certainty of getting Ellie safely back to him, with Felix as well.

"That's …. shit."

It seemed to sum it all up for me, with as much heartfelt feeling as I could put into the word.

"Yeah. I used to say that a lot myself." He admitted. Then he slapped the table top, looking across at Cormac and Manisha.

"So, now that's sorted, how about you explain *exactly* who the fuck has our loved ones, our friends?" He growled, and I saw the tattoos on his skin glimmer with latent fury. A stray thought hit me. Maybe Terra was having to play by the laws of the Realm, but that didn't mean She was out of options and entirely dealt out of the game. Not by a long shot. "And how we get them back and make sure the bastards who took them never see the light of day again?"

I grunted an *amen* to that.

Chapter 11

"*Chimerians*? Geez, that's a bloody stupid name for a bunch of psychotic supped-up devil's rejects." Gregory growled, shaking his head as Cormac finished bringing up to speed on where we'd gotten to. "Sounds like one of those bands my parents listened to back in the Sixties."

"Someone obviously agreed, given how they chose to call themselves Scarecrows instead." Cormac replied. "Probably due to the horrific disfigurements the surgeries done on them caused. I am surprised they didn't opt for the Frankensteins or some such moniker."

I cast my mind back to the two attackers, clad in those all-encompassing beetle suits. Something had been obviously wrong with the first one, his arms freakishly oversized. Possibly grafts taken from some Real creature, to imbue unnatural strength. A small ogre, maybe?

"But be that as it may, we cannot underestimate the threat these individuals pose." Cormac continued as he tapped the papers from his compiled file. "If they are indeed the chimerians from Second World War or products of further investiture into the project now revived, they will be highly motivated, skilled and accomplished at succeeding against formidable odds. We know nothing of their directives, what mission they are committed to achieving nor who is aiding them, or if they are acting alone. Which I think is doubtful, given the obvious collusion of senior OPS members to cover up their continued existence. We do not even know a location to track them to, given their obvious proficiency with portal keys. To sum things up, we know very little at all at this moment."

Something tickled my memory as I listened to Cormac list out just how much information we were missing, how in the dark we still were.

"Ok, I get that Terra can't just click Her fingers and end these bastards," I looked over at Gregory. "But can She at least tell us where they're holding Ellie and Felix? She must be able to get a fix on either of them, surely? *Find my witch* app on Her phone or something?"

Gregory grunted a laugh but then shook his head.

"You'd think immortals would get this shit, wouldn't you?" He told me with a sigh. "No, that's the first thing I asked Her myself. According to Her, they're blocked somehow. Some sort of veil, cloaking device or whatever. It's like they've dropped into a hole and vanished. Just the sort of thing you'd expect some shadowy security organisation might use, which points a fairly big bloody finger in my book."

That it did, but even as I directed my gaze back to Cormac, the memory clicked.

"*The Doctor*" I recalled, sorting through my memories of the attack. "The bastard who jumped us. He was all for killing me and Jess, but then his mate showed up and said things were fucked up. That they had to move to the *secondary objective*. And that *'the Doctor will want to deal with the two witches.*' His exact words."

"Well I doubt he was talking about Doctor bloody Who." Gregory growled, but I saw something spark in his eyes. It wasn't all fucked up. We had something to work with. "But which doctor? And what's this secondary objective, if the first one was to silence you both?"

I had a cold, cold feeling in my gut and looked back over at Cormac. It couldn't be.

I'd seen the bastard *die*. Horribly.

"Robert Knox was a doctor. Famed for it, if you believed half the shit he said." I grated, clenching my hands into fists at the ugly suspicion. "And you said he refined some of the medical procedures first used on the *chimerians*. If that bastard is somehow still breathing …"

Cormac shook his head, the scent of him telling me how certain he was.

"Robert Knox is deceased. Dead. Expired. No longer part of our problems." He told me with complete confidence. "We collected his remains when we cleaned up after that debacle at the Southbank Centre, where *unnamed someones* left evidence of otherworldly events just lying around everywhere. For anyone to discover."

I grunted, knowing the agent had a point. When the shit had hit the fan, and Morgana was reborn, we'd tried to stop her. Thrown a lycan Alpha, our strongest fighters as well as our consultant witch and me at her, but the Shadow fae had slapped us down like someone swatting annoying flies. I'd been *skinned* trying to reach her, but I'd at least managed to hurt her, screw up her plans just enough to give us a chance to fight back, another day.

Of course, that had set in motion the whole *Mortal Realm invasion*, as well as Terra's poisoning, Elspeth's capture and Gregory's corruption into Morgana's pet killing machine. I'd lost Terrigyle Munstrum, and almost lost my own life let alone that of my mortal love. And it had all ended with the birth of the Harrowed Queen … so not *quite* the happy ending I or anyone could have hoped for.

But, fuck it, we'd tried.

"OK, let's put a pin in Robert Knox for now." I grudgingly admitted, not wanting to fully believe the bastard was dead and buried until I'd stood on his sealed grave. And even then I'd worry … "So if not him, then who the hell is this doctor, and where the fuck are these *chimerians* holding up if Terra cannot locate them?"

Cormac shuffled some of the papers in front of him, then sighed.

"Right now, I can only hazard some guesses based on the few details we have." He admitted, and I could tell just how much he hated doing so. "There is the fact my superiors have sealed not just the files on the chimerians but also on the DOPA research team your mother was involved with, those individuals tasked with capturing Herne the Hunter the first time. The fact they are all dead, documented and certified, makes as little sense as the chimerians being an active unit still. Give me twenty-four hours, and I should have some more answers. Something firmer to base our next steps on."

"Jessica might not have twenty-four hours." I growled, thinking of how wan and frail my Alpha had looked when I saw her. Despite her unnatural strength and lycan healing abilities, the shit they had used on us was beating her. "Maybe if I speak to the other Alphas when they show up, get them involved, they can find something …"

Cormac shook his head, raising a hand to stop me even as I saw Manisha about to reply.

"Morgan, the lycan Alphas will not be coming here. Nor will any of your pack, or any known associates. Anyone that could lead the chimerians to your location." He told me with certainty. "I am well aware of Ms Walker's instructions to her pack, but I have interceded and made sure you and she remain off the grid, and have nothing for either my organisation or those who have tried to kill you once already to use to find you. That is simple good sense, and not anything I will agree to changing at this moment in time."

I snarled, my anger finding a direction again. How dare he lock us away, keep us here and any assets who might help in the search from meeting us? He had no right …

"Morgan, think for a moment." The Ivory fae interjected, glowing eyes focused on me as if she was reading my thoughts. Which was entirely possible. "You have uncovered possible evidence of mortals breaching the Accords. Acting in such a manner contrary to their agreements with the Courts. That has led to these mortals rashly attempting to silence you, ending the lives of innocents and endangering the life of your Alpha. Yet all this is purely mortal concerns, and nothing the Courts might decide to act upon, until we have actual proof to bring before them."

"But think of what might happen should these mortals learn of your location, of where your mortally wounded Alpha lies?" She continued, forcing me to think beyond my anger, my urge to do *something*. "They will most likely, in their arrogance, send these grey men to finish their task. Using stolen portal keys, they would breach our abode here on sovereign territory, and I and my companions would be forced to defend you both. Leading to death, maybe theirs, maybe ours. But there would be blood shed, violence done. And what would you think my Lord Oberon would do upon learning of this?"

I closed my eyes, clenching my hands together and mentally throttling my rage until it slowly, slowly slipped back under my control. Dammit, she had a point. A fairly fucking huge one.

"The sod wouldn't give a shit who was to blame. He'd just come and squash as many mortals as he could, to make the point no-one messes with the Courts." I growled out, seeing her nod in agreement. "We'd be looking at another incursion, but this one where the mortals kickstarted World War Three themselves. Oberon would make Twilight's invasion look like a fae picnic in comparison, and Terra wouldn't have a leg to stand on to counter him."

"Fuck."

Manisha nodded, her expression although alien still managing to convey understanding and sympathy.

"Given the recent developments, my finding Shadow agents in our Court and your knowledge of this no matter how slight, my Lord Oberon considers you out of favour until you prove your worth to Ivory once more." She told me, and I gritted my teeth against the stab of frustration I felt. Of course Oberon would use this fuck up to slap me back down again. The upstart Redcloak, the mutt who his Lady had gifted special privileges to. He'd probably been chuckling for fucking hours when he saw his chance. "Hence when Cormac contacted us, even as we felt your distress, we were forced to relocate here and not to Camelot Herself. But my Lady sees further than her Lord, and knows the dire consequences which threaten to come about if this matter is not handled … carefully. Hence her desire imparted to me, to enlighten you of the wisdom of inaction, and not charging headlong into danger."

"But I do it so well." I growled back at her but then shook my head, relenting. "Fine, Cormac. Go do your thing, you've got a day. But any longer, and I'm going to start my own search even if it brings those bastards running. I'll just make sure I lead them away from Jess, and this place. Maybe find a nice deep shithole to drop the fuckers in."

Gregory snorted at my bravado, whilst Cormac just sighed.

"Given the recent interaction you had with them, I would normally advise caution." He replied, but then smiled at me. "However, knowing who I am speaking to, we both can agree that would be an impossibility."

With that, he slipped the papers back into the folder and pushed himself up from his chair.

"I believe that is it for now." He told us coolly. "I shall return tomorrow with whatever I have uncovered, and we can plan accordingly from there. Until then, I would ask that you sit tight and take advantage of the Ivory Court's hospitality. And please, do not contact anyone ... partners, friends, packmembers, as I *cannot* guarantee who will be listening. For now, remain off-grid. As you know, mobile phones do not function in the Real, but please refrain from any other efforts to speak to anyone. At least until I have more knowledge to share."

Shit. With everything that had happened, my brain was now only playing catch up on the impact this had on not just me, but those around me. In my life. Dependant on me, in one way or another. Bear, stuck at home for over a day without me to walk him, feed him. Sarah, all too familiar with the sort of trouble I got myself into, not hearing from me.

Cormac must have guessed from my expression where my thoughts had run off to, as he smiled reassuringly.

"Do not worry, Morgan." He told me with no trace of patronisation. "Dr Conner has been made aware that you will be away from home for a few days on pack business, and she is staying at your residence to look after your ... *companion*. And Mr Price is under the impression his daughter is with you, and may not hear from her for a short while. Those matters were dealt with, to make sure no one might think to put your loved ones to question to locate you. They are safe."

I grunted, not entirely convinced of that statement but nodding my thanks all the same.

"You'd better watch your own back," Gregory commented dryly to Cormac, expression grim. "If whoever is calling the shots for these grey men is in your backyard, maybe your *superiors* even, then they'll be after you as soon as they find out you're still snooping where you shouldn't be. Could already be."

Cormac smiled thinly, nodding to the once police detective.

"Thank you for your concern, *Mr* Allen," He replied, stressing the civilian title. "But snooping is what I do best. That, and I make a mean watermelon margarita, but we can discuss cocktails when this matter has been properly settled and those to blame duly dealt with."

With that, the OPS agent left the room, closing the door softly behind him.

Chapter 12

Twenty-four hours passed slowly, painfully slowly. But also so far too bloody quickly. Since the whole concept of quantified time was invented by mortals, I'm never surprised when it doesn't make sense.

With Cormac off information gathering, Gregory, Manisha and I hashed over everything we'd talked about, everything we'd discovered. And came to the same conclusion that we still knew jack-shit, and faced an almost impossible task.

Fine, we knew the grey men … Scarecrows … chimerians or whatever were after me, and it was *probably* due to the disappearances I'd uncovered, and me poking my nose where I shouldn't. But we didn't know who had pointed them at me and shouted *kill*, nor in fact if this was about Herne and the Harrowed Queen … Harry … or something totally unrelated. We also didn't know what their objectives were, given how they'd switched goals when they'd failed to kill us straightaways. And we knew fuck-all about whatever had been used to poison Jessica. The somehow almost living alternative to wolfsbane that coursed through her veins as she lay in a room not far away, slipping slowly closer to death's door.

Like I said. We knew jack shit.

Gregory excused himself after I'd sworn for the hundredth time and forcibly stopped myself hurling my coffee mug at the nearest offending wall. He cited talking to Terra again, to see if anything had changed, if there was any chance she had picked up a trace of where Elspeth and Felix were. I had to figure even OPS or DOPA or whichever shadowy mortal organisation might be calling the shots with the chimerians wouldn't know how to bug the Goddess of the Mortal Realm, and that however She and Gregory communicated, it was safe and secure. Bully for them.

Manisha kept me company as I switched through the various stages of frustration, anger, mild despair, self-recrimination and back. Wash, rinse and repeat. But eventually even the Ivory fae seemed to have exhausted her immortal patience and suggested pointedly that we should go check on my Alpha. To take my mind off my own maudlin' thoughts and grim certainty that this time we might be well and truly fucked. Beyond the level of fucked-dom I've faced to date.

I sat with Jessica for a long, long time, telling her what we'd found out, who we thought were after us. Who had our friends. The Alpha was conscious, but there was no hiding the strain it was taking on her to stay that way as sweat soaked her skin and dark shadows grew deeper under her eyes. Her breathing was laboured, pained, and those grey orbs she fixed the world with at every moment, showing only inner calm and unbreakable strength, were now filmed over with pain and exhaustion.

"Ah'm not quite ready tae join mah love just yet, Morgan." She told me with quiet reproach in her voice as I flinched, realising I'd let my frustration and fear bleed from me like week-old sweat. "So dinnae ye fuss and waste yer energies worrying over me. Focus. On Elspeth. On Felicity. They need yer strength, yer full attention right now. Ah'll last till you bring them home safe and sound, an' nae a moment before."

"That's good to hear." I told her gruffly, shoving down everything I was feeling, locking the emotions away as tightly as I could. "Coz you *know* just what sort of mess is likely to happen if you leave me unchecked for any length of time. The pack, too. We need you."

"The pack, ah cannae argue with you." She replied with a small smile, lifting one hand and waving for me to take it. I did, feeling her erratic pulse through the contact, the clamminess of her skin, the *wrongness* soaking through her. The poison, killing her. But I also felt *her*, my Alpha, someone closer to me than my newly found mother, my murderous and possibly insane fae grandmother or even my bestial and immortal father. Jessica was my rock, and that simple touch reminded me just how strong was the bond we shared, and just what I'd do to keep her safe, keep her alive.

Anything. Everything.

"But as fer you needing me?" She continued, quirking a small smile. "Ah think it is past time you started believing in yerself, Morgan. And realising you are not just some simple lycan, a catcher of pets and doer of good deeds. Yer steps resound through this Realm and all others, whether you feel it or nae. And it is high time you started tae use the gifts you have, and believe in yerself."

I went to snark a reply, one of a hundred glib responses slipping easily onto my lips. But Jessica gripped my hand back, stopping me as she held me with her pained eyes, fixing me as only she could.

"*Believe*. Because ah do." She told me, letting me feel the truth through our touch, our connection. "You are destined fer great, maybe terrible things, Morgan Black. You have the blood of immortals running in yer veins, and only you can decide what future awaits you. But know yerself, fer ah fear you'll be tested far beyond anything you've faced before we're done this time."

Tested more? I grunted, shaking my head. I'd faced down Arthurian immortals, snarked the Lord of the Ivory Court in his own home and bumped shoulders with the oh-so-shit scary Queen of Shadow. I'd uncovered the long lost and missing Court of Twilight, brought back Odin to sit his wrinkled arse back on his throne, and gone head to head with Madb's sister *and* the Death of Immortals made flesh.

Just how much worse could things get? And why the fuck was it always *my* problem?

Jessica obviously read my confusion and frustration, nodding once to show she saw her point had been made before she collapsed back onto her pillow.

"Now, if you dinnae mind, ah will get on with the matter of *not* dying, but feeling wholly shite and probably being unconscious." She told me matter-of-factly, even as two of the fae healers stepped to her bedside, the air around them pulsing with the power they were channelling fight the poison killing her.

I took the hint, and exited the room with only one last glance to freeze her in my thoughts. How she looked, slumped and grey faced, trembling and sickened. I slotted the image beside my last glimpse of Felix, of Elspeth, knowing all three needed me to save them. And there was *no* fucking way I was going to let anything happen to them.

More than had happened, I ruefully told myself with a slight mental kick.

The Ivory Embassy was not a building I was familiar with, having never needed to stay at their convenience. But Manisha and the other Knights seemed to be under instruction to make me as comfortable as possible, to feel home from home … except that I was missing one massive furry trollhound as a companion, constantly on the lookout for a sausage or roasted chicken, or a squirrel to scare the living piss out of.

Instead, I had to make do with a sparring hall and gymnasium the size that ancient Greece probably offered for its Olympians. It had been outfitted with all the toys any serious exercise nut might need … no mortal devices that required electricity, but instead good old-fashioned weights of every conceivable … well, weight, sturdy bars set up in cage-like constructs to climb and hang from, weighted bags to punch the living shit out of and much, much more. There was a sparring ring, with ropes and padded corners, as well as a small armoury's worth of dull-edged weapons for training or fun, whatever took your fancy.

The ambush, explosions and poison had put me on my back for a full two days, well, almost and I needed to see what sort of state I was in. So I pushed myself, forcing every muscle, every sinew, putting every part of me through its paces. It *hurt*, a lot … but I'd had worse. Being skinned by Morgana still topped my worst experiences as duly noted, and this was way lower down the list. My body was finally healing, knitting itself back together as expected, leaving only scars and the ghosts of injuries suffered to fill my dreams and haunt my nightmares. Poetic, but unfortunately true.

Anger helped keep me going, as I piled on the weights and pushed hard until I felt my limbs tremble, my muscles burn. Rage that Jessica was dying, fury that some psychotic fuckers had come after us and caught us unawares. All-consuming, blazing pissed-offness that two very close friends were in harm's way, suffering who knew what fucking what.

That thought stopped me, dropping the pushbar and letting weights crash down behind me as I say back up on the bench. This wasn't the first time one of my friends had suffered kidnap and worse, had been taken against her will for nefarious reasons. But I'd been able to sense Felix still, I'd been linked to her through my Court-given gifts. And if anything, that link had grown stronger as she explored her witch nature, her craft tightening the cords woven between us as comrades, friends. Pack.

I settled myself down on the thickly padded mats, letting my breathing slow and my heart settle inside my chest as I closed my eyes, trying to focus on Felix. Picturing her in my mind. Hearing her voice in my ears. Her scent filling my nostrils. Building her brick by brick, until she stood bright and solid behind my eyeballs. *Where are you?*

I threw out the question, hunting for her. Searching for that weird link that had messed my head up the last time, any sort of vision, any hint.

Anything.

Nothing.

I'm no witch, warlock or sorcerer. Magic just isn't something I *do*, so I was probably getting it all bloody wrong. But it *felt* like Felix had simply vanished. Wiped clean, erased. Not a shred of a scent to follow.

Fuck!

I let the anger roar out of me, leaping up from where I'd sat and grabbing down one of the ornate weighted poles from the nearest wall. I needed to hit something, and a large punch bag happened to be closest. I hammered at the thing, pounding it again and again with all my energy, picturing the bastard who had attacked us, the grey man or whatever the bloody hell he was, and me smashing him again and again until he was just a bloody pulp.

The weapon snapped with a shivering crack, pieces flung across the gym floor. Without thinking, I strode back over to the wall and grabbed down its paired twin, and went back to pounding out my frustration on the punchbag. Again and again … until with a crunch, the entire frame gave way and the material split, spilling the solid core onto the matts at my feet with a muffled thud.

A quiet, discreet cough behind me brought me back to myself, as I caught the familiar scent of the watcher. Turning, I found Manisha looking at me from the door to the gym, her fae eyes calm but with a slight trace of humour flickering in the golden orbs.

"I'll pay for the damages." I grunted, setting the admittedly bent sparring staff down to rest by its shattered partner.

"It is of no matter," The fae knight told me with a curl of her lips. "Though Ser Galahad might be a trifle upset, as those were his favourite training staves. But that is not the reason I have come."

"Cormac's back?" I guessed, but she shook her head.

"No, Morgan." Her smile slipped and I felt the cold stab of fear punch me in the gut. "It is your Alpha. Her condition worsens, and our healers fear her strength is not enough now to fight the poisons afflicting her whilst remaining alive. I have come to fetch you, for they will be placing her in … a *coma*, you said to say."

I snarled, feeling my own helplessness threaten to choke me. Damn it, how had things gotten so bad so quickly? I'd just been speaking to her … but I drew a calming breath, throttling the fear trying to drown me in its cold embrace. It wasn't helping anyone.

"I'm coming."

They let me sit by Jessica's bed as the healers gathered around her. My Alpha looked like shit, skin sodden with sweat that plastered her hair to her skull and soaked the sheets beneath her. The greyness had leached all colour, all life from her, and she shivered and shook with every ragged breath she took. I gripped her hand, feeling the searing heat of the poison burning inside her, as she locked her pain-filled eyes on me one last time.

"Find them, Morgan. Ah'll be … waiting … fer you." She spoke with a few gulped breaths, before sinking back into the pillows.

Manisha gripped my shoulder, gently pulling me away as the fae closed ranks around her. I stopped at the door, looking over my shoulder, but Jessica was lost from sight as golden fire surged in the air and magic sparked to life all around. Then the Ivory knight closed the door behind us, leaving me standing in the hall with her. Feeling lost, broken. Like someone had torn something precious from inside me, leaving only a gaping wound behind.

"They will do all within their power and art to keep her safe." Manisha told me gently, laying a hand on my shoulder. I nodded, more just at the truth in her words than from my belief in what she was saying. The Ivory fae would do everything they could to help Jessica.

I just had to hope it would be enough.

It *had* to be.

Chapter 13

I was summoned back to the meeting room eventually.

I didn't have the strength to go back to the gym after seeing Jess put under, despite Manisha offering to spar with me. The rage and fury were definitely there, but both weighed down by the fear for my Alpha's life. So instead I'd gone back to the room I'd woken up in, and laid out on the bed, just trying to *be*. And not think too hard.

When sleep refused to come, I pulled out my mother's journal. The book I'd grabbed from her shattered and ruined home, the place where Baba Bohdana had bound her murdered spirit into the form of a fetch. With the help of a beaten down and desperate goblin mage, who my mother had taken pity on.

No good deed truly ever goes unpunished.

I'd initially thought I might learn a bit more about the woman who had birthed me, to understand her maybe. Know her reasons for what she did, how she had fallen in love with my father and made the decisions she had had to, which led to her disappearing into the Wyld and eventually her death.

Then, after her revelation as we were leaving the Wyld, hinting at a connection between her old work colleagues and the strangers who had been in league with her own murderer, and who had stolen away the Lord of the Wyld, let alone a whole bucketload of Real creatures … well, I'd begun thinking the journal might have a darker purpose. Reveal some of the shit they had been up to, who they were. Where they might be.

After the first hour of reading, I realised two things.

One, that DOPA or at least the scientific subdivision that my mother had belonged to, had been up to some serious Accord-breaking and entirely fucked up shit for way longer than these disappearances indicated.

And two, I was really, really *regretting* finding and now reading the bloody book. And what it told me of Black May.

Margaret Black had been employed by DOPA as an expert consultant to help with the crafting and binding rituals to firstly draw Herne the Hunter to the Mortal Realm and then bind the immortal elemental once he had appeared. But it also seemed my mother had had proficiency or at least more than a passing interest in the biology of supernatural creatures, and had advised on several separate projects that Dr Zarkof Bremmer had also been involved with, pre- and also during the planning of the clusterfuck that had resulted in pretty much everyone involved in it dying.

Nov 4th Dr B asked for my unbiased opinion on specimen CV478-7P's reaction to electrical stimuli. Shows some signs of diminished aggressive behaviour after repeated applications. Possible use to pacify in conflict situ. My findings inconclusive as specimen CV478-7P expired before …

Dec 18th Team required samples taken from specimens BF408-8 though to 15 to test theory of regrowth capabilities under extreme conditions of heat, cold, chemical interference, vacuum and various other harmful environments adverse to homo sapiens. I assisted on request, as I needed fluid samples for my own rituals …

Mar 23rd We tried combining ritual crafting with electromagnetic field interference to induce vulnerability in specimen RG209-7Z. Specimen displayed indicators of pain at the higher range of electromagnetism but appeared to recover itself from my own rituals. Possibly feeding off the magic I channelled directly. Have suggested to Dr B and the team we can try introducing variants into the rituals, to affect behaviour if this is indeed a method of interaction we had not considered before …

There were pages of tightly scribbled notes, always with only initials of the DOPA men and women who my mother had worked with or for, detailing a long list of experiments performed, along with a disheartening list of failures due to 'specimen expiration'. Oh, and never any reference to actual *what* those specimens were, only codes. But knowing the Real as I did, there were enough hints about their strengths, their weaknesses for me to identify them.

Goblins, sprites, dwarrowkin. Trolls, ghasts and grimms. Just the sort of unaffiliated fae creatures that wouldn't be missed if they just happened to disappear. Lost souls, slipping between the cracks and not worth the Courts' time to investigate, nor the mortal Authorities if any evidence of such activities were uncovered.

It truly sucked, especially that my mother had shown so obvious an emotional detachment to such appalling acts against the Accords. The lack of empathy was just plain shitty.

Amongst the daily details of experiments completed, either successfully or more usually not, I did however find nuggets of information that stopped me from hurling the bloody book across the room in disgust.

…. Required JB and his goons to remove suits before approaching my workspace. Dr B knows the dampening effects seriously mess with my rituals and craftings, and I won't be blamed for another failed test run just because some gorilla is too stupid to listen to instructions …

… Still have no clue as to what Dr B and Dr VW are up to in the sublevel. Told its just DOPA storage down there, but somehow my security clearance is insufficient to provide me access to somewhere they supposedly keep the replacement lightbulbs. Yet I'm allowed access to the black lake and every other level. Makes no sense. Bureaucratical bullshit …

… Bumped into new team member today. Dr R. Not on roster and not noted in any schedule. Asked his area of expertise, found myself being lectured on cellular replication … re-imaging imprinting … but JB appeared like magic and told none of my concern. Shuffled him off, just one more secret Dr B is keeping. I'll be happy when I'm done here …

Dr B was obviously Dr Zarkof Bremmer, and JB had to be Jurgen Blass, the head of Security. I fitted Dr VW as Erunt Von Wyndham, their paranormal physicist but I couldn't remember there being anyone with a last name beginning with R from the list I'd been shown.

The dampening effect struck a jarring bell in my head, reminding me how the attacker had fiddled with his suit just as Ellie had appeared, calling on her craft to kick his arse across London. Like he'd been cranking up something. Whatever it was, it had almost flattened me, and definitely affected the witch. Like some sort of interference, weakening anything Real related.

Just the sort of thing DOPA might want its soldiers or guards to have to hand, when handling situations involving non-mortal targets or antagonists.

I also couldn't help but wonder what the head of the project had been hiding at their DOPA base, that needed such a high level of security if my mother had had access to everywhere else. The story about storage was obviously bullshit, but if she'd been allowed where they were planning to keep Herne once they trapped him or in laboratories where they were keeping Real creatures as test subjects, I couldn't figure what that left in terms of black op secrecy.

The mention of the black lake I squirrelled away, in case we needed something to help identify the mysterious location. There couldn't be that many DOPA facilities with something like that, surely.

I'd closed the book and was examining my feelings about my mother, about what I felt she'd written … what it said about her, when a knock broke me from my thoughts.

"You're needed." Manisha told me, as she opened the door to see me pushing myself up off the bed.

"Cormac's back, right? Don't tell me it's anything else …" I half growled, shoving the journal back into its pocket.

The fae shook her head, expression, for a fae, troubled.

"Cormac is not here. But … well, you must come anyway. Better you see, than I say anything."

I grunted, shaking my head at the typical fae cryptic crap. Even now, with everything I had going on, Manisha couldn't just tell me something straight. That would be too bloody easy.

She led me back to the same meeting room, from the little I'd memorised of the outpost's floorplan and layout. Opening the door, she motioned for me to head on in, grinning as she caught my sigh and obvious reluctance to enter first.

"You are in my house, Errant. My rules." She told me, brooking no argument.

I growled under my breath, but decided it wasn't worth pushing. I still reckoned the Ivory Knight could knot my arms behind my back and fold me like origami if she so wanted.

Greg was already seated, looking around as I entered. He'd been staring at the only other occupant. And it wasn't Cormac Smith. Obviously so.

I stopped a foot in the room, eyeing the grey suited figure. Instantly recognisable, but entirely out of place given the circumstances.

"Where's Cormac?" I growled, as the woman turned to face me. "I didn't take you for his personal runner. Just someone who likes stabbing people and writing nasty binding contracts to fuck them over …"

The OPS agent smiled thinly, shrugging.

"I'm many things, Morgan Black. Messenger, contract taker, provider of beverages and assorted biscuits … whatever is needed. Whatever my employers tell me to be." She glibly told me, but bells were ringing in my head, jarring and discordant. Something was not right here, at all.

I shook my head, my wolfy senses crying alarm.

"No, I don't buy it. There has to be more flunkies than you in OPS, yet you seem to be the one on hand whenever I'm involved. You just keep popping up." I replied, eyeing her warily even as I felt Manisha move to my side so that she was not blocked. "I'd say I'm flattered, but I've recently been informed the organisation you work for might not have my best interests in mind. So pardon my wariness."

I waved at her from head to toe.

"Plus, this … this isn't right. I don't know if its glamour, a veil or what. But you aren't who you pretend to be." I tapped my nose, grinning nastily. "This doesn't lie. So who are you?"

"Oh boo, you've caught me." She smiled back at me, stepping around the table. Even as she moved, her image shifted and shimmered, until I faced another very familiar figure. "Would you prefer this, instead?"

Sarah Conner stared back at me, batting her Spanish eyelashes and smiling a delicious curve of her lips. Then her image changed again.

"Or maybe this? Possibly something more hierarchal?"

Jessica now looked at me, un-poisoned and unharmed. She set herself down on the edge of the table, looking at me even as she tapped the ever present keypad against her thigh.

I'm normally down with playing games with idiots, but my patience was stretched to breaking and seeing Jessica flaunted at me in good health and not dying broke what little control I had left. I crossed the room in two loping strides, catching the figure up by her throat and pulling her up so that she dangled from my grip even as I leaned in and snarled into her face.

"Tell me who the fuck you are or I'm going to rip that mask right off your fucking bones." I growled, letting my Wyld strength burn in my veins as I easily held her off her feet, For her part, the newcomer simply settled her hands on my forearm, easing the pressure on her throat, eyes fixed on me and smile a savage cut that had no place on my Alpha's face.

"Enough!" Manisha barked from behind me, and the Ivory Knight stepped to my side. She set her hands on my arm and pushed down. I snarled, resisting, but she shot me a look that told me I should trust her, that this wasn't what it looked like.

"Let her go, Morgan." The fae asked me gently. I spat a snarl, but wasn't about to fight my comrade and friend over an idiot trying to piss me around. So I just unclenched my hand, dumping the woman's arse down hard on the table.

"Thank you." The Ivory Knight told me, before turning back to the newcomer and talking to her in sharp tones. "This is no time for games. Introduce yourself, and what news you bring. I will brook none of your usual gameplay this day."

"My apologies, Ser Knight. I had thought simply to lighten the mood of this sombre gathering some." The woman slipped off the table, still smiling but there was a sharp glint to her eyes as she looked across at me. "No harm meant."

She backed up a step, and her form shifted once more. Revealing a short, slim Ivory fae clad in the OPS suit from before, with hair of alternating copper and gold highlights. Eyes of shimmering amber burned with unbridled glee, as she looked over at Manisha.

"However, I believe the duty of introductions should be yours, Ser Knight." She glibly commented, that smile of hers sharp as a knife. "Since I am already acquainted with the guests of our Lord and Lady, no matter that at least one of them knowest not of this merry occasion. If you would be so kind?"

Manisha sighed, then turned to face Gregory and I.

"Gregory Allen. Morgan." She spoke to us with a formal dryness to her voice, masking her personal feelings at that point. "I have the … pleasure of introducing Puckerillian Neth Esmerell. The Ivory Mask, servant of Lord Oberon and oft times Lady Titania. The High King's *Little Knife*."

I caught the emphasis on the last title, knowing this was something the Ivory Knight was damn sure I needed to know.

"Thank you, Manisha Na Pendragon Cie." The fae replied, and gave us a deep, low bow.

"But since we are all friends, here," She told us, that smile glinting like the curve of the moon. "You can call me Puck. Merry met, my good fellows!"

Chapter 14

"Puck. As in Shakespeare's *A Midsummer Night's Dream*?" Greg asked, shaking his head at finding another fantasy and fairy tale stepping off the shelves and into his life. "That idiot?"

I couldn't blame him.

"Harsh criticism, but fair given that was exactly what I wished the wordsmith to say about me." Puck replied with a small laugh as she settled down onto one of the chairs around the table. "It helps in my … ah line of work, if I am considered less than I am. Foolhardy, reckless and lacking in wit."

"And a bloke." Greg commented dryly, to which the fae shrugged.

"It was a time when only the male of your species was considered suitable for lead roles. In politics, in war, in any matter except the kitchen or spawning more of your kind." Puck shrugged. "Not that much has changed, but I have still had fun influencing those who yet play my part. Next time you attend so comic an entertainment, look you to the sex of who plays my role. Male I may be written, but yet female am I oft times played by."

"You're a spy. Planted in OPS's ranks to keep an eye on the mortals. Right?" I spoke up, the surety clear in my head. "How the hell can Tits or Obie get pissy at finding spies in their own Court when they pull the same shit with the mortals?"

"Well, I am not admitting anything that might lead to repercussions for my Lord, nor the Lady of Ivory," Puck told me blithely, smiling innocently. "However, if we are talking pure hypotheticals, then I might suggest there is always a need for those of us willing to get our hands dirty, so that those in positions of responsibility do not have to. And so that they can be assured of where the dirt might arise from, to avoid it becoming more a of a mess than can be cleaned easily? But no-one likes finding dirty undergarments in their own clean laundry, do they?"

"That's about the sort of bullshit nonsense answer I was expecting, yeah." I growled, looking over at Manisha. "You have anything to add?"

"The King's Little Knife serves a purpose in the Ivory Court. As do I. And you, Errant." She replied dryly, eyeing Puck who blew her a small kiss. "No matter my personal feelings on what Puckerillian does or does not do for the Lord of Ivory, I believe we should listen to what brings her to you this day. I fear the news will not be of any of our liking."

"Little Knife. Like *knife in the back*?" Greg spoke up quietly, looking down at the table and his hands as they were laid before him. "I knew a couple of people who had titles like that. I know the sort of things they did. What I arrested them for. You like them?"

"Sometimes a thread needs to be cut, delicately. Quietly. Out of sight, so as not to cause any knots forming." Puck answered brightly. "I make sure there are no tangles, one way or another."

"Yeah. Thought as much." The ex police detective looked across at me, and I knew exactly what he was thinking without saying a word.

Assassin.

I grunted, storing that nugget away until I had the time to deal with it as needed.

"Fine, so what's happened?" I settled down into a seat, as Manisha took station by the door, closing it firmly behind her.

"Cormac Smith has been … detained, is probably the best way to describe it." The fae spy started, earning a snarl from me and a sign from Gregory. "Six agents arrived at his office earlier this morning, and he was escorted from the facility. To be held whilst a formal tribunal is convened into his wilfully ignoring direct orders from his superiors. And to be questioned about your whereabouts, as there is some thought your disappearance so soon after an attack on OPS is significant. Possibly indicating a link."

"Shit." I growled. We'd warned him ... Gregory especially ... that his digging into the *chimerian* project might draw heat. But he had been sure of his own safety, a bullet-proof mentality that I knew a lot of mortals maintained until they actually got shot. I'd thought Cormac of all people would be cleverer than that.

Just goes to show, everyone has the same potential to play stupid.

"Cormac must have known that they were coming for him. He instructed me that if he was taken, that I should come find you and share what he'd found. That we'd work out what to do next, and not to be concerned for his safety." Puck went on, as she drew out a similar folder to the one Cormac had brought along before. "So here I am. And here it is."

"And Cormac trusted you to help? You've fooled him like everyone else, and he thinks you're just a nice helpful office assistant to come lend a hand when needed?" I snarked, given how off this all felt. Cormac was a suspicious bastard, not a trusting fool. Puck might be the greatest fae spy, but no way would the Agent Smith he knew so easily trust another when he knew so much shit was going down inside his own organisation. When he wasn't sure who to trust. "And how the hell have you done that? They have detection devices and shit up the wazoo. You should have had your cover blown the moment you stepped inside their doors!"

The Ivory fae spy sighed, cocking her head and looking at me for a moment before answering.

"I expect the recent trauma you have been subjected to, along with the previous trials faced in the Wyld, have led to your faculties not working at their most optimum. Explosions can cause that, I am told." Puck finally quipped before splaying open her hands as she explained. "You are right that I would have triggered the trickier alarms created by the mortals no matter my amazing skills and god-like talents ... if I had not been given the very means to make them accept me for whom I wanted them to see to be."

"And Cormac Wessen Smith would not simply trust some simple subordinate with such sensitive materials or the matter of his personal enquiry against his superiors' directives." She continued as I forced my grey cells to keep up. "Unless he trusted that individual to be exactly what he thought they were, and knew their motives and the value of using them to keep his secrets. Because they were not part of the mortal conspiracy he found himself in."

"He knew." Greg followed through, as things fell into place.

"Yes. Cormac Smith was aware of my true nature, and my allegiance." Puck shrugged. "He once told me he preferred knowing exactly where my Lord's chief spy was and what I was hearing, than not. *Better the devil you know*, I believe the quote he used was, though I do not think of myself as demon or devil. Possibly impish, maybe I would allow."

That did sound like the man I knew, the corkscrew way his mind would work. But still …

"How did he find you out?" I had to ask, since I had to assume Puck was well versed in keeping her identity hidden whilst out snooping for Oberon.

The fae shook her head.

"That is a tale for another time, either in a life of death situation or where we have access to far more alcoholic beverages than are supplied in this wayhouse. Both of which scenarios occur frequently where you are concerned, I am led to believe." She told me with that smile again. "Simply accept the fact that Cormac *did* know, and that I was one of very few that he could trust to bring what he had found out, without risking this information passing into the hands of those who hunt *you*, wolf."

Manisha had already made her thoughts clear, so I shot a look across to the only other potentially sane person in the room. Greg had a wary expression on his rugged, lined features, eyes narrowed in thought. Chewing over everything he had heard, using his experience and gut probably to lead him.

Catching my look, he took a breath, then nodded once. It was all we had, and sometimes you just have to jump off the cliff edge and hope it's a short drop and a soft landing.

In my case, usually soft *and* very smelly.

"Fine, let's say for now we believe that what you've said is true." I told Puck, not really caring how bad that sounded. She was a spy, used to deceiving and lying as easily as she breathed. Maybe more so. If she got upset at my tone or accusation, she could go cry into a pillow later. "What did Cormac find out, before he got picked up?"

Puck opened the file and spread out several sheets of paper. All of them handwritten, obviously made by the agent in haste given his scrawl.

"Agent Smith was looking into details of a DOPA project team that are listed as inactive and deceased, and was referencing redacted DOPA facilities which any of that team might have any links to, no matter how tenuous." Puck ran her finger down the pages, as she spoke. "He was running cross-checks against a terminated project involving mortal enhancement … ah, your *grey men*. All official channels of information for that particular subject have been locked down, but Cormac was digging in the archives to find the copy of classified data which the organisation retains in case of disaster recovery enaction."

It sounded like Cormac, despite his doubts, had been following the lead my mother provided. Pointing her finger firmly at her old colleagues and workmates in DOPA. Which meant there was sufficient evidence to make him suspicious … which was good enough for me. It gave us a direction, at the very least.

"Hmm, it seems he identified three suitable sites removed from case files, their details intentionally buried. Each with anomalies which might indicate they are not extant but still in use." The fae spy ticked them off her fingers. "A site in Bavaria, Germany. The second in

Tanzania, Africa and the last in an odd place called Transdniestria, Moldova."

"*Kleiner Hügel*, Little Hill for the German site. The *Bone Pit* for Tanzania and *Ozero chernil*, the Lake of ink for the Transdniestrian facility."

Two things rang alarm bells in my head. The chimerian who had attacked Jess and I, I'd detected a Germanic or possibly Afrikaans accent through the beetle helmet he wore, as he prattled on about torturing and killing us. Which could point to the Little Hill or the Bone Pit as possible homes for the fucker.

But the second ... I reached into my pocket and pulled out my mother's journal, flicking through the pages until I got to the reference I remembered.

 ... . *Yet I'm allowed access to the black lake and every other level* ...

Lake of ink. Black lake. Coincidence?

Nah, not a chance.

"What's the deal with the last one? And where the hell is Transdniestria?" I grunted, my knowledge of geography spotty at best. The Mortal Realm was made up of fairly large lumps of land which I could name, but as soon as we got any more detailed I quickly became lost.

Manisha stepped away from where she guarded the door, tapping the wall nearest her which swung open to reveal cupboards stocked with a variety of paraphernalia. From this, she took a long rolled up parchment, held together with cord and looking like an extra from some medieval film-set where everyone wrote with quills and said *verily* and *thou* a lot.

The Ivory Knight walked over to the table and deftly untied to the cords binding the roll together. She then rolled the parchment out across the table top revealing … blank parchment. Empty of anything, not even a watermark or stain from a coffee mug.

"Show us *Transdniestria of the Mortal Realm*." The fae spoke clearly and with a commanding tone, as I felt the faint buzz of magic light the air in the room.

The next moment, ink began to etch its way across the parchment's surface. Firstly broad strokes defining a long valley-like segment, jagged from the top left hand section of the parchment down diagonally to the right bottom corner. Then finer lines picked out a river running along its left-hand edge, with roadways and towns, villages and other habitats picked out with elegant grace. Rolling heights were marked as gradients sloping down to the southern end, with the map's surface rising up to match the topography, giving us a three-dimensional view of the small country. State. Slice of very confused land, or whatever it was.

"Neat trick." I told the fae, who smiled with a glint in her eyes. "Very *Harry Potter and the Marauder Map*."

"Where do you think the author got the idea from?" She shot back at me, with the given knowledge that the fae always meddled and messed with mortals, whether in real life or dreams. They couldn't help themselves.

Puck leaned over from where she sat, and pinched a section of the map so that the rest of the detail greyed out. Instead, the part she had caught between her slim finger spilled out to allow us to see it in much greater detail. Colours blossomed and the map took on a much more animated visual, almost as if we were staring down on the place itself from on high.

"Well that looks like the arse end of absolute nowhere." I growled, seeing high cliffs and sparse trees, scrubby bushes and not a lot else. One road wound down a corkscrew path, but the uneven ground was split by streams and small waterfalls that vanished into pools of inky blackness. No buildings, no development. No scars left by the mortals to show they had ever been there. "What's with the water?"

"Do I look like I'd know the answer to that?" Puck quipped back at me, before checking back on the notes Cormac had made. "Agent Smith listed some power readings recorded at the site over the past thirty years. Too low to warrant investigation, considered possible faulty recording equipment. And there is a note to talk to locals about disappearances, and also strange findings washing up in the rivers and pools. But nothing that warranted an OPS investigative team's time or expense."

"Someone's going to feel bloody stupid if it turns out they've had a bunch of psychotic ex World War nutters squatting at their supposedly empty, secure site." I snarked, eyeing the map for any sign that the place hid a DOPA facility. Was the base of operations for a bunch of genetically perverted assassins, or in any way was something other than a rugged landscape of crumbling cliffs and deep running pools of blackened water.

If it *was* there, they'd done a brilliant job hiding it away to make sure no-one accidentally stumbled on their front door.

"Supposedly the facility was closed down in the late nineteen eighties. All DOPA related projects removed, everything stripped to leave nothing behind and the facility closed and decommissioned. Too high a cost to refit it for serviceable use." Puck commented as she read from the notes. "Cormac identified and contacted several individuals previously stationed there before its closure. It seems the facility gained a bit of a reputation for being haunted. Strange noises heard, items going missing. That sort of thing. Just the recipe to unnerve your run of the mill mortal and convince them they should not be there."

"Cormac also looked into any possible links between these grey men and the deceased team you identified as possible co-conspirators." She flipped to the last page, eyes narrowing at what she read what was written there. "None of those named would have been of an age suitable to have been employed by DOPA at the time the chimerian project was active."

"Bugger." I growled, knowing that had been a suspicion knocking around my skull having seen the sort of experiments my mother had witnessed, even taken part in, with those colleagues in her time working for DOPA. "I really thought …"

"But …" Puck held up a hand, forestalling me. "He did find one Doctor Gertrude Schneider in the list of operational staff who worked on Chimera as a surgeon of all things. Employed as part of the surgical team tasked to perform the procedures on the mortal soldiers. Who later changed her name to Bremmer, upon marrying Dr Theodore Walter Bremmer. Whose son, Klaus Bremmer, married Ingrid Fuhler and had two sons, Stefan and …"

"Zarkof. He was her grandson." I grinned savagely. "And granny dearest probably told bedtime stories to her little boys, all about the top secret work she did to help win the war."

"If she did, she was in breach of the oaths she took to keep such knowledge secret." The fae spy mused quietly, then smiled a quick curve of her lips. "But I would presume that the mortals were so paranoid from such sloppy behaviour and poor oath keeping, they instigated the bindings I now get to inflict. So some good came of this."

"Good, yeah. Right." I grunted, remembering the effect the binding had on me if I tried to tell anyone about High King Bran or what I'd seen at the OPS site. Convulsions, loss of muscle control, blacking out … oh what a lark.

"Oh, and his final finding which he requested I impart was probably what led him to being detained." Puck commented dryly as she reached the last page from the folder. "Incidents that occurred at the same time of the attack outside the Tower facility. Where your Alpha and you were ambushed and mortally wounded."

"I remember it, thanks." I growled, feeling my wounds give phantom throbs even as my mind cast back to Jess. Lying in a coma, dying. "You think he found out what the *secondary objective* meant?"

"I believe so." The fae replied, tapping the sheet. "It would seem that a secure storage site was accessed with the current codes and a number of items removed. Which normally would not have been cause for concern, but the destination for the requisitioned equipment was left blank and when the guard queried this, he was told the details were above his security clearance to know. Which is against current protocol, as *all* details need to be provide to remove anything from OPS storage."

"The guard also noted he couldn't describe the agents who requisitioned the equipment. He had their names recorded, but any other detail seemed to slip his mind." She continued, reading the notes. "Equally, when Cormac checked the security footage, someone had tampered with this as well. Nothing to show the individuals who had posed as OPS agents and had taken ownership of a select number of crates, the content listed as *historic technical equipment, last usage c1940s*."

"World War 2." Greg confirmed with a sigh. "I assume the guard in question didn't note these individuals turning up in armoured suits of a beetle-like nature? Or is that covered by *can't remember anything about them*?"

"Nothing like that." Puck confirmed, but I just shrugged.

"Doesn't matter. It might have been other grey men, or they ditched the suits to look more authentic." I hazarded, knowing this was a detail which didn't matter much. "Maybe they only wear them when expecting to fight or something. Or who the fuck knows. They were chimerian, I bet my life on it. And they needed old-school equipment that dated back to when they were kicking around. Not the sort of shit you can just pop down the shops for these days."

"That's it." Puck slipped the pieces of paper back into the folder, settling back into her chair.

"It's enough. Cormac found a connection between the chimerians and the people from the photo. He also got us a location for where the bastards might be hiding." I let a savage smile bend my lips, as my frustration and anger abated with the knowledge we had something to go on. "All that, in about twenty-four hours. That's pretty bloody impressive."

"Oh, one last thing." Puck nodded in agreement before looking across at me, her amber eyes glittering. "Nothing that Cormac Smith discovered, but involving him all the same."

"When I received notification that he had been … *detained*, I made efforts to uncover where he had been taken." She told me, and I felt my smile stiffen a little. More bad news, I just knew it. "Cormac Smith was not detained at our own facilities, nor was he transported to any other site that I could readily identify. He was not placed under house arrest, as the mortals say. In effect, when he left his office in the company of those OPS agents, he vanished. And no-one seems to know where he has gone. Or who the agents were who took him. Or who in fact ordered his detainment in the first place."

"And that tells me one thing, and one thing only." She told me with a sharp smile. "These enemies of yours who have your friends? They now have Agent Cormac Smith too."

Yeah, that pretty much was about as bad as I was expecting.

Chapter 15

"Well, that sucks." I grunted, but then clapped my hands together.

"Still, at least it's simple now." I told the room, earning a grunt of a laugh from Greg, as well as cocked eyebrows from both fae.

"Pardon my obvious and unpardonable ignorance, but how so?" Puck enquired politely.

I gestured at the folder in front of her, those three simple pages that had helped identify the bastards set against us. The fuckers who had our friends. And where the cowardly sonabitches were hiding.

"All we've gotta do is open a Way near the place on the map. Hunt till we find the backdoor to this oh so secret facility, kick it down and go get our friends. As well as the antidote to the shit they put into Jessica." I growled, loving the simplicity of things. Too much had been complicated, but this … this was nice and straightforward. "Then we bring the place down on the fuckers' heads so they aren't a problem anymore, and head home. Clean, straightforward and easy."

Greg coughed, trying to fight the smile tugging at his grim features.

Puck and Manisha exchanged a knowing look, before the Ivory fae spy took a breath.

And spoiled things.

"Sorry to … I think the term is *'rain on your parade'* but I feel it necessary to point out one or two little holes in your straightforward and simple plan." Puck told me, that smile of hers so sharp it almost drew blood. "Only small ones, but pertinent, I have to say."

I rolled my eyes but settled back in my chair, making the universal *get on with it* gesture with my free hand as I slurped down a cup of coffee that against all odds was still piping hot.

"Thank you." Puck commented with a winsome smile before ticking items off her long, slim fingers. "Firstly, you make a not unforgivable assumption that this *Ozero chernil* is where your foemen reside. We have no definitive proof of this. No sightings of them, no certainty which cannot be contested. Simply some reports of odd activity in the area, some fluctuations in power and a name from a journal you hold."

"Secondly, even if this is the location of their stronghold, we do not know where it is. Just it's general vicinity. We have no idea of its interior, how to access it and find those we seek."

"Thirdly, I look around this room and see a lycan Redcloak, a mortal anointed by the Goddess of the Mortal Realm, an Ivory Knight-Captain and myself." She smiled, holding a hand to her chest. "Whilst I understand your faith in my humble talents, and I *up your game* as they say, we will need more than this to face off against these grey men, and whatever else lurks unseen in this mortal stronghold."

"And finally, we cannot simply open a Way to this place, for if it is like any of the other facilities I have studied whilst serving my time with the mortals, then we would trip whatever alarms lie in wait and waltz in blindly to our well-deserved deaths. Aiding no-one, except those who seek your death already."

"Apart from that, your plan is a resoundingly *great* idea, and one I personally whole heartedly endorse!"

I growled, knowing the fae was making perfectly valid points … but thoroughly disliking the manner in which she made them. Especially with that smug, sickle smile slapped on her face.

It seemed I was not the only one.

"Puckerillian! Remember yourself!" Manisha snapped, her amber eyes blazing with anger. "The Errant is recovering from grievous wounds. His Alpha lies at death's door and his friends have been taken by his enemies, for purposes unknown but doubtfully for their own wellbeing."

"Oh, I don't doubt at all. They are probably being tortured *horribly* even as we speak, arguing over Courtly etiquette." Puck quipped back, and I let my growl ratchet up a notch, not caring if I caused any further trouble. The Ivory Court could probably cover the costs of redecorating a room at the waystation if I just happened to wreck it, teaching an arrogant fae spy to watch her words.

"So, what? You want us to waste time proving we've got the right place?" I snarled, stabbing a finger at the three-dimensional model from the map. Map out every bloody possible entry and exit route? Come up with fallback plans for any and all eventualities, get a clear idea of what sort of opposition we might face going in? That sort of stupid shit they teach you in OPS?"

"And which would undoubtedly end in the deaths of your friends, as well as Agent Cormac Smith. Let alone give these individuals the time they need to complete whatever it is they are seeking to do." Puck smiled back at me, wholly unfazed by my snarl. Bloody fae, knowing just how tough they are, makes them the cockiest fuckers around. "But you are right, that is what they teach the mortals to do in their secret organisation. The rules to follow, the laws to obey."

"Which both Cormac Smith and I agree, in this situation, we should completely ignore."

The fae spy pulled out another sheet of paper from her pocket, unfolding it and laying it on top of the folder.

"Agent Smith guessed his imminent danger, and laid out some initial thoughts on how we should proceed." She told me, tapping the piece of paper. "And I have certain … experience in dealing with these sort of matters. On my way to bring this information to you, I have formulated the basics of a plan of action which I believe gives us a bare minimum chance of success. But I must warn you … due to your being on the mortals' watchlists, we will have to do things my way."

"Think outside the box, huh?" I growled, still not best pleased with the glib fucker of a fae. But if she was our best bet to get Ellie, Felix and Cormac home safe then I could swallow her shit. For now. "Won't be the first time."

Puck laughed, a sharp sound full of tinkling bells and underscored with the shattering of glass.

"Oh no, Morgan Black." She look me in the eye, and smiled savagely. "You most certainly will be *inside* the box."

Oh, I really wasn't looking forward to working with this fae. One fucking bit.

Chapter 16

I truly hate flying.

Well, that's a lie. The actual act of moving through the air, gazing down on the Earth and seeing it displayed in all Her beauty … it's not a bad thing. Not that I've done it, but seeing it on television, captured by drone or film-crew … it looks pretty amazing.

But the way mortals fly? It's barbaric.

Locked in a metal tube, sat in row upon row of tightly-fitted seats like battery chickens or pigs shoved away in their cages in farms. Said metal tube filled with enough flammable material to make a very pretty explosion in the air if anything mechanical happened to go wrong, in any number of possible ways. The air inside the plane circulated and recirculated to carry every cough, sneeze, cloud of obnoxious perfume or cologne to every single passenger where they were crunched up uncomfortably in their *Spanish-Inquisition* designed chair. Every sound magnified by the confined space, but despite this mortals finding the need to shout, bellow, scream and shriek to be heard by someone less than five feet away.

And all this whilst employees, having to slap on smiles against every circumstance they are faced with, walk up and down offering snacks and hot or cold beverages, and answer every inane or random question with reassurance that all is fine … when the whole thing is a clusterfuck waiting to happen.

No, flying the mortal way is something I hate having to do, and will avoid at all possible opportunity.

Puck, it seemed, knew of my feelings on flying commercially and had found a suitable alternative for getting my arse to Transdniestria. One that had her brand of humour written *all* over the fucking thing.

"Since we are unable to use the Ways to approach our goal, and you cannot simply utilise any of the normal mortal routes to get yourself there, we are left with few options to move you from here to where you need to be." She told us, smiling like the Bayun Cat, and I had to guess this particular fae was equally crazy. "There remains one service I am familiar with that I know will not trigger any alarms nor reveal your presence on mortal security."

We were in a box.

A crate, in truth. A cargo crate.

"I believe this is a service used by mortals to smuggle other mortals across boundaries, to avoid the attention of their law enforcement officials." Puck had commented, showing a knowledge of people smuggling, which surprised me not at all. Fae got mixed up in all manner of mortal shit, and the more morally corrupt the action, the more chance an immortal was involved. They did it for kicks and giggles, usually, rather than for financial gain. "But whilst such services utilising motorised land-based vehicular transportation are at risk of discovery from surprise inspections or the like, this method to transport goods or even people circumvents such chance exposure."

Which in layman's terms meant shoving us in a cargo crate in the Real, and opening a Way to a small storage facility filled with similar boxes of equal size and marking. Then having said containers, with us hanging on for dear life inside, transported to Gatwick Cargo Terminal where we were jostled and knocked about as the wooden crates were packed into the hold of a transport plane.

"Arranging for you to be delivered where we need to get to is no difficult task." Puck smugly explained, as we had digested the news of our travel arrangements. "Misdirecting mortals is a game I have been playing for many, many years. The manifests will state your flight is headed from the United Kingdom to Hong Kong, as we distribute required goods to OPS global facilities. It's just paperwork, and you will be simply hidden in the deck, so to speak. Shuffled amongst enough materials to cover your presence."

"Then, due to unforeseen technical issues, the flight will need to make an emergency lay over at … oh, looking at the flight path, I would say Camenca." She had resized the map to show the full geography of Transdniestria, stabbing a finger down to show the airport's location. "Gremlins will serve, providing just enough of a complication to force the flight to land and the issues to be investigated whilst not putting yourself at risk. That will provide enough time for you and your companion to be relocated from the plane, and to meet our assets on the ground.!

"Child's play, really."

Childs play indeed.

Puck refused to reveal any more of the plan, which was frustrating as fuck, but I figured I was in her hands for now. Until we had gotten somewhere closer to our goal, and I could start thinking more clearly, and feel better about my chances of not fucking everything up for everybody by putting my size ten foot in the wrong place.

Like I had a habit of doing.

With our immediate future agreed, Manisha had led me from the meeting room with a simple *please follow me*. I wasn't going to refuse so polite request, so gave a nod to Greg, knowing I could rely on the ex-detective to ask any and all pertinent questions whilst I went to see what it was the Ivory Knight wanted.

She led me back to my room, where I found a new set of clothes and some familiar yet new toys laid out on the bed.

"Your clothes were beyond salvaging when you were brought here." The Ivory Knight told me, nodding to the clothes I was wearing. "Those raiment's might do for meeting other guest of this place, but they are hardly suitable attire for an Knight Errant going about his quest. So our seamstresses have made an effort to provide you with serviceable clothing, akin to what you are used to. With some ... differences."

I grunted, fighting my innate doubts around accepting gifts from fae. Or any Real creature in fact. They usually came with a hefty debt owed or a nasty surprise lying in wait like the proverbial rake in the grass.

The trousers were multi-pocketed like the combats I had been wearing, and made of a black, grey material that felt hefty enough to withstand decent wear and tear. The top was fitted, making me wonder just what those seamstresses had been up to whilst I was lying unconscious on the bed, but made of the same material. There was a simple jacket that went with it, kitted out with more pockets and straps to secure anything I might want to. It felt padded in all the right areas, but light enough not to restrict my movements.

A pair of sturdy combat boots completed the ensemble, solid enough that I couldn't dent the toe despite using a fair amount of grip. Probably *not* metal toe-capped, but good enough to keep my pinkies in one piece.

"The garments will repel water, heat and cold as well as being resistant to bladed strikes and blunt force trauma." Manisha told me, as I hefted each piece. "We salvaged whatever we could from your own clothes, and stored them in your pockets by wherever we found the items. A hood folds out of the collar to protect your head if need be, and there are gloves in the pockets of the jacket for your hands if you so need."

Each garment bore the Ivory flame brand, but someone had decided I needed a little more personalisation. I held up the t-shirt, with a detailed wolf's head and red-cloak embroidered over the heart plate. Each piece had the same somewhere.

"I believe those who made these garments for you thought a Knight Errant should have a sigil. Since you use no shield, nor wear any banner, this is the best they could do." She told me with a chuckle.

Setting the garments down, I then checked over the tools provided for me, with a mixture of wariness and delight.

Two sheathed shortswords lay crossed over, in supple leather scabbards. Beneath them, a dozen long knives were looped into belts that looked like I could attach them under my jacket or over my thighs. Even possibly down my back. Anywhere I might want to hide something with an edge. Twenty, I counted, throwing knives like triangular sharks teeth were arrayed beneath these and finally a thickened stave with what look like metal studs set along its top length lay at the bottom.

"Enchanted?" I enquired, remembering the Shadow knives that the Morrigan had gifted my house-guest dryad to help her protect my home. Those things had granted her inhuman speed beyond even her own, an ability to slide through shadows and a penchant for bloodshed that had little to do with her Wyld nature but instead drew from the darker Court.

I had serious misgivings about using anything that had magic mixed into its making, given how unpredictable the stuff was. It's all well and good seeing heroes chuck spells around with wands willy-nilly, or slay deadly foes with gleaming swords that never blunt or can cut through anything but they never show the flipside … the poor fuckers having magic explode in their face because of a mis-used artefact, or the knights crumpling to the ground dead after having their life drained by said sword to power its cutting ability.

There's always a price, and I would rather not pay it in the first place, thanks.

"Your feelings on using tools enhanced by our smiths is not a secret, Errant." Manisha told me with a wry chuckle. "These weapons are expertly weighted and have edges to cut through most materials without needing to be imbued. They will not grant you greater skill nor strength in battle, but can be relied on to function as your own would at all times."

"However, there is one thing you need to learn." She told me as I slipped one of the swords free and tested it with a few twirls and stabs. "Hold up the blade, and call on your Ivory mark. Keep *heat* firmly in your mind, or you will default to summoning your armour."

I did as the Knight told me, taking a breath and holding up the sword even as I thought of flames burning brightly in my mind's eye.

Without any effort, the blade of the sword began to glow, pulsing with contained fury. The metal shimmered from dull red through molten orange to white-hot brilliance so that I had to slit my eyes to stare at it.

"The weapons are a channel for your Ivory brand, and this will work for you and you alone." She told me as I let the weapon cool by the quickest route I could … thinking of those flames extinguished. The sword darkened back to its regular colour and when I tested it gingerly I found the metal cool to the touch. Perfectly crafted so that I didn't set fire to its sheath when I was done with the bloody thing. "You can summon such fire to all of the weapons except the stave. That one *is* enchanted, and will allow you to unleash stored lightning into anything you strike with the studded end. It has enough potential for a hundred or so strikes."

"Oh goody, my very own taser." I grunted a laugh, glad I had something non-lethal to wield. That might sound odd given I was headed into the lair of mortal aberrations that had already tried to kill me once, let alone any other horror that lurked in the shadows … but there was equal chance I'd run across minions, mortals caught up in things beyond their control or just idiots stumbling into my path as they are wont to do. Having something to knock them out, whilst not taking their lives, would make my Alpha very happy when I had to report back how this shit went down later.

If she survived, coz no fucking way was I telling this story to her ghost.

Jessica was going to be ok, because I was going to find a bloody antidote and save her life. No other option was conceivable.

"You'd best change. Puckerillian never takes long to go about a task, so most likely your transport awaits even as we speak." Manisha told me. I nodded, then nodded again to the door.

"Mind waiting outside then? Privacy, you know?"

The Knight laughed.

"This embarrassment over your unclothed body is endearing, Errant." She told me with a wicked smile. "You lay in a torpor for quite a while, and I or any other might have had their way with you or at least enjoyed the sight of you naked whilst you slept. And you would be none the wiser."

"I'll just have to hope you had a book to read, a poem to write or some paint to watch dry. You know. things *way* more interesting than ogling me." I replied dryly. Fae were just plain weird. "And oh, yeah trust your honour that you would not do anything like that without my consent."

Manisha snorted a laugh, most un-fae like, but acquiesced with a gracious nod of her head. She strode from the room, leaving the door ajar behind her so that one last, lingering chuckle followed her out.

Bloody fae.

I quickly kitted up, getting a feel for the not-my clothes and not-my weapons. Everything was comfortable, not like the feel of new clothes never worn before, and the weapons felt right in my hands as I spun through a few basic moves before settling them about my person. I'd just have to trust that their makers knew their business, and harboured no grudges towards me that might lead to embarrassing situations like everything vanishing at the most inopportune moment.

Immortal senses of humour, they can run to that level of inanity.

"Oh, one last thing, Errant." The Ivory fae popped her head back round the door, letting her eyes rove over me professionally. "A warning, maybe not needed but still best voiced."

"Go on, hit me." I sighed, rolling my shoulders for whatever bad news she had to impart.

"If you keep asking, as a lady I will not be able to refuse you much longer." She snarked, before her voice grew serious. "It is the matter of

Puckerillian. Her involvement in your affairs should never be simply accepted, but something to be very wary about. As my Lord's *little knife*, she is tasked with orders none of my Knights nor I would consider right or proper. Her actions cloaked in shadow, her moves unseen. Yet there should be no doubt that when she strikes, she strikes true and to the heart."

"Watch my back around the lunatic fae. Got it." I snarked back at her, but saw a glimmer of anger spark in the other's amber eyes. "Hey, just joking."

"And that is why I am worried." She replied, shaking her head. "You jest, when you should listen. My Lord is *displeased* with you, Errant. And those who earn his ire … it never ends well for them. Be wary, Morgan Black."

With that, she slipped back through the door and left. Leaving me with that existential dread settling in my stomach, that I was just being warned to not trust the very person I was having to put my faith in, if I had any chance of finding my friends. Of saving my Alpha.

This was a fucking mess, alright.

I reflected on all this as I dragged my thoughts back to the present, and my current predicament. The crate in which I was slouched creaked and groaned, and I tried hard not to think of all the ways this particular part of our plan could go wrong. Which, in truth, there were quite a few.

"You chewing over something, that's obvious." Greg grunted, where he sat across from me. He was dressed in rugged, outdoor clothing obviously well used and looked after. I'd never figured the ex-detective as the outdoor-se type, but then again I didn't know half of what had happened to him since his elevation to guardian for Terra. Coming back from the dead, being bound to an immortal and gifted with supernatural powers … that would change anyone.

"Oh, just enjoying this entirely sane part of a plan I don't know much about, trusting in someone I've been told to *not* trust, and trying not to think of what the fuck happens if gravity decides we shouldn't be this high up and moving so easily through empty air." I growled, closing my eyes as the crate rocked and groaned again. Turbulence, just a bit of turbulence was all. Perfectly natural.

Greg chuckled.

"Nervous flyer, huh?" He guessed, and I shrugged a nod. Look at me, able to admit my weaknesses. "Don't worry, I get it. I'm the same about open water. You know, looking down and seeing nothing but blue running to black underneath. Nothing to stop you if you just sank and kept on sinking. Can't watch films like *Jaws* or anything like that. Not even *Blue Planet*."

It was an effort but I bit back the urge to mock the man, knowing he was just trying to help in his own way. Find common ground, show I shouldn't feel embarrassed at being messed up this way.

Gregory Allen was a good man, no matter what he'd done before. That hadn't changed.

"You armed?" I tried switching conversation, to take my mind off things. "You know, for when we eventually get out of this box and find the fuckers we're after?"

He nodded, loosening his coat to show the snug harness fitted under one arm. The black butt of a pistol nestled there, nothing too big or cumbersome, alongside several slotted cartridges.

"Got a backup, just in case I lose this one." He told me, and from how he shifted in his seat I guessed it was one of those back holsters that look cool in all the movies, but are a pain in the arse in real life. At least when you want to sit comfortably. "Silver-threaded loads, 9mm. Enough to put down anything man sized, and significantly discomfort whatever else is bigger if I hit it somewhere sensitive. Did two years firearm training, so I shouldn't blow my own foot off."

I nodded, even as he reached down and picked up a sheathed shortsword he'd stowed beside him.

"And in case those fail, I've still got this." He unsheathed the weapon and I immediately noted its singular nature.

"Wood?" I guessed, since the blade had the wrong hue for metal.

"Yeah. White oak, blessed by Terra so it handles like a normal sword. Cuts pretty much anything, but I can make it blunt if I just want to send something sleepy-by-by's instead of killing it." He told me with a small smile. "Pretty indestructible too … I tried cutting it but blunted a diamond-tip hacksaw just to prove the point."

I noted how he handled the weapon, an ease in the way he angled to look down its short length and then with a flick of his wrist, sheathing it once more and placing it on the crate by his feet.

"Getting good at that." I commented dryly, seeing him look back at me with a lot going on in those pale blue eyes of his.

The man I'd known as a Detective Inspector Gregory Allen of the mortal City of London constabulary had not carried a gun, not even a pocket knife. He had faced hardened criminals with only his instinct, years of training and his fists, and he had rarely if ever had to rely on those. He had fought with his brain, out-foxing the lawbreakers before violence ever threatened.

Yet since his return from the dead, I'd seen Greg handle weapons with uncommon skill, starting with his slaying a Twilight fae whilst the bastard had the rest of us locked down and at its mercy. Which it hadn't had any of. Morgana had stolen him away when Ellie walked into the trap the fae had laid, making him her Knight and gifting him with suitable armour and weapons as well as further enhancing his combat training through a disgusting slug embedded in his head.

All in all, I still was not entirely sure I knew the man who sat opposite me, at ease bearing weapons and talking of killing. Compared to who I knew had lived behind those eyes of his before. Who Elspeth MacElvy had fallen in love with, and risked her mortal existence by breaking the Accords to save.

He eyed me for a long moment, before shaking his head.

"It still troubles me. That's what you're wondering, right?" He admitted, leaning back and slipping free the gun from its holster in one smooth movement. "But Terra explained it as a reason She agreed to bring me … well, back, I guess. Why I'm a guardian, not a Redcloak or whatever you are. I take life only to protect it. She didn't want someone comfortable with killing. She wanted someone used to shielding those that need protecting."

I could almost hear the Goddess speaking through him, and his runic-script arcing over the side of his face pulsed in times with the words. He held the gun steady, pointed downwards, but I knew how quickly he could move now, how easy it would be for him to raise and fire.

And then he smiled grimly.

"But in the case of the bastards who took Elspeth?" He told me, his own anger a righteous spark burning in his eyes. "I'll have no problem putting them in the dirt, and ending their sorry existence."

"Amen, brother." I growled, wholeheartedly agreeing.

Chapter 17

We'd been flying for what felt like forever, but had probably only been a few hours.

Puck had fitted the crate with refreshments in case we got hungry or thirsty on the way, but apart from the seats fitted with straps, there was little else in the container. No ports to look out of, nothing to get a feel of how the flight was going, or how long we had left.

Given OPS was probably monitoring any and all ways of tracking me, I'd agreed to keep my mobile phone off so that I didn't ping any towers and allow them to work out my location. Greg had been the one to think up that, probably saving us all manner of trouble since that thought hadn't even occurred to me amongst all the other shit bouncing around my head.

I *had* flicked it on once, just long enough to activate and download any messages I might have received in my absence. I told myself there was no way that could have fucked things up for us, that even the mighty OPS needed an active signal longer than I'd allowed to find me.

Otherwise Hollywood had been lying to me for a long, long time.

I checked through the texts I'd gotten since the attack. There were the usual messages from my daily life in the Mortal Realm … Royal Mail informing me several packages had been delivered (crates of my favourite wine, and black pudding sausages I bought wholesale for my ever hungry trollhound), my mobile service letting me know I could upgrade to the latest model at a perfectly reasonable price and get a wholeload extras for free if I acted quickly … that sort of noise.

Then I found Sarah's messages. She had left me three, deciding not to leave me voicemails so I guessed all was well with her. That helped loosen several knots I'd let form from worry in my neck.

Hey, just me. Letting you know I'm at home safe with Bear, drinking your good wine and demolishing the charcuterie you left in the fridge. Got the message you are off on a hunt, so just take care and get yourself back home in one piece. We miss you, mi lupo.

Me again. Sorry not sorry. When you get home, you need to tell me what really happened at Tower Hill. You vanishing just after an attack like that tells me the terrorist story is so much mierda, it stinks. So fess up wolfboy.

Ok I'll stop filling your phone. Maybe. Probably not. Some people from the Spook squad visited me at work. Asked after you. I told them to speak to Cormac Smith but they said he is unavailable. Not sure what's going on but just want you to be ok. Come back when you can. Mi amor.

I couldn't help but laugh at the tone of messages from my mortal love, but at the same time felt an overriding surge of relief knowing she was safe and well with Bear. The fact OPS had questioned her about where the hell I'd disappeared to wasn't a surprise at all, and at least they seemed to be playing by the rules. Not pulling any stupid blackbag shit, like they had when Cormac 'arrested' me to bring me in for questioning.

It still felt completely fucked up to be on OPS' hitlist though. After the trouble and pain I'd personally been through, working alongside them against firstly Morgana and her mortal puppet, Robert Knox. Then the horror of Lykaois, a creature of the Wyld Court intent on regaining its glory. Cormac and I had shed blood, broken the rules and generally forged bond of comradeship at the very least … I'd been trusted with the secret of High King Brann, which was no small thing.

Yet here I was, on their Wanted List. A 'person of interest', because I'd maybe stumbled on the fuckery that at least one of their superiors was up to. Just my bloody luck/

"Did Puck give any idea when we'd know we were near Transdniestria?" Greg asked, speaking up from the silence he'd fallen into after our little chat.

I shook my head.

"Nope. Just we'd know it when things happened."

Of course, Fate or whatever immortal being that had dogged my life with ill-fortune and bad luck was listening, and chose to act right there and then. Of course it did.

Something gave a metallic screech from outside the crate, and both Greg and I felt the plane shake and vibrate as if struck. My lycan hearing picked up a stutter in the otherwise steady drone that I had gotten used to tuning out, the rumbling roar of engines pushing however many hundred tons of metal though the air giving an agonised groan.

"That's not good." I growled, seeing Greg's questioning look as I sank back into my seat and began pulling on the straps to secure myself. "Better lock yourself in. I think it's about to get …"

Bumpy.

Bloody gremlins.

The plane dropped suddenly, lurching as the engines gave a grinding roar. At least one coughed and began to make seriously painful noises, even as the metal outside our crate began to rattle unhealthily.

Greg grabbed hold of the sheathed sword as it jumped into the air, securing it on his lap as he fumbled for the clasps to fasten him in place. Half unwrapped parcels of pastrami on rye slapped at me from where they'd been sitting, whilst water bottles bounced around the small space to splash cold liquid over us both.

Whoever was piloting the plane was using every trick they knew to keep the thing flying, as we bounced down again and then tried to level off, leaning sharply to the right before the metal tube rolled to correct itself. I swiped pastrami off my face, cursing the little bastards who I knew Puck had hired to 'divert' the aircraft. With something mechanical, just enough to convince the pilot he or she needed to land.

Not wreck the fucking plane. But it seems the little horrors hadn't got the memo, or just liked their job *way* too much.

Greg gritted his teeth as we dropped again, as metal around us shrieked and groaned in an wholly unnatural way. We both hung on as we were bounced from one side to the other, my head bouncing against the back of the crate as we jerked and rode out what felt like one massive bucking bronco ride, thousands of feet up in the air. With nothing between us and a very thorough pancaking if things didn't settle down sharpish.

Outside our temporary accommodation, I caught the sound of snapping cables and the crunch of suddenly freed crates crunching against each other. Our own one shuddered as something slid into it, the shielded wood that protected the contents … ie us … from conventional scanning equipment splintering from the impact.

The engines whined, then roared, stuttering on the verge of giving up. Then, finally, the craziness settled … the plane levelling off and righting itself. I slowed my breathing, seeing Greg do the same as I felt the plane begin a slow, calculated descent. Whoever our pilot was, they'd decided enough was enough. This bird needed to land.

"When this is over, remind me to have a word with Puck about what constitutes a good plan, and what is bloody insane." My companion told me, and I grinned nastily.

"No worries. I'll even hold her still so you can get your point across."

When I was confident the fucking gremlins weren't about to crash the plane, I unstrapped myself and started brushing off all the food that had hit me as we'd bounced through the air. Greg slipped from his seat, picking up the water bottles and settling them back securely.

With things once more squared away and looking less like an upturned dumpster, we both settled in. To wait.

And wait.

We felt the plane land with a reverberating thump that vibrated through the crate underfoot, and heard the squeal of tyres hitting tarmac before the brakes were applied. The whole plane shuddered around us and we were pressed into our seats as we slowed and finally came to a standstill.

What felt like an age later, I caught the hiss of hydraulics as the cargo bay door was activated. Something on wheels entered the hold, and I nodded across to Greg as the crate was jostled by prongs sliding underneath. We rose slowly, and then slid backwards with far more skill than I would have credited whomever was driving the hauler.

We thumped down once more, and I heard the rumble of a much smaller engine kick to life. A truck, definitely. But who the fuck was driving, and why were we still stuck in the bloody box?

The transport slowed and halted, but I wasn't able to hear much other than some muted conversation that sounded like I was listening through a brick wall or underwater. The shielding on the crate was definitely messing with my hearing. Then we rumbled into motion once more.

Checking my phone, I counted off half an hour's drive before we turned again and then slowed to a halt. Movement outside the crate had me pushing up from my seat, Greg joining me, as I faced the sound of sudden movement. Metal being applied to the solid fastenings keeping the crate sealed.

The back wall finally creaked open, crashing down to let sunlight filter into the box.

"Thank you for flying *Puckerillian Airlines*." The Ivory fae glibly recited, peering in around the edge of the crate. "We trust you had a pleasant flight, and we hope to see you again on your return flight home."

"Fucking funny." I snarled, as I stepped out of the crate, followed by Greg.

We were in the back of a large, military style truck with a high curved roof overhead and sides fastened down to conceal the interior. Basic seating, little more than planks, ran on either side, with handhold dangling at intervals for those not wishing to 'enjoy' the bench-style arrangement.

Puck jumped down off the back where she had waited, unsubtly putting herself out of immediate reach. That just left Greg and I, and the person who had helpfully let us out of the crate.

The stranger looked down at me, given the bastard was easily seven foot tall and built like the lovechild of Arnold Schwarzenegger in his prime and the Rock. On steroids. Corded muscle was visible from his neck downward, over massive forearms and even visible through the combat trousers he was wearing. The word wasn't ripped, this was shredded or even minced. Though *mincing* I've heard means something different and this particular specimen might take exception if I used that term for him.

Clad in combat fatigues, an under-armour fitted t-shirt and a military-style jacket with the sleeves ripped off, the man grinned down at me as he hefted the crowbar he'd used to open the crate.

Oh, and his skin was the dusky grey of hewn stone, pebbled like rock. Granite, maybe.

"We welcome you warmly to the Pridnestrovian Moldavian Republic." He spoke with a heavy, Slavic accent. Possibly Russian, but more likely one of the separate countries who had managed to escape the clutches of the angry paranoid great bear. Ukrainian, Moldovan, Poland … take your pick. "We eat some bread, drink some *divin* and compare scars. Make friends quickly."

"Janus, not now!" Manisha barked from outside the truck, and the grey skinned man sighed, shaking his head.

"Angry lady says we must do this later." He told us, setting down the crowbar and jumping out of the truck to thud on the ground outside.

I looked over at Greg, who shrugged. We didn't really have many options, since hiding in the truck would get us absolutely nowhere. So I rolled my shoulders, took a breath and went to find out what sort of madness the insane Ivory spy had planned for us.

It was a cold day as I poked my head outside, the air cleaner than London's by about a million miles. There was still the taint of mortal habitation, but tuned way down. We were parked in a tree encircled clearing, a dirt track leading back to where I guessed the road lay. Around us, the gnarled and twisted trunks still had plenty of leaves attached but most were the gold-brown of autumn, soon to be shed to leave the boughs bare.

A couple of picnic tables had been set to one side of the clearing, and a half-collapsed hut could have been the remains of an old roadside café, possibly offering tar-strong coffee and sandwiches filled with artery clogging bacon. If that was something they did over here.

The grey skinned man was standing to the side of the truck, tree-trunk arms crossed and expression closed as we disembarked from our hulking taxi. Taking the time now, I caught sight of the massive bowie knife he had sheathed on one hip, matched on the other side by an evil looking throwing axe. I'd been expecting a pistol, given his attire since everything about him shouted *ex-military* but then again, maybe he couldn't fit his stubby fingers through the trigger guard.

Two more were sat at the picnic table. Black haired, thin faced, the man and woman were definitely related. Probably brother and sister if I were to guess. The man was dressed in faded denim, ripped and patched with what I thought looked like biker motifs or possibly again, military insignia.

The woman wore a ragged dress, somewhere between grey and black, thrown over leggings and chunky biker boots. She had her hair in braids, tied up and kept in place with long black needles. Possibly chopsticks.

Both had intricate tattoos on their fix-thin faces, mimicking each other left to right, right to left. Both carried slim throwing knives and sickle shaped swords, hung about their person, again mirroring each other. One right, one left.

A fourth stranger stood almost opposite me, scanning the treeline, the way we had come. Keeping an eye on our surroundings. Alert, focused. He was clad in loose clothing coloured a mixture of earth and natural colours, and his skin was streaked with what I guessed was camouflage grease. Eyes of brightest yellow briefly flicked over me, then moved on. Constantly roaming.

He carried a long, powerful looking rifle. The first gun I'd seen of the group. The type I guessed military snipers used, with rags wrapped around it and the scope's cap open and ready for use. He also wore a bulky handgun on one hip, and I saw a long knife's hilt peeking from one boot top.

The final figure was possibly the weirdest of them all. She stood off to one side, slowly twirling with her head thrown back and eyes raised to the clouds above us. Long, grey hair caught in ragged braids and clumps fell down her back, with small bone charms clattering as they bounced off each other. She was dressed in baggy trousers and a ragged top, with an old cloth rucksack slung over one shoulder and a black webbing belt slung across her chest. From which hung a variety of green bulb grenades, black tubular explosives. Even a few sticks of orange dynamite. Wires and several more tubes stuck out of the rucksack as she circled in the dirt, arms held up like a child playing windmills.

Oh, and she carried a sawn-off shotgun belted at her hip, slung with a brace of fat cartridges. Like some old Western gunslinger. And she was singing quietly to herself, some nonsense that I still recognised.

"Cause baby, you're a firework. Come on, show 'em what you're worth...'

Beside these five strangers, Manisha looked downright normal, clad in loose earth-tined clothing that could have come straight off the *hiker's guide to looking fashionable*. Only the massive sword sheathed at her hip, and the wolfshead mace slung over her shoulder looked out of place as she nodded across to me in welcome.

I settled against the back of the truck, even as Greg moved to my left, seemingly stretching his legs but making sure that if this was going to go wrong in any way, he had me covered. Five strangers, all of them armed. At least one heavily with mass explosives. If things did go sideways, it would be loud.

"Morgan Black. Gregory Allen. Well met this day." Puck spoke up, walking from the side of the truck where she had waited. Still keeping out of my immediate reach, as if she knew how much fun her little helpers had had with us as we sat defenceless in that bloody crate. "We should get going, now that we are sure of your well-being, but I believe you would benefit from some introductions?"

"Yeah, introductions would be good." I agreed, letting my gaze wander over everyone even as my senses told me all I needed to know about the five others. "And maybe an explanation as to why five half-fae lunatics kitted out for a small war seem to be part of our small group now?"

Puck chuckled, along with the stone skinned giant and the two sitting at the table. The watcher didn't break from scanning our surroundings, and the old woman kept spinning.

"Janus, I believe you have met." She indicated the giant, who grinned and reached into a chest pocket of his jacket to pull free a large hipflask. "He is what you might call our tank."

"Dah. Now we drink and show scars?" He lifted the flask to his lips as his free hand went to the broad belt keeping his trousers up.

"Troll?" I assumed, even as everyone else shouted "No!"

"Ha! Later then. But it *will* happen." Janus growled after tasking a long swig from the flask and shoved it back into its pocket.

"The twins. Trix and Dix. Experts with quite the reputation for breaking into impossible places, and getting out again despite the defences arrayed against them." Puck turned to motion to the pair seated at the picnic table. Hearing their names, the man pushed himself up and gave a short bow, flashing a sharp smile. His sister gave a sigh, walking a slim throwing knife over her knuckles with negligent ease.

"The idiot is Dix. I'm Trix." She told us, dark eyes lingering on the pair of us before focusing back on watching the silvered weapon flickering around her slim fingers.

"Shadow fae." I nodded, recognising the tattoos as similar to ones I'd seen on the skin of other fae from that Court, on multiple occasions when I'd had to deal with Madb or the Morrigan.

"Then there is Hunter. Our eyes and ears." Puck moved on, waving to the man standing with his rifle held loosely, eyes still scanning our surroundings. "Not much of a talker, but invaluable all the same as a scout without compare."

"Shapechanger." I knew those yellow eyes, far from the amber glow of the fae. More animalistic, close to those of Lykaois but even more so the shapechanger bastard who the Lady of the Lake had had as her second in command. The fucker who had tried to kill me numerous times before I ended his life in the Natural History Museum.

Hunter nodded, once. Without even looking in my direction.

"And finally we have Mother." Puck pointed to the woman still slowly twirling. "Every group needs someone versed in both field medicine and explosives. With her, we gained two for the price of one. Plus she cooks a mean spiced borscht."

"A love of making things explode? Got to be gnome." I sighed, remembering my old pal Terrigylle Munstrum. A complete nut for weapons of all sorts, but most especially anything that went bang with excessive force.

"These fine and upstanding citizens are in *my* employ, signed and paid for under Ivory Court jurisdiction. Procured under article eight hundred and fifty-three, section twelve I believe. *An emissary of any Court may engage the services of residences of whichever Realm they shalt find themselves in after receiving a duly authorised invitation. For the purposes of their visit or to address Court business as understood by all parties granting them aforementioned* invitation. As to *why* you are meeting them, that is simple." Puck finished with a smile as she spread her hands wide. "For I believe I have located an entry-way to the facility we seek, but it will take *all* our combined skills to enter.

"Let alone if we wish to ever leave."

Chapter 18

The large minivan sped along the motorway, with Manisha driving whilst Puck, myself and Greg stretched out along the spacious rear seating. A second van, behind us, held the group of mercenaries the Ivory fae had hired as support, plus all their own personal gear.

We had left the military truck in the clearing, Puck assuring us she had arranged for it to be picked up and driven onward by a third party, just in case anyone thought to track it. It was destined for a long journey across country.

Just to be sure no-one linked it to our transport and our presence here, I'd helped smash the crate Greg and I had hidden inside to little more than kindling and pile the fragments behind the rusty hut. I wasn't ashamed to admit that I pictured Puck's face a few times as I hammered the thing into bits, after the whole gremlin stunt.

"One thing's bugging me." Greg spoke up, his voice quiet and thoughtful. There was little traffic on the road, and from what brief views I'd seen of Transdniestria so far, I wasn't expecting anything like the continuous background thunder I always associated with London. Even when I'd gone further afield, finding my arse dropped at Glastonbury by my Shadow fae grandmother, there was noise. Out here … not so much.

"Only one? I am impressed, gentle sir." Puck mocked lightly, but then motioned with one hand for him to continue.

"All this. The crate, the transport. The flight inspection allowing us off the plane. The papers allowing us to travel as some sort of *'archaeological expedition exploring old church tunnels'* discovered out of town in the middle of absolute nowhere." Greg listed off the items Puck had detailed as we loaded ourselves into the truck after introductions were done. "All done by you. The same person. Don't *certain people* have checks to flag up this sort of thing? Your fingerprints all over this, won't it alert *certain people* as to what you might be up to?"

Puck shook her head, smiling.

"*Certain people* would indeed be interested why a simple assistant to Agent Smith was sending large crates of office equipment to the Eastern offices. Or why she was booking the use of ex-military transport vehicles in a country we no longer operate in, or why she was hiring criminal talent of specific skill sets and arranging for illegal forgeries to be produced to grant travel access through said country. For individuals including one member who is currently on their red list, targeted for investigation."

From one statement to the next, as she spoke, Puck changed. Shifting from the Ivory fae to the mortal OPS agent I was familiar with. Complete with quill pen. Then to another woman with long black hair and a far larger body frame wearing civilian clothes. Then to a ginger haired man, bearded and business suited, then to another older man with grey hair and glasses. One to the next, to the next.

"The fact is, if I had done all those things, indeed we would be in trouble." Puck shifted finally back to her original form. If that was in fact her face, and not another glamour. "However, the tasks needed to get us where we need to be were completed by various individuals, both inside OPS and outside. With nothing to connect any of them at all. So please, save your worries for other, far more relevant concerns."

Greg grunted, shaking his head but accepting the explanation. When dealing with fae, you always took the chance when asking a question that the answer wouldn't really what you were after.

"Ok, what have you told our new friends? Because I'm guessing not the whole truth." I spoke up, nodding to the van following along behind us. "And where did you find them? *Rent a goon squad dot com*?"

Manisha laughed brightly, whilst Puck smiled with little humour.

"We keep track of *interested parties*, let's call them. Individuals who we know traffic in the sort of knowledge and equipment which OPS retains. Who are known to access sites illegally, or interrupt transports of sensitive materials to sell on for their own profit." Puck replied brightly. "Agent Smith supplied links, ways of coordinating an on the ground team to offer us support for what we need to do. I simply expounded on them, and made sure I found the skills necessary for this endeavour."

"As for what I've told them?" The fae smiled thinly. "Only that we are looking to access a closed site that once served as a DOPA test facility. That some friends of ours went ahead of us, but we've lost contact with them. We simply seek to find them, whilst any materials we uncover are there for the team to take and use as they see fit."

"So you lied to them then." I growled, not surprised at the deception.

"I would say I simply withheld knowledge that is not pertinent to them performing their assigned tasks. To get us into the facility, to safeguard against anything we might come up against and to facilitate our escape with the people we seek." Puck rebutted with a shrug. "Each member of the team is used to dangerous situations, involving non mortal elements at the very least. They have proved themselves resilient and reliable, as long as we pay their fee and let them take what they find to enrich themselves. It is not much to ask, if it means Cormac Smith, Felicity Price and Elspeth MacElvy are freed and returned safe."

"And Herne, and Har… the Harrowed Queen." I added, ticking them off my hand. "And hey, those other creatures the chimerians have been stealing away too. We don't leave anyone behind."

Puck nodded with a sharp smile.

"Them too." She held out a hand, for me to shake. Her grip was cold, hard like I was instead shaking the hand of a statue. "Personally, I intend to leave this site a smoking ruin, and those who have perpetrated these acts unable to ever do so again. So yes, no one gets left behind."

I settled back, accepting her words but remembering Manisha's warning. Puck was Oberon's tool, with his agenda front and central. I'd be an idiot if I forgot that at any point.

The motorway wound through rough countryside, with craggy mountains rising up on one side of the road whilst the other had a drop off leading down to a wide, deep river called the Dniester running cutting through rock and earth. I caught sight of white caps on the surging water, telling me it was fast flowing and strong. Not that I intended to go swimming anytime soon, but I liked to know these things.

Warning signs posted along the road were easily understood even though they were in a foreign language. Falling rocks, the possible chance of boulders to come bouncing down and strike anything in their path. I kept an eye on the craggy heights as we drove along, as ever suspicious of sudden attack, of being vulnerable.

I'd been ambushed once. Not again.

We stopped at a checkpoint, guarded by serious looking mortals dressed in serious military fatigues and bearing serious looking guns. Puck had requested that we divest ourselves of all obvious weapons, packing them away from sight but still easily reached in case the shit hit the fan. So whilst Manisha handed across our travel documents, Greg and I just smiled at the guards who peered into the van, eyeing us suspiciously.

Both fae proved fluent in the local dialect, one of either Russian, Ukrainian or Moldovan – which was also known as Romanian outside of Transnistria. Puck had been a veritable mine of information now that we were out of the crate and part of the company again. There was lots of scowling over our documents, whispered conversations and a visit back into the border office to make a phone call before the guards lifted the lightweight striped gate and waved us onward. We *could* have simply driven through the obstruction, but I figured the guards with their heavy weapons had orders to turn such offenders into so much mulch and wreckage, helped along by a larger calibre gun sat on top of the border office building.

We continued on, winding around the craggy mountainous landscape, encountering more signs of mortal habitation now. Villages, even small towns, seemed to sprout up as we followed the main thoroughfare and I let myself soak up the feel of where we'd landed.

There was a vast difference between London and where we were now, with wider roads and far more open spaces in every built-up area we passed through. The buildings were not crammed in like lego blocks stacked together, and there were a lot more flagpoles flying national colours on show and odd statues like solitary tanks on show as we drove past. Lots of statues of men in heavy coats looking very serious, or on the back of horses wielding curved sabres defiantly.

There was also a lot of gold on show. White walled places of worship topped with bulbous towers of glittering gold, majestic crosses rising up into the sky. Murals etched in gold and silver, of saints or other important figures staring down on the lowly mortals from on high. Tens of feet high.

Trees were to be seen everywhere, not just lining the rocky heights of the mountains but filling the mortal towns and villages, lining the roads and in little green spaces. They made a welcome counterpart to the frankly grim statues I'd noted, trying to lessen the harshness of the stone figures set to guard over the populace. Or watch them.

If any of those buggers were actually gargoyles, I *really* didn't fancy meeting them late at night in the dark.

We passed through another checkpoint, this one manned by a bunch of mortals in different uniforms. Manisha and Puck went at it again, slipping fluently into conversation whilst Greg and I sat back and tried to look as innocent as possible of anything they might find interesting.

"Moldovan." Puck remarked, nodding back towards them as we passed through again with little difficulty. "For such a small slip of land lying between much larger countries, it is bemusing the number of guards set to watch and ward a simple gate that divides one bit of ground from that which lies on the other side. When they are both one and the same."

"Yeah, well, that's because it's *their* bit of ground, and the people on the other side of that pole are the sort who want to take it from them. And they've both spilled blood to own it." I summed up, my knowledge of the whole *Russian – Moldovan – Transdniestria* mess based purely on what I managed to read in the Ivory wayhouse before we were packaged off into our crate. Thankfully, whilst they had not had internet access or Google, the fae always had scryers to hand, ready to answer questions if suitably bribed.

I needed to replenish my stock of decent chocolate, note to self. The shit they make in the Real just doesn't come close.

"It makes no sense to me. There is no power in owning dirt." Puck commented, waving her hand at the outside world. "It doesn't care who walks upon it, what flag they plant. Dirt is dirt."

I went to reply but Greg held up a hand.

"I think I got this one." He leant forward to look across at Puck his craggy features intent. "Your mistake, and what I'm learning about people like you that I meet nowadays, is you all think in terms of power. Who has the most, who has more that you can take from them. Who has less, so you can dominate them. That sort of idiocy."

"But these people? Most normal people? They never have *any* power." He nodded out the window as we passed through one town, at the passerbys walking the streets. Sitting at coffee shops. Talking, complaining, laughing. "All they have is the patch of dirt they are born on, they are raised up on. Where they find work on, meet friends and loved ones on. Raise a family of their own on or just live their own life on. And the dirt they bury their friends, their family, their loved ones in. Where they themselves are laid to rest. The same dirt, sometimes different, but where they call home. Their *own* land. And for that, they will fight. Bleed, suffer and even die to keep a hold of it and make sure no one else takes it from them."

"Because it is *theirs*."

He smiled grimly.

"And if any one of you immortal buggers ever understood that simple fact, you'd probably stop making so many silly mistakes and actually do something good with all your *power*, your endless lives. Maybe make some real changes, help those without power with some of your own." He rolled his shoulders, settling back into the seat. "But that's about as likely to happen as a duck farting the National Anthem. So I guess we'll just keep on going, fighting over dirt."

Funnily enough, Puck had no witty comeback, no glib reply to give. Something she saw in Greg's eyes stopped any of her expected response. Good to know even the fae respected Terra's chosen. Or feared what pissing off one of her champions might do.

We drove in silence for a while longer, looking out the windows with our own thoughts. The road began to wind up into the mountains, buildings falling back behind us and leaving us surrounded by jutting rocky cliffs and sharp drops down to the roaring river. All vestiges of civilisation left back with the flags and the cafes and the neat tidy parks.

"So you think you found a way in?" I finally spoke up, conscious we'd been quiet for a while. Not uncomfortably so, but I reckon enough thinking time had been done. "How'd that happen?"

Puck smiled, the moment forgotten. Put aside. Just the way immortals and mortals glossed over what they don't want to ever hear. Normally, the truth.

"Those on the ground assets you were questioning, the help I arranged for us." The fae reached down and slipped some notes from a satchel she carried. "I asked them to look for anomalies. Hints that might lead like breadcrumbs to our goal."

"And they found them."

"Missing persons reports. Hikers, tourists, even some locals." She leafed through the papers. "Never enough to cause too much concern or warrant any proper investigation. Only for the locals to know not to go near a particular place, to never go walking amongst a certain set of hills or near particular rivers and pools. All in one general place, which they are happy enough to tell you about. If you ask the right questions."

"And just as helpfully, historical reports filed of strange bodies found floating in the black pools which locals warn against ever visiting, and say never to swim in. *Childlike but wrong. Deformed like they had suffered radiation poisoning or something.* Some examples of what was reported." She flicked to another piece of paper. "Several such instances were put to the local law enforcement agencies over the past few years but on each occasion, evidence was misplaced after an initial investigation, and cover stories issued. *Damaged animals mistaken for mortal bodies. Practical jokes played by younger mortals to scare or confuse others. Deformed-birthed mortal children caused by contamination linked to drinking fouled water or bathing in prohibited waters.*"

"And finally, rumours and gossip of a place where mortal technologies suffer impediment. Disruption in phone services, computers and such." Puck flicked to the last page, running her finger down what was written there. "Nothing, again, of enough magnitude to have required investigation but the locals have been happy to share this when tasked for … *oddities* to be aware of, for a scientific team investigating the country."

I nodded at the simple truth, given so much of what us Redcloaks worked from in the Mortal Realm was word of mouth, rumour more than hard fact. Anything that we needed to handle, interactions between mortals and creatures of the Real, tended to be talked about over alcoholic drinks down the pub or shared as campfire horror stories rather than anything well documented, evidenced and proven. Mostly because OPS did such a good job of hiding the truth, and keeping a lid on that sort of shit.

"Individually, these matters tell not much of a story." Puck finished up, folding up the papers and storing them away. I noted at least seemed to have been written in thick crayon, and had to wonder which of our team mates had delivered that masterpiece. "But together they were enough for me to suspect where the facility might lie. And thanks to our very own Hunter, we have found a set of old tunnels leading off one of the black pools the locals warn never to visit, which seemed just a *little* too taken care of. No animals nesting in them, a lack of detritus blocking them. Not even any mortal artwork painted by bored youths on a dare."

"That is where we will start, and I trust find what we seek."

Great, more tunnels. I'd crawled through the sewers of London Upper to talk with the once Lady of the Lake, to hunt miscreant trolls who were kidnapping children for ransom or on the orders of a deranged doctor, and stomped my way through the passageways of London Lower to hunt down traitorous lycans and to rescue captured mortals from that selfsame medical lunatic. One way or the other, I always seemed to be heading back into uncomfortable, stinking environs.

That was the only good thing about not having Bear along for this one. It took *forever* to get the stench out of his fur.

Damn I missed the fuzzball.

Chapter 19

Puck refused to give any more details of just how we were getting into the facility, if the tunnels were what she thought they were. Instead, she simply sat back, having revealed as much as she wanted to, and watched the countryside whisk by.

Bloody mysterious fae bullshit.

Eventually, Manisha followed some unspoken instruction from her fae colleague, and turned off the main roadway. The throughway we were now on was far narrower than the motorway, with solid walls rising on each side and no visible roadmarkings or the now familiar warning signs about falling rocks. Obviously a less than well-travelled route.

We bounced along, steadily rising, seeing no other traffic either coming the other way or ahead of us. Just the two minivans, slowly destroying themselves on the stone-strewn road.

The Ivory fae turned off down an even narrower track, this one rutted and half overgrown. The van gave vocal squeals of complaint as we lurched from side to side, in and out of the ruts, and forcing us all to grab hold of the seats and belts to keep from spilling all over the interior.

"Hey, *demolition derby*!" I growled as I narrowly missed smacking my head on the side bar. "You know where you're going, right?"

"The Guard Captain knows where we need to get to." Puck announced instead. "You might want to take a moment to re-arm yourselves. We are almost there."

It takes some skill and more than a little luck to not accidently hurt oneself whilst clipping swords, knives and any other weapon whilst on what was sort of like a rollercoaster. Even sheathed and with little chance of getting cut, there's always the pommels and grips to get bashed by or to dig into ribs or other tender places. Let alone Greg having to reposition his guns under his arm and behind his back.

Somehow we managed to kit up without doing ourselves any serious injury, as we turned off down another track. We were definitely in the mountains now, with scrubby trees sprouting from anywhere they could set down roots. I could smell water close by, hear the slow chuckling of it in hidden streams or rivers, and the bite of cold was fiercer up here. I even reckoned we had rain coming, looking up at the grey sky with clouds heavy and soaked, ready to drop.

We finally slowed and stopped, Manisha putting us into the barest of clearings. Rocks jutted up from the ground like snaggled teeth slowly worn down by the harsh climate, and scrubby bushes spilled out from under the few trees nearby, sharp thorns glinting.

Clambering carefully out of the van, I set my feet on the ground and leant back against the vehicle. Letting my senses reach out, searching. For anything out of place, anything that might let me know we were in the right place. That my friends were close by.

Nothing.

Just the bareness of unspoilt wilderland. The cutting breeze with the threat of rainfall, possibly a full blown storm lurking at the periphery. And not a single birdsong, animal cry or sense of anything living anywhere around me to be felt at all.

So. Maybe not 'nothing'.

Greg stepped out beside me, stretching his back before rubbing his hands together briskly. He was dressed for the outdoors, but we were definitely far from the pleasant temperament climate of London.

The other minivan rumbled up the path and slowed to a stop beside our own. Almost before it had come to rest, the side door jerked open and Janus hopped out, thudding to the ground. Hunter followed him, immediately stepping away and scanning all around us.

Trix, Dix and Mother exited from the front of their van, the twins immediately moving to the rear and opening the doors to start unpacking various backpacks and crates of equipment. Given how we Redcloaks tended to only take what we could carry in pockets or at most a simple pack, I did wonder at just what the team were planning on doing with all the stuff they'd brought … it looked like we were either hosting a full-scale party or preparing for a mini war. Or possibly both.

With my attention on the unpacking, I only realised Mother had stepped away from the van when she pushed a large cup of something steaming at me. Reflexes had me take the mug and not spill anything even as she rattled off a short, sharp statement and then stumped back off. Less of the airy-fairy windmill of before, more the grumpy gnarly gnome to be seen in her demeanour.

"Mother says you too skinny. Can see your bones. Need to fatten you up." Janus told me with a bark of a laugh and a toothy grin. "Better eat up, else she will just keep coming back. Does not take *no* for any answer."

I stared dubiously down into the container, seeing mysterious objects swirling in what looked like melted fat amongst a brown-like sauce. My nose was conflicted by the various aromas spilling from the cup, and I usually did not trust myself to eat or drink anything I could not immediately recognise, at least partly.

"Drink up. Is her version of *galushki*. Dumpling soup." The half troll told me, slapping his chest loudly. "Will make scrawny Redcloak like you big and strong. Like me. Much more better than how you are now."

I winced, feeling the muscles in my neck tighten at the appalling phraseology used. Beside me, I heard Greg muffle a chuckle, turning away so I couldn't get a glimpse of his face. The bastard.

Knowing I really had no choice, and what was likely to happen if I refused a simple gesture of goodwill this early on in our partnership, I took a breath and lifted the mug to my lips. And let the hot semi sludge pour down.

"Mmmm yum. Very good." I gulped down everything, feeling the melted fat coat my tongue and the small dumplings slide down my throat to hit my stomach like little lead cannonballs. Everything else sort of glooped down alongside them, and I bit down a rumble of complaint from my innards. "Can feel it doing good already."

Janus slapped me on my back, almost jolting the dumplings back up again, and laughed quietly.

"By time we are done here, you will love Mother's cooking." He joked, but I bit down hard on a rebuttal about chewing on my own arm instead, and simply nodded back at him.

"So, troll right? Mother or father?" I asked to move the conversation on, discreetly turning the mug upside down behind my back and letting the remains drop to the ground. A quick scuff of my heel covered the evidence.

Janus gave a bark of a laugh.

"Mother. Father was soldier in Russian Ground Force, reassigned to Siberia for dereliction of duty. He got drunk a lot, did very stupid things." He explained in his broken English. "Siberia did not help with that, and he got into fight with some *ruska roma* … gypsies might call them. Killed one, hurt more. Matriarch of the family cursed him, drove him mad. Made him fall in love with my mother, hoped he would die. She would kill him. Instead, I happened."

It was the sort of story that the darker fairy tales used to cover off. Some idiot mortal crossing a witch or someone with the gift, and being cursed to suffer for the rest of their admittedly shortened life. Making a man love a troll *should* have meant one thing, and one thing only … but then, Fate or whatever joker was watching at the time must have had a moment of genius. Creating a half-troll for the fun of it.

"Mother left baby with him, otherwise probably have eaten me." He grinned, chuckling that thick laugh of his as he took out the flask again and took a swig before continuing. "Tried to be many things. Troll. Man. Found no-one wanted me to be one or other. Laughed at, mocked.

Bullied until I got big enough to hit back. So … here I am, being both. Now I am one laughing. Ha ha."

"Yeah. Ha ha." I accepted the flask when he offered it across, taking a sniff and smelling the strong alcohol inside.

"Kvint brandy. Best there is." Janus told me and I just nodded, taking a pull and swallowing down the burn. It wasn't a Malbec, but it helped push the chill of the wind back a little.

"Good. Now we are comrades. Not brothers, as no blood has been shared, but comrades still." The big half troll told me, slapping my shoulder in a friendly manner. It still made things ache, but compared to how I woke up not so long ago, it was nothing.

Greg waved the flask away when the half troll offered it.

"I'm good, thanks. It's against my religion." He told him with no trace of a smile, completely serious. "But don't worry, if he's your comrade then so am I."

Puck clapped her hands, ending our little dialogue.

"Gentle folk, let us gather to discuss how next we proceed on this epic adventure." She rolled off brightly, making me wince. I figured she *had* to be putting it on, since no-one would believe she was some simple mortal if she spoke like that in OPS.

Trix and Dix finished packing up two rucksack with all their kit, and sat themselves down on them to listen. Mother squatted down and sat on a flat rock, spreading her legs to show her old battered boots, complete with metal toe caps shining. For his part Hunter remained where he was, within earshot but able to scan back the way we had come to make sure nothing or no-one snuck up on us.

Janus, Greg and myself joined the small gathering, as Manisha stepped away from the mini-van. She had shifted outfits, her look now more outdoor ranger with padded upper body armour and a pack, and her weapons hung comfortably within reach. Not quite the full Ivory Knight armour, but enough to mark her as a fighter.

"We must proceed by foot from now on, due to the terrain becoming ... troublesome." Puck spoke up, indicating a path that led off into the sparse treeline. I could make out a rough track winding into the rock, the sides closing in to make the going snug. "Hunter will range ahead and mark the way for us and warn of danger, should it approach."

"Due to the confines of the path, we should walk in single file." She continued, looking around the small group. "I suggest our own formidable Manisha take point, followed by Morgan and Gregory. Then Janus, Mother and Dix and Trix. I will humbly take the rearmost point, to ward against anything following us and to remove what little trace of our passing we leave. Is that reasonable?"

The twins shrugged.

"We normally run interference at the rear, so to speak." Trix commented, whilst Dix nodded in agreement. So far he hadn't said a single word, at least that I'd heard. "If you want the job, that's one less thing we need to worry about. Just do a good job."

"That will *not* be an issue." Puck told her a little tartly.

"What should we expect?" I asked Hunter, since he had already done a recon of our destination. "Anything to worry about?"

Hunter shook his head, setting his rifle down and shrugging out of his jacket. Next went his trousers and undershirt, and finally his socks and boots, leaving only his dignity covered with a pair of dark boxershorts.

Then he dropped these too.

"Geez, Hunter! Warn us before you do that!" Trix sighed, averting her eyes as if offended. Mother cackled, eyes firmly fixed on the nude shapechanger. I didn't check whether Puck or Manisha were ogling him, since it was none of my business.

Hunter crouched down, onto all fours. His body rippled, shaking as if fevered whilst cracks and pops heralded a complete reshift of his anatomy. Fur burst through his skin, and he gave coughing grunt as his skull reformed.

I'd never watched a shapechanger change form before, and found it oddly disturbing. For lycans, the change was pretty much instantaneous, nothing like the torturous slow motion idiocy you see in werewolf movies since that would probably equal extinction for our race if we had to wait that long to face an enemy.

But Hunter's way was definitely slower, as he took the form of the creature he wanted. Building it out of his own flesh and bone, down to the exact DNA of the thing. We had suits to shift between but we were never *true* wolves.

Whereas after a long moment, Hunter faced us as a large timber wolf, fur dusted and grey like the rocks around us. His eyes gleamed yellow from within the canine skull, but otherwise he was an exact copy of the creature.

With a low huff, he trotted off along the trail we were meant to take. At the first turn, I saw him cock his leg and realised he intended to mark our way in the simplest of ways. There was no way my lycan nose was going to get misled, but for anyone else, they'd just see the stain of an animal marking its territory. Clever.

"Hunter did not come across any sign of trouble when he scouted here yesterday." Puck answered for him, hefting a small pack that Manisha had set at her feet. "The path leads into a small crevasse which bottoms out at a pool of this black water. The tunnels we are looking for are within a cave set to the lower side of this, easy to miss unless you are looking for them. No man, animal or anything other has left marks anywhere along our route to indicate we are not alone here."

"Yeah, right." I growled, shifting my weapons and checking they were loose in their sheaths. "It's always when things look harmless that I'm the most nervous."

"And that is what makes you a cynic, and probably due an ulcer." She quipped back at me with a sharp smile. "The walk should take us no longer the fifteen minutes but the weather is increasingly antisocial so I suggest we start off. Unless anyone has any other questions or objections to raise?"

Mother shook her head as she stomped over to where Hunter had undressed. With deft skill she packaged up his clothes and strap his rifle to a small rucksack, which she added to her own load without any sign of inconvenience. Gnome-stock, meaning she could carry heavy loads without issue, and probably arm-wrestle me or Janus without breaking sweat.

The twins looked at each other, sharing that same unspoken communication that I began to think meant Dix didn't speak at all, and relied on other means instead. Trix caught me looking, and grinned as she waved her fingers in a spooky manner. I'd let Elspeth dissuade the half-fae of that sort of behaviour when we got to her, given how many times I'd earned a thump for suggesting that was how magic was performed.

No-one said anything, so Puck nodded once.

"Good then. Let us be off on our journey, before Mother Nature decides to loose her displeasure upon us." The Ivory fae motioned for me to start off, with Greg following.

Nice and easy. No sign of trouble, nothing for us to worry about, this early on.

I should have known it wouldn't last.

And it'd be me who got hit, first and foremost.

Chapter 20

We'd gone maybe fifteen, twenty metres along the path, taking one sharp turn and following Hunter's scent markers when it hit me.

Hard.

It was like, taking one step to the next, I crossed some sort of threshold. Nothing that I could see, but instead a feeling like I'd brushed against an electrical fence or plugged myself into the mains by accident.

My vision darkened, as my ears suddenly popped.

"Morgan? Is that you?!"

Felix's voice whispered in my head, sharp and unmistakable.

"Felix? Where the fuck are you?" I reached out to stabilise myself, pressing my hand against the hard rock and packed earth of the ravine where we were. Around me, the rest of the group had stopped and I could feel the questioning looks being thrown my way.

I held up a hand, waving off distractions as I tried to concentrate.

Felix's voice came and went, like there was static or something blocking her.

"My god Morgan! I've been trying … weeks … reach you. Elspeth's with …. They put us glass cells … can't do anything. Nothing seems … work. Magic … blocked."

I focused on her voice, trying to make the link stabilise somehow. It was the connection between us, the one forged when she was last kidnapped, just made stronger by her own magic now. But I had no clue what I was doing, making it up and half-arsing around with something I had no rights being able to do.

"Felix, listen. Where are you?" I reached out, with whatever I had inside me, whatever it was she had linked to. "Can you show me?"

"*...Gonna ... try ...*"

My vision tunnelled, and for a moment I looked out on somewhere completely different. Rocks and mud were replaced by metal and glass, smeared with old dust and other substances. Scratched in places, but uncracked. Unbroken.

Looking round, I saw through the smeared glass, saw inside the next cube. The next cell. And staring back at me, red hair tangled and face bruised, but otherwise alive ... I saw Elspeth. She had her hands pressed against the glass wall dividing us, but her green eyes were locked on me.

"*Ellie?*" I asked, but it was with Felix's voice.

"*Morgan?*" I saw her mouth move, though I couldn't hear her speak through the glass. "*Where are you?*"

"*I'm coming. We're coming.*" I told her, wanting Felix to hear it as well.

"*Hurry.*" She mouthed, just as I felt the link between us start to shred and tear, like paper ripping.

The next thing I knew, I was back in myself, leant against the hard stone. Greg was beside me, pale eyes fixed on me. Manisha was a step behind, with Puck peering round her shoulder, whilst the others kept an eye on our surroundings. This wasn't the time to be stopping, I knew.

It hadn't exactly been my idea.

"You ok?" Greg asked me quietly, and I nodded, taking a moment to calm myself and slow my thudding heart.

When I'd managed to get things straight in my head, I straightened back up again and looked over at my companions.

"All good. Just, ah ... thinking of our friends. You know, like I wish I could just speak to them. Let them know we're coming." I hedged, not wanting to share my mysterious link that I had with Felix, with our mercenary companions. I wasn't ready to trust complete strangers that easily. "It all just caught up with me, I guess."

Janus grunted a laugh.

"Redcloaks ain't so tough." The half troll grinned, shaking his head. "Less wolf, more kitty."

I bit back any retort I might've wanted to share, instead only concerned about staying upright. Magic, whatever the fuck it was, really messed with my head. Just another good reason for a mutt like me not to mess with the bloody stuff.

Instead, I caught Greg's eye, and saw him nod once without saying anything. He'd understood. That was what mattered.

When I was fairly sure I wasn't going to fall on my face, I motioned for Manisha to get going once more. She flashed me one enquiring look, slim eyebrow cocked and telling me I hadn't fooled her, then started off again. Following the path.

I paced behind the Ivory Knight, trying to recall every details of what I'd seen. Glass cells, almost like massive specimen containers. Scientific equipment, definitely. And the scratches, the marks on the glass, those looked to have been made by something or somethings from the *inside*. Like prisoners, trying to break free. Maybe.

Through Felix's eyes, I'd also caught sight of figures moving outside of the glass, a view of a larger open space with stairwells and platforms leading off to Gods knew where. Something of the DOPA facility hidden away beneath our feet, hopefully. And more of the containers or prisons close by. Ellie and Felix weren't alone, they weren't the only ones being held captive.

Somewhere down there, Herne and Harry … the Harrowed Queen … were also imprisoned. An elemental immortal centuries old, and the death of immortals merged with a Shadow fae ages old. Whatever the facility was using to keep them locked down, it was impressive.

Two things nagged at me as we traversed the ravine, the path starting to slope down to where I guessed the pool awaited us. One, Felix had tried to tell me something about magic being blocked, which made a load of sense if these arseholes were imprisoning witches, immortals and creatures to whom using the craft was like breathing. And I remembered how the chimerians who jumped us had done something on their suits that messed with Ellie and Felix, when they tried to channel their craft as well.

So, if that was the case, how the hell did Felix and I manage to share our thoughts, and me see through her eyes for even a little bit of time? If that wasn't magic, I didn't know what the fuck it was. Wishful thinking?

Second, Felix had said something like she'd been trying to get through to me for *weeks*. And the inflection I got from that was not one or two, but a lot longer. But even with me being on my arse for two days, and then us having to wait for Cormac … then Puck, to come back and plan our insane rescue attempt, we hadn't been gone long enough for that to be fact.

So either they'd been drugging her so she had no idea of the real passage of time, or something really fucking weird was going on in the DOPA facility. The one we were just about to break into.

Ah, fun times.

We reached the pool without further incident, Manisha motioning for me to go left as she took the right. The ravine had proven little more than a goat track at the end of it, forcing us to half stagger, half hop our way down, but it then levelled out even as it opened on both sides.

The pool lay before us, inky and still. Rocks led down to its shore, and the liquid lapped at the pebbles and shattered boulders, leaving inky droplets staining their surface. It looked to be about thirty, maybe forty feet from one side of the other but there was no clue as to how deep it ran. Even though the pool was as still as a mirror, waterfalls fed it from on high, the gushing liquid sinking into the pool in almost surreal silence, whilst inky water ran off down several passages carved into the rock. There was no stink of stagnancy, no build up of weeds to indicate the water was trapped, just an inky blackness. Impossible to pierce.

I checked my surroundings, alert for watchers both physical or otherwise. Mortals use electrical devices for surveillance, drones and cameras which when used against themselves are virtually undetectable. But to a lycan, you might as well paint them pink and have fireworks fired off at their location, given we can pick up the whine of their power-supply as well as tickling that *'we're being watched'* feeling.

Magical surveillance can be a bit trickier to detect, as Felix had smugly showed Jess and I by stalking us under a bloody impressive crafting. But even through the Veil itself, that border between Realms, I'd felt the Morrigan watching me when she'd been spying me out all those months ago. So I knew what to look for, so to speak, to make sure we were alone here.

Finding things safe, I motioned to Manisha and the rest of the of the party where they lurked in the ravine. Puck immediately headed off to the side where her Ivory companion was, and where I could see some sort of shelving in the rock. The caves, and pipes, I had to guess.

Trix and Dix began checking the clearing for any other hidden entry points, obviously having gone to the school of *use natural camouflage to hide secret doors*. Why waste effort and energy making entrances blend in, when you can just hide them behind a nearby bush or inside a suitable boulder. It's what you learn from watching far too much *Scooby Doo*.

Meanwhile, Janus, Greg and I moved over to look at the black pool.

"What do you think makes it so dark?" Greg asked as he squatted down, running his fingers through the stained water. It left a residue on his fingers, like ink, that dripped off his skin like droplets of dark blood.

Ok, yeah, my thoughts were a little grim. But I was still a little shaken from my contact with my friends. Knowing the shit we faced, to get them home safe.

Mother shuffled over, and let loose a torrent of words which had the harsh soviet twang to them, again making me think the half gnome was local, from this region or close by. Janus cocked his head, then grunted before looking back at us.

"Mother says there is local legend." He expounded, nodding to the pool. "Young woman, long ago, used to come bath in pools. Said to have magical properties, make her beautiful, live longer. Old wives tale, but woman did not care."

I grunted out a sigh, knowing as soon as someone mentioned an *old legend*, and *old wives tales*, then this never, ever ended well. Not for the person involved, and normally not the suckers who had to clear up the mess afterwards and deal with the repercussions.

"Woman's mother not like her sneaking out by herself. Tried to stop her from coming here." The half troll continued, and even Greg shook his head. He had had children, he knew what *don't go there* meant to them. "Young woman still went, snuck out all alone. Some bad men follow her, drunk on bad beer and brandy. They do bad, bad things to young woman but not kill her. Leave her broken, shame-filled."

"The men go back to village, drink more and fall asleep. No think of what happened to young woman. She crawled back to pool, and is said to have called on Devil himself. Given her soul, to revenge herself on wicked men. Devil tells her to get into pool, and when she does, water darkens from her blood. Blackens, as runs from her broken body. Sinks into depths, and is lost."

"Black water poisons whole watercourse, even underground streams running all way down to village. Wells fill with it, pours from taps and showers, filling troughs for animals. Everything sickens, babies born deformed, disease runs rife. Village priest calls town together to pray, beseech God for cure. Drunken men still alive, hiding their shame."

"Whilst priest calls on God for forgiveness, doors flung open and black water gushes in. Rises up into form of young woman, thought long dead and lost. She points to cowardly attackers and names them cursed, blames them for sickness and death. But men deny her, calling her devil. Priest tries to cast her out, and even her own mother turns from her."

"So woman names whole village cursed. Water will remain black, poisonous until men or their children or children's children admit wrongdoing. Throw themselves in black pool to appease her spirit."

"Legend say if you are here alone at night, can hear her sobbing. Spirit still crying for justice."

Yeah, that's about as bad as I thought it was going to be. The shit mortals do to one another, it would be unbelievable if I hadn't witnessed so much of it myself. And that devil … one of the creatures of the Real, seeing a chance to fuck with the lesser creatures, just another game to them.

Janus grinned, and reached down to pick up a stone from the ground.

"*Or* maybe just minerals. Iron, magnesium … in rocks, leaching into water as runs down from mountains." He hefted the stone before tossing it out into the middle of the lake. "Degree in chemical engineering. Not just a pretty face, ha!"

I'd noticed the Ivory fae join us as Janus told translated Mother's story, but neither had made any sort of comment or interrupted. But now Manisha moved with inhuman speed, hand open and catching the stone before it had even travelled a foot from the half troll's throw.

She looked across at us, casually dropping the round rock to the floor.

"Best not disturb the pool. We do not know what might have been set to watch this place, as a guardian or just something settling where it knows it will not be disturbed." She told us with a small smile. "There *are* no creatures alive in the vicinity, after all."

"Ivory Knight is paranoid." Janus shrugged but showed no signs he'd taken offence.

"Doesn't mean I'm not right." She shot back, showing she knew that particular mortal saying.

Me, I just had a flash back to *Lord of the Rings*, when the company were outside the gates to Moria. Where one of them tossed a stone into a lake, rousing a tenticular horror that had been set there to guard the way in. Personally, I was happy *not* to be tangling with any bloody-minded calamari that might be lurking within the black waters.

"If we are done poking around, we should head on inside." Puck instructed, as the two half fae returned from their fruitless search for hidden entrances. Since there was nothing else to do, and the black water was giving me the creeps with its stillness, I nodded in agreement.

At that moment my senses pinged, and I turned … but it was only Hunter, padding into the clearing. I assumed he'd been making a circuit of the place, hunting out any sign of danger, but the wolf was at ease and showed no sign that he had encountered trouble.

The shapechanger padded over to where Mother waited, the second pack resting beside her. With more painful organic noises and unwholesome bodily movements, he returned to his mortal form, start bollock naked again.

"You know, I think he likes showing his bits off." I told Greg, who grinned but forbore to comment. Trix earned a thump from her brother as she ogled the other's naked body far too long, but Mother simply laughed and unpacked his clothing.

Fully dressed, the shapechanger hefted his rifle and looked over at Manisha and me.

"Nothing out there. No animal, nothing." He finally spoke, his voice rough. There was an accent, possibly Native American maybe, but given his ability to look like anything he ate, who the fuck knew where he'd come from, what nation he'd been born to. "It's not normal. Something's scared it all away."

"Yeah, that's hardly surprising if this *is* a top secret research facility for the mortal security services." Manisha replied dryly, and nodded off to where she and Puck had been poking around. "We're heading in."

"I'll follow. Make sure nothing's watching." Hunter instructed, and paced off to settle down amongst the rocks, rifle tucked in and his eyes fixed on its scope as he began a slow sweep.

Leaving him, the rest of the company followed Puck around the shoreline of the black pool, all of us avoiding touching the dark water. Whether it was cursed or just contaminated, there were enough stories of bad things happening to anyone exposed to it to make us all steer clear.

The overhang of rock loomed ahead, a shelf that extended out over the water. Run-offs from above splashed down into the pool but did not cause much of a ripple, given the viscosity of the stuff flowing. We had to duck a little to enter, but the roof then opened up, allowing us to straighten.

The pipes were instantly obvious, metal circles extending out of the rock like lifeless gigantic worms. Despite their age, they were free of corrosion, and another sign of their oddity was the lack of cave vegetation clinging to them. I'd have expected moss or algae to have swarmed over anything out of the sunlight, even mould or fungi. But they were almost pristine.

"What makes you think this is a backdoor to the DOPA site?" Greg asked, the once-detective obviously not having spent as much time as me down in sewer tunnels and the like, to know when things didn't look right.

"Follow me. You'll see." Puck replied with that annoying smugness that made my fists twitch. Just another supercilious fae, convinced of their own superiority. So far, Manisha seemed to be a rare exception to their arrogance.

We had walked maybe five minutes down the darkened pipe, with our mercenary friends pulling out flashlights to light our way, when the whispers started.

At first I thought it was just the wind, caught down here and tickling at the very edges of my hearing. But then I caught words, faint but insistent.

"You do not belong."

"Go back."

"You will die here, far from the light."

"Your death approaches!"

I twitched my head round, trying to locate the direction they were coming from but it was impossible. The whispers shivered in the air, from one place then another, constantly changing. Fucking annoying.

"Ok, what the fuck's going on?" I growled, earning a broad smile from Puck as she motioned for us to stop. We stood in the broad pipe, and I could tell everyone was hearing what I heard, as eyes darted around and hands settled on weapon hilts.

"Trix dear, if you would?" The Ivory spy asked the woman, smiling in the near darkness. "I believe, of you both, you are the more accomplished at finding what is hidden?"

"You might say that." The half fae replied, but cast her torch around the tunnel as we all waited. The whispers kept coming, stronger now, and I could sense a threatening undertone growing, like water growing more agitated before the tidalwave struck.

"You will die!"

"You are lost, alone in the dark!"

"You will never see the light again!"

The voices began to rise to a howling shriek, and I snarled as I pushed against their insistent verbal assault. Greg held his hands over his ears, jaw tense from gritting his teeth, and the rest of the company all showed that they too suffered. Only Puck stood, calm and untroubled, as Trix chased across the tunnel ceiling.

"Your end comes!"

"Die!"

The words howled around us, pushing at us with almost physical force now. Tearing at our clothing as if we were in a strong wind, lashing us and drawing blood from sharp scratches across any bared skin.

"Trix! Whatever you're doing, do it faster!" Janus bellowed, one arm over his eyes to protect them. Even the tough half troll was bleeding from scratches the words were inflicting.

"Got you!" She almost crowed a moment later, torch directed above us. Where a patch of the pipe seemed to shimmer and shift under her light, writhing in the illumination. "Fucking wards!"

She reached into a pocket and pulled out a fistful of what looked like green dust, which she hurled upwards at the patch of metal. It billowed out as if blasted from her hand, coating the metal and sinking in. Immediately, the shimmering haze vanished, revealing lines of scrawling fire written into the pipe's metal, intricately done.

The green dust flared, and the fiery lines gave a last, sullen burst of luminesce before they faded and died. With them went the wind and shrieking abuse, the pipe settling into silence around us once more.

"Word Ward. Standard protection for all DOPA sites of a security classification of *sensitive* and above. Exposure to its effects lead to mental instability, deafness and physical harm. Even death if it is allowed to run its course. Exactly as the mortal manual describes." Puck explained as I swiped at the thin cuts the magic had made on my skin. They were already healing, the indirect nature of the ward allowing it to bypass my lycan immunity. Fucking nasty things. "That should tell you we are exactly where we need to be, and also explains the lack of animals inhabiting this otherwise hospitable abode."

The spy then smiled brightly, nodding ahead of us where the pipe ended, and smooth blank rock faced us. Featureless, unforgiving and very solid except for a single door set in its frame. The sort of door you see used to seal bank vaults, submarines and even airlocks. There was no handle, no keyhole, nothing to allow anyone entry from our side.

She rubbed her hands together theatrically.

"Now, how about we stop fooling around and crack this nut, shall we?"

Chapter 21

We all stood back, having been gently ushered that way by Mother as she set her backpack down and went to work. It helped that Janus had loomed behind her, glaring at anyone looking to crowd the half gnome at her job.

She inspected the door, tapping it gently and leaning in to taste its surface with a quick lick of her tongue. Ruminating on whatever that told her, she nodded to herself and began tapping at the rock around the portal, leaning in to lay her ear against the craggy surface. Finding whatever she was after, she then leant back against the door, whispering so quietly that I couldn't understand what she was saying. But it looked like she was having a conversation with the bloody thing.

The seconds ticked by, and I bit down on my natural inclination to say something, try to hurry the whole thing along. With people I knew, I wasn't too worried about pissing them off but the mercenaries were still pretty much unknown to me. The last thing I wanted was to let my smart mouth fuck up our chances of success before we'd even go through the back door.

Wisdom cometh with age, supposedly. With me, its more like hit and miss.

Eventually Mother stomped back to he pack, and began rummaging around inside its voluminous contents.

"Old stone, old metal. Strong still ,and it's a stubborn sod. Wants to remain shut. Set in its ways like all old men." She mused to herself out loud, shaking her head. "Won't be convinced, won't be bargained with. So only one thing for it."

The half gnome pulled out a large jar, screwed down tight and bound shut with wire. She then extracted a thick brush, the sort you see in hardware stores for the really big paint-jobs.

"Janus, I need your height." She waved him over, and he joined her without hesitation. I had to assume they'd worked together before, and knew each other well enough not to question. "An inch, maybe two should be enough. Remember, none of it on you. Even your thick skin won't be proof."

Janus grunted, smiling and patting her on the head in a familiar way. He was quick enough to sidestep as she went to thump him, snatching the brush free with deft skill.

"Everyone back up a step. This bit, never know quite what will happen." Mother told us, waving us back several feet further up the pipe.

The half troll gingerly opened the jar, and my nose immediately twitched with acidric sharpness. Whatever the stuff was, it was strong, though I also weirdly got the scents of herbs and spices. Not something I'd associate with anything as corrosive as what the jar contained.

"Was trying my family's recipe for *zhur*. Think I overdid the gunpowder and citrine a touch." Mother told me, seeing me react to the smell. "Melted the pot, the stove and put a tidy hole in the floor beneath. Scared the tenants below me half to death. Good times."

I was *definitely* going to be eating my own food on this hunt, that was for sure.

Janus, meanwhile, gingerly began spreading a line of the substance from the base of the door, all the way around it. The half troll was careful not to touch the metal, only painting the thick liquid on the rock itself. He was quick, avoiding any splashbacks or drips, and after a few seconds he stepped back. The brush was in ruins, all the bristles gone and the handle already beginning to droop and melt so he dropped the stub to the floor. Where it began to bubble and hiss from contact with the pipe.

He quickly closed the jar up again, having used only a third of its extremely corrosive contents, and handed it back to Mother, who settled it amongst the rest of her gear in the rucksack. I had to wonder just what else she was carrying in there, and the risk it presented if she accidently fell or was knocked. She carried enough munitions on her person to make a very large hole in wherever she was standing, let alone whatever she had hidden in that pack of hers.

Mental note. Keep the half gnome away from fire or anything that might trigger her. For the wellbeing of everyone.

"Now we see how stubborn he is." Mother grunted, and nodded at the rock wall. "And whether Mother can break him, like all the others."

It took a moment, as we watched expectantly, before the line of corrosive substance began to bubble and hiss. Little flecks of flaking rock spat down from the line, hitting the pipe at our feet and causing sparks to fly. Then the line darkened, hissing as the acid ate its way inward. Smoke billowed up to coil and twist above us, leaking out towards the pipe's mouth and the fresh air.

The rock around where Janus had painted began to crumble and flake, revealing a thick line eaten right the way through. As he had coated the rock *under* the doorframe, the metal slab gave a sharp groan and slumped, slowly but inevitably falling to the floor with a resounding thud. Dust and powdered rock billowed up into the air, and we all covered our faces to stop ourselves breathing in the crap.

"Ha. No man beats Mother!" The half gnome crowed, settling her rucksack back onto her shoulders and grinning broadly. Trix laughed sharply, whilst her brother rolled his eyes, telling me this was an old, old joke between them.

Puck snapped her fingers, bringing everyone's attention back to her.

"Now, before we traverse inward, let us discuss what to expect." She told us all, looking across at me. "Morgan, you are in possession of a record of one who worked here before. Any insights you would like to share with the company?"

It was like being at school, and having the teacher invite a student to share the sweets they'd smuggled in with the rest of the class. It was more than a little disconcerting how easily the Ivory fae slipped into that role.

"There wasn't much about the facility." I offered up, thinking through what I'd read, what my mother had written about. The secret experiments, the things she had seen, had done. Definitely nothing I wanted to share. "Except, there was something in the basement. Something Doctor Bremmer and his team didn't want my … ah, her knowing about."

"Truly enlightening." Puck snarked, then shrugged. "It is of little matter. DOPA facilities tend to follow a set pattern, to allow their mortal staff the ability to navigate the confines of each one without needing much time to orientate themselves."

She snapped her fingers, but only sparks burst from her fingertips, sizzling out in the cold air of the pipeway.

"Damn hex blockers." She cursed, sighing theatrically before reaching into a pouch and pulling out a pad and pen. "If you could give me some light please, we'd best make this quick. In case anyone … or anything heard us knocking."

She quickly sketched on the paper, detailing what we should expect.

"The main entrance should lead into a secure waiting area for visiting officials to be checked in, with guard posts to prevent any unauthorised individual progressing any further than the front door." She tapped the top of her drawing. "If we had attempted access there, we would have faced far greater security, and a mightier door to prevail against than this one. Proof against most mortal munitions and science, and layered with suitable materials to block magical means of entry as well."

"Beyond, there will be at least one large briefing chamber, along with offices and conference modules for discussions involving non-DOPA staff and visitors. Security will have at least one room located nearby, but their command centre will be far deeper inside. Made to be unbreachable in case of an outbreak of violence."

"Corridors will run between the offices, with living quarters, recreation centres and a canteen set on the floor above. Accessed most likely by stairway, given the age of the facility. Any service lifts will have been utilised for moving assets or equipment between floors only, and the habitats designed to be locked down in an emergency. Securing staff safely away from anything that might have escaped".

"The sublevel, below us, will contain laboratories, research facilities and all the necessary paraphernalia to complete whatever experiments the mortals were involved in at this site. The security command centre will be located there as well, along with whatever controls were built into the facility to purge accidents or erase the entire building if it was in danger of being taken over."

"Finally, the basement level. Normally utilised for storage of the larger, bulkier equipment and generators to keep the facility running. As well as at least one entrance or egress for larger vehicles to being in test subjects or materials, to then be transported to the level above." Puck looked over at me with a smile. "However, as Morgan has noted, this facility has at least one surprise awaiting us."

She tapped the drawing with her pen, marking an ex to the bottom left.

"I believe we are here, at one of the venting stations on the top floor. Probably from the kitchens. Meaning we will be entering the accommodation block, and have three levels to descend."

Janus looked at the drawing, his knobbled skin furrowing on his forehead.

"These friends of yours, they here already, so you say?" He queried, and I nodded. "You think we find them at very bottom of this dump? Why not elsewhere?"

Puck looked over at me, letting me field the obvious question.

"As I said, there's something in the sub-basement, something they wanted to keep hidden. It's where they'd have headed." I lied, shrugging my shoulders. Keep it simple, that's what they always say when telling lies you *really* want believed. "They found another way in, but it shut behind them. Now they're lost somewhere inside and we don't have communications with them. Just the fact they'd be heading to the bottom."

"Can't you, like, howl at each other, if these are friends of yours?" Trix asked brightly, earning a chuckle from Hunter and a snort of laughter from Janus.

I shook my head, but Puck decided to take back the conversation, possibly knowing some of the answers I was already thinking of voicing.

"If matters were that simple, we wouldn't be employing your most delightful of services, and offering such a bountiful of compensation for your time and assistance, now would we?" She smiled showing the sharp whiteness of her teeth. "To be clear, they are out of any communication range, at least for the present time."

"That *bountiful compensation* …" Janus grinned, and Puck sighed.

"As agreed, you can lay claim to any technology you decide is of suitable value that you find whilst we search this facility, and you are able to carry it out yourself. Without mechanical or arcane assistance." She told the full company, and I winced. Basically the Ivory fae was opening the lid on anything DOPA or OPS had left lying around this place, or anything the chimerians had managed to steal and store here. That covered a lot of stuff, some of it probably quite lethal in the wrong hands.

Then Puck allayed my fears, at least a little.

"However, I do reserve the right to withhold any item we come across, whose usage would threaten the Accords, or pose significant risk to the mortals of this Realm." She added, earning a grunt from the half troll, full of disappointment. "I am fully authorised to recompense you instead, in untraceable currencies of your choice."

"Are we done?" She asked, and since no one decided to argue, she waved to the open door hole. "Then, let us begin. Keep an eye out for any old surveillance equipment, or traps set for foolish adventurers seeking their fortune."

Or idiot lycan, come looking for his family and friends, I told myself before joining Manisha on the inside of the facility.

The space beyond the door was a non-descript corridor, wide enough for myself and Greg to stand beside each other without touching. The ceiling was a normal mortal height, so Janus ducked a little as he brought up the rear. The overhead lights were dark, and the air smelt stale, old. Like nothing had passed through here in a long time. That also explained the dust on the floor under our feet, puffing up as we moved inside.

When all of us were in, Janus reached down and, showing his unnatural strength, carefully picked the fallen door up off the floor. With more care than I thought he possessed, the mercenary gently slotted the portal and its surrounds back into the hole he'd made with Mother's acid. Stone grated as he wrestled it into the jagged gap, but the door finally settled back in place.

It wasn't perfect, but to the casual eye it would look like the thing was still in one piece, still solidly blocking entrance to the facility. And if we needed a quick way out, I had no doubt between us, we could knock the thing back out again.

With the door back in its place, all light from the pipe was blocked off. Trix and Dix cast their torchlight around us, illuminating the dust and grime covered corridor, and the door at the far end. Closed like it's twin, but this one set with a spin-wheel locking mechanism.

We let Mother inspect the mechanism, the half gnome toying with the bandolier of explosives she wore as she poked and prodded the wheel. Then, with a grunt of disappointment, she pulled out a can of very familiar blue and yellow colour, with a red spray cap.

"WD40. One of the most useful things mortals ever invented." She shot back over her shoulder as she liberally sprayed the juncture between wheel and door, and the hinges. Then she waved Janus forward. "Counter-clockwise, if you would please?"

The half troll gripped the wheel, then bunched his muscles and slowly turned the locking mechanism. It resisted but he ground his teeth, muscles bunching under his body armour, and finally the wheel started rotating. Something clunked as he did a complete revolution, and the door swung slowly open without even a creak.

Dead, cool air gusted out to us, carrying the scent of dust and decay. Silence rolled in as we waited a long moment, alert for the shriek of an alarm, the cry of security or the thump of feet heading our way.

Nothing. Dead and silent.

Like a tomb.

Manisha looked over her shoulder, and I gave her a single nod. No going back now.

We headed in.

Chapter 22

I think I've mentioned before, but building, habitats, abodes … they all have a feel to them. A presence, a sense of what their history was, imprinted into their very substance. That feeling you get as you step over their threshold, either as a welcome or a warning.

The DOPA facility … it felt *wrong*.

The door led into what looked like an old pantry, shelves set on every side, dust-laden and bare. Everything was metal, not a soft surface to be seen. Metal trays, pots and pans, all the required utensils for en-masse cooking were stacked haphazardly, covered in cobwebs and dust. A door opposite led out of the room, again with a spin wheel lock. They definitely had a thing for those, I had to guess they'd been in fashion when this place was put together.

Not helpful for any poor sod laden down with trays of food, but hey. Who ever thinks of the working stiffs who have to use the bloody thing?

Quietly, we moved to the inner door and I noted the complete lack of footprints or tracks marring the dust on the floor. No-one had come this way in a long, long time. Not even vermin.

Janus eased the new door open, this one not needing Mother's ministrations, and poked his head out into the darkness beyond.

"Kitchen. Dining hall. Empty." He told us in a hushed voice, and pulled the door open to allow our entry.

We files in, fanning out on each side so as not to clump together in case of a sudden attack. Flashlights flickered firstly over the large kitchen with large stove tops and ovens big enough to fit as many children as a witch might fancy. All cold, all covered in dust. Sinks with taps covered in more cobwebs, and large metal units with pull out drawers filled with corroded cutlery, kitchen knives and utensils.

Then the beams shot out onto the main room, revealing trestle tables sat five deep running the length of the room with uncomfortable-looking foldable chairs pushed under them. Salt and pepper containers sat on each table, mostly buried in grime and dust, and several decaying heaps of paper hinted at someone's old newspaper, left to gently decay.

The overhead lights were off, controlled by a bank of switches on the far wall by another closed door. A large posterboard ran the length of the right hand wall, with bits of faded paper tacked to it. I squinted at one under the light of a torch, finding it a menu displaying a weeks-worth of breakfasts, lunches and dinners on offer. All in English, which was initially surprising given in which country we stood. But then I remembered this was a DOPA site, and the general mentality of that populace … speak it loudly enough, write it enough times, and the foreigners *will* understand.

We ghosted through the refectory, nothing of interest to the team apart from Mother who poked at various stored foodstuffs before turning away with a grunt of disgust. The next door led out into a wide corridor, with signs hanging from the ceiling indicating *Restrooms A-H, Shower Block A, Toilets* and the like. Some were hanging loosely by broken chains, others had fallen to the floor, smashed by something. Cubbyholes in the walls held fire extinguishers behind smeared glass, whilst dry and dusty water fountains had been set at intervals to service the staff. Everything was caked in grime, cobwebs and more dust. Without a single track to show anyone had been this way for a long, long time.

With Manisha and Janus now taking the lead, we moved along the hall carefully. Whilst Greg and I, as well as the Ivory Knight and spy, had our weapons sheathed but close to hand, our mercenary companions were not so shy and taking no chances.

The half troll carried his throwing axe in one hand, whilst the twins had their sickle swords unsheathed and carried over opposite shoulders.

Hunter had slung his sniper's rifle over one arm, and instead had his handgun gripped low and ready.

As for Mother, the half gnome had her sawn-off shotgun cradled in her hands. I caught sight of markings etched into the barrel of the gun, and guessed it packed far more punch than the standard mortal weapon should.

All in all, enough firepower and weaponry to make anything we disturbed think twice before tangling with us. Without the rest of us needing to change suits or ready our own weapons.

I should have known better.

Pacing down the hall, I poked my head into one of the rooms marked as a restroom. Standard cubicle affair, with a metal frame bed, a desk and chair. Some cupboards for clothing and drawers to keep all the crap mortals took with them wherever they went.

Everything was dust covered and caked in yet more cobwebs, thick as string. Nothing to make the place feel personal, like anyone had lived there. Or that housekeeping had been round in the last century or so.

But still, something felt off to me. A niggling feeling at the back of my skull, one I had long gotten used to trusting to tell me things weren't right. I didn't reckon I needed to switch suits just yet, but still eased the fae sword I'd been given in its sheath, making sure it was nice and loose.

Greg caught the movement and raised an eyebrow, but I just shrugged. If the shit hit the fan, I trusted him to react and manage himself, given he was now a guardian of Terra, the Mortal Realm goddess.

We carried on down the hall, Trix and Dix poking their heads in other rooms but finding nothing. Corridors branched off on either side, but a sign still attached to the ceiling told us the stairways were ahead of us so we carried on. The mercenaries were obviously well versed enough to know anything valuable in terms of personal belongings would have been retrieved long ago, and whatever had been left that might have value would be down below.

And that's when my senses pinged. We weren't alone anymore.

"Hold up." I told the team quietly, taking a breath and focusing. I shut down everything about my companions, both friends and strangers, and looked for whatever had tripped me, whatever was out of place.

Hunter walked up beside me, scanning the darkness ahead. I could tell the shapechanger also felt it, the way his yellow eyes searched around us.

"What is it?" Puck asked, as she and Trix roved their flashlights over the corridor. Ahead, the stairway was encircled with an iron railing, black and pitted, with a sign above it stating *"Ground Floor"* needlessly. The corridor ended maybe twenty feet beyond, with a pair of doors set firmly in the walls, both closed and covered with webs.

"Something … more than one thing, and they are taking their time. But getting closer." I nodded to Hunter, as my senses told me the same thing. But something more.

"I'm getting goblin. But not normal … definitely something weird about these ones."

"Bah, goblins. Green skin runts." Janus grinned, tapping his axe in his hand. "Crawl in through holes, make nests where they can. My axe make short work of the ankle biters, no sweat."

"Cocky, isn't he?" Trix looked over at her brother, resting her sickle sword on the dusty floor. The other half fae grinned, pulling out a wallet and unfolding a note from inside.

"Seriously, you want to bet?" She plucked the money from him, and added a second note from one of her dress' many pockets. "Fine, I'll take your twenty on him needing our help. Five minutes."

I shook my head, knowing everyone was different and I wasn't there to judge how this lot dealt with tense situations. Just needed them to do their job, and get us safely where we needed to be.

Janus moved in front of Manisha, who stepped back, giving him room. The half troll rolled his shoulders, tossing the axe from one hand to the other.

"Closer. Very close." I smelt them, the particular goblin taint strong in my nose. So familiar from my recent brush with the Wyld, but disturbingly different. Tainted, wrong in some fundamental way. "Should be right in front of us."

The darkness around the stairwell was lit up with torch beams, crossing to cover the entire corridor, exposing every possible obstacle or route the stubborn bastards might use. Air vents, crawl spaces, whatever.

Nothing.

"We should be able to see them." I growled, shifting to look around us. Trying to work out what we might be missing. "They're right on top of us."

"Well unless they've learned how to be bloody invisible, they obviously aren't." Trix commented dryly, pointing at the blatantly empty space in front of Janus. "You maybe sniffed too much dust on the way in? Got you smelling shadows?"

I shook my head, looking over at Hunter. The shapechanger was fixed on the corridor, muscles bunched and eyes slitted. Trying to work out what the hell was going on.

"I watched a movie once." Greg spoke up quietly, slowly drawing his sword. "There were these marines, sent in to save some settlers who had made their home on an alien planet. They found themselves cut off, stalked by monsters. They knew they were coming, they could see them on their scanners but couldn't see them even when they should have been able to."

He slowly pointed with his sword. Upwards.

"They came through the ceiling."

Shit.

"Give me a leg up." I told Janus, who eyed me uncertainly before shrugging and setting his axe back on his belt. Then he cupped his hands, giving me a stirrup to stand on.

"Here." Puck gave me her flashlight, even though I could see well enough in the shadows and gloom of the facility. "Watch your head."

I set my foot in the half troll's palm, and boosted myself onto his shoulder, turning so I faced in the right direction. He grunted, bearing my not inconsiderable weight, and gripped my thighs to steady me.

Crouching, I was now level with the ceiling, just over my head. It was composed of large square sections criss-crossed with metal, each one large enough to be four feet maybe across. The stink of goblin-kind was strong in my nose now, as well as a foulness that was not normal, nothing I'd smelt before. And now I could hear a scraping sound, the rasp of something against something else. Possibly organic, possibly not.

Gently, carefully, I pressed up against the ceiling section over my head, and flicked the flashlight so that its beam carved into the darkness in front of me.

And then I poked my head through the hole.

Chapter 23

The torch's brilliance stabbed out, illuminating a space maybe three feet high, created for all the pipes and electrics to be run and hidden away from the space below. Just the sort of thing you find in any facility, office building or place of business that mortals create when they have a shitload of gear to keep the temperature pleasant and all their necessary equipment working as needed.

What they didn't normally have were the things my light fell on.

Goblins. But not.

Crawling towards where we stood, the creatures were emaciated, their knobbled skin tightly wrapped around withered muscle and bone. Even their natural green colour was muted, greyed and webbed with blackened veins. They stank, the normal goblin musk masked with vicious chemicals and foul rot.

But far worse, black hairs bristled from their skin, long and fibrous. These were what were rubbing together as they moved, rasping like scratched metal. Each goblin's limbs were crooked like multi-jointed legs, clawed and spiked without humanoid hands or feet. And the ugly fuckers had eight limbs, far too many for my liking. Like miniature smelly, scary as fuck *Kali's* from mythology.

The flashlight shone on yellowed bone, their skulls warped and uncovered by flesh or skin. Eyes that had no pupil, but were simply full-blind white, fixed on me and their jaws were engorged, stitched or held together with metallic staples oozing pus from each incision. Spiked, twisted teeth jutted out in every direction, some more like tusks or fangs, and the goblins gaped their jaws and hissed at me with snakelike, barbed tongues.

These things were *wrong* in every way possible.

And then they scrabbled forward in a frenzy to reach me.

"Fuck, down! Down!" I shouted, tossing the torch down and slipping off Janus's shoulders as quickly as I could. "They're right on top of us!"

And the bastards burst through the ceiling plates, dropping amongst us.

I yanked out my sword, Changing even as I settled on my feet and calling on the Ivory brand as the twisted creatures hissed and shrieked as they landed. They were bent over like monstrous spiders, using their lower limbs to stabilise themselves and lashing out with the second double pair. They screeched as they came at us, skittering towards us with frenzied rage.

"What the fuck are they?" Trix shouted, her sickle sword lashing out and carving a spiked claw as the nearest creature tried to skewer her. Dix warded her back, his own sword dancing with inhuman skill, batting aside the strikes of the spider-goblins, drawing black ichor-like blood instead of the usual silver fae blood.

"Stinking ugly-arse gobbo freaks!" Janus bellowed, smashing his axe into the skull of one as it scratched and stabbed at him. Gore exploded, even more foul smelling than the creature it came from, as he grunted and levered his weapon free.

The monstrous goblins kept dropping, more than a score of them filling the corridor all around us. Hunter drew careful aim as he dodged those trying to claw him, his handgun barking and blowing limbs apart so that the creatures scrabbled and slumped amongst their seeping gore.

"You always help me meet the most interesting of beings, Errant!" Manisha told me dryly as she rolled her sword down the limb of one spiked horror, slamming the edge into its exposed neck. More ichor spread, splattering across the walls and over the creatures as she summoned darts of fire to her free hand and burned gaping holes in the nearest enemies.

Puck, for her part, drew a slim rapier of silvered brightness which exploded in flames as she darted and cut like some musketeer or swordswoman of medieval times. She was smiling cruelly as she poked the tip of her burning blade through eye-sockets and up into their gaping maws, carving her way through them and letting them fall.

Mother, however, did the most damage which hardly surprised me. Gnomes might be small, but their ability to inflict disproportional damage compared to their size was well known. Her altered shotgun blasted out a tongue of fire, and I realised she had dragons' breath shot loaded. The runic markings made sense, given how normal mortal weapons would be damaged beyond repair after using too much of that shot, the heat buckling and ruining the barrel.

Instead, her weapon savaged the spider-goblins like a miniature comet, hammering into three and shattering them into hairy, spiked ruin. They scrabbled like spiders, burning and shrieking as they curled up and died.

"Dix!" The half shadow fae cried out, catching my attention. Her brother was no longer at her back, instead he was pinned to the corridor's wall, encased in sticky webbing. Two of the creatures made horrible hacking noises, and spat out more goo in ropy strands that slammed into him, pinning him further. His sword was caught, stuck as well, and he made grunting noises as he tried to free himself.

I didn't stop, feeling the Ivory mark ignite inside me and channelling it as I'd been instructed into heat. My sword shimmered and blazed, shining bright as I lashed it across the back of the nearest goblin. Its hairy skin burned away, the meagre muscle severed and smoking as I hewed through its upper torso.

The other goblin turned, sensing its danger, and spat a mouthful of the webbing at me. But I twisted, letting it splatter behind me, even as I hammered at the thing with my free hand, claws extended. The creature squealed, a half cut-off sound as the sharp edges bisected its misshapen jaw and shattered its skull.

Mother's weapon boomed again, and three more creatures exploded in flames. Janus stomped down on a wounded goblin's skull, grinding his boot through its bones and squishing the brains out with a vengeful roar. Manisha and Puck had piled bodies around them, whilst Trix warded her imprisoned brother.

Greg, I noted, had four dead goblins lying around him, their bodies cut apart with a skill I knew he didn't possess when he was a simple police detective. His expression was set, but the tattoos on his face shimmered with fury, and I revised my thinking on Terra being completely out of the game. I'd had my suspicions, but seeing her guardian standing unscathed with the dead around him, I figured she was just playing her cards carefully.

Normal goblins would have cut and run after losing this number of their kin, but the horrors refused to quit. Forcing us to burn, skewer and carve them apart until finally the last drew a shuddering rasping breath before collapsing in a pool of its own innards.

I turned back, seeing Trix lower her weapon with a grimace.

"Ok. brother, you can get down from there now." She told him as she tried to wipe gore from the edge of her weapon, finding it sticking and refusing to shed. "We've dealt with all the big bad guys trying to kill you."

She cocked her head, smiling a hard smile as he replied silently to her.

I kept the heat powering through my fae sword, and went to start cutting the webbing holding Dix against the wall, but Trix waved me away.

"No need. He just needs to stop lazing around. It doesn't fool anyone." She told me, as her brother rolled his eyes and sighed.

Then, closing his eyes, he breathed calmly a few times … and I watched as an exact copy of himself stepped *through* the webbing, and slid free. For a brief moment, two exact copies of Dix stood side by side, and they looked at each other and grinned before the one within the webbing crumbled away to dust.

"Temporal Translocation." Trix told me with a shrug. "Means the slippery bugger can walk through walls, get out of anywhere he's been stuck, that sort of thing. As long as it doesn't take more than five breaths for him to get beyond where he's running from. After that, he's stuck wherever he appears. Solid rock, halfway through a chair. You get the idea."

"Neat trick." I growled out, realising this was probably key to his ability to get himself out of tricky situations, like being locked in a cell or behind a closed door. Handy for someone who made a living breaking into and out of places.

"These gobbos, they not normal. What the fuck are they? And why they attack us?" Janus grumbled as he scraped remains off his boot. He prodded one of the corpses with his axe, spearing its skull and pulling it up to examine the battered, burned body. "Looks like spider fucked a gobbo. Made ugly babies."

"Those sods will screw anything." Trix replied with a smile, but Puck shook her head.

"I believe these are not natural creations, birthed in any manner of copulation." She told us, slipping her cleaned rapier away. "Looks at the markings on their faces, the joins at the extra limbs. Do they not remind you of *surgical* scars? I do not think it much of a stretch to suggest these are Frankenstein-type creations, hybrids brought together to create something new. Something more than the two were."

"As to why they assaulted us, I am again hazarding a guess," She continued as I examined the corpse. The Ivory fae was right, the sections where the extra limbs were attached showed signs of scarring, let alone the staples and stitches embedded in their unnatural jaws. "But I believe, like you said, goblins will nest anywhere. We have been unlucky to stray into theirs, and they reacted with territorial ire."

"A nest would indicate a queen or female, if they followed arachnid morphology." Greg pointed out, and I felt a cold shiver run down my spine.

"What the fuck would a queen of this lot look like?" Trix asked, and I guessed her brother had the same thought, given his horrified expression.

"Bigger. Uglier. Nastier. And not anything I'd like to hang around to meet." Greg replied dryly, and I growled my agreement.

"Let us proceed beyond the boundaries of the creatures' domain." Puck instructed, as Janus and I pushed bodies aside to give us a clearer path to the stairs. The floor was still sticky with ichor and spilled fluids, but at least we wouldn't have to clamber over the hairy, spiky corpses. "And let us take this as a gentle warning to be on our guard, for this facility holds many secrets. Some quite possibly worse than these unfortunate creations."

I decided if this was the sort of shit we were going to face, I was staying in my worgen form.

"You know, if those chimerians *are* here, we've just run the front doorbell for them, right?" Greg whispered to me, and I huffed an agreeable grunt. "Just saying. Eyes open from now on."

I wanted to snark back at him, something like *Goodness, I'd been walking around with them closed this whole time!* But I just snapped my wolf jaws closed and bit down on the urge.

Instead, I focused on that link between Felix and I, the tether that had allowed her to pull me into her mind somehow. Not to talk with her, but just to make sure we were in the right place. And I felt it, that familiar sense of her, not cut off anymore but lingering in the back of my mind somehow.

Close, definitely close. Yet also weirdly still feeling like we were also at a distance too. Askew, like we were at different angles. It was hard to make sense of it, but something was interfering. Probably the containment they had her in, to stop her using magic to escape.

The important thing was, we were in the right place.

The stairs curved back on themselves, running down to the level below. Dust muffled our footsteps and no-one used the railing given how thick with grime the metal was. Torchlight lit our way, flicking up to the ceiling every other breath to make sure none of the monstrous spider-goblins were lurking in wait, but either we'd killed them all off or more likely they were lurking at a safe distance, nursing their hunger.

We emerged on the ground floor, weapons held ready, eyes searching the gloom. That sense of wrongness was only getting stronger, a churning in my stomach now like I'd eaten rotten fruit or something. A taint, definitely coming from inside the facility, in with us. Possibly the chimerians, possibly something worse.

The stairs ended in a large foyer, with a curved reception desk set against one wall. Posterboards behind this displayed tattered notes, a faded calendar from the late 1970s when the facility was still operational. Security warnings, the usual fare for governmental sites secure in their own importance. A dried up and cobwebbed waterfountain stood mournfully to one side, alongside a broken metal stand that still held the remains of several dated magazines and publications.

Puck shone a light up to illuminate a set of hanging arrows still firmly attached to the ceiling. To our right, the main entrance and security, and to our left, offices and conference rooms. Ahead, down a dark corridor, the sign indicated another stairway leading to the sublevel. Where the laboratories would be found, as well as the route to the lowest level.

I pointed to the way ahead, but Janus shook his head, pointing to the office route. I growled but the half troll just shrugged, turning his back and heading off to ransack whatever had been left behind. Trix and

Dix followed him immediately, whilst Hunter and Mother lingered for a moment.

We couldn't split up. I knew of too many fucks ups which had ended that way because idiots decided *safety in numbers* was for suckers or wimps. We'd already walked into one horror-fest but managed to escape relatively unscathed … that wouldn't continue if we split up and weren't covering each other's backs. Plus the mercenaries had been hired on the proviso they could collect anything they could find. Not letting them go hunt, even if it meant wasting a few minutes, would just lead to bad blood between us.

And the only blood I wanted belonged to the chimerians and whoever was pulling their strings.

So I sighed and motioned to Hunter, giving him ten fingers as a sign of how long they had.

He nodded, Mother halting her dance from one foot to the other and grinning manically at me before turning on her heel and hastening after the shapechanger. I looked over at Greg, reading the same frustration I knew I felt on his gloom-cast features. But I could only shrug, and head after the mercenaries.

We found them quickly enough, their professionalism showing in the way they went through the rooms in the left wing of the floor quickly, not wasting any time. They obviously had items they were on the lookout for, passing over desktops with indifference and instead burrowing into drawers and under tables.

Trix and Dix were paired off, whilst Janus seemed to be working solo. Hunter and Mother began their own scavenging, as the rest of us held back to watch out for anything hostile headed our way.

The half troll appeared from underneath a bank of desks, trailing wires and boxed units that had the look of vintage computer parts. The sort that made whirring noises and clunked a lot, and were made before mortals decided that smaller was better.

"What do you need that junk for?" Greg asked, showing more knowledge about such matters than me. I tried to stay clear of anything more technological than my phone and possibly my smart tv. Though that latter one was pushing it as well given the arguments I'd had whilst standing over it with remote in hand, swearing as it refused to find a channel or film I'd *just* been watching.

Turns out *accidently tripping whilst carrying a purely ornamental movie prop and sticking it through the television screen by complete random chance* wasn't an acceptable excuse for spearing the bloody thing with a sword, according to my insurers. Go figure.

"Junk? Ha! This not junk!" Janus grinned as he expertly stashed the stolen equipment away in his pack. "'State of the art technology', at least for Russian military services. Even civilian infrastructure. Whole country run on *junk* like this. Foolish mortals pay very well for quality equipment in mint condition like this."

"Whatever. Mind finishing up here, so we can head down and find our friends?" I growled, my worgen jaws as ever adding bite to my frustration.

"Maybe reason friends not answering is they met those spider goblins already?" Janus shot back at me, as he finished tucking his stolen gear away. "Maybe they not so good at making gobbos fuck off?"

I shook my head.

"They're alive. I know it. But we need to get to them quickly."

The half troll snorted, but shouldered his pack, and using two fingers, whistled sharply. Trix and Dix appeared from another office, the brother stuffing oddments into his rucksack whilst Trix eyed the gloom with sharp eyes. Hunter reappeared, the pockets of his flack jacket bulging, along with Mother who didn't look to have taken anything. Nothing suitably explosive for her tastes, I presumed.

"We done here?" I asked, checking each of the mercenaries before looking across at Puck and Manisha. Neither Ivory fae had tried to stop the others from looting, but had not joined in themselves since they were here for entirely different reasons. I still wasn't sure *what* the Ivory spy was about, but I trusted the Knight Captain at least.

Puck waved back the way we had come,

"Pray lead us down, Redcloak." She smiled sat me, and the glitter of her eyes made me wonder if I had interpreted that first word right. *Prey* felt like it could have done the job equally well.

Chapter 24

Off down to the laboratories we went.

That weird feeling got stronger as we descended the stairs, torchlight flickering over the walls and ceiling, everyone conscious all manner of nasties could be lurking below waiting for us.

This time, the stairs led us to a security station, set so that anyone descending would have to confirm their details before being allowed onward. This consisted of a gate of grimy metal blocking the way onward, and a desk at which I assumed a guard previously sat. Their job, to check IDs, probably off a list and otherwise look menacing at anyone foolish enough to think to try to sneak past for a peek where they were not allowed.

The desk had been shoved to one side a long time ago, given the build up of detritus piled against it, but the gate was firmly closed and locked. There was another guard station beyond, obviously containing the control mechanism for opening and shutting the gate, far enough away that there was no chance of reaching it and bypassing the security even with the longest arm or niftiest tool.

Mother took the lead, borrowing a torch to inspect the gate's locking mechanism. We waited as she poked and prodded the metal, humming in an off-tune way to herself. Finally, she drew a slim pipe from one of her many pockets, inserting this into the lock where a key could be fitted. She peeled a little of its wrapper back, then stepped away.

"Might want to look your pretty eyes away." She sang to us, and I saw smoke start to spurt from the roll up. "Bright lights about to shine."

I shielded my eyes, just as bright sparks ignited and metal shattered with a sharp shriek.

"Lock-breaker. I stole it from the mortals." The half-gnome chuckled as she pushed the gate, and it grated on its hinges as it swung open. "Very handy to scare off anything that comes looking to pee on my vegetables too. Cats especially, the evil little shits."

We passed through the security gate and station, and found ourselves facing another large door. This one fitted with another spin-wheel lock, but of a size to suit most bank vaults. Janus and I grabbed the over-sized wheel and began to turn it, finding the mechanism sluggish and stuck with grime and age. But with some swearing and a lot of effort, we got the thing moving in the right direction.

It swung open slowly, pulled outward to reveal a sealed door at least two feet think, with rods that extended into the walls on either side to further secure the door. A faint hiss also told me the thing was pressurised, sealing the area beyond away from anything that might have been released in the upper sections of the facility.

Or possibly sealing away anything that got loose in the labs. There was always that option too.

Beyond, the facility changed. Dramatically.

A wide corridor of medical white lay ahead, illuminated by the group's torches. Floor, walls and ceiling were all the same hue, immediately putting me in mind of a hospital. Doors marked by hanging signs above them as *Lab 1, Lab 2, Bloodworks* and more led off the main corridor, and I caught sight of large windows set in the walls to show what was taking place in each. There was little dust, little grime … instead the place looked almost untouched. New.

It was creepy as fuck.

Manisha motioned us forward in pairs, and I took her side as we moved into the new section. This didn't look anything like I had seen in the link with Felix, and when I quested for her … hell, it felt like the right way of describing it … I didn't get a sense of her being any closer. So I doubted we'd find them this easily.

My mother's diary weighed heavy in my pocket, a grim reminder of what we'd most likely find instead.

Our footfalls were muffled on the medical wing's floor, softened purposefully so as not to intrude on the work being carried out. The team came to the first set of laboratories, and shone their torches through the windows to light up what lay inside.

The labs *should* have been empty. Neither DOPA nor OPS were known for leaving expensive equipment lying around when they vacated a premises. Not only to stop such items falling into the hands of enterprising individuals such as our mercenary companions, but also because they like every Government body kept strict lists of all their assets and hated misplacing even a single pencil.

But they weren't.

Instead, the torches lit over two rooms fitted out for full surgical procedures. Large tables with restraining straps and padded belts, chains and pins to lock in even the most powerful of *patients*. Cupboards with glass fronts held glittering instruments … saws, picks, knives and scalpels of every size and shape. Clamps, grips and staplers, needles and surgical spools of thread. Enough equipment to stock a medium sized hospital, in each room.

But what *didn't* belong in any normal hospital room were the full-sized metal frames set against the walls, fitted with more restraints and extendable bars which could be adjusted to fit any body that was strapped into it. These were fitted with drainage tubes and injector ports, to have syringes fixed into them to deliver or take whatever samples were needed. They looked like modern day racks, straight from the torture chambers of the Inquisition, and were fitted with wheels so they could be moved to allow access to the rear area of anything constrained in their deadly embrace.

Faded drawings were tacked to notice boards, detailing inhuman morphology in minute detail. Trix shone her light on the skeletal structure of a goblin's body, beside which was a sketch of a gorgon's head and close-up of one lone eyeball, extracted from its socket. The anatomy of a beast's hand and forearm, showing where the claws could be retracted into the skin, almost but not quite akin to a mortal. The enlarged heart with exposed ribs of an ogre's chest, splayed open and each vein outlined in detail.

"What the fuck is all this?" The half fae swore, playing her light over the lab. The units still bore signs of staining, fluids spilled over them and soaked into leather. Etched into metal. Blood and other humors from the creatures the scientists had worked on.

I felt eyes on me, and in the gloom found Puck staring at me, her expression easy to read. This one was for me to explain.

I reached into my pocket and drew out my mother's journal, flicking it open even as I motioned for someone to shine a light on the page. Then, speaking slowly so my worgen jaws didn't mangle the words into unintelligibleness, I read out what had been written.

September 15th. Dr B brought me into Lab five to help with an experiment in detached stimuli. Specimen HS-313-5E had had its wings removed but evidence persisted it was still connected mentally to them and sensed anything affecting them. And the wings themselves continued to exist without decay. But subject had been unwilling to interact with Dr B and colleagues. He believed, due to my field of expertise, that I would have better luck engaging with and forming a bond with the subject.

Dr B informed me I should attempt to deceive the subject into believing its wings would be surgically reattached once the tests were completed, its freedom granted. However I decided the truth was more likely to elicit a response, and informed Specimen HS-313-5E that its future was one of pain and misery, and that it would never be allowed to leave the facility. All without Dr B's knowledge, of course. None of the facility staff can communicate with the subjects so my deceit will not be known.

Specimen HS-313-5E simply nodded, and told me to tell Dr B it would respond to any test as best it could.

September 16th Dr B called me into his office, to inform me that overnight, Specimen HS-313-5E had terminated its own life. Shed its own blood with a talon newly grown overlong even though they had removed all its nails and broken all its fingers to render it compliant. I suggested the specimen had simply disbelieved the rather implausible lie I had been given to tell it. Dr B seemed unsure how to respond, but I believe he accepted the lie. If he continues to seek my help, I might eventually learn what he and his team are up to in the sub-basement … the life of one fairy is surely worth knowing that.

I closed the journal, looking around the small company. Dix looked sickened, dark eyes wide as he stared through the glass at the instruments that had been used to cause so much pain. Trix eyed me coldly, the set of her jaw in the gloom of the corridor an obvious sign of where her thoughts lay. Mother simply shook her head sadly, ringing her fingers as if she needed to wipe a residue from them.

Janus grunted, nodding to Hunter.

"Same shit, different boss." He voiced his contempt, as the shapechanger nodded. "Seen mortals do worse to each other. Why surprised they would do it to things they don't understand. Is second nature to them."

"It's a breach of the Accords, is what it is." Trix spat back, dark eyes flickering with anger. "That book you read from. It's a diary, someone who worked here. Someone you know? Is *this* why we're here, for this shit? Coz if so I'm rethinking what me or my brother are doing being involved. I … *we* don't any part of anything like this."

I shook my furry head, as I slipped my mother's book away. But it was Greg who replied, patting me on the shoulder to let me know he had this.

"That book is Morgan's mother's diary. She worked here, *as a consultant* but wasn't a part of the work DOPA did here. She was just in the wrong place, and had to make some tough decisions." He spoke quietly, and I bit down on anything I might want to say that would contradict him. "We're not here to answer for, or try to bring back, anything that was done here in the name of science, research or whatever lie they used. Our friends … loved ones, they are who we are after. If I had my way, I'd bury this place with all its secrets, and make sure it never ever sees the light of day again. That's the truth."

"Then why are we standing here, wasting time?" Trix waved a hand down the corridor. To where access to the sub-basement had to be. "Let's go find these lost sheep of yours and get the hell out of this creepy shit hole. Before anything else attacks us, right?"

"Should search …" Janus began, but the half fae cut him off, hands settling on her knives.

"We should search shit, and leave this stuff to be buried like the nice man said." She told him, staring up at him with no concern over the fact he out-muscled her and loomed a good two feet over her. "I signed up for a simple snatch and grab, not this level of stupidity. This stuff stays here, and we leave all together. Or you can try your luck getting out past those spider-goblins and whatever else is living down here without my or my brother's skills."

The half troll stared down at her, then sighed and shrugged.

"Is probably too big for bag anyway." He grunted, earning a wolfish grin from me.

We set off, looking for any sign of stairs leading down. Or possibly the goods lift which I presumed had to exist, to transport the creatures they had worked on up from the transports they were brought in on. No way could they have used the front door.

Trix sidled up to me as we walked, conspicuously keeping her eyes away from the glass windows that showed fresh horrors depicted in graphical detail on the walls, hung on posters and showing in folders left on countertops. DOPA had been unusually careless at leaving traces behind of their Accord breaking activities, which made me wonder just what they were playing at.

Where were the OPS watchdogs, doing their job and cleaning up after their inconsiderate and idiotic colleagues to make sure no-one found out what they'd up to?

"That journal, it was written by your mother?" The half fae asked quietly as we walked. I noticed Dix kept exactly an arm's length from his twin, and never seemed to move further from her. Like they were attached, linked somehow that none of us could see.

I grunted, patting the pocket where the book sat.

"Don't mind me saying, but she sounds … not right." Trix commented dryly, and I let out a growl of a chuckle, shaking my head. "Not the sort of woman I'd like to meet, if you know what I mean."

I shrugged, knowing nothing else needed saying. My mother … Margaret May Black or Black May … was neither a good witch or a bad witch. She was the reason a bunch of DOPA scientists and workers had died, but had saved Herne the Hunter from enslavement by the mortals. She had done things in the Wyld to cause immortal creatures to fear and loathe her, even want her dead … but she had had me.

I still had not made up my mind whether her being back from the dead, even reborn as a Crone of the Wyld, was good or bad. I was still waiting for the shit to hit the fan, to help me decide.

The corridor branched, with more labs on the right and a security station set on the left. The command post, overseeing the laboratories' safety, making sure nothing got in … or out. I motioned to the left, thinking if there was going to be a way down, it would have been guarded as an extra security measure.

Of course, that didn't mean it *still* wasn't guarded.

We moved quickly, none of us wanting to hang around a place where so much pain had been caused, where death had been inflicted clinically and coldly with no care for those who did the dying. I could see enough in the dark to avoid the trolleys that had been left parked alongside the wall, probably used to transport body parts or fluids taken, whilst larger gurneys had been stored in a dead end we passed, stacked and ready for any bodies.

The security station was a nodule sticking out of the wall, with glass windows webbed with wire to make sure they wouldn't fully shatter if struck. Inside, when Trix shone her torch, we saw seats enough for a full half dozen guards with controls for the security door as well as other switches that had to be for the lights, the air conditioning and anything else mechanical down here. Jackets had been left over the back of two of the seats, as if the guards had simply stepped out and would be about their rounds, and a set of walled cabinets at the rear of the room looked the perfect size for rifles and any munitions they might have been armed with to keep the place safe. Several long, white Haz-Mat suits completed the grim spectacle, hanging near to hand in case something hazardous leaked.

Janus looked longingly at the office, but Puck shook her head and motioned for us to keep going. We paced passed it, but I couldn't help but look back, trying to see if there was anything marked as *Lift* or *Stair access to basement* marked handily for us to use.

One of the chairs had moved.

I stopped, looking through the glass, not entirely sure I was remembering things right. The half dozen seats, two with jackets over their backs ... except now there was only one jacket. I saw the second one crumpled on the floor, and one chair now stood at an angle, in exactly the position it would be if someone had gotten up from it to go to the door of the station.

Which was now open.

And then things got *messy*.

Chapter 25

"Morgan!" Greg bellowed. "Chimerian!"

I whirled, even as several torch beams lit over Greg as he struggled, sword drawn but his wrist captured as he in turn tried to force a large, bulky handgun out of his face and up to the ceiling.

The figure he was grappling with was immediately recognisable, clad in weird beetle armour with antenna protruding from the back and helmet. A hump over its shoulders and back was revealed to be some sort of power unit, with a fan whirring near the base, and dials and valves on the thing measuring who the fuck knew. Pipes ran from it into the suit, obviously working like an astronaut's pack and providing oxygen and other necessary vitals to the sod inside.

The bastard had gotten past us, walked probably right by me and I hadn't even twitched, hadn't felt a thing. They must have been hiding in the security module, and heard us as we entered through the gate. Then waited till we passed, probably meaning to either shoot us point blank in the back from behind, or make a break for wherever the rest of the fuckers were to warn them.

Somehow, Greg had not been fooled. Point one for the mortal guardian.

The chimerian's finger clenched on the trigger and a short blaze of bullets hammered out from the gun. Narrowly missing Greg, spewing out in a storm of sparks and fury. Trix and Dix ducked out of the way, whilst Janus gave a bellowing roar, ripping free his hand axe and hewing at the arm bearing the weapon.

But the armour it wore was extraordinarily tough, the axe bouncing off even with all the half troll's strength behind the blow. The chimerian snarled something guttural, wrenching round and kicking out with one thick leg that bent oddly, booting Janus in the abdomen before he had a chance to block. Even as the half troll folded, gasping for a breath, the chimerian wrenched itself free and hurled Greg into Janus.

With its wrist freed from his grip, the handgun rose, pointing point blank at Greg as he staggered, fighting to regain his balance …

But I slammed into the bastard, knocking the arm up and sending the ensuing volley of bullets into the ceiling.

"Not this time, bastard!" I snarled, punching hard into its lower back. Right into the pack, making the whirring fan scream and stutter. Metal bent under my blow, but the chimerian twisted, the body in the armour shifting in ways no ordinary mortal should be able to, and slapped me across my muzzle with the arm bearing the gun. The other arm bent in entirely the wrong way, and folded so that the hand at its end could reach a large dial.

Memory sparked, of the chimerian outside the Tower doing exactly the same thing when Ellie attacked, knocking us all flat. Vulnerable. And me getting a knife in my guts.

"Hell no!" I howled, grabbing at the limb before the chimerian could activate whatever the fuck it was they'd created to mess with their enemies.

It was like wrestling a snake, the arm within the armour folding and moving in ways it shouldn't. Not if it there was a normal skeleton in there. The bastard's fingers managed to shift the dial one click round, and I felt *something* slap at me, sapping my strength and making me want to throw up everything I'd eaten in the past day. But it was faint, far less than what they'd used on me at the ambush, and I bit back a mouthful of bile and yanked at the arm, pulling it away even as it writhed and slithered in my grip.

And then the bloody thing detached. In my hands.

No blood in fact, no gushing wound. I was just left gripping a writhing arm that ended in a solid metal joint that had been ejected from the armour. The chimerian shoved at me with its free limb, smashing

Janus in the face with the pistol as the mercenary finally got past Greg, knocking him back with a grunt of pain. Pushing off the half troll and running back the way we'd come.

Janus and Greg were out of range, Trix and Dix were cowering down at the floor level, and Manisha and Puck had gotten ahead of us all, leaving the way back where we'd come from open.

Except for Hunter and Mother.

That sawn off shotgun of the half gnome's boomed, the chimerian sensing the danger far too late to turn, to avoid the shaft of flame that roared from the barrel. The slug detonated against the beetle armour with a ringing thud, even as fire scorched all over the figure as it staggered and bent over. Mother flicked the breach open with practised skill, popping the spent cartridges out and loading a fresh pair without even looking.

The chimerian was just straightening back up when Hunter fired his own rifle, the weapon almost completely silent compared to the small cannon Mother used. But the bullet hit the chimera with far deadlier force than Janus and his axe, sending shards of the armour flying as it shattered the bulbous headpiece and slammed into the chimerian's skull beneath.

Even as the grey man writhed, handgun flung aside as it spasmed in agony, Mother's second blast hit it, striking it in the ruined helmet. Something made a nasty *cracking* noise, and the chimerian slumped to its knees, bubbling noises coming from inside the wrecked faceplate of its armour.

Silence settled in the corridor, broken as Janus spat out a mouthful of blood from a split lip.

"What the fuck was that thing?" Trix demanded as she pulled herself up from the floor, eyes wide as she looked at the savage holes ripped in the wall beside her. Smoke hissed up from the holes drilled through the metal and stone, and driblets ran from each one to carve fresh tracks in the surface. "And who the fuck shoots *acid* bullets?!"

I tossed the arm, still jerking and twisting though more slowly now, to the floor beside the slumped body even as Greg came up beside me, sword held level and ready in case the bastard moved.

"You saw it. How?" I growled, but he just shrugged.

"Don't know. It's like when we were at the Southbank." He admitted, eyeing the fallen soldier in its weird armour. "When that Twilight fae jumped us. I could see it, could move when all you lot were locked down. Terra still can't explain it, so don't expect me to have the answers."

Greg had come back from the dead, infused with life energies stolen by Robert Knox and blessed by the Goddess of the Mortal Realm. Making him altogether a very different man from the one who had died trying to protect the woman he loved from a monster, my half-brother. I shouldn't be surprised he could do things no mortal could, but one of these days I was going to get an explanation from someone about what had happened … how he'd changed.

Because the only other creature who had undergone something similar was Morgana, and she had ended up sacrificing her reborn life to birth the Harrowed Queen. A hybrid monster not entirely from the same dominion, realm or whatever you wanted to call it as the rest of us, and something that for whatever crazy reason thought of me as its father.

A thing I *still* didn't know what the fuck to do about, given its murderous capacity.

Trix and Mother shone their torches on the slumped soldier, as Greg and I stood over it. Janus glared down at it, rubbing at his swollen jaw from where he'd been hit. Hunter was investigating the bullet holes in the walls, Dix shining his own torch on the damage wrought as the shapechanger poked the indents made with a metal rod he'd pulled from a pocket.

We were two short.

I looked back up the corridor, to see Puck and Manisha standing where they'd stopped, when the chimerian attacked. The Ivory spy had a torch and was shining it back our way, whilst the Knight stood off to one side. In the gloom, her amber eyes glittered as I started walking towards the pair.

"You'd best make sure it's dead. They have a troubling habit of weathering significant damage and coming back for more." Puck told me dryly.

"You know about them too?" I remembered Manisha admitting to knowledge of the wholly fucked up mortal experiment, so it did not surprise me that Oberon's chief spy was aware of the bastards too. As ever, everyone else seemed to know more than I did.

"Anything else you'd like to share?" I growled, but it was Manisha who replied.

"One thing, Errant." She told me, voice calm, level.

Then she spun, her Ivory armour igniting over her body with flickering flames even as her massive sword appeared in her clasped hands. Already swinging downwards.

The edge hammered into nothing … which spat and ran with fire as the figure was revealed. The Knight had struck at an angle, the scalpel-sharp edge overcoming the strength of the armour and carving deep into the body within, bisecting it from right shoulder down through its ribcage and out in one massive cut.

The chimerian's arm, holding another handgun of similar size and pointed at me, juddered and dropped, its round expended as the finger convulsed on the trigger and blasted a hole in the floor a foot from me as blood gushed from the mortal wound. The figure folded, its hip shattered from the sword exiting its body, and collapsed face first to the floor in a widening pool of gore.

"They always travel in pairs." Manisha finished, as she played fire along the length of the weapon and burned off the fluids staining it. "And the trick is not to look for them, but for the things around them that betray their presence. Disturbed dust, footfalls, displaced air or even the sound of a mortal weapon about to be fired. Things they cannot hide."

"Uh, ok. Thanks." I growled, knowing she had just saved me from serious harm. I wasn't sure how badly bullets made of acid would fuck with me, or how long I'd take to heal any damage done but I was comfortably glad not to be finding out.

"You are very welcome, Errant. Now, shall we take a look at these two?" She reached down and grabbed the dead chimerian by its armour, easily picking it up off the floor as blood drained from it. "Mayhap to see what we can learn of them?"

With the Ivory fae dragging the very dead chimerian behind her, we rejoined the others even as Greg was leaning over the one who had attacked us. He was checking around the armour's neckline, as Trix shone a torch on the body.

"Thought I saw … ah, yep." He carefully unclipped several catches, the suit making a faint clunking sound as locks disengaged. Carefully, sword set to one side but close enough to reach, the ex-detective lifted the shattered helmet clear.

Revealed, the chimerian's face was a mess of burned skin and blackened blood, the hole made by Hunter's shot perfectly centred in its forehead. Mother's second blast had sloughed away flesh, revealing grey bone underneath made brittle by the extreme heat of her dragonbreath ammo.

But there was more than enough still visible, illuminated under the brilliance of the torchlight, to show this was no mere mortal, no simple man hidden away in armour. This was a monster, no doubt about it.

The grey man's mouth had hinged open, revealing a narrowed and protruding jaw fitted with crooked teeth more suited to some crocodilian species than a man. And the skin not burned by Mother's blast was scaled, grey in shade like those of a python. One lone eye had survived, bloodshot now but still unnatural in that the pupil was much larger than any normal man's and a vivid scarlet. Akin to the vicious eyes of goblins, I recalled.

Puck leaned to inspect the dead man's face, prodding at it with one finger.

"Originally taken from a naga, I would say. With goblin orbitals implanted for vision in the dark." She picked up the detached arm and carefully bent it in ways that would have meant breaking bone normally. But the arm simply flopped in her hands, pliable until rigor mortis set in. "They must have refitted this creature's entire skeleton with that taken from one of the naga, to allow such motion. Handy to allow it to move unexpectedly, and lose limbs without catastrophic injury. Like a lizard, detaching its own tail. Extraordinary work, really."

"And the other?" I growled, eyeing the dead chimerian warily. It … he had to be dead, given his injuries. But I wasn't about to trust these fuckers to start acting sensibly.

Manisha deftly flipped the catches on the second soldier's helmet, tossing it aside casually. Revealed this chimerian was a woman, the body shape hidden before now under the weird armour. She looked relatively normal, especially compared to the other grey man, with mortal skin and a normal looking face. But when Manisha thumbed back her eyelids, she too had goblin eyes, and the Ivory fae pushed the collar of her under-armour down to show two engorged muscles or something set below her jawline.

"Probably the vocal chords and mouthparts taken from a siren," The Knight surmised, flicking up the dead woman's lips to show teeth sprouting from gums like some creature from the sea. Definitely aquatic. "If she had had a chance, I believe she would have been able to cause significant harm to use with her voice alone."

"Good thing you made sushi of her then." I couldn't resist, earning a hard smile from Manisha and a chuckle from Puck.

"Indeed. These grey men are an abomination, but one has to admire the skill used to create them." The spy commented, shaking her head as she pushed herself up from where she had crouched. "I can only presume they did not attack together and so cause us much greater inconvenience due to orders. One to engage any intruder, the other to hold back and alert their comrades if the need arises."

"Look, you can even see differences in their armour." She pointed to the first corpse. "His pack appears fitted with some sort of amplification device. Possibly the sort that was used to render you and your Alpha and friends helpless before. Whereas the second one is more compact, modelled I would suggest for stealth and speed of movement. Without the same sort of heavy equipment. A scout, whereas the first is the tank …"

"Oh dear."

I looked up from the dead woman to see what had caught Puck's attention.

Trix was standing a few steps back from us, expression furious as she held the handgun dropped by the chimerian. The one fitted with acid bullets.

Pointed directly at us.

Chapter 26

"You *lied* to us."

The half fae accused, dark eyes shining in the reflected light of the torches.

"This was meant to be a simple rescue mission. Find your friends, who had got lost in an *abandoned* mortal facility." She parroted, almost spitting the words. "With the chance to raid anything left behind. Simple, easy."

She pointed the gun at the dead bodies.

"Instead, we've been attacked by fucked up goblins that look like spiders, found ourselves arse-deep in Accord-breaches and then these fuckers tried to kill us!" She spat, looking from Puck to me. "You recognised them. You know them. You were *expecting* them. You lied."

I checked out the rest of the team, just to see how they were taking the revelation. Dix was staying close to his sister, hands on his knives. Janus was still rubbing his jaw, but he smelt of slow burning anger too, the sort that normally blows up spectacularly and leaves a body count in its wake. Hunter was a closed book, the shapechanger giving nothing away, whilst Mother just smiled as she stowed her handcannon away and hummed quietly but discordantly to herself.

Puck raised her hands slowly, in a *let's be calm here and not do anything rash* gesture.

Unfortunately, Trix was a little too wound up for that sort of thing, and her finger on the trigger tensed, almost firing. But for Dix laying a hand on her shoulder, stopping her from doing something we'd all most likely regret.

Puck blatantly ignored the fact the half fae had almost shot her, instead smiling with that sickle smile of hers.

"Trixina Del Elouqin, I lie to *everybody*." She admitted with absolutely no guilt. "It's part of who I am, what I do. The trick is knowing if the lie is meant to help you, or maybe not so much."

She gestured at the gathered group, amber eyes bright in the corridor's shade.

"You all were brought here to perform tasks well within your breadth of experience, with the promise of lucrative remuneration for a few days' work." She instructed quietly, as I kept my eyes on the mercenaries, watching for any sign of dissent, of trouble. The last thing I wanted was a falling out just after we'd tangled with some chimerians. Who knew if the fuckers had raised an alarm, or if more of them were on their way?

"The level of risk, I admit, I *fudged* slightly." Puck shrugged again, reaching over and placing one finger on the muzzle of the handgun Trix still aimed at her. "But according to your resumes, you've all been in what I believe were high-risk situations, and walked free to find further employment with all your limbs attached."

"And," she continued, "It's not like any one of you were in a position to turn down the opportunity I offered. Given your ... ah predicaments?"

Puck looked over at Janus, eyes glittering.

"Janus Kováčik. Wanted in several countries for crimes ranging from property damage, grievous bodily harm and distribution of stolen property to manslaughter." She recited as if from a list. Which I had no doubt she had somewhere safe. "Of three very disreputable individuals who you thought were simple ruffians and traffickers, but one who turned out to be an agent for the mortal authorities under cover. I believe you were awaiting extradition when I facilitated your accidental release."

"Hunter. Real name ... well, you know I know it." She moved on, eyeing the shapechanger who simply nodded, yellow eyes glittering. "Wanted in connection with several disappearances of prominent members of the illegal wildlife trade. I believe there is a bounty out on you dead or alive, for not an inconsiderable sum. For your head. Not the rest of you."

She then looked across at Mother, who smiled back at her.

"Mother Meredith Kamiński. Wanted for the unlawful destruction of several financial institutions, including the *Bank of Moscow, Bank Otkritie Financial Corporation, Gazprombank* and *SberBank* sites which were found to be holding undisclosed volumes of gold belonging to individuals not easily identifiable. Gold which was destroyed in each case due to the ... ah *excessive* heat applied by the explosives used." Puck commented dryly. "I believe there is also a bounty set for your capture by the Russian police services."

Mother gave a curtsey, patting her bandolier happily.

Puck then looked back at Trix.

"And lastly, the twins. Trixina and Dixiam Del Elouqin." She nodded to them both, still blithely ignoring the gun pointed at her. "Wanted for multiple heists and raids on seemingly impregnable vaults across the Mortal Realm. Contracting only when the site to be broken into is suitably challenging, like ... oh, a DOPA facility with *eyes only* security rating maybe. Both of you were hiding out in Florence when I found you. Your assets seized, and the authorities only a step behind me with warrants for your immediate arrest and internment. In silver and cold iron lined cells."

"The fact is, you all need this job to pay for your continued existence outside of confinement, or to elude those who hunt you. Wishing you dead." She finished up, gently pressing the gun barrel down with her finger. Trix resisted, but Dix leant his head against her own, and after a moment she sighed and relented. "Yes, there is risk. I would not have brought the Knight Captain of the Ivory Court, nor a renowned

Redcloak and a guardian of the Mortal Goddess herself along if this was going to be a picnic."

"But we are in this to the end. Together. That is no lie." She eyed everyone coldly, all humour gone from her gaze. "We seek lost companions, as I said. But there is something going on in this facility, something abominations such as these two are guarding, which affects this Realm. All the Realms. And we need to understand it, and stop it. If you try to run now, the things lurking below, who must know of our presence by now, will hunt you down and kill you slowly. Painfully. In ways you have not even dreamed of."

Then she smiled wickedly.

"And that is if I don't find you first. Which I have done once already." She clapped her hands together, turning her back and presenting it to Trix. "So, if you wish. Go ahead, shoot me but make sure you don't miss. Try to run. See where that gets you. Or hand that gun over to Morgan, and let's get moving before more of these sick creations of mad mortals come hunting us."

Trix grimaced, her grip on the gun tightening and its barrel lifting fractionally … before Dix shook his head, placing his own hand on the weapon.

"Oh fuck it. I wasn't *going* to shoot her." Trix growled, shaking her head and jerking the gun from her brother's reach before offering it to me by the grip. "Well, not to *kill*. Fine. Have it."

I checked the safety was on the thing, before sliding it into a spare pocket so that only the butt end stuck out. I don't particularly like guns, given how they can make even the most idiotic mortal a killer with little or no thought required. But against the chimerians, I'd be happy to make an exception.

Plus I really wanted to find out what the fuck these things were firing. Acid bullets, what was that all about?

"Uh, Morgan. You might want to see this." Greg motioned me back to the dead bodies. Oh goody.

"What's up? They not dead enough yet?" I hazarded, knowing just how things tended to happen around me. It would just be my luck to find out there was such as a thing as *zombie* chimerians.

He pointed down, and I looked at the grey man Hunter and Mother had dispatched. Someone shone a torch helpfully, illuminating the corpse.

Nope, still dead. In fact …

As I watched, the scaled skin began to flake away, the burned bits turning to black ash. Flesh withered away and the bones underneath began to crack, then crumble. Within moments, any trace of the chimerian was gone, even the blood spilled disintegrating into nothing. Leaving only the shell, the armour, to show he had existed at all.

"Oh, that is another thing we learned of these grey men." Manisha commented, as she gazed at where it … he had lain moments ago. "If you should breach their armour, they wither and fade. As if the very air is poison to them."

"Huh. So all need do is get them to take kit off, and they go kaput?" Janus grinned, looking around the group. "Ladies, any volunteers to take one for team? Get funky with the freaks?"

Mother rolled her eyes and shook her head, whilst Manisha eyed the half troll coolly, cradling her gleaming sword. Puck laughed sharply, but it was Trix who replied.

"I'm pretty sure these freaks would prefer to get *funky* with someone a little closer to home. Another freak." She smiled sweetly at him. "So why don't you give it a try? Show them those big muscles of yours. Worth a shot … for the team."

Janus scowled, not finding as much humour in the half fae's retort as she did, and not helped by Dix miming him mincing around, flexing his arms.

Before this broke out into anything physical, I coughed hard, jerking their attention to me. Reaching down to the second corpse, I freed her pistol and handed it over to Janus.

"If there are more of these bastards hanging around here, you'll need something more than that axe or knife." I instructed him, wolf jaws making the words sound like a snarl. "Try not to shoot yourself in the foot."

He expertly checked the gun over, sliding out the cartridge of weird-arse ammo before clicking it back in place and chambering one bullet. Then he stuffed it into his belt, something no sane person would do with anything loaded.

Sanity, however, was something I was thinking Puck had forgotten to include on our checklist when hiring the team.

"If we are done, we had best proceed with haste." Puck spoke up, eyes glowing in the gloom. "Or if you prefer, we can sit around and await more of these charming individuals to play with?"

"We're going." I growled, and Greg nodded in agreement.

People to save, bad guys to kill.

This time, Puck had Greg lead with me keeping him company. If the mortal guardian of a goddess could shrug off the chimerian's camouflage, then I was happy to make him our mine canary. Ready to sing at any hint of trouble.

The corridor led straight on, past more laboratories, more facilities used to commit all manner of horrors on those creatures captured and contained here. But then we spotted signs hanging from their chains, attached to the ceiling.

Stairs to sub-basement.

Sub-basement Lift.

Bingo!

The stairs and lifts were guarded by a second security station, glass windows embedded with wire and with enough seating for another half dozen guards to keep the way down safe.

Given what happened last time, we made sure Greg looked over the room whilst we hung back, ready to unleash hell on anything lurking there. But he eventually shook his head, giving me a thumbs up instead. All clear of lurking invisible bastards.

The lifts were fronted by heavy duty folding doors, and were of a size that could accommodate a small truck if needs be. Plenty of space to transport all manner of creatures of the Real, from ogres all the way down to gremlins. With space for guards, cages and whatever else they had used to move the captives to their short-lived futures as test subjects for the fucked up and morally corrupt.

Puck had told us there were odd power spikes at the facility that had been recorded, so I figured there might be enough juice for these things to still be working. However, I had no desire to be trapped in a box with no idea what waited for us below, and with the chance the chimerians or whoever else was lurking here had rigged the lifts with something especially deadly for intruders.

Plus, they'd most likely make one helluva racket, even more than our little run in with the spider goblins and then the chimerian guards. And we *were* supposed to be sneaking around, not drawing attention to ourselves.

So, we took the stairs.

With torches lighting our way down, we kept our footfalls as quiet as possible as we descended. This stairway wound down and around, going back on itself several times meaning I could tell we were headed deeper than one simple level. The air grew noticeably colder, and that sense of wrongness also increased, like spoiled meat. Not quite something rotting but still not right in some fundamental way.

It made my head ache, that was for sure.

We finally hit the sub-level, the stairs finishing in a large cavern that had been dug out of the bedrock. Steel girders and pillars braced the ceiling high overhead, with electrical droplights running in banks from one side to the other. These were caked in cobwebs, thick strands disappearing into the darkness. All too reminiscent of the crap the spider-goblins had strung around their hunting ground.

The floor was bare concrete, scarred and marked but free of grime and dust. Electrical cables ran in thick bundles down the walls, and pipes led from the ceiling to wherever the generators, boilers and machinery lurked to keep the facility running. A few massive crates, marked with black letters and numbers, sat off to one side, but otherwise the space was empty.

We spread out from the foot of the stairs, Janus with the chimerian's handgun out and eyeing the gloom on all sides. Hunter kept his rifle cocked against his shoulder whilst walking, a move practised well enough to mean he didn't trip over his own feet. Trix and Dix had throwing knives ready in their hands, and Mother had her shotgun primed, a mad grin on her wrinkled features. Enough firepower to ruin anyone's day.

More ceiling signs helpfully indicated the way to the *Black Lake*, *Storage*, *Garage* and *Transport Access*. Less helpfully, nothing pointed to "*secret hideaway*" or anything so useful in telling me where the bad guys were lurking, but then I never expected things to be that easy. Nothing so far had been on this hunt.

However, my mother *had* mentioned the Black Lake in her journal, and I got the impression there was something significant about it. Apart from the ominous name, that is. So when the answer doesn't present itself in shining lights and fireworks, pick the creepiest, weirdest sounding location to try first, when hunting psychotic Frankenstein monsters.

There was no talk now, all of us feeling like there were eyes on us. The sense of being watched, of danger lurking close by. Instead, I simply pointed to the *Black Lake* sign, and motioned for the group to head that way. No way was I going to make the rookie mistake of splitting us up.

We took the lake's exit from the large storage room, following a twisting corkscrew tunnel that we immediately noticed had railings fitted to the floor. Probably for some sort of transport system, though there had been no engines or wheeled machinery of that sort to be seen where we'd come down. But the tracks were there, rusted and filthy with old grease.

The tunnel continued for maybe ten, fifteen minutes then opened out in front of us. By then, I'd caught the tang of water in the air coming from ahead of us, and guessed we were about to find out where all the black water up top fed down to.

Casually, we poked our heads out of the tunnel, expecting cries of alarm, gunfire … hell, anything really.

Nothing happened, so after nods between the group, we stepped out … and stopped, silenced by the view that opened out before us.

Chapter 27

The Black Lake was well named … a vast underground pool of ink black water, utterly still yet without the taint or stink of stagnancy. The tunnel opened out onto a concrete landing that had been built on top of the shoreline, creating a platform fitted with railings and even a squat pier leading out into the dark water.

Lights, their filaments unlit, were fitted along the landing's railing since there was no way anyone could have hung them from the ceiling as this was lost from sight far overhead. Instead, I figured they were meant to simply light the way for whatever was being transported from … or possibly to the lake, not anything else lurking out of sight.

The rails ran onward from the tunnel, crossing a junction that ended at the far end of the platform with several large, wheeled trailers parked there. These were heavy duty vehicles, with what looked like vintage engines fitted to them like the sort seen on old trucks that belched out lots of black fumes. The sort that might work no matter what sort of magic was tried, given the low level of technology involved in their mechanics.

The second set of tracks continued on from the junction and led out onto the pier, all the way to the end. Several intersections allowed for carts on the rails to brought right to the edge of the concrete jetty along its length. The reason for this was immediately obvious, given the large flat-bed boats lined up and bound to the pier with thick ropes, stationed at these intersections to allow carts to be bought onboard or their cargo offloaded.

And, ignoring the spider-goblins and the two chimerians we'd encountered, there was the first indication that the facility was not as deserted as it was meant to be. In the thick grime on the floor, distinct bootprints and markings, showing where someone or someones' had passed, with smaller sized prints indicating they had not done so alone.

I knelt down by one of the small prints, pressing my worgen snout near and inhaled carefully so as not to get lungful of dust and crap. Yep, as expected, I immediately got the scent of Felix, carried from her small boots. Along with her, I found Elspeth, both bound to the non military bootprints that escorted them.

They'd come this way. They were definitely here.

I bit back the urge to howl, both from joy at finding them but at the same time rage at their being taken. Given how large the cave was, I hated to think the sort of echo I'd make, and that would wake up anything that might be hiding in the shadows.

Puck and Manisha walked out onto the pier, and I followed them with Greg a step behind. The rest of the team remained on the platform, the twins moving to check the wagons whilst Hunter and Janus kept an eye on our surroundings, expecting trouble.

Stopping with the other three near the edge of the pier, looking over at one of the boats, I told them in a quiet whisper what I'd found.

Puck nodded, motioning to the still, black water.

"It makes sense. If these grey men are using stolen portal keys to move about undetected, using such a body of water will only aid their endeavours." She sighed as I cocked my head, confused. "Still water is a medium through which one can travel, if one has the knowledge or the power of a key, where one wishes to go. It … *assists* with any such crafting. Hence how the Lady of the Lake was so powerful in this Realm, and could move where she wished."

"But running water negates magic, and really fucks up anything that uses it if they are dunked in it." Greg countered, equally at odds with this tid-bit of information. "Hence the reason witch-finders used to dunk witches in ponds to prove them guilty, or remove all their magical powers."

The Ivory fae chuckled quietly, shaking her head.

"Typical mortals, getting things so wrong." She admonished with a sickle smile. "Had those witchfinders of old happened across a real witch, a crone or the like, then they would have learned to rue their error … for the brief moments they yet remained alive. They only tormented and murdered innocent mortal women, without skill or talent. Still water, pools and ponds, these are places where magic may flow and be used. Running water, that is what disrupts and destroys."

"No, this is how they have moved about unseen." She continued, waving at the boats. "I presume they retain powerful enough portal keys to open ways anywhere within this Realm, to any body of water near to where they need to be. The Thames, for example, in your most recent interaction with them. Then they simply opened another way, linking their escape route to the site of their ambush. Fooling anyone attempting to track them, since the running water of the London river would have wiped all traces clean once they left."

"Also a handy place to dump anything they were finished with." I growled, seeing the pier's edge stained with old ichor and blood. The far end of the jetty had no mooring for a ship, instead it ended abruptly, with railings on either side but nothing barring the end. Perfect to slide corpses, body parts or whatever into the black water from a cart. "How much you want to bet there's a load of skeletons down there?"

"No bet. I can see them." Manisha told me, her amber eyes glowing in the gloom as she gazed down into the lake. "The restless dead, I see their shades eternally bound to their broken bodies. Lying deep within the darkness, forever hidden. Their screams silent but neverending. This is a place of death and despair."

Not creepy *at all*, thanks.

I motioned to the tracks, grinning a wolf's snarl.

"I can track them now. Their scent. We need to head back." I rolled my shoulders, feeling the burning urge to be gone from here, finding our friends filling me. This was the best chance we'd had so far and I didn't want to …

Darkness engulfed me.

"*Morgan! Are you there?*" Felix's voice erupted in my head as I felt everything blur around me.

"Felix. We're close. I've got your scent." I told her, thinking the words and shoving them through the link between us.

"*I was getting worried! It's been like a day since I got through to you!*" She shot back at me, and I felt my confusion bleed into the link. A day? I knew I was bad at time keeping but there was no way it had been *that* long since we spoke.

"*Something's got them all upset. I think they know you are here.*" She sent through the link, as well as a blurry image of beetle-clad soldiers moving past the cell she was in. Guns held in hands, a sense of urgency about their quick, hurried movements. "*I don't know how long until they take us to see this doctor. I'm scared, Morgan!*"

"Just hold on. We're coming …" I tried to reassure her, but something intruded suddenly. A presence, a weight that crushed down on the link and severed it before enveloping me. And a very different voice rang in my head.

"Ah, so that is what has been bothering me." The voice drawled, Germanic accents thick in its tones. But there was something else, a jagged edge that spoke to me, reminding me a little of when I'd spoken to Robert Knox. The sharpness of madness. "I'm not sure who you are, or how you are talking to the little witch, but we won't be having any more of that behaviour. No, I will deal with you momentarily, so feel free to remain where you are. I won't make you wait long."

The darkness crushed down on me, and I snarled as it felt like I was shoved back and away. Back into my body, finding myself kneeling on the grimy pier, with my three companions looking at me expectantly. And more than a little concerned, from what I could pick up from them.

"Felix?" Greg asked, and I nodded, taking a gulp of breath and rubbing my furry skull to shake the ache.

"Yeah. And … no." I snarled, before explaining what had happened. What Felix had said, then my brush with that other person.

The two Ivory fae eyed each other, then Manisha shrugged.

"It was too much to hope that we would avoid drawing attention, given our recent encounters." The knight shrugged, pointing to the tracks. "If you have your friend's scent, then we had best try to get to them as quickly as possible. But be wary of whatever trap this *other* may have laid for us. I like not its invitation."

The mercenaries accepted my quiet and quick explanation of why we were heading back, none of them commenting on the source of my knowledge that a trap possibly lay ahead of us. They trusted a Redcloak's nose, and his instincts, since we were known to be familiar with fucked up situations and having a long list of people, mortal or otherwise, wanting us dead.

I had to figure I'd only picked up on Felix's scent, and that of Elspeth because of the connection between the young witch and me. It had somehow cut through the interference, allowing me to lock on to her, when before whatever the chimerians or whomever I'd spoken to were using had masked them completely. Which is why the fucker had cut me off, thinking that would work.

But I had them now, and no one was going to stop me finding them.

We went back through the tunnel at pace, me leading as the scent blazed in front of me like landing lights, leading me to them. The group followed closely behind, keeping a watch for any sign of ambush.

Back to the stairway, still empty of threat. I took a moment to orientate myself, and found the trail leading me to where the sign indicated *Storage*. I now remembered my mother had said something about Dr Bremmer and the team being up to something in the storage area, so guessed the scent was leading me true.

The new tunnel was wider than the one leading to the Black Lake, probably to allow vehicles like forklifts to deliver equipment of a size and volume that the facility had needed to function back when it was officially active. Lights hung from the ceiling, unlit and grimy, and there were more tracks in the floor, meaning equipment … or captives had been taken this way as well. More likely equipment that had been brought by some access through a waterway, before the chimerians started messing around with portal keys.

We moved quickly, and entered a large storage room moments later. Massive shelves of metal reached up on every side, with crates stacked tightly against one another. Most were almost buried in cobwebs and dust, the writing on them illegible.

I caught Janus glancing at them with a hungry expression, obviously interested in finding out what DOPA had left behind. But the scent took me past them, so I caught his attention and motioned him to keep moving.

The half troll snorted, shaking his head in frustration but he kept pace as we moved deeper into the warren of shelving units. The footprints and tracks clearly marked passage through the storage centre, meaning whomever had passed this way had not been too careful about concealing themselves. Sure of their own secrecy, all too cocky … just the sort of thing psychopathic and mentally unstable failed experimental super soldiers might do, given their indoctrination and belief in their own supremacy.

The sense of *wrongness* was palpable in the air now, enough so that I could see it affecting everyone in the company. Dix and Trix kept shaking their heads as if to clear them from a headache or hangover, whilst Janus was chewing his jaw like he was trying to break rocks. Hunter darted glances all around, his seemingly calm persona definitely showing cracks, whilst Mother wore a grimace of mild pain, and no longer danced or hummed as she walked.

For our part, Puck and Manisha wore the serene countenance of the full blooded fae, but I could tell they sensed the strangeness in the way the spy was unusually quiet and refraining from making sarcastic comments for the sake of it, whilst the knight had her sword unsheathed and wore her armour. Ready for battle.

Greg's tattoos were glowing in the darkness, illuminating his features in stark detail. I could sense his worry over Elspeth from his scent, his need to see her safe. Tangled up with a growing rage towards those who were keeping her, who were putting her life at risk. Far from the calm, unflappable detective I remember winding up on numerous occasions.

The trail led me through the maze of empty shelves, the few crates left by DOPA now far behind us. The tracks continued to be easy to follow … until they weren't.

I looked at the blank wall in front of me, having almost walked into the bloody thing, I was concentrating on the scent trail so much. Shelves just like the ones we'd passed rose up to over double my own height, empty and clad in dust. The tracks simply vanished a few steps before the edge of the lowest metal spar, but led nowhere else when I looked around. The passage formed by the shelves ran off to both my left and right, but there the dust was undisturbed, untrod. And there was no scent of my friends coming from either direction.

They just … stopped.

I looked at the shelves, at the wall behind in case I was missing something obvious. A door handle, a sign saying *secret lair*. Hell, even an enchanted imp head telling me to fuck off and go bother someone else. All the normal stuff people decorate their lair door with. But I could sense nothing.

"This it?" Puck walked up to the shelves, knocking her knuckles against the nearest one and making a dull ringing tone. "You sure that nose of yours led us here?"

I growled, even as I questioned the fact myself in my head. Could I have been misled? Tricked? Had I just walked us into some sort of trap, like the cartoon lambs prancing into the wolf's lair?

Was I calling myself a *lamb*?

"Ok, Trix. You're up." Puck called the half fae over, indicating the wall. "Wolfie here thinks this is the way in. A door, something hidden. Which I believe you have proven is your speciality once already. Care to earn a two-for-one bonus?"

I stepped back to give her some room, as she began examining the shelving carefully, with the beam of her torch illuminating the dusty and grimy metal. The half fae poked around, peering under the units and then checking the rock wall beyond, making clicking noises with her tongue as she tapped at one section, then another.

Then Trix reached into another of her belt pouches, pulling out more sparkling dust. She puffed this out in one breath, watching as it shimmered up like a curtain, illuminating the entire unit in front of us. She cocked her head, as if hearing something, nodding to herself.

"Well, there's good news and there's bad news." She drawled as she turned back to us, scrubbing her fingers clean on her leggings. "It's a door, definitely. The whole thing you're looking at? It's fake. A complete fabrication, built to mimic its surroundings perfectly. Us looking at it only strengthens the deception, as we're *expecting* to see shelves and the like. All the way here, we've been subtly guided to only see what the clever fucker who made this wants us to see. *Not* a door."

"So how do we get it to open?" Greg asked, tapping the metal shelf. It still made a solid sound, a perfect copy even though he in theory wasn't touching it but whatever lay underneath. If Trix was right.

"It's bound to a phrase. A prescribed set of words, something personal to whomever put this together." She sighed, shaking her head. "Could be their birthday. Their favourite song lyrics. Hell, it could be utter nonsense they made up just for this very purpose. Pretty much impossible to guess."

Fuck.

"I'll try some of the more obvious pass-phrases, since I'm assuming a mortal is behind this?" Trix offered, and I nodded, trying not to let my frustration get the best of me. "Otherwise, well, there's always Mother …"

I looked over at the half gnome, thinking of the amount of munitions she carried, the way she had dealt with the first door to the facility. There was little doubt she knew her business, but the first obstacle had been simple … a matter of cutting through rock. Here … a magical door that was clever enough to camouflage itself with its natural surroundings, and influence us to believe the lie? I reckoned it would take more than her gunpowder soup to get through, and whatever that took might not only alert our enemies that we'd blown open their front door but *also* bring the whole facility down on our heads.

Not the outcome I really wanted, even as a last resort.

Leaving Trix as she started throwing out phrases like "*Open Sesame!*", "*123456*" and "*Abracadabra!*" I slouched off to go lean against one of the other shelves … this one *probably* real, enough to support my weight.

The rest of the mercenaries settled in to watch every possible way an enemy might come from, though they knew only Greg and possibly Manisha would spot any more chimerians creeping up on us. Anything else, like the spider-goblins, they'd deal with happily.

I couldn't believe we were stuck on the front door step, with the bastards now knowing we were somewhere close and every moment we wasted, they were able to ready themselves to greet us appropriately. We'd lost the element of surprise, and it wasn't like the things we faced were simple pushovers. The chimerians were psychopathic killers, trained to tackle Real monsters and walk away, but they paled to whatever the hell had cut my contact with Felix short … that voice in my head. In the brief moments I'd had when it spoke to me, I'd felt the wrongness of it. It stank of power, and more than a little insanity.

Never a good mix.

Just get me inside! I snarled in my head, wanting nothing more than to hurl myself at the door and smash it down, break my way through. Old school, sometimes it is the only way.

And that's when I found out I wasn't as alone as I'd thought I was.

Open the journal.

The voice whispered in my head. Not Felix, nor some crazed thing. Familiar, but still unexpected.

"Mum?" I queried, having heard her voice not so long ago. Having met her in the crafted space Herne had taught her to build, a place they could meet without harm inflicted or any fear of their connection being discovered.

Open the journal. I shall aid you however I may.

Black May's voice echoed in my head, a sharp bite to the words that I figured were part her own, part the newness of her becoming a Crone of the Wyld. Taking the place of the rotling who had killed her the first time.

Never one to look a gift horse in the mouth, or any other body part to be honest, I pulled out the battered journal and flicked it open. The pages riffled by themselves, pushed by an unseen hand, until they stopped at a section marked with several photos.

The last one.

She directed me, as I spread the black and white images out. Greg stepped to my side, helpfully shining a torch down on the photos since we were still in almost all-encompassing gloom apart from the illumination we'd brought along ourselves.

The photos were of various individuals, ones I recognised as people from the main photograph my mother had shown me. To first prove the identify of the mysterious beetle-clad kidnappers. Standing in various poses ... working, talking over a water fountain, smiling foolishly. Typical mortals, just going about their daily lives.

The last one showed a man sat straightbacked at his desk, wearing a stark labcoat, thick spectacles and a very serious expression. Everything about him shouted *official*, even to the way the desk was neatly laid out and everything in its exact place.

The picture, behind him.

I focused on the background, seeing the wall of the office where he sat covered with framed certificates of one form or another, all set below another photograph of a man standing by a blackboard covered in chalk-written equations. With the words highlighted below ...

"Now I am become Death, the destroyer of worlds."

"Oppenheimer." Greg identified the man shown, and I recalled this was the mortal scientist's famous quote taken from I believe Hindu scripture, when he saw the first ever detonation of an atom bomb ... which he had masterminded.

Dr Bremmer's favourite saying, whenever he gave a speech or address

My mother's voice whispered in my head, and I grimaced at the realisation of the sort of man she had worked alongside, if this had been something he had said a lot. Something he had built his perverse experiments upon. The man had been fucked in the head, to say the least.

With no better option springing to mind, I tapped the words and nodded to Greg. I still was in my worgen suit, and there was every chance I'd mangle the saying enough for it not to be recognised. This task was far better suited to someone else.

Greg walked over to Trix and spoke to her softly, earning me a look back over her shoulder with one eyebrow cocked and a definite *you think you know better?* look illuminated by her torch. I just shrugged and nodded.

"Whatever." She mouthed, and waved the guardian forward.

Greg stood in front of the shelves, as the rest of the company gathered in case … well, in case anything happened. Once everyone was in position, he squared his shoulders and spoke the phrase out loudly.

For a moment, nothing happened.

Then, the gloom around us thickened suddenly, gaining depth and weight as it pressed in all around. The shelves, the rock, everything in front of us shimmered and melted away as if sucked down a long funnel. We only had a moment to swear, gasp and generally wonder what the fuck we'd done, before we were pulled into the swirling maelstrom …

And found ourselves suddenly elsewhere.

Chapter 28

We *definitely* were no longer in the DOPA facility.

Either that, or whoever had created the portal or door we'd just passed through had also decided on a complete makeover for this section. Based on *Dante's Inferno*, perhaps.

We found ourselves in a large room, carved out of the bare rock. On second thoughts, carved wasn't really the right word, since when I focused on the walls, they looked more ... *melted*. Fused even. Dribbles of molten stone running down from floor to ceiling, looking almost more like veins than anything else. It was disconcerting, to say the least.

The first sign of power still being utilised were the functioning strip-lights attached to the ceiling, but these were of some strange substance as they bathed the area in an almost bloody hue, and they pulsed as if the power-source was not constant. Almost like a pulse, instead.

In fact, the odd lighting wasn't the only thing messing with my senses as I took a moment to settle myself after our displacement or transportation. Whatever had happened when Greg opened the door. Things felt ... *off*, nothing immediately definable but there was a strangeness to our surroundings that had my skin prickling and every warning in my lycan bones triggered.

All telling me one simple thing.

This was *not* a good place to be.

"You sense it too, wolf." Puck told me, her features painted in bloody tones by the lights. I was really struggling to tally the Shakespearian trickster with the reality of this fae, in any way. "Something at odds with your sense of rightness. Yet a question you cannot immediately answer, beyond your understanding."

"But not yours." I growled, seeing her smile sharply and nod. "What's wrong with this place?"

"Think back, instead. Recall where once you might have felt such … *oddness*." She instructed mercilessly. "Mayhap a time of struggle and strife, when your now companion was instead your enemy. Your hunter."

Gregory Allen had only ever been my enemy once. More than that, a pain in my furry butt, but only once would I have thought he sought harm against me. And that was as we sojourned through Twilight. But when had I felt this …

And then the memory sparked.

… the newly born Queen struck at the empty air ahead of her. A rip appeared, widening into a massive tear into which she hurled herself. Darkness shone from within for a moment, a bottomless depth in which things stirred, vast beyond imagining and wholly alien to anything of these Realms …

I'd felt the same weird wrongness when I'd looked on the Way the newly-born Harrowed Queen had ripped in the fabric of the Real. When she had escaped beyond all our reaches, beyond the very dominion of the Realms. Back to where she came from, at least that part of her that was the death of immortals.

The Beyond.

"Yes, you now understand." Puck nodded, gesturing around her. "This is the truth of this place, and it is both simple and complex. Someone or something has crafted a pocket dimension at the bottom of a mortal facility, warded by a portal of magic."

"Yet the very nature of our reality has been bent, twisted and altered by something more … there is a weak point, a tear. Some point within this place where the Beyond and our Dominion have been connected. A breach between realities. A wrongness that mimics the nature of this Harrowed Queen, but on a much greater and dangerous scale."

Things had just gotten a *whole* lot worse.

Pocket dimensions, I was familiar with. Troll-holes, like the one Terrigylle Munstrum had lived in and used as a place of business and storage, were commonplace where Real creatures lived and refused to obey the simple rules of the Mortal Realm ... like paying taxes or rent for the square footage of space they needed to live in. Instead, they crafted entire palaces out of cupboards, quaint family homes inside a single all-be-it size ten shoe, or cozy hideaways to stash their golden hoards from treasure-seekers or giant lizard killers in the case of most surviving dragons.

The magic needed to create these was relatively simple, according to Elspeth. It needed to be constantly maintained, however, otherwise Reality had a habit of playing catch-up and closing down the bolt-holes ... whether or not anyone was in them or not. That tended to be fairly terminal for anything trapped inside ... image the bubble you are in bursting when at the deepest part of the darkest ocean trench, and all that water and pressure rushing in.

'Splat' doesn't quite cover it.

Mortals could create bolt-holes with a bit of learning and some skill. Witches often made their cottages larger on the inside, to accommodate an actual functional toilet and space to store all their books for example, and warlocks often crafted 'wizard towers' that looked as skinny as fashionable jeans for mortals, but contained enough space for all their robes, pointy hats and dusty libraries ... let alone the armies they often housed to keep them safe.

So I was not all that surprised to find a troll-hole stuck at the bottom of a DOPA facility, given the highly intelligent and learned individuals that the government tended to employ ... and the cost saving advantages of having an off-the-books storage space to stash as much crap as they might want.

The issue here was the link to the Beyond. That was not good for anyone.

Mortals exposed to the Real often went insane, driven mad by the sheer impossibilities of a Realm were everything was possible, where the laws they 'knew' existed did not in fact apply. A place of every dream and nightmare overloaded most mortals' mental infrastructure, resulting in foaming at the mouth maniacs, religious fanatics hearing any number of deities in their heads. Or cold, cunning despots intent on overseeing as much bloody chaos as possible.

I had *no* idea what a mortal's exposure to a place that made even the everchanging laws of the Real seem dependable in comparison might cause. The sort of insanity, paranoia and utter frightening psychosis that could sprout like weeds, uncontrolled.

And that's where we stood.

No problem.

"You said they knew we were here?" Trix spoke up, pointing to the single tunnel leading off the room. "Well, us standing around here means they can come find us and kill us real easy-like. How about we get our arses in gear and go find these friends of yours, before that happens?"

Janus and Dix exchanged high fives, obviously enjoying the sarkiness of the half fae, but I couldn't fault her argument. Nor it seemed could Puck.

"Onward then. And prepare for ... well, anything." She smiled back at Trix, shaking her head apologetically. "However, I must point out Morgan and Gregory were the ones to open the way to this place, so I am sorry Miss Del Elouqin but you forfeit the bonus. Better luck next time."

Trix's response was short, blunt and predictable. Which earned a few chuckles around the company, but Puck simply rolled her eyes and turned away, choosing to ignore the jibe.

We headed down the tunnel, steps fashioned from slabs of black stone forming stairs which led us down in a slow curve. There were no other openings that we passed, meaning the only way trouble could come was from in front of us ... but conversely there was nowhere for us to duck into and hide if needed. We'd just have to meet whatever came at us head on.

Finally, Hunter motioned us to slow. The shapechanger had taken the lead, and now he peered round the edge of the tunnel with his rifle kept ready, crouching down to minimise his outline against the tunnel's bloody light. For a long moment he scanned whatever lay ahead, then gestured for us to join him.

It was a sight to behold.

A central shaft dropped away in front of us, rising upwards from where we all crouched. Impossibly huge. If this *had* been build in the Mortal Realm, it would have taken out a sizeable chunk of the mountain in which the facility had been built and would have required immense effort to excavate, let alone keep from falling in on itself over time. It reminded me of images I'd seen of olden day mortal missile silos, built to house the weapons of mass destruction that had never been deployed, but still lurked as a deterrent or threat depending on who was speaking.

Fixed to the sides of the shaft were several walkways, with stairways attached to allow passage up and down. I recognised the design from the mental image Felix had shown me, realising that meant the glass cells they were kept in were here somewhere. Close by.

But what dominated the view was a strange, intricate structure that descended from the ceiling high overhead. A network of blackened steel poles fixed together in a confusing pattern ran from the top of the shaft down its entire length, with cables entwined throughout the whole structure. This shrank in size as it descended until, as I looked carefully over the edge of the platform where our tunnel ended, it stopped at the very bottom of the shaft. And at its inverted pyramidal tip something hung in the air.

It wasn't a Way like I'd ever seen, nor was it any sort of gate or portal that I was used to. It refused definition, altering its shape and size with unsettling frequency … a frequency I realised matched the slow throb of the lighting. The cables made sudden sense, when I realised that somehow this thing … maybe a doorway to the Beyond, maybe something from there, it was powering the facility. Hence the inconsistent and only sporadic energy spikes from the main site, when all the energy they needed to get up to whatever fuckery it was they were doing here came from that thing.

Walkways ran from the platforms to the central inverted spike, for maintenance or some other purpose maybe. These were set haphazardly down its length, so that if someone fell from one, there was a good chance they'd plummet the entire way down without landing on another bridge to prevent their death. But cables were strung from each spar, crisscrossing between and beneath them like some vast web, so there was always a chance of snagging one of the thick black tubes to stave off death by splatting.

Down one level and across from where we lurked, I saw a large tunnel leading off the causeway. There were no guards, nothing to indicate this was any different from the other entrances I could see on the other sections of causeway … except for one thing. From there, I felt an unmistakable, undeniable presence. Not Felix, nor Elspeth. Not even Cormac Gregory, if he was indeed down here.

Herne the Hunter. My father.

My friends were elsewhere, somewhere on the base level of the shaft if my lycan senses were working as they should. But I wasn't entirely convinced I could trust myself, given there was a thing from Beyond messing with my head. The only way to be sure was to go look, as quietly and quickly as we could.

"Now we must take our separate ways." Puck spoke up suddenly, and I felt the urge to groan. "For there are many tasks we must overcome, and cannot do so if we remain together."

"That's a stupid idea, when we don't know how many enemies there are here." Trix hissed back, gesturing at the strange structure in front of us. "We should find a place to hold up, lay low and send out a scout to get intel. Not go blindly walking into whatever trap or ambush they've no doubt laid out for us."

"We simply do not have time for that." The spy told her, shaking her head. "No, there are critical objectives we must meet, and to do so, we must separate. I to gather evidence of whatever Accord breaches are taking place, for our Lord and Lady and the other Courts. With me, I shall take Hunter as I believe his skillset will prove useful to the ask."

She looked across at me, and I knew she'd sensed the same thing as me. Herne's presence.

"Morgan and Greg, to find their friends and loved ones, and free them." She instructed next, revealing the mercenary streak in her as well. Cold and callous with her next words. "There may be other captives here that we should seek to release, to act as a distraction to the guards here as much as for their own wellbeing."

Then she looked across at the mercenaries.

"And you, to seek out any power source or controller for this place and to shut them down. Given you will face the strongest opposition, I suggest my companion Manisha accompany you and lend her strength of arm to your endeavours." She explained, but I caught the cocked eyebrow from the Knight, telling me she had not expected this either. "If they are drawing power from the Beyond through that tear below us, they must have converters in place to translate what is essentially alien and unusable energy into something friendlier to this Realm. Find that, switch it off however you can. Then we will regroup, I would suggest at the lowest level to decide how best to end this connection with the Beyond permanently."

I could tell I wasn't the only one who thought splitting us up was a bad idea, but Puck had made valid points. And a larger group would be easier to spot, and ambush, whilst if we divided we could maybe help out anyone caught, if we got enough warning.

To that end, Manisha handed out small smooth stones of grey-black hue, with a rune carved in their surface.

"A whisper-stone. If you are in need, grip it and whisper what you will." She told us, giving me an a particularly long look. "Our own stones will shiver, and by holding them, we will hear what you have spoken. But only use it for emergencies, for its power is not unlimited. It will however connect to its paired stones no matter where they are."

I pocketed the one she passed to Greg and I, unsure just what the Knight had been trying to tell me, or whether I was just imagining her weighted attention. It's fair to say hints are generally wasted on me.

Manisha kept hold of one stone, whilst Puck took the third. I had a moment's flashback, to standing in Twilight with two Norns, seeing them hand across a charm that would mask me from being recognised by anyone, and a twin to make the bearer look like me. And how that had ended …

No-one was going to die, pretending to be me. Or being a distraction for me.

Not again.

Hunter shared a nod and several fist bumps with the rest of his team, another sign they weren't complete strangers and had been on the job together before. For her part, Manisha simply exchanged a cool look with Puck, not saying a word but I figured they were still speaking, given the spy's decision on the groups.

Then, without any further word, Puck and Hunter slipped out of the tunnel entrance, sliding silently away. Greg gave me a nod, and we headed out the opposite direction, my eye on a stairwell leading down.

I wanted to reach Felix and Ellie, not forgetting Cormac and even the troll brothers I knew had been taken. But first, I had to get to Herne.

Maybe he would be in good enough state to help deal with the chimerians and their boss, whoever that was.

And there was still Harry to think about, and wonder what the hell they'd wanted her for. The link to the Beyond, and a creature originally from there … it had me worried.

We slunk carefully around the metal platform, keeping an eye out for any movement. Any sign of trouble. Felix had told me they were onto us, which wasn't surprising given the noise we'd made dispatching the spider-goblins let alone the two chimerian guards. But the massive chamber was eerily still as we circled the level we'd entered at.

Almost *too* quiet.

And that sense of being watched pressed in on me, a presence that was all around. Pervading both the gloom and the bloody-hued lit space we made our way along. I had to stop myself looking over my shoulder, gritting my teeth and softly growling at the incessant urge to check around me.

We made it to the stairs without encountering any enemies, and ghosted down them.

The next level was much like the one we'd entered on, with a metal walkway strung all around the walls and stairs leading up and down. The entrance from where I felt Herne's presence was on the other side of the chamber, with several more openings dotted around the rock face but no clue as to where they led.

No guards, no obvious traps waiting to spring. It was thoroughly disconcerting.

Greg seemed to think the same, scanning our surroundings intently but than shaking his head to tell me there was no sign of the chimerians. No one hiding, waiting to pounce. No little red dots settling on us, telling us we had guns pointed at us. It was like the place was deserted.

They couldn't have just fucked off, could they? Used a portal key and run?

That made no sense.

So, pushing all my worries aside until I needed to deal with them … or they built up enough to overwhelm me, I crept around the gantry until I reached the tunnel mouth. And peered carefully inside.

The tunnel was short, leading to another door with a wheel-lock and looking like it should have been featured in a crime movie or heist where the heroes or villains face an impregnable vault to crack. It was the sort of thing to either stop anything from getting *into* what lay beyond it, or imprisoning something truly powerful from ever getting out.

Given what I sensed lay beyond it, I reckoned it was the latter in this case.

And the door was *just* the sort of make and model, that it would have been really nice to have had our resident experts along who specialised in sneaking into places … or using their highly suspect recipes to carve their way through any obstacle.

Instead, I just had me and Greg. So my options for getting past the locked door were limited, to say the least.

There was a chance I could break the mechanism, if it wasn't built for inhuman strength. Possibly snap whatever rods the wheel moved and open up the door that way. Or I could bugger up the whole thing and make it so that it *never* opened … that was definitely an option as well.

Greg was great at spotting bad guys hiding from sight, and dealing with them when they were found out. His lock-picking skills, I had to admit, were probably woefully unpractised. Him having been one of the people who arrested and jailed those who were skilled at breaking into places, not doing so much of that himself.

Hmm.

Use your sword. Cut your way in.

My mother's voice helpfully whispered in my head, but for a moment I had to wonder if she wasn't still recovering from her death and reincarnation as a Crone. The door was a solid slab of metal, definitely a good few feet thick at least. I'd need an acetylene torch or something to make a dent in it ...

Or an Ivory fae blade, through which I could channel my Court craft to make it hot as hell.

I grinned nastily. Oh, this was going to be fun!

The metal hissed and popped as I applied the point of my white-hot blade to it. Just as my mother had expected, with a little effort on my part, the sword cut into the door and began slicing through all the hidden mechanisms, locks and bolts that shut it tight against intrusion. Sparks flew out, as I carved my way up, across and then down, shearing through everything I could as quicky as I could.

Something made one final crunch in the mechanism, and the door juddered and slowly swung inward. I made a note to ask my mother sometime when she had a chance to watch the *Star Wars* series, to have me recreate an iconic scene with my version of a lightsaber. But that could wait.

With Greg covering me, I pushed the door fully open and stepped into the new chamber.

But then stopped, as the horror of what lay within became clear.

Chapter 29

Nothing had prepared me for what lay revealed before me.

The closest I had come to anything like this, my mind reminded me as I stood just inside the cut door, was when I'd gatecrashed Robert Knox's secret hideaway he'd built in London Lower. Where he'd been keeping the young women he had kidnapped to dissect and use their body parts to build Morgana a new body.

We'd saved one young mortal girl's life that day, but I'd lost good friends, packmates too. As ever, it's never totally good or bad, always a mixture.

This … this was far, far worse.

The room we'd entered was a laboratory, that was immediately obvious. Shining metal benches and workstations had been fitted to the melted rock floor, gleaming in the bloody hue of the overhead lights. On these, all manner of apparatus had been set up, with microscopes, distillers and a whole host of other equipment I recognised from the television shows I'd watched but had no clue as to their name or function. Things with rubber tubes and glass bulbs filled with murky liquid sat alongside small refrigerators filled with test-tubes carefully arranged in rows and labelled with indistinct lettering.

Along one wall, an entire bank of what looked like vintage computer cabinets stood, with blinking lights and reels of tape whirring away, chattering and clicking like something from a dated science fiction movie. It reminded me of the equipment we'd seen in the offices and working spaces back in the facility proper, but these were powered on and doing something other than gathering dust.

After that, it got weird.

Lit by the red hued lights, massive glass containers stood upright further into the room. These were set into sealed plinths and plugged with multiple hoses and metal brackets, chunky blinking displays set squarely on the front of each cylinder. Liquid filled each one, from top to bottom, with bubbles rising lazily up in steady streams.

And each cylinder held a body.

I ghosted over to the nearest tower of glass, followed silently by Greg. And peered in.

The body was supported on some sort of apparatus, a black mask fitted over its nose and mouth and fitted with tubes that disappeared down into the base of the container. Other tubes were plugged into veins along the naked arms, legs and neck. Each of these pulsed with some sort of thicker liquid, slowly draining into or out of the body. I wasn't sure which.

It looked dead, no matter the fact the face mask obviously was supplying air to the body. No movement of the chest indicated a breath drawn, no pulse of life in any vein that I could see. The body just hung on its frame, liquid encasing it, bubbles rising up gently past it.

I did a quick count, looking past the first cylinder. There was more than sixty of the chambers, which meant over sixty bodies like this. What the fuck was going on here?

Greg was by my side, looking at the body in the glass tube too. Then he tapped my shoulder, and pointed to a label I'd missed on the glass.

Ingless. P. Variant Delta 10.2. F

The last bit meant jack shit to me, but the name? *P Ingless?* That struck a worrying note in my head.

I pulled out my mother's journal from my pocket and leafed through to the note I'd made that I'd slipped beside the photograph of her old colleagues.

Petra Ingless. Biomedical Expert.

What the hell?

Exchanging confused looks with my companion, I showed him my list. He grunted, obviously remembering the name too, and gestured at the rest of the cylinders.

"We need to check the rest." He whispered, and I nodded. This was just getting weirder by the second.

He took the left, I took the right and we headed off around each of the giant liquid containers. Alert for trouble. Unsure of just what the hell we'd found.

I peered in the cylinders, checking the names on each.

Ingless P. Variant Delta 10.3. F

Delta 10.4. F

10.5 F

I counted six cylinders containing the same bodies, all of them floating on their racks. Masks covering their faces, eyes staring blankly at nothing. The same moles, the same imperfections. These were identical, copies of each other.

Beyond, the next cylinders held a different body. Female, thicker and shorter with black hair. Still completely naked, masked and with tubes inserted into her arms and legs. A black tattoo marking her left forearm, of a moth or butterfly.

I checked the label on the cylinder.

Monrose E. Variant Echo 11. 4 F

Eselle Monrose. Lead Liaison, according to my mother's journal. Whatever that meant.

Counting them, there were seven copies of this body. All in exactly the same state as the previous ones. All looking dead, even with the fluids flowing through them. I was willing to bet we'd find versions of all the names on my list, all the people in that photograph my mother had made sure I saw. People who had died years ago, with nothing to indicate foul play except the timing.

All of them having previously worked together at this secret facility, doing Accord-breaking experiments on creatures from the Real. Up to their eyeballs in black-bag operations. Yeah, this wasn't creepy *at all*.

I moved back out from the cylinders, and Greg joined me a moment later.

"I counted three names from your list, all on tubes with bodies in them." He told me quietly, expression grim. He obviously sensed how weird and fucked up this was as well. "There's a bunch of empty cylinders too. One each from the names, and several belonging to *Bremmer Z*. A couple are cracked, looks like either something hit them from the outside, or they broke from within."

"Something getting out, maybe."

I grunted at *that* cheerful thought.

"I reckon I know what these are." He continued, tapping the nearest cylinder. "They're clones. Like, copies of the original people. Like Dolly the Sheep, but humans instead. I didn't know we had started doing that … there were always so many problems reported in the news. Genetic failures, degradation, mutation. Bad stuff like that."

Copies of the original. Those words sparked in my head, along with Cormac joking about ghost stories.

The team were all dead, he'd told me. *Their identities confirmed from the bodies themselves. No chance of an error.*

But what if they had had copies of themselves, all tanked up and ready to be used to stage their deaths? What if the mysterious reason they had all died of natural causes or such was down to them not actually being the real people at all, and instead just tools to be used to deceive people into thinking one thing, when the truth was very, very different.

What if the scientists my mother had worked with, trying to trap Herne, were still alive ... and they'd decided after failing the first time, to enlist some more help and try again?

And this time, they'd succeeded.

Fuck it, I needed to find Herne.

Find him ... my mother's voice echoed in my head, spurring me on.

There was nothing else we were going to learn from the floating clones, so I closed my eyes and let me senses point me where I needed to go. Off to the right, beyond the cylinders. With Greg following, I headed in that direction, the need for answers quickening my step. Too much had happened, too much made no sense.

The laboratory opened up around us, with what looked like a viewing platform set to one side, with a long glass window looking out over what lay beyond. Wide steps and a ramp led down, and I felt Herne's presence more strongly as I took the stairs, knowing he was close. And from what I could sense, not in a good way.

That turned out to be a *major* understatement.

The chamber below was circular, a large door standing open that would seal the entire unit off the from the rest of the lab. The door was over a foot thick, and looked to be made to create a complete airtight seal, as well as having four thickened rods to slide into the surrounding walls to further lock it in place. Thorough security, yet redundant given the door stood ajar.

Inside, the walls were almost brilliant white, clean of any grime or dust. Instead, intricate runes had been inscribed across every surface, scrolling all the way over the ceiling and on the floor as well. I stood in the doorway, and could feel the strength of the warding, the layers of protection built into the chamber. All to lock down and keep the single occupant from breaking free.

Herne rested upside down on a gantry, his body bound to a set of X spars spreading his arms and legs to what would be an uncomfortable position for anything mortal. He was bound with iron and silver, wrapped around his arms and legs, encircling his neck. And he was completely naked, his robes and armour, any clothing stripped from him.

Revealed, Herne bore the resemblance of a mortal man. Heavily muscled, marked with white whorls and script that stood out from his dark skin, shining through the thick hair that clad him. His head was animalistic, heavily bearded and with thick brows that made him look almost bestial, helped by fangs that jutted from just behind his scarred lips.

His eyes were dark holes, staring at from under his brows. Alert, aware.

In pain. From the horrors that had been visited on him.

Antlers had once jutted from his forehead, branching up and over his head when he wore a hood to hide himself away. These had been broken, torn away at their roots so that the flesh around the shattered roots was torn and inflamed. From there, the flesh on his left side on his face had been stripped away all the way down to the bone, and even there, sections had been removed from his skull to expose the flesh underneath.

Herne's right arm ended at the elbow, with nubs of bone jutting from under the circlet binding the limb to the spar. His legs both ended at his knees, the bones of his knee caps pinned by more iron needles and with tubes inserted into the flesh. His ribcage was visible, the dark bones gleaming in the bloody light of the chamber, and more tubes were nestled between the curved ribs. Worming their way into his body, his organs.

The Hunter had been split and splayed like some laboratory animal, for what purpose I could not understand. But it tore at me, igniting the fire of my rage, to see him so weakened and humbled. My father, the Lord of the Wyld.

Broken.

Then one eye in his head fixed on me, the other only a dark hole in his skull.

And he spoke to me.

Chapter 30

"Son."

I was standing elsewhere, suddenly no longer in the chamber with Herne's broken body. Instead, it was like I was surrounded by shattered mirrors, fractures in the very air. Cracks ran everywhere, shards spinning past me as I looked around me.

To see Herne in a large broken pane. Wrapped in his old clothes, hood hiding his features. Horns returned and arcing over his head. Just like I knew him, not how I had found him.

But even this wasn't entirely true, as I immediately realised. His form blurred, bits falling away into dark smoke. Like he was bleeding into the fractures and cracks where we stood.

In fact, I realised Herne showed in many of the fractured, shattered fragments whirling slowly around me. This was like the place where I'd met my mother in the Wyld, where she had asked me to choose between Felix and my newly found half-sister Briar. To stop an evil Crone from taking control of the Wyld, and returning my mother back to life … not an easy choice.

I'd taken door number three, saving both Briar and Felix, and still stopping the insane Crone. I'd *slightly* annoyed Terra in the bargain, but hey, can't make an omelette without cracking at least one eggshell.

This time was different. I could sense that this time, this safe place was ending, fragmenting as Herne lost control. Hell, the state he was in, I was surprised he could hold it together this well.

"Son." He repeated, voice cracking and slipping between a whisper and a shout. *"Must warn you … Must ask you …"*

"What the hell have they been doing to you?" I asked him, but the image in the large shard broke into shreds of dark smoke and vanished. Instead, his voice came from another fragment, to my right as I turned to follow his voice.

"Fed on … me. Drank my blood." He snarled, the baying of hounds, of wolves throbbing in his voice. *"But they did not know … Changed them, foolish mortals …"*

They'd *eaten* him? Fuck, this was way beyond even the nastiest shit I'd read in my mother's journal, way worse than the madness I thought possible. I mean … if these were the scientists my mother had worked with, then I'd figured they might have been trying to trap Herne again for the original reason … as a weapon, looking to bind him some way to the Mortal Realm as a deterrent against the Courts.

But they'd been feeding off him? I mean, what the actual fuck?

"Who did this?" I asked the image of my father. "Was it the same ones who tried to take you before? When you and my … when you took Margaret Black back to the Wyld?"

The image nodded once, as black smoke bled from it.

"Same but … not." He replied rather unhelpfully. *"Before they were … but petty mortals. Now … perverse soldiers of mortal madness. And betrayers."*

Perverse soldiers of mortal madness? That had to be the chimerians. As for betrayers, I reckoned that had to be Baba Bohdana, the fungoid Crone who had also killed my mother, as it turned out.

"You … come too late to free me. But you can still … save me." Herne told me, slipping from one fragment to the next, me following him as the shards twisted and turned in the air and the cracks grew larger. *"Not much time. Must … free others. Stop them."*

I felt a spike of pain and sorrow in my mind, an echo that I knew had to be my mother. She knew the truth, had seen what they had done to the elemental she had given up her entire mortal existence to be with. He wasn't walking out of here with the rest of us, not with the level of damage they'd inflicted.

I wasn't sure how he would be walking anywhere at all.

"What are they doing here? Why are they messing with something from the Beyond?" I pushed, knowing I was running out of time to get any answers, any hint of how deep in the shit we were. "Why the fuck were they feeding on you?"

Herne flickered and bled smoke, vanishing from one shard to reappear in another before he answered.

"Madness. Wanted me ... stopped. Ordered to ... take me." He explained slowly, a painful whine like a shrill bite in his voice. *"Madness ... seeking utter ruination. Took me to stop ... me. Took the other to ... use. As a ... channel. A loci."*

I'd been wanted answers, but everything Herne was telling me simply raised more questions, like a game of whack-a-mole. Everytime I hit, another furry bastard sprouted from a hole.

Someone had ordered Herne's capture. To stop him, but from doing what? And the other? The only one who had been with him when he was taken was ...

Harry. The Harrowed Queen. And they had kidnapped her at the same time as Herne. But she wasn't in a room, partially dissected. No, they needed her for something else. A channel. A loci.

The Harrowing was from the Beyond, which was what gifted it the power to be the death of immortals. And the lunatics running this shitshow had something from the Beyond hooked up and running this ultra secret lab, and doing Gods knew what else. Two things from outside our dominion, and Herne was saying they needed one as a channel or loci. A focal point.

What the hell was going on here?

"Son ... you must ... end this." Herne whispered, as cracks ran up all around me. Splintering, revealing darkness behind. *"Free me ... Only you ... can. Then stop them. Or we all ... end."*

"How? How do I help you?" I didn't even know how I could leave this place, get back to the lab. And how could I end Herne's torment? He was strapped into a massive warding, containing his essence, binding him in place. Making him vulnerable, allowing these bastards to chow down on him and drain his life. All I had were some sharp tools from the Ivory Court, which were great at opening doors and dealing with run of the mill Real critters … but Herne was a Power. I didn't know the first thing of dealing with something on his level.

The image of Herne appeared before me, and raised a right arm made whole. Somehow the image pushed *through* the glass, the finger extended and appearing without shattering the glass or whatever it was where he stood.

I braced myself, forcing myself not to flinch, as the digit gently pressed against my forehead.

And then I knew.

"When you are … done, do this one last thing." He told me, as images blazed behind my eyeballs. *"My … gift to you. My … legacy. Use it … wisely. Son."*

"Ah fuck, no. You want me to … ? I came here to *save* you!" I groaned out a snarl, the knowledge undeniable as it sat in my mind. The one truth Herne wanted me to know. How to help him. "And what the fuck, I don't want your legacy. I'm not going to be the next bloody Lord of the Wyld. Briar is the new Lady, and I'm not taking that from her. Not for you, not anyone. *Dad.*"

Herne somehow managed a chuckle, even though it was riven with pain. The laboured breath of the prey, about to meet its end.

"My … legacy. Not my … throne. You'd make a truly … awful Lord." He told me, the dark hood lifting enough for me to see the glint of his eyes. The shine of a fang as his lip lifted. *"You will … have need soon enough. We are of the same … blood. The beast is in both of us. Take … mine. Use it … wisely."*

There was nothing else I could do, but nod. As the cracks widened and the shards splintered and fell all about me, Herne held me with that last look. A promise asked, a promise made.

"Beware. Betrayers … come in … all colours."

His last words echoed in my head.

Then I was back, standing before him in the doorway. Greg behind me, the mutilated body of my father hanging before me.

And I knew what I had to do.

It wasn't magic. The wardings and bindings in the chamber were to lock Herne down, weaken him enough to allow his captors to be able to wound him, do thoroughly shit things to him. Not stop anyone else from acting, as that would limit what they could do themselves.

But they had probably written something there to react against magic, since if there was a slim chance anyone might come to rescue him, the surest bet was it would be someone or something from the Real, using magic. So I was guessing there was a nasty surprise awaiting anyone trying *that* in the room.

Instead, I closed my eyes, huffing my breath through my jaws and focused on one thing as I held out one hand just like I had been shown. And called on it. A simple thing, something I had carried with the simple desire to return it to its rightful owner when I sat his hairy arse back on the throne where it belonged.

Now, I was going to return it in a different way. Not a way I wanted, but one I'd promised to do.

All too easily, all too quickly, I felt the weight settle in my hand. Rough against my skin, the carven surface thrumming with innate power. And heavy with all the death that had soaked into it over the centuries.

Opening my eyes, I found Herne's spear lying where I had summoned it. The spear he hunted with, that for him he could throw as many times as he liked but it would always return to him. Now given over to me.

I just had to do one thing.

"Wait here." I growled at Greg, not knowing how long I'd been gone, in communion with my father. It could have been a heartbeat, it could have been an hour. But my companion simply nodded, turning to look back the way we had come, keeping watch.

As I stepped into the chamber.

Nothing blew up under my foot, no alarms triggered to shriek in my ears. I walked slowly forward, coming to a stop as I faced my father. That one remaining eye was locked onto me, his bestial features strained from the agony of what he was suffering but in that lone orb I read his greeting, and his thanks.

His head jerked, once. A nod.

I set the spear point against his broad chest, over his heart as it pulsed slow and erratically within the cage of visible ribs. His nature would not let him die, they had left him enough strength to remain alive no matter his own wishes. Alive, for them to continue to feed off him, use him for their purposes.

It had to end.

"Goodbye. Father." I huffed out the words, feeling them wrench at something deep inside me. And I leant down on the spear, with all my lycan, Wyld and Court-blessed strength.

His body arched one last time, that lone dark eye widening and a gasp bursting from between his clenched teeth. Then, like in the shattered room where we had spoken, the Lord of the Hunt bled away to black smoke, the restraints clattering down against the spars as his body vanished.

Bright blood coated the spearhead, and I acted without even thinking. Just following his instructions. The cut stung as I slashed my other palm with the sharp spear's edge, his essence burning as it boiled off the metal and into me. His last gift, the legacy he'd promised, I felt it. A darkness somewhere deep inside me, taking root.

A part of him, with me from now on. Always.

I'd just killed Herne the Hunter.

I'd just ended the life of my father.

I stared down at the spear in my hand and then, again without any real thought, dismissed the weapon back to wherever the hell it went when it wasn't being used.

Then I turned back and walked to the door, seeing Greg standing there waiting. Expression grim, but the questions thankfully set to one side for the moment. He'd seen the state of the immortal, and I'd explain things after I'd processed them myself.

With little effort, I pulled the door closed, shutting the last resting place of Herne away. For now, I told myself. Herne was a greater Power, and I was bloody sure this wasn't the first time he'd been dealt a mortal wound. Creatures of the Real could come back, if they so chose. Odin had confirmed that fact himself. It just would take as long as it needed, if there was enough of a reason for the Hunter to restore himself.

A son, up to his wolf chops in trouble. A lover, mother of his son, returned from the dead. One or two reasons, I could think up on the spot.

At that moment my pocket vibrated. Not my phone, but something else.

The whisper-stone.

I yanked it out, holding it in my hand as it pulsed with urgency.

The next moment I heard Manisha's voice, filled with unexpected emotion. Not quite fear, but definitely disquiet. That was bad enough, given it was the Knight talking.

"If you can hear me, we've found the *what did you call them? … ah ok* … controllers for the power to this place. But there are other things in here than grey men. Worse things. Something attacked us, a creature I have never seen it's like before. It or they can … hold on … by the Light it's back! More of them! And Hounds! They can use … Watch the shadows! They're coming for …"

Then the stone fell silent.

"Shit." I growled, shoving the stone back in my pocket.

"Trouble?" Greg asked, and I bit back the urge to say something suitably snarky in response. So far, *everything* that had happened since I got back from the Wyld could be called trouble.

"Something's attacking Manisha and the others. Not chimerians. We gotta go help them." I growled, gesturing back the way we had come. "She sent a warning, something about watching out for the shadows."

"Useful." He commented dryly, looking around at all the lightless corners and darkened sections not lit by the blood-hued lights.

I didn't bother replying, instead keeping an eye on my surroundings even as the events of the past few minutes buzzed around my head. There was a stab of sorrow, an aching sadness, that had to be coming down the link with my mother, since I hadn't known Herne well enough to feel his loss so keenly.

But it had been *my* hand that had ended him. You don't kill an immortal Elder and simply shrug it off. There would be hell to pay, when the current crisis was dealt with. That I knew with cold certainty.

We made it back into the main room with the glass cylinders and clones, and headed to the tunnel leading to the shaft where we'd come in.

But stopped, as a low growl throbbed in the air. I felt a difference, a presence even as my ears caught the click of talons on stone. Greg halted as well, eyes narrowed as he searched around for the source of the sound.

He didn't have to wait long.

From beyond the tall tubes, a pair of thick bodied dogs stalked. And it was immediately obvious these weren't simply mortal guard-dogs, Dobermans or Alsatians. No, they were easily four foot at the shoulder and massed easily the same bodyweight as the guardian at my side. They were black as night, fur stiff and bristled, but their eyes … the orbs glowed the same violet and scarlet hellish hue as bled from the Beyond breach.

Both canines stalked slowly towards us, mouths gaping showing rows and rows of sharks teeth. Saliva drooled from their lips, ropes hanging down to glisten in the gloom.

I'd never seen their like before, but the sense of them … I don't know how, and it wasn't my immediate concern but they *felt* like the Hounds my father had used in his Hunts. Those creatures taken, altered in form and used to chase down those unfortunate enough to earn

Herne's attention. Sometimes it had been packmates, fellow lycans caught whilst on hunts of their own.

These though? These were *wrong*. A taint running through them like spoiled milk or rotten eggs.

I tried to reach out to them, as any lycan can to any living beast. Not exactly talking to them, but a bond linking us that at times could allow one of my kin to calm an angry animal, to silence and subdue a fellow predator. I'd used it more than a few times when a mortal's pet chihuahua wouldn't stop yapping and frothing at me whilst out walking Bear ... my trollhound happy to let me handle the little monster whilst he focused on more important matters.

It always worked.

Except now.

The Hounds simply cranked up their snarls, their eyes blazing as I felt my attempt to reach them rebuffed. Slipping off them like water touching hot oil. These were definitely *not* like anything I'd come across before.

"This the trouble Manisha ran into?" Greg asked, casually easing his sword clear of its sheath. I shrugged, as I slipped my blade free, cracking my neck and grinding my teeth. They might be nothing I'd seen until now, but I bet they bled all the same.

"No, we won't be having any of that." That other voice whispered in the air, and this time I could see that Greg heard it as well. Not in my head anymore. Cracked, maddened and wrong in so many weird ways. "You are intruders in my home. Unwanted guests. I have your companions, and now I have you. I want answers, and you **will** talk before I am done with you."

My senses lit with danger, even as I realised what the Hounds were.

A distraction.

The shadows boiled around us, tentacles lashing out to wrap around us, ensnare us. I summoned fire to my sword and lashed out, carving them apart even as I snapped my wolfen jaws onto black threads to shred them. But they simply vanished like smoke, yet those entangling my limbs felt as strong as iron.

Greg was hacking and slicing all around him, but the shadows burgeoned and buried him. I heard his cry as they piled all over him, but I could do nothing as more wrapped themselves around me. Pinning me, smothering me.

I gasped for air, but the shadow limbs crushed my chest, forcing all air out of my lungs before smothering my jaws so I could not breathe. My vision swam, fire burning in my chest as I tried to reach for my Ivory armour, the ice of Shadow. Anything to help free me.

My last sight was of the Hounds, sitting on their haunches, eyes glowing with madness. Still as statues.

Then … blackness.

Chapter 31

I struggled back to consciousness, surprised to find I was still breathing.

Still alive.

That was someone's mistake. A bad one, in my humble opinion.

Ignoring the throbbing headache that being choked unconscious always leads to ... and yes to clarify, this wasn't the first of them I'd experienced, the last one being when a Redcap Wyld psychopath tried strangling me to death ... I shook my head and took in my surroundings.

We weren't in the lab anymore. We were somewhere far worse.

I was kneeling on the floor of the lowest level, where the breach to the Beyond hung. From above, the gantry we'd traversed had hidden details of the ground floor, but now I saw the glass and metals cages that Felix had shown me. Where they had been imprisoned. They lined one wall, more than forty of them, and I could see other figures huddled on the floor of each cell. Goblins, fae, trolls ... I spied two familiar creatures staring back at me, one with a wooden leg. The Bung brothers.

They glared at me, obviously deciding this was my fault they were imprisoned. Good to see the whole *thanks for saving our lives* had lasted as long as I'd expected it to.

Felix and Elspeth weren't in their cells. Instead, they stood to my left. Both looked tired, still wearing the clothes from when they had been taken except they were both barefoot. I couldn't sense any injuries on either of them, so that was at least one good thing. But they both wore frightened expressions, obviously more clued in to what we faced than I was. For now.

Across from me, I saw an area hidden by shadows, cloaking whatever it was they had stashed there. The darkness rippled like water, obviously under someone's control ... and I thought back to the way Greg and I had been attacked, how the shadowy tentacles had struck like they were being directed, controlled. This wasn't anything any mortal scientist, no matter how learned, should be able to do. This stank of Real involvement.

The breach hung in the air, rippling and shifting in ways that only added to the dull throb of my headache. I saw now it was caged in some sort of structure, copper rods fashioned delicately all around it and cabling running from this to the shadows beyond. For what purpose, I had no clue but I figured it couldn't be for anything good.

Beside me, I saw the rest of my companions. Greg, kneeling. Manisha standing tall and straight. Janus, Dix, Trix and Mother all sat on the floor. We had all been stripped of our weapons, our packs removed and pockets searched. Everything had been set out on a series of tables to the side, piled up almost without any regard to their destructive nature. They sat alongside cargo crates and other storage boxes, piled haphazardly that spoke of a certain type of mind that ignored clutter like background noise.

My mother's journal was missing, but I couldn't see it amongst the piled equipment. It had to be somewhere, but I had a niggling concern that its disappearance meant something. Something bad.

I caught sight of our guards, chimerians in their beetle armour. Carrying stubby rifles and those pistols loaded with acid, their bulbous helmets glistening unnaturally in the crimson light. One caught me looking, and tapped a long knife sheathed at its waist. It made a cutting motion across its throat with the other hand. The fucker from the ambush, I was willing to bet.

There was only thirteen of the grey men that I could see, surrounding us or up on the gantry above. Not as many as I had thought there might be, but then I remembered Cormac saying that the project had been burned, the test subjects eradicated to the best of the mortals' ability. A few stragglers slipping through the traps set for them made sense.

But I'd expected more ... that if a secret, fucked up bunch of psychopaths had been running loose for decades, they'd have at least tried to increase their numbers. Make them operationally strong again. A force to be reckoned with.

Maybe they had. Maybe the others were off doing shitty things like ambushing people and trying to kill them. Or maybe they'd failed, not found anyone capable of surviving the ordeals of becoming one of their own ... more likely given what Cormac had said about the procedure, how many had died as failures.

As the OPS agent popped into my head, I immediately caught sight of him. And what they'd done to him since his capture.

It wasn't pretty.

Cormac Smith was lashed to a structure similar to the one I'd seen Herne bound to, though this one was made of simple metal spars rather than cold iron and silver blended. He was also right-side up, stripped down to a pair of dark shorts and hooked up to various IVs and bags of fluid. His body was surprisingly muscular, scarred from his encounters with the Real and the conflicts he had been involved in before, fighting to preserve peace in the Mortal Realm.

Bruises tattooed across his body showed the tender care his captors had bestowed on him, and one eye was swollen shut. The other, however, was bright and aware as he fixed it on me, crooking battered and split lips into a semblance of a smile.

"Great rescue." He mouthed at me, and I just shrugged. Fuck it, we'd at least found the ungrateful bastard. Anything more was a bonus in my book.

Six of the unnatural Hounds prowled around the chamber as well, their black fur bristling, their maws gaping with jagged fangs. None of them made any move towards us, simply happy to pace around and look menacing. Obviously commanded simply to add to the threat in the chamber … at least for now. Two more sat on either side of Cormac, an unnecessary guard and a bit of overkill for a simple mortal bound to a cross frame, I thought.

I had to guess he'd given them more trouble than they had thought possible from one simple man. Go, Cormac.

My wandering gaze finally settled on the last members of this merry gathering. And they were definitely the oddest of them all.

Four of the six figures wore white labcoats, the sort you see in every television show or movie where a hospital or research laboratory features. But the clothing was definitely sized for men and women of normal stature, and so hung off them oddly. Their limbs were too scrawny, too elongated, their bodies too bony. All four of their skeletons were prominent, jutting shoulder blades under the coats, elbows and knees sharply defined. Their skulls were bald, the bones oddly planed and pushing through the flesh, but I still saw something in each face. An echo of what they might have looked like before.

Something I'd seen, only a short while ago. Floating in the glass cylinders, staring vacantly back at me.

These were the scientists, the ones from when the facility had been a fully functioning part of DOPA operations. But they were changed somehow, the mutation or whatever gone horribly wrong. They weren't mortal anymore, nor were they creatures of the Real … and I wasn't sure what that left them.

The fifth member wore no labcoat, instead it wore clothes more associated with private security. Dark padded leggings and an undershirt, with a flak jacket thrown over the top. It too was oddly deformed, but more hulking than the first four, more bestial. Its muscles were ribbed where they showed, thickened veins writhing like worms over skin that was dusty black and oddly stonelike.

But all five had nothing on to the last one. The one standing beside the rippling, shifting breach. Staring at me.

Tall. Far taller than any mortal man. This figure bore the same deformities as the others, but far more pronounced, as if it had had longer to change. Its skull had lengthened, rising up like a deformed egg behind, its features stretched and mutated. The nose was now mere slits across a bony snout, and the jaw had narrowed to almost like a jutting eel's maw.

It wore long garments hung off a scrawny, bony frame with growths that jutted out from its shoulders and back. Almost like spines. Yet I was certain of this thing's identify, even though it looked nothing like the man I had seen in pictures from my mother's journal.

A journal that it held up in its hand, as its red-violet eyes fixed on me.

"Where did you get this book?" It … *he* demanded angrily, waving the book.

I ignored the creature for a moment, the thing that I guessed was all that remained of Dr Zarkof Bremmer, as I checked my companions one last time. Though we'd all been disarmed, no-one looked to have been significantly or seriously hurt. Just bruised, battered about a little. Still in good shape.

And I noted one more thing.

Puck and Hunter were missing.

Dead? Maybe. Or maybe, just maybe, they'd managed to evade capture and were lurking somewhere nearby. I had to hope that was the case, and that they weren't instead lying cold and stiff in the shadows.

"I asked where did you get this book?!" Dr Bremmer angrily snarled, looking across at each of the company, but coming to rest on me again. Lucky me. "You. You are the lycan I was *ordered* to eliminate. My chimerians almost had you, almost brought me your head as I instructed them. Did you enjoy the taste of my wolfsbane variation? I am surprised you are still functional, given the dose I understand you received. Your companion, the stronger one … she is still alive?"

"Yes. And patiently waiting for me to bring home the cure for the shit you pumped into her." I growled back, keeping a reign on my rage for the moment, I'd use it when I felt we had a chance of getting out of this in one piece, with everything and everybody. Including the cure for Jessica. "So how about you just hand it over, and save yourself some serious pain?"

Dr Bremmer cocked his head, then utter a dry, nasty laugh. He reached into a pocket of his clothes and pulled out a small test-tube, filled with glittering silver liquid.

"You wish me to give you this? My panacea for all ills, ailments and poisons … including the one your friend must be currently … dying from?" He snarked, before slipping it back out of sight. "Then answer my question. Where did you find this book? I will not ask a third time."

He held up the journal, eyes burning with unchecked fury.

I needed to play for time, to learn as much as I could about this new bunch of lunatics. What they were up to. What the fuck they'd been doing with Herne. And that meant stringing them along as much as I could, delaying whatever they had planned for us. As I reckoned it was nothing we'd enjoy, nothing good for our ongoing health, based on our recent interactions.

Plus I figured it was worth a gamble, seeing if I could slap the smugness off the fucker who had endangered my Alpha's life. Kidnapped my friends. Caused so much trouble for one single mortal.

And there was always the hope Puck and Hunter were just waiting for the right time to cause a distraction, give us the chance to break free. I needed to give them time, if they still lived.

So I tossed the dice, and played the truth card. Mixed metaphors, I know but I'm terribly at playing games.

"I found it in my mother's home." I told him, slapping a wolfish smile on my worgen features. "Which makes sense, since, you know, she wrote it."

Dr Bremmer, the thing he had become, froze. The other five freaks exchanged bug-eyed looks of shock, breath hissing from their malformed lips. Even the Hounds stopped pacing, their violet-red eyes dimming for a moment as if something in their heads had been switched off.

I caught Ellie looking across at me, expression easy to read. Unfortunately. She slowly shook her head, and mouthed *oh Morgan no* to me, making me instantly wonder just how badly I'd fucked up.

"Your *mother*?" He spoke slowly, the words hissing from his malformed jaws. "You dare tell me Margaret Black survived that day?! That she lived to spawn you, and her blood flows through your veins? That bitch … what she did to us … the curse we suffer … and she *lived*?!"

I pushed myself to my feet, facing him as he stepped away from the breach, towering over me. Locked my eyes on his own, and grinned my most annoying smile.

"Yeah. She survived. And lived long enough to have me, and see all your plans well and truly fucked up." I replied, seeing the rage boil in him. Good. Anger caused stupidity, was my general rule of thumb. "In fact, she's the reason I'm here, fucking up your plans *again*. Ruining your little schemes, exposing your shitty secret. So what are you going to do about it?"

The creature that had once been the head of the research team stationed at this facility snarled, fingers clenching so hard around the journal that its spine creaked and the cover cracked.

"Seize him!" He commanded, and two of the chimerians pushed through my small company, shoving Greg and Trix to one side as they latched onto my arms, pinning me in place. Not that I was going anywhere.

"There's a simple way to tell if you are lying. Blood never lies." He hissed knowingly, motioning to the guard holding my right arm. "Note I did not say painless …"

I let the chimerian pull it up, knowing I could probably arm-wrestle the bastard easily enough to cause trouble but then they'd probably use their stun on me, and knock me sideways. I needed my wits about me, if we were getting out of this in one piece.

Dr Bremmer leant down, his back creaking and flexing to allow his malformed head to draw near my flesh. With his free hand, he raised one finger that was tipped with a dark talon instead of a nail, and lashed it across my bare skin delicately.

The talon had to be sharp as a scalpel, as I felt it slice into me with ease. Blood burst free from the wound, and I snarled in disgust as he craned his face down and latched his lips over the cut, sucking on the blood with obscene pleasure.

After a moment, he freed his mouth from my skin, his tongue slithering over his lips to clean them. His mad eyes stared at me for a long moment, then a cruel smile slipped over his features.

"The child of Margaret Black, you are indeed!" He hissed with obvious delight. "Oh the irony! To think of how long have I … have we wanted to revenge ourselves on the witch who cursed us, who wronged us so badly. The pain and torment I wished to visit on her. And now … now her own flesh and blood kneels before me, come of his own accord!"

"I shall visit such pain on you, lycan, you shall cry for mercy. But I have none." He crooned, and I snarled at the sick lust and delight I felt seeping from him ... from the other twisted mortals. "And when we are done, we shall drain your blood, feast on your flesh. Your ending will be one of misery and despair, for the foolishness of coming here."

Yeah, it looked like Elspeth was right. Admitting whose child I was *hadn't* been the best idea.

Go figure.

Chapter 32

Dr Bremmer cocked his head, those eel jaws twisting with a seething smile.

"But I would be remiss if I did not *also* consider who fathered you. Whose blood also fills you. You are a child of the Hunter. The spawn of the Lord of the Wyld Court. He whose bounty we have been blessed with."

The twisted mortal stepped back, waving to the Hounds as they resumed their slow pacing around us.

"Your father's flesh, his blood. His essence. Such power contained in one being." He crowed with dark pleasure. "After feeding upon him, I discovered I could summon these creatures, and command them. Loyal only to me. And the darkness … it answers to me now. It is mine to command as well, as you so foolishly all found out."

He made a curling gesture with his hand, and shadows bled from the wall behind and beside him, curling and coiling like eels over his fingers, over his skin. It was creepy as hell to watch, but not the scariest thing I'd seen by a mile or ten.

"Your mother is to blame for all this." He suddenly snarled, gesturing at his colleagues, at the tanks containing the captured creatures. "With what we thought was her dying breath, she cursed us for trying to trap a force majeure, a being of untold might far beyond our ability to understand. That we would pay for our crimes against him, against everything he stood for. Seeking to imprison the unimprisonable, to tame the untameable. Make a being like the Hunter serve mere petty mortals."

"Instead, we were marked for death. Our lives draining away like water through our fingers. Like sands through an hourglass. Her curse was nothing we could heal, nothing all our vaunted science could cure. Our dreams were haunted by the Hunter's hounds, drawing ever closer until we could run no more. Death came for us all." He hissed, the frustration of decades released in his breath as he recalled what had happened. "The weak went first, until only we six were left. And our time was short, our fate seemingly inescapable."

"We tried everything that human science could offer, broke immutable Laws and solved problems that had dogged the greatest minds for generations in our desperate search for a cure. Dr Ingless perfected the cloning process, transferring our own consciousness to blank copies of ourselves with only minimal loss of secondary emotions, harmless memories. We hoped the curse would be left behind, bound to the shells we had once inhabited. But the mark stained our very spirit, and would not wash away so easily."

He spat out the words, fury and loathing staining each one.

"It did afford us the means to fake our deaths however. To disappear before we were imprisoned by our own inferiors. Locked away, without any chance to save ourselves and only the surety of our approaching end granted us. The fools believed the staged demises, wrote us into their ledgers and closed them tight. Forgetting us, leaving us to strive to find a way to defeat the doom your mother so cruelly cursed us with."

"I'm taking a wild guess that you *still* failed.." I snarked, finding the truth not just in Dr Bremmer's snarl but in seeing several of the other warped scientists hiss and flinch with fury.

My mother had proved to be cleverer than them. More vengeful. They had been beaten by not only a woman, but a witch. Something anathema to their science. No wonder they'd been pissed.

"From what I read in her journal, you lot well and truly deserved whatever she and Herne cooked up to pay you back for your dumb-ass attempt to trap an Elder of the Courts." I mocked with a growling chuckle. "I mean, for a bunch of clever mortals, that was *stupid*."

But Dr Bremmer cackled a laugh that rang out in the chamber, sharp as broken glass. Not the response I was expecting.

"And yet here we stand. We **survived**. She knew not what we found in this place, this window to another universe, another reality. Only the worthy selected to understand its existence, and we swore to protect its secret even as we fought for our very lives." Dr Bremmer gestured at the breach, his hand tracing the air over the cage almost lovingly. Possessively. "And we were rewarded for our service. What science could not heal, we found answers from beyond her reach. Beyond the understanding of all lesser men and women."

"*He* spoke to me. Reaching between realities, connecting our world to the limitless beyond … *he* answered my darkest despair." The doctor crooned, and I felt the hairs on my arms rise. Ok, this *was* starting to get way creepy now. And who the fuck was this 'he'? "It was he who first showed us how to craft this hideaway, forestalling the ravages of time and slowing the grains of sand of our lives as they sped away. He who whispered secrets to me in his first voice, that I shared with my colleagues … my brothers and sisters. He who then blessed us with his second voice, teaching us. Showing us the truth of what we had to become. For we brothers and sisters have transcended, advanced far beyond the weak creatures we once were."

It is never good when mortals get involved with creatures of the Real, let alone the Beyond. If something had reached out through the breach, had heard Zarkof Bremmer's desperate begging to be saved, then

I had little doubt we were looking at an angel of mercy or a creature simply out to do its good deed for the day, to earn its merit badge.

No, this thing, this whisperer of secrets, this creature of different voices definitely did not have the well-being of a bunch of mortals at the heart of its concern. Far from it.

"So, what? This friend told you to start kidnapping innocent creatures? And, what, Herne and anyone with him was like the next step up? You'd got your amateur kidnapper badge and were going for the *utter villainous bastard* merit?" I had to have answers, to know if we were just dealing with a mad mortal who had stared too long into the Abyss and began talking to the supernatural version of a sock puppet, or if there was something much nastier that needed putting back in its box. "And me? You said you were ordered to deal with me? By this same thing, your 'special' friend? Which voice did he use, first, second or a whole new one of that fuckery?"

Dr Bremmer snarled angrily, so caught up in his rant that he didn't see I Was just goading him to get answers. One of the others, either Dr Corin Blasé or Eselle Monrose given they still looked a little like female mortals, tried to interrupt him but he hissed at them and they cowered back.

Easy to see who was in charge here, no matter his words about them being family. Bound together. His brothers and sisters … up until anyone challenged him.

Useful to know.

"To him, you are just an annoyance in his eyes, a troublesome flea to be quashed. Your fate was left to the foolish mortals who think themselves our masters, who know not that he speaks to them, through them as well." He hissed back at me, eel jaws gaping evilly. "Aging fools, thinking to command me. Us. They desire to use the science we discarded to extend their own miserable lives, in repayment for keeping our secret. Wishing to escape Death's jaws, but unworthy of *his* truth. The truth that has elevated us far beyond them. We bargain with them, allowing them to think they are in charge, that we are merely their servants as we once were. They turn a blind eye to our … forays, cover up the disappearances and we grant them a few more years, a handful of time for them to squander like all lesser lifeforms do."

Our fruitful conversation was interrupted suddenly by Cormac, coughing to clear his throat before speaking up as he hung on his frame. Voice rusty and pain-filled, but still clear enough for me to tell how pissed off he was.

"Thanks for confirming my suspicions. Sir Gerald Montgomery-Scott." He pronounced the name with a snarl of his own, eyes narrowed and jaw a hard line. "CIC of EO … Commander In Chief of Extraordinary Operations. My boss's boss. The old man. He's been diagnosed with terminal cancer, according to the rumour mill. Aggressive too. Turns out he'll do *anything* for a chance to live longer. Even deal with chimerians and rogue DOPA scientists."

"Yes, the old fool thinks the answer to avoid his own death lies in our failures. An easy man to fool, eager and desperate to believe anything I tell him." Dr Bremmer mocked, reaffirming my faith in mortals and the fact they'll do pretty much anything to stave off the inevitable. Even deal with fucked up creatures like the one standing in front of me. "But a necessary tool, to allow us to complete our mission. The reason for all this."

The altered mortal scientist waved one bony arm at the troll-hole they had built to house the rent in our dominion, the way through to the Beyond.

"And what's that then? You've got to tell us, it's in the rulebook." I quipped, knowing this was it. The root of all our problems, the knot I needed to untangle to bring everything crashing down. What was driving Dr Bremmer and his cohort to kidnap creatures across the Realms, what had led to me here, for everything that had happened to come to pass.

Including me having to end my own father's physical existence.

That fact still shook me, the memory all too bright and clear in my head. When we were out of this mess, safely back at home with everyone healed and hale, I reckoned I'd be needing some serious downtime to deal with *that* little matter, and what it meant for me. Just me, Bear, Sarah and several good bottles I'd been saving for a real shitty day.

But Dr Bremmer turned away and instead of answering me, he stalked with entirely the wrong sort of steps for a mortal's bone structure over to where Cormac hung. The hounds slunk away from him at his approach, cringing down and their weird eyes narrowing, telling me no matter that he controlled them, it was not from loyalty but through fear.

He didn't notice.

The scientist reached out and pulled the OPS agent's head back up from where it had slumped after he'd spoken, the effort to speak obviously draining his strength.

"I can sense your doubts, lycan. Your unspoken derision of the truth I have told you." Dr Bremmer hissed, mockery dripping from his jaws like acid. "Yet if what I say is untrue, then how do you explain this? We searched for suitable candidates for ... *recruitment* into the chimerian ranks, as per our agreement to secure their services. Men and women, children. Of all ages, those who met the original criteria for Operation Chimera."

"Yet none of the those we tested proved able to pass even the first test, the base requirement for creating a chimerian. Too weak, too sickly. Enfeebled from lives wasted and squandered." He explained, and I felt that cold sharpness in my gut, telling what something I did not want to hear. "None of them possessing the *conviction*, the single-minded devotion to see them through the first stage."

"But your friend here? Agent Cormac Smith? He has proven most resilient. A true candidate." He confirmed and I bit down on the snarl I wanted to loose. "Now that we know what we are searching for, my brothers and sisters and I should be able to find suitable candidates from the OPS' own ranks. Imagine, an army of chimerians once again operational, bound to our cause. We will be *unstoppable*."

"*He* ensured our success when we once again faced failure. He whispered to the foolish mortals, and sent us one of their own to prove where our sights should be set." Dr Bremmer hissed out a snicker of a laugh, eyes burning brightly. "Now do you see *his* majesty, in all that *he* has wrought?"

"Never … going to … happen." Cormac panted out the four words, sweat dripping from his face, eyes narrowed with barely contained fury. They'd tortured him, experimented on him and unless we stopped them, were going to turn him into one of the very monsters he was tasked to fight, to keep from ever causing harm to the innocents he protected.

Mortals always paid a price when they dealt with the Real. Gregory Allen had, and now it looked like Cormac Smith was headed the same way. And there was fuck all I could do about it right now.

"What cause? Why do you need a fucking army?" I growled instead, needing to have my answer. Only then could I fuck up whatever they were after, if I knew where I needed to poke a stick into which wheel.

Dr Bremmer let the agent's head fall, and turned back to me, grinning gruesomely.

"Our cause? *His* cause." He hissed, and motioned to the breach. "It is simple. We have been shown how broken our world is. How cruel and self-serving are the men and women in power, how selfishly they rule and impose only those laws that serve their purpose, benefit their own selves. And how the corruption has spread from our dealings with devils like those in your company. Those fair of face, but dark of heart."

He pointed a long, talon tipped finger at Manisha, standing tall and proud even though she had been disarmed, taken with the rest of us.

"We have forgotten the lessons of long ago, and fallen under the sway of these creatures and their false ways. So I have been chosen … *we* have been chosen to end it. All of it." His eel-jaws gaped, his eyes burning bright with madness. "And you, lycan, you made this possible. *He* told me that, his first voice whispering the truth to me."

"Behold, our chosen vessel. To usher in the new era …"

"Of death. And utter destruction."

Chapter 33

Dr Bremmer gestured and the shadows hanging in the air beside him rippled and drew aside like curtains.

Revealing what lay hidden beyond.

The Harrowed Queen.

She lay strapped to another frame, her inhuman form bound with silver and iron like Herne's had been. But there were other metal restraints binding her as well, ones which glittered with a violet shine that I had never seen before. Alien, something used to bind a creature from Beyond if I had to guess.

Her black skin was marked with multiple wounds, healed scars and damage that told me she had been in a serious fight, and not walked away unscathed. Some of the wounds looked fresh, only recently inflicted but others had had time to heal, meaning these might have come from when Herne and she met. When the Hunter tracked her down. I still had no real idea what Herne had been thinking, going after her alone, but I'd been told he'd taken on the responsibility of finding this thing as a fatherly act. To me.

I reckoned that said a lot about how much … or little Herne knew about being a dad.

She was naked, her breasts flattened under a strap wrapped across her upper body, and more straps wrapped wound her triple joined legs and hoof-like feet, crisscrossing over her elongated forearms and binding tight those clawed hands of hers. Other than that, she was unclothed for all the world to see.

But it was her expression that struck me, as she raised her head and those ropy tendrils that were her version of hair fell away from the face she had taken from Morgana when she was reborn from the Shadow Fae's very flesh.

Then, standing in the arena in Twilight, her eyes had *burned*. Aflame with the fury and alienness of the Harrowing, a thing not of our dominion, a creature of hunger and destruction without any recognisable consciousness behind. Simply a creation to wreak utter ruin wherever it was unleashed.

But now?

Now I read something utterly different in her eyes as she gazed across the distance at me. Something I *never* thought to see in those orbs of darkness.

Fear.

Whatever had happened after she fled Twilight, it had marked her. Badly. The Lords and Ladies of the Courts had hunted across the Realms for any trace of the would-be Queen, seeking her children that she had left in both Realms and destroying them utterly when they were found. Oberon had made it clear she was an utter abomination and needed obliterating down to the smallest molecules of her being, and even newly-returned Odin had not challenged that sentiment.

But she had vanished, back to the Beyond it was thought. Seeking something, aid maybe. Kin to bolster her forces for her return, to challenge for a place in our dominion. Or just to get away from the murderous pack of immortals hell-bent on her utter destruction.

Whatever the reason, it had been Herne who found her. But instead of slaying her, he had … what? Captured her? Escorted her back to the Wyld? Something had happened between them, leading to them both returning to his Court. In the image I had seen, she had not been his prisoner. He had gone alone, seeking her himself. Without his Hunt, without the warriors of his Court to slay her.

And now here she was, bound and broken. Filled with fear, with the knowledge of what the fuck Dr Bremmer had planned for her. And it scared her.

That terrified me.

"Behold our vessel. Our angel of deliverance." Dr Bremmer stalked over to where the Harrowed Queen ... Harry was bound. I noticed that as well as being tied to the frame, she had tubes running from under several of the bindings, which glittered from whatever substance filled them. So they were either pumping shit into her, or extracting from her like they'd done with Herne. I wasn't sure which would be worse.

The scientist turned serious *Frankenstein's monster* gently caressed the obsidian skin of her cheek, and Harry actually flinched. A mingling of the death of immortals and oh so powerful Morgana ... and she *flinched* at the thing's touch. That told me a lot, and none of it good.

"She is of the infinite, a shell awaiting only its true purpose. From *his* home. And *he* has decided this joining of our worlds is the perfect host. For *his* entrance, for his triumphant coming. To wipe away the unworthy, to heal all that foolish humanity and corrupt devils have ruined." He crooned, gesturing at himself and the other scientists. "Like us, melds of two worlds. We will be the Adams and Eves, the first ones of a whole new species. *Homo Gloriosus*, I shall call us. The Ones of Glory. And all lesser unworthy creatures will fall to darkness and be lost, those that we do not bless with the duty of service to us. As is only right. This curse I shall level on *you* this time."

I digested what he had said, letting it spin around my grey cells for a few moment before formulating my careful and considerate response.

"It's my honest opinion that you, mate, are fucking nuts. You know that?" I growled, shaking my head and pointing at the breach. "Anything that has been talking to you through that hole or whatever it is is *not* going to be helping you out of the goodness of its heart. If it even has one.

Things from the Beyond ... they're *alien*. They don't think like us, and definitely don't want what's good for you."

I waved a hand at him.

"I mean, take a fucking look at yourself! Whatever this thing is, it didn't *save* you. It changed you, from the man you were to ... I don't know what the fuck you are." I snarled even as Dr Bremmer eyed me with cold, glittering intensity. The sort of stare you find called *snake-like*. "Yeah, my mother cursed you. To die. Not to turn into ... this."

"It's no use, Morgan." Elspeth spoke up from where she stood beside Felix. I noticed something I'd missed from before, when I'd first seen them free of their cells. Both women wore metal restraints, glowing the same ivory sheen as the ones on Harry. The devices were fitted on their wrists, and I caught sight of similar clamps attached to their ankles, given both had been stripped of their footwear. I figured they were some sort of blocker to stop the witches using their magic, which made the fact Felix and I had spoken through our link even more odd.

"There's no arguing with him. He's wholly under that thing's influence." The witch told me, shaking her head wearily. Ellie normally tried to see the best in people, give them the chances they need to do the right thing. Not jump to immediate conclusions like I did. I think it was some sort of immortal wisdom Terra bestowed on her.

But with Dr Zarkof Bremmer, she wasn't wasting any effort.

"He's not the first to fall for the whole *agent of change* and *wipe the slate clean and start again* offer from a mysterious Power. The Nazis did when they thought Adolf Hitler was calling the shots, as did the Crusader Knights when they thought God spoke to them of *cleansing the infidel*. The French had their Bonaparte, whilst Russia had Stalin. All who spoke to *something* that offered them their dream of world domination." She continued, going to scrub her face but pulled up short by the manacles restraining her. I saw the wrist and ankle sets were connected, allowing only a limited range of movement. Someone *really* didn't trust witches ... go figure. "There's a whole mythos about beings who offer up such bargains to those foolish enough to listen. H P Lovecraft was credited for its creation, but it dates back a lot further than one lone mortal man."

"Cthulhu."

"Bless you." I snarked back, as the word meant nothing to me. "What's that when it's at home."

But it was Greg who answered, taking a step towards his love before stopping as an ominous growl erupted from the nearest shadow hound.

"Cthulhu. Supposedly a bunch of scary-arse gods called the Great Old Ones. Cthulhu is one of them, kind of like an octopus stuck on the head of a man with bat wings and weird slit eyes. You know, just your average tentacled horror." The guardian of the Goddess Terra commented dryly, stepping back slowly. The hound settled back, its lips curling over its jagged shark teeth once more. "The rest are pretty much what you'd imagine as gods of darkness and fear … tentacles, fanged mouths, too many eyeballs, copious amounts of slime or flaming balls of death. That sort of idiocy."

Dr Bremmer reared up to his unnatural height, eyes slitting and his mouth twisting in a rage-fuelled snarl, but Greg ignored him as he went on.

"If I remember, I think they're all supposed to be asleep or something, and Cthulhu is their priest with the alarm clock to wake them up. Or something. Except he can't, unless certain parameters are met. There's a whole bunch of them … Cthulhu, Azathoth, Nyarlathotep, Yog-Sothoth, Dagon. Loads more." The guardian continued, shrugging his shoulders. "When I was a detective, way back when, we arrested a whole family who thought the liar god *Nyarlathotep* was talking to them through a weird clay figurine they'd found on holiday in Eqypt. It convinced the father, the mother and two teenagers to kidnap and murder five complete strangers before we caught them. I remember all the stuff they had, the research and everything. We had to read the brief to help interrogate them for any more victims they might have had stashed away.

Took me weeks to stop seeing freaky shit in the mirror when I looked away, or shit in the shadows. Never went to Egypt either."

"Utter idiocy, but then idiots will believe anything."

"How *dare* you speak of what you do not know!" Dr Bremmer snarled, stalking forward From his group, I saw the hulking one, or who I figured to be Jurgen Blass - their old Head of Security, raise his hand and go to speak, but the enraged doctor simply slashed a hand in their direction. Shadows boiled in the air, rearing up then lashing out to knock his own people back a step, a slap down if ever I saw one. *"How dare you utter the sacred name!* I shall wrench the tongue from your mouth for such blasphemy!"

The warped scientist towered over the guardian, seething with rage, taloned hand raised to strike.

And that's when Greg suddenly smiled, and things literally went boom.

Chapter 34

A massive explosion rang out from above us, loud and sharp. I saw pulverised rock and metal burst from the tiers above and come raining down all around, even as sirens began wailing like screaming banshees.

The blood-hued lights flickered and died, even as the thrumming sound I'd grown so used to in the troll-hole went shockingly silent. Someone had pulled a plug, and it seemed to have fucked up a whole lot of things if the alarms were anything to go by.

The breach to the Beyond spasmed in its cage, and I couldn't help but think its constantly shifting pattern began to grow more chaotic, less fluid. Spikes erupting from it, as bloody violet light blazed all around it in a sudden corona of agitation.

Emergency lights flickered on a moment later, even dimmer than the red illumination of before, as Dr Bremmer snarled a curse, clenching his raised hand into a bony fist.

"What is happening! What have you done?!" He demanded, but it was one of the chimerians who answered him.

"They've either got accomplices we didn't find on the first sweep, or they set timed charges we didn't see." The grey man spoke matter-of-factly, even as he slid that long knife free from its sheath. Yeah, I knew this one, his South African tones all too familiar. "Whichever, they've done damage to the converters on level three. Maybe knocked out the relays completely. We've got maybe an hour, an hour and a half to fix what they've damaged or it'll be a cascade dump of all the energies you've routed from that … thing, like I warned would happen if something ever happened to the rig you had us build."

"Well, fix it then!" The doctor snarled, and the chimerian nodded before turning to motion to two other bug-suited soldiers.

But I ignored them, as Greg leant over to whisper to me.

"I needed him close. Remember the arena. What I did to you?" He told me quickly, and I realised whilst I'd been stringing out the doctor to learn whatever I could before I made any plans, my friends hadn't been idle. "It'll work the same. Sort of. But I can't control it like before. Everyone around me, up to five metres, they'll all be affected. You understand?"

The arena. Where Morgana had made Greg fight me, as her chosen Knight. Where I'd found out he had come back from the dead with a few tricks and gifts, one in particular that almost cost me my life.

He could switch off the supernatural stuff. Make anyone he faced mortal. Vulnerable.

This was going to get *messy*.

Dr Bremmer snarled as he reached over to grab at me, dragging me close as his eel jaws gaped and the stink of his breath washed over me.

"You will tell me what you have done. Who else is out there. Or I will begin feeding your companions to my hounds. Bit by bit. Whilst they still live!" He hissed, but I just grinned a wolfish smile and lifted one hand, single finger raised in a world-known gesture.

"Do it." I growled to Greg.

That weird unnatural sense washed over me, like someone had dumped a bucket of water over me. Cold, cold water. In the next breath, I realised I'd Changed, no longer able to keep my worgen suit in the wake of his greater gift. I was back as a mortal.

The effect on those around us was way more profound.

Dr Bremmer staggered back, his body spasming as if he'd been electrocuted. Nothing seemed under his control, as his limbs bent and twisted in all directions. Beside us, the nearby shadow hounds simply snuffed out, vanishing into black smoke with screaming yelps, as Greg's gift negated their very existence.

The chimerian with the knife and the two he called over to instruct, as well as two more of the bastards immediately started convulsing before crashing to the ground. Groans and screams erupted from within their helmets, as their altered bodies began to fail. Everything that wasn't theirs, bound to them unnaturally, all failing to function. I could only imagine the pain they were suffering … and grinned savagely at the comforting thought.

I waved my hands at our little group, shouting to be heard over the screams and blaring alarms.

"Don't ask. Just listen." I told them, seeing Trix about to do just that. "We're all mortal right now. No Real tricks, nothing supernatural. Just mortal. So let's grab some weapons and stop these insane fuckers from bringing a world-destroying entity into our backyard. And don't get shot!"

I saw movement from across the way, as two of the altered scientists hurled themselves at us from their small group. Either to aid their fallen leader, or simply seeking to kill us for whatever we'd done, I had no clue. Their twisted faces were distorted into snarling masks, their mouths gaping wider than any mortal mouth should and showing fangs lengthening from their jaws. Like snakes or something. I swear I could even see things moving on their backs, as if wings were growing.

But as soon as they crossed the invisible threshold of Greg's gift, they tumbled to the ground, their bodies convulsing and refusing to obey their commands. Shrieks of pain and screams of fury were ripped from their throats, the sounds making the moment that much sweeter to me as I loped to the table bearing our gear.

Janus reached it a moment later, the big half-troll looking decidedly odd with mortal skin and softened features. He was still big, still heavily muscled, but looked fragile compared to his normal self.

"When this is done, you and I have little talk." He grunted at me, reaching to pluck his axe up as well as the spare handgun we'd taken from the dead chimerians. "And this thing? Better not be permanent, or we have *bigger* talk."

"It's a date," I told him with a grin before nodding to the remaining chimerians outside of Greg's influence. "Just don't get shot, ok?"

"Ha. Take more than these weird bug men to take me down." He grunted with far too much self-confidence in his own indestructability to stay safe.

Greg reached the table and he pulled his sword and stun baton free. As I strapped on my weapons, I looked across at the guardian, seeing his expression fixed in fierce concentration. So this was something he had to focus on to make happen. Good to know. We needed him conscious and unhurt, to keep the nulling affect going.

"I can't keep this up much longer." He told me as I passed him the other pistol we'd taken from the dead grey man. Woman. Whatever. He had proven to be an excellent shot, and was more comfortable with firearms than I was anyway. "So if you have a plan on how to get us all out of here now I've stirred the hornet's nest, I'd appreciate if we got on with it smartish."

"How did you know when things were going to go bang?" I queried, knowing there was far too much coincidence to the two events to have happened randomly. Yeah, I'm a suspicious bastard but life has taught me that's no bad thing.

"Because *I* told him." A voice whispered in my ear and I gripped the table hard, pushing down the urge to spin and punch the figure who appeared beside me. Smiling brightly.

Puck.

"Merry met, good companions." She quipped with a laugh, as she looked around the room. "It looks like matters progress much as I expected. We had best be quick if we wish to ensure success of this venture, with everyone unharmed that we wish that way."

Bloody Ivory sarcastic bloody fae.

Gunfire cracked out, and I ducked instinctively. But there was no impact nor splash of acid. Instead, there were cries of alarm from the untouched chimerians, those atop the first level looking down on us. Guards, watchful for any reason to open fire with their large bore rifles. But my eyes immediately spotted one slumped figure, acid having eaten through the shattered faceplate and into the head underneath. Whilst another chimerian took aim and laid down covering fire at those others still standing.

"Hunter." Puck confirmed as she quickly handed out weapons to the rest of the group as they hurried over. "I presumed we had best have at least one useful asset located in their ranks, to sow discord and confusion when we broke you from your captivity."

"But … how the fuck did he …" I remembered the size of the shapeshifter, and there was no way he'd have been able to squeeze himself into one of the squat, beetle suits. Unless … "Oh fuck. You mean he … ate …?"

"Just enough to take one of their forms, yes." She replied lightly, then shrugged. "However I believe he mentioned something about *a bonus for services rendered outside of his agreed parameters.* Chowing down on a mortal soldier blended with several Real creatures through perverted science and magic, and of … let's say … vintage years did not seem a particularly enjoyable act for him, no matter his racial habits."

Ellie and Felix had joined us with stumbling steps, Greg wrapping his arms around the red-haired witch as soon as she drew close. Felix thumped her head into my chest, something between a sob and a groan escaping her lips as I gave her a comforting hug.

"God, I am so glad to see you, you great lump! For real." She told me, looking up at me. I could see the tear tracks through the grime on her face, the evidence of her suffering since she had been taken. And I would make those bastards pay for every moment she and Ellie had been their captives. "It's been torture, not knowing if you were alive after the ambush … then finding you … then losing you again. What took you so long?"

"You're in a troll-hole. Time moves differently here. Slower." I replied as I grabbed hold of the restraints around her wrists. The metal was foreign to me, greasy under my fingers and there was no way in hell I'd be able to break it whilst I was just a mortal. Affected by Greg's gift. "I'll explain everything when we're out of this lunatic asylum, and safe."

"You'd better." She told me with a rough edge to her voice, a crackle of the new Felix, witch-in-training. I had to remind myself occasionally that she wasn't just the young woman I'd known from making friends with her father, and had had to carry home from partying beyond her curfew on more than one occasion.

Those had been simpler times. Safer times.

Another person paying the price for coming into contact with the Real.

With everyone re-equipped, we quickly overturned the tables where our gear had been shoved and spread out to give the remaining chimerians less of a large target to aim at. Three of their number were down, two of them writhing in the grip of whatever meltdown Greg's gift was causing them. The third, the bastard with the knife, had managed to get onto his hands and knees and was slowly crawling away from us with snarls of pain echoing from his helmet.

Alongside them, the two malformed scientists were still screaming and writhing on the floor, as their mortal bodies rejected whatever changes had happened to them. For his part, Dr Bremmer was slumped on the floor near the breach, shaking as if in the grip of a high fever, uttering gasping breaths from his gaping eel jaws. Saliva and blood dripped from the spiked teeth where he had bitten through his own flesh, in the grip of so powerful a shift *back* to his once self.

Why they hadn't fully changed like me or those members of my group had, I didn't know. I was a mortal right now and the half-bloods were all altered as well, appearing as mortal versions of themselves. Manisha remained herself, an Ivory fae, but I could tell she was suffering from the weird effect Greg was able to project, clenching and unclenching her hands and breathing deeply to calm herself.

Trix seemed the most horrified of what had happened, running her fingers over herself and staring at her own hands with an expression I could only explain as revulsion. She and her brother now were smaller, plumper versions of themselves, with pale pink skin that looked like it needed a healthy dose of sunlight, and no trace of their Shadow fae heritage to be seen. Except dark eyeliner and a possible goth-girl caste to her makeup.

Gunfire cracked out, and we ducked as acid splashed out to eat into the metal and stone from each strike. On the next level, Hunter had downed another chimerian, but the remaining three stationed there were concentrating their gunfire on his position, forcing him to duck for cover now that his ruse was exposed.

Below, that left four chimerians beyond the range of Greg, with the four remaining altered mortals untouched as well. And Harry, strapped to her frame, jerking at her restraints uselessly. She was still caged, still bound to the breach and whatever mad plan Dr Bremmer and something from the Beyond had cooked up where she was the sacrificial lamb.

Oh, and not to forget the ticking clock, a countdown to when we all were truly fucked. From a catastrophic meltdown caused by Mother's personal brand of exotic explosives destroying or severely damaging the controls keeping whatever bled from the Beyond in check. The breach was growing more frenzied, shivering and shaking with jagged splits erupting at its outer edges … growing closer and closer to the cage crafted around it. I had no idea what would happen if the breach broke free, but I figured the best place to find that out would be as far from the thing as possible, putting as much distance between us all as I could.

We just needed a little luck. To get out of this immediate mess in one piece, and deal with all the fuckery that was threatening to spill out into all-out apocalypse.

Not much to ask.

I *should* have known better.

Chapter 35

Gunfire hammered all around us, as the four chimerians sought to pin us down and put a stop to whatever we were doing to their comrades, their employers. None of them had identified Greg as the one they needed to shoot, so they just fired off shots with their rifles and handguns in the hope they hit the right person and stopped whatever it was we were doing to them.

Janus, Trix and Dix were huddled behind one overturned table, bits of it having been chewed apart by acid strikes, whilst Manisha and Mother crouched nearby, partially protected by some cargo crates dumped and left once their contents was removed.

That left me, Greg, Ellie and Felix since Puck had vanished off into Gods knew where again. Probably seeking to avoid the effects of the guardian's anti-supernatural aura, since of all of us I figured the sharp tongued and all-too-full-of-herself Ivory spy would hate being made mortal the most.

Turns out, I was dead wrong on that. Close, but still no cigar.

"Urgh! I can't stay like this any longer!" Trix screamed out, ducking as another shot shattered the table near her head. "It's not enough these fuckers are trying to kill us, but what the hell have you done to me and my brother!?!"

She drew out her knives, holding them professionally but cringing at the sight of her wrong-coloured skin, her softened physique.

"I'm going to gut these bastards, then someone better turn us back to how we were, or they're next!" She snarled, before hurling herself up and out from behind the table's protection.

Dix tried to grab her, pull her back to safety, but she slipped from his grasp with ease.

It seemed, unfortunately, that was *all* she was able to do with ease. Turned out her quickness and agility were born from her Shadow fae blood. Which Greg had momentarily robbed her off. Her mortal side definitely hadn't blessed her with any amazing agility. In fact, pretty much the reverse.

Her foot slipped on some spilled fluid on the rock floor, and she stumbled almost as soon as she was clear of the table. She windmilled, struggling to keep her balance as she slid and staggered like she was drunk. Exposed, in full view of the chimerians who waited beyond the boundary of the nulling field.

I saw one of them swing its gun round, the rifle's muzzle pointing right at the off-balance half-fae. Dix saw the danger, shouting out to his sister and rising up to go after her, but Janus shoved him down as more shots erupted along the table's length, shattering chunks off it.

Trix turned, her eyes wide, mouth already forming the words that were going to be her last ones. Looking back at us, at her brother.

"*Oh shi…..*" She screamed, as the gun barked.

Manisha appeared from behind the crates, reaching out with one arm to shove the woman away, out of danger. The Knight couldn't summon her armour, but simply threw herself at Trix. Hurling her to the side, without thought to her own safety.

As the bullets shattered over her outflung arm, impacting and discharging their deadly payload.

The acid bathed the weakened Ivory fae's skin, burning through cloth, then into the flesh beneath. The Knight snarled out a string of curses as she stumbled, but grabbed at Trix's collar and yanked her in the direction of cover with the one arm she still had that worked. The pair sank down behind the crates, Trix breathing in short, sharp bursts whilst Manisha dug her fingers into her burned, wrecked flesh and cursed even more loudly. I caught the stink wafting from the wounds, and met her eyes as she took several deep breaths … then clenched hard.

The remains of her left arm thumped to the ground, even as she ripped free some material from her undershirt and scrubbed her wrapped hand against her trousers to wipe off the acidic residue. The wound had cauterised itself, so little blood flowed from the severance, but I bit back down on acid of my own at the sight of the Knight's shoulder. Where until moments ago a whole arm had been.

Fuck.

In the next breath, Puck appeared out of thin air, long curved knives unsheathed in her hands. She was behind the chimerian who had shot Manisha, and her eyes blazed with righteous fury as she jammed the wicked blades under the bulbous helmet with all her inhuman strength.

Blood fountained from the rent armour, gouting out over the soldier's chest. But the fae wasn't finished, sawing the knives' edges through flesh and bone until the body dropped away with a crash, leaving the head balanced on the two blades. Severed, with ragged bone showing amongst the pumping spurts of blood.

She snarled, tossing the gory trophy aside as she whirled to face the surviving grey men. Who took one look at her feral expression, and the body of their comrade at her feet, and all came to the same conclusion. This was a cluster fuck, and nothing they needed to waste any more lives over. As one, the three soldiers loosed a barrage of bullets at Puck, at us, at the whole room and fled.

The remaining four warped mortals, scientists and security guard, snarled and hissed with fury but fear glittered in their bulging eyes as they took in the sight of their soldiers fleeing, the dead sprawled on the floor. Their leader at our mercy, unreachable. And then they fled too, howling as they darted back towards open doorways in the lowest chamber.

That left the chimerians up on the walkway, but the Ivory fae spy shot me a savage smile as she *licked* the blood from her weapons and vanished, reappearing with devastating swiftness behind the soldiers as they focused their fire on Hunter. Blood slicked through the air as the fae carved into them, leaving two dead and the last one fleeing down a side tunnel firing their rifle to ward her off.

The bloody fae was *enjoying* herself.

I pushed myself up as I realised there was no-one shooting at us anymore. The bastards had fled, leaving Dr Bremmer and the other two warped scientists at our mercy, along with three of the chimerians …

Two. Even as I checked, I found the one with the knife missing. He must have escaped when our eyes were on Trix and Manisha, dragging his altered body clear of the effects of Greg's field before *retreating to a more favourable position* as well.

I wanted the bastard for what he'd done to me and Jessica, but I had more pressing matters to deal with. One, in fact that I wasn't letting escape me.

I strode over to Dr Bremmer, hauling him up with all my mortal strength. Whatever had been done to them, the changes to their bodies, it had left them hollowed out. A shadow of themselves, and I found I could hold up the doctor with little strain even with my weakest suit's muscles.

"You've lost. Your allies are dead or run off to hide someplace. So give me the antidote." I snarled into his weird as fuck face, seeing his eyes wide with fear and horror, his hands scrabbled at my arms as I shook him. "Don't speak, just fucking do it or I *will* tear you apart to find it. Do it!"

He hissed and cursed, but flinched as I freed one hand and clenched it into a fist, raised to strike. I *wanted* him to resist, to give me an excuse to pulverise him for all the shit he had caused. What his madness had led to. Actually, I knew I didn't even need one … but Felix was watching me with those dark eyes of hers, and I knew in the moment that one of us had to do things the right way, not just what would make me feel a whole lot better.

With one of his own taloned hands, he scrabbled at his clothing, reaching for the pocket where the vial was stored. His body still shook, still refusing to function properly as Greg's gift bled all the supernatural powers and strength from him.

I had it. The cure to heal Jess. The bastard behind the kidnappers. My friends were safe. Fuck it, we'd done it. All I had to do was get us away from here, and work out what to do with the fuckers who had caused so much hard, done so much damage in their twisted desire to see the world pay for their own pain.

All I had to do was …

"Morgan Black. Son of Herne ne Eachthigheirn. Child of Black May. I summon you."

The words rang in my head, sharp and loud like clambering bells.

The Morrigan's voice, summoning me.

"Oh you have got to be fucking kidding me!" I snarled out loud, shaking my head and thumping one hand to my ear as if that would stop the noise. "No fucking way!"

"Morgan Black, child of my child. Blood of my blood. I summon you!"

I could feel the power of her summons dragging at me like a whirlpool's grasp in the ocean, even as Greg and Ellie looked over, surprise and shock mirrored on their faces. Felix reached out to grab hold of me, but her fingers somehow slipped *through* me, as if I was smoke.

"Morgan Black. Knight of the Shadow Court, by your allegiance to Madb, Queen of Shadows … I summon you! Thrice called, you WILL answer!"

And just like that, I was someplace else.

Coldness hit me like a physical blow, stealing my breath for a moment as I fought the urge to shiver. The light had changed, brightening from the dullness of the emergency bulbs in the troll hole to something like daylight but sharper. Edged in cool blue.

Ice.

Black and blue hues shimmered on all sides, reflected off a myriad of facets, sharp edges and fracture lines. This was Superman's Fortress of Solitude if he had ever thrown in the *good guy* towel and gone seriously to the Dark Side. And then employed a bunch of goths to outfit his new abode.

Ragged banners hung from poles crafted of whitened bone, splintered from weapon blows or teeth. Blood stained the cloth in mismatched patches, some massive splashes whilst others were just thin rivers or specks. All spoke of tokens taken in battle, wrenched from the dying grip of someone's enemy and displayed as a reminder of the victories, the dead left behind to rot and ruin.

Alongside these were the broken weapons taken as spoils of war. Massive swords of all design, curved axes meant to carve flesh not wood. Wolfhead hammers like the one I knew Manisha had taken from an ogre who challenged her authority … resulting in much pain on his side, and her gaining a new toy to play with.

Manisha. Her arm. The memory of what had just happened stung me. I knew she was an Ivory fae, able to shrug off injury that counted as *mass destruction* for mortals, but it had shocked me to see her so badly hurt. Whatever the fuck was going on here, I needed to end it quick and get back … to stop anything else bad happening to my companions, my friends.

Here. I put all the ice and damaged weapons and gory trophies on display together, and came up with one simple conclusion.

I was in the Shadow Court.

Mabd's home.

This was not good.

I stood on a platform of raised ice, steps leading down to a large open arena carved from more frozen water. No effort had been made to make the footing any less treacherous than black ice was normally, no rugs thrown down, nothing to get a good grip on. If you did not have the grace and balance of the fae, you were royally fucked if you had to step onto that skating rink.

Tiers rose on every side, and filling these were the minions of the Shadow Queen. Every fae and Real critter of the Court, horrors of every fairytale and old wives' story, jostling and snapping and snarling at each other … even as their attention focused solely on me.

Across the way, over the other side of the arena, a single raised dias stood with steps leading up to its flattened top. And on this a single throne stood, carved from bone and ice, looking like *the* most uncomfortable item of furniture ever developed. Arching over it was the skull of an elder dragon, so huge that it could have opened those jaws in life and swallowed a double decker bus without flinching. Its gaping, hollowed eyes glittered with blue-green fire, given it a semblance of life that warned me the thing wasn't as dead as it looked.

And under it, sitting sprawled bonelessely atop the throne, sat Madb. Clad in her dark funeral rags, still the size and aspect of a child. With long straggle hair knotted and twisted into dreadlocks of every shade of a bruise, her porcelain-ash skin stark against the clothes she wore.

And her dark eyes were fixed on me as well, even hidden as they were behind a sweep of fetish-tied locks.

"Morgan Black." The Morrigan spoke up from beside me, standing like the scariest scarecrow in the world. Leaning on her spear and clad in her armour and raiment of war. Her dark eyes also gazed upon me, and her expression was typically inscrutable for a fae. Tow of her bodyguards perched on her shoulders, transformed into crows with blood-red eyes and ugly purple tongues which they waggled at me as they both opened their beaks to hiss.

"What the fuck's going on?" I asked her with as much tact as I could manage, still raw from being pulled from the troll-hole to the Real.

On television shows like Star Trek they make translocation look easy and comfortable, but right now it felt like someone had scrubbed me from head to foot with itchy wire wool. And then splashed on some vinegar to *sooth* me.

The Morrigan looked across at me with those dark, bottomless eyes of hers and I felt a sinking feeling. There was no sardonic smile, no sharp quip at my obvious failings … none of the usual banter I 'enjoyed' with my grandmother, on Herne's side. Instead, she was ice cold.

Chill as death.

She slammed the butt of her spear down onto the ice three times, each time the cracking sound echoing out across the arena. Stilling the Court, so that all of the gathered creatures grew silent. Watchful.

"Morgan Black." She intoned solemnly, sending another chill down my spine that had nothing to do with the temperature around us. "Knight of Shadow. You are summoned to appear before Madb, Queen of the Shadow Court. To answer for Her Majesty's displeasure, to atone for your grievous contravention of the sacred oath that binds you to her."

She shot me a hard look, dark fire burning in those orbs of hers.

"To suffer your punishment, as is only right."

Fuck, things had just gotten a *whole* lot worse for me. Terminally so, maybe.

Chapter 36

Someone, somewhere was having a right bloody laugh at my expense.

It was the only explanation for how I could be standing in the Shadow Court, about to be punished by a psychotic fae for reasons most likely all in her own head, and as detached from reality as they could possibly be.

"Look, I don't have time for this!" I snarled, glaring first at Madb, then back at the Morrigan. "I had the bastard. The one who poisoned Jessica, who tried to have me killed. Who kidnapped and *fed on* Herne, for fuck's sake! Send me back, so I can finish that shitshow before the fucker slips away!"

"You are in no place to demand anything, pup." The Morrigan told me dryly, resting on her spear. "The Queen has summoned you, and here you will stay until she is satisfied your punishment has been served."

"Didn't you hear me?" I growled, facing off against my fae grandmother. The Mistress of War herself. "This bastard *fed* on Herne. Your son. He had him staked out, drained and fucking dissected! I had to … I had to do what he asked. His final bloody wish. Don't you *care*?"

The Morrigan met my anger with frigid control, not a muscle twitching on her face as she looked at me for a long moment, before replying.

"What you speak of is a matter of blood. *This*, this is a matter of duty." The Elder fae instructed me even as growls and snarls echoed from the tiers on all sides. The Court was growing restless, but none dared raise their voices too loud, with all eyes switching between the silent

Queen and I. "You will learn that there is a time to listen to your blood. When to accept who you are, what you are. Here and now, you are about to be taught a different lesson."

"One of duty. One of consequence."

The Morrigan left my side, walking down the ice steps without even a waver or slip, effortlessly balanced. She stalked to the centre of the arena, and bowed low to Madb sitting on her throne. Then the Shadow Herald turned back to face me.

"Knight of Shadow, you are brought here to answer for your crimes." She repeated loudly, her voice echoing around the chamber. "But before these are voiced, you have not yet properly greeted your Queen."

Madb shifted on her seat, raising her head and shaking back the dreadlocks to lock her eyes onto mine. I felt the weight of an Elder being press on me, a being old beyond ages, and of terrifying power.

She spoke one word.

"Kneel."

A simple command, one little word. But backed by just a shred of her might, it felt like she had dropped a mountain on my shoulders. My legs quivered, muscles protesting as I locked them tight, back popping loudly as I squared myself up and gritted my teeth.

"I don't kneel to *anyone*. You know that." I snarled out my reply, letting my beast fill me with strength. A touch of the Wyld on me, that savagery gifted me by my father. Yet it felt different this time … altered somehow. Stronger, more savage than before. I knew my eyes burned yellow now, as I resisted the urge to Change just yet. Let them see me as a mortal, standing tall.

Well, tall-ish. Even I couldn't help but hunch under the strain, as Madb added another drop of her bottomless might to the effort, to make me bend. Make me prostrate myself before her.

"Not. Going. To Happen." I snarled, muscles burning.

The sensation of being squashed under a giant's foot held for a moment longer, then vanished. Yet instead of looking upset at my defiance, Madb wore a sickle of a smile. Pleased beyond herself, which quelled any confidence I felt at resisting her.

"See. You will not even show proper deference in front of the rest of the Court. You belittle your own Queen." The Morrigan told me pointedly, but I shook my head, not taking my eyes off Madb.

"You gifted me this knight-schtick, this *bond* to the Shadow Court." I reminded the two Shadow fae, ignoring everyone else. They weren't my problem. Yet. "I never asked for it, never sought it for myself. You gave it to me. So I'll show *due deference* to the Queen of the Shadow Court when she quits playing silly buggers with me, and stops wanting to use me to show off how powerful she is. I'm no-one's stress doll, and I don't like being squeezed."

Whispers echoed round the Court, even one or two snickers of laughter, until Madb casually raked her eyes over the gathered monsters. Silence settled back in like a heavy drape, everyone and everything freezing under that ice cold lash.

"Speak on, Herald." She instructed the Morrigan, who nodded once.

"Knight of Shadow." The Herald was obviously acting as the prosecution's lawyer, Madb not deigning herself to tell me what I'd done to piss her off this much. It figured … I might have been treated a little differently by some members of the Courts recently but deep down to the bone, to most of them I was just a Redcloak. A mutt. Third rate citizen. And to be treated accordingly.

"Did you or did you not discuss the existence of Shadow fae working in the Ivory Court recently with members of said Court?" The Morrigan enquired coolly, and I felt my stomach lurch. That bloody thing again.

Of course it would come back and bite me *twice*. Not good enough Manisha had gotten pissed finding out I knew about the planted spies but …

Hold on. I'd been in an Ivory wayhouse at the time we spoke …

"How the hell did you know … ?" I started before logic caught up and knocked on my skull with steel-toe cap boots. "Shit. You have spies, and spies *on* spies. The ones who owned up and buggered off were the obvious ones, sacrifices that probably expected to be killed in the event they were found out … leaving your deepcover buried and undetected. Hell, did one lot even betray the others to keep their cover? That's cold, even for you lot."

The Morrigan shook her head, her rune-twisted braids clashing softly.

"It matters not. You spoke, and confirmed the knowledge of the Queen's pawns in the Ivory Court. Betraying her trust, betraying what it means to be a Knight of her Court." She told me but it was my turn to shake my head.

"Uh, no way." I tried a rebuttal. Maybe I should have shouted *objection!* "Firstly, all I did was acknowledge that a body I came across whilst investigating the theft of *Excalibur* from the Ivory Court turned out to be under some sort of glamour. Pretending to be one thing, whilst being another. I didn't … I still don't know of any more spies *your* Queen has slipped into her cousins' home without them knowing. And I don't want to know."

"Plus, if we're talking about what it means to be a Knight of any of the Courts," I added with a snark, shrugging. "So far all that looks to require is a desire to beat the living shit out of anything that pisses off the Lord or Lady who commands you. Nothing in the fine print about keeping secrets that you didn't even know were secrets in the first place!"

"Ignorance is no excuse in this matter, even such as deep and all-encompassing as yours continues to be." The Morrigan shot back at me, earning a few more chuckles around the Court. "The fact is, you spoke of matters you should not to individuals who at times have been considered the Queen's foe. And will again, no doubt."

"Moreover, the Queen has requested your presence and your skills on multiple occasions. When situations have construed to require a Knight's talents to resolve a matter of import." She continued, her dark eyes narrowing. "I have born missives to you, and you have denied your Queen's request, and put your own business before hers."

I scowled, remembering the Morrigan's warning in *Good Deed's* office, where she had summoned and controlled agonising pain through the Shadow brand I wore. She'd told me then that Madb was losing patience with my inability to drop everything every time she whistled.

"That business you say I put before hers?" I queried, letting my tone tell one and all what I felt of this accusation. Not impressed. "Would you be speaking of the time I had to drop everything to go stop Oberon from killing Titania whilst under the influence of Morgana? Where, in fact, you sent me anyway? Or the time I had to haul arse into Twilight to stop Morgana from fucking up all the Realms so she could play Queen of the Hill over all our rotting corpses?"

The fae went to reply, but I held up one hand.

"Or, and this is probably my favourite, when Madb decided I should be the next Lord of the Wyld when Herne disappeared. Her pawn on the throne, so she could control that Court too?" I enquired, and heard more than one indrawn breath around the chamber. It was one thing the Courts working against each other to further their own power but it was never spoken of. Never a light shone on one of their plays for power. That was simply not done. "Is that what's got her knickers so in a twist? That I put my half sister on the throne instead, and let Wyld look after itself?"

I knew I'd gone too far with the knickers comment as the Morrigan shook her head slowly, turning to look back at her Queen and giving one simple shrug. That was all it took.

Madb rose from her throne slowly, stepping to the edge of the dais to face me. She still was only four feet tall, but her shadow stretched far and high behind her, a monstrous creation that in now resembled her child-like form.

Then she addressed me.

"Knight, my Herald has told you of the offenses you face, and you have denied none of them. Given no good cause for your actions or shown us another truth than the one we know." She told me, her voice skipping along like she was singing a nursery rhyme. One of the old ones, involving blood and bones. "My Herald has told you that I brought you here for one purpose only. To learn a lesson … that of duty, and of consequence."

"That lesson is now due."

I took a breath, calming myself as I stared back at the fae Queen. Time was ticking away, the longer I let this drag out the further Dr Bremmer would have as a headstart to escape, or of bad things to happen to my friends I'd left behind in the troll-hole. I had to get this over with, and maybe the path of least resistance was the way to go …

"Fine. I offer you my apologies for the disservice I have done you, whether intended or not." I tried to make the apology sound as formal as I knew the fae of the Courts loved to be, even though it sounded like something from Shakespeare's woeful attempts at prose before he got the right thread. "If there is a punishment I must suffer, let's get it over with."

Reaching up, I pulled my Ivory top layer over my head, stripping down to only the leggings and boots. The cold bit at me, but I refused to Change, even though fur would be bloody useful right now. Let them deal with me at my weakest. And I'd *still* walk away from here.

"What's it to be?" I enquired, looking around for a fae or Real creature dressed for the part of doling out punishment. Black hood, various implements of torture hanging off their belt … that sort of thing. Maybe she'd get that freaky Boogey Man she used as a jailor to mete out what she had in mind … he looked the part even on his best day. "Forty lashes of the whip? Water-boarding until I'm almost but not quite drowned? The rest of your Knights getting to put the boot in and break a few bones for my impertinence?"

The Morrigan sighed quietly.

"Even when you try to make things aright, you have no control over that tongue of yours." She quietly told me. "Remember what I told you. There is a time for duty, and a time for blood."

Madb raised a hand and the Herald quietened.

And the Queen smiled.

Possibly one of the scariest things I'd seen in a whole, trust me.

"No, Knight. I have nothing so banal in mind." She told me, and made a simple gesture in the air.

The air at the sides of her dais melted away, and I felt my heart stop in my chest.

On the right-hand side, a cell was revealed. Of ice and bone, the bars wide enough for me to see what … who stood inside. Encased in bonds of ice, and with spears of the jagged, razor-sharp stuff growing inwards towards them from every direction.

Sarah. My mortal love.

She was held in an awkward position, the ice holding her bending her so she was arched backward, arms bent behind, legs spread as if she was intending on doing squats. But her head faced forward, and she looked at me with plain and simple terror writ across her gorgeous features.

On the left, a much large cell squatted. Within, a large form was held upright by manacles of ice and chains of bone, tight enough around each limb to hold the heavy creature in mid-air despite its bulk. Resting just above a nest of frozen spikes, twisted and corkscrewed to cause the most amount of pain when entering a body plummeting down on them in the grip of gravity.

Bear.

My trollhound also faced forward, and his great head sagged with pain and weariness, but his eyes were fixed on me. The stubby ears perked up, and his jaws gaped to pant out a single whine of greeting.

Fuck.

Fuckity fuckity fuck fuck fuck!!

"What the … ?" I snarled out the start of my question, but stopped as Madb's brow creased in a frown. Immediately, the spikes in Sarah's cell grew, slipping closer to her bare skin, brushing her unprotected flesh. And Bear dropped an inch as the chains slackened slightly, nearing the deadly spikes under him.

So I shut up.

The Queen smiled, nodding before speaking.

"As my Herald told you, this is a lesson. Of Duty. Of Consequence." She told me, laying a hand on her heart and pointing at me.

"Duty."

Then she waved her hands at my love and my trollhound.

"Consequence."

"What will come to pass this day, Knight is simply this." She slowly stepped down the dais, her ragged dress brushing the ice and making swishing sounds. "You must choose. You have earned my wrath, but I *choose* not to punish you directly. You are of still use to me, and I need you able to function at your best."

"No, you will learn of the consequence of your actions this day, and carry the pain you are owed for the rest of your life." She stopped at the bottom step, motioning. Bulky figures issued out of gaps between the seating on either side of the arena, to stomp across the ice and form up between us. Knights, I had to think, in their black ice armour. Gnarled hobgoblins, hulking ogres, lithe fae. The *other* Knights of her Court, lined up to place themselves between the Queen and I.

"You must choose, Morgan Black." Madb told me, her voice dripping acidic pleasure, and I felt my world end as her words crashed over me. "One must die. Your mortal lover, or your beloved companion. Only one can you save."

"Choose, and the matter will be settled between us."

"Just … choose."

Chapter 37

I looked from Madb's malevolent, hungry expression to the Morrigan's cold, implacable stare.

"You have *got* to be shitting me." I told them both, fear warring with rage inside me. "This isn't … you're just playing with me. They're not really here. I left them safe and secure back in the Mortal Realm!"

The Morrigan shrugged, her lips finally crooking into a hard smile. Not one with any humour to it.

"You left them safe and secure behind wards writ by whom?" She reminded me, and I felt my stomach sink even lower, reality hitting me hard. "You are foolish indeed if you thought we would gift you wards of Shadow without any means for us to access your abode ourselves. I believe the mortals call it a *back door*."

She motioned to the prisoners. Bear dangling ever more closely to the spikes beneath him, Sarah stretching as far as she could away from the needle tips lancing into her skin.

"This is no trick. They are no glamour nor illusion. This is *real*." The fae told me, voice hard, tone dead. "You must make your choice, or both die. Whatever you choose, you will have to live with for the rest of your life, the pain your choices and decisions caused to be. This is on you, Morgan Black, so choose. And choose wisely."

"And quickly." Madb added, tapping one slim hand against her thigh. "I have little patience, and will take any sign of indecision or prevarication as your unwillingness to save even one of those you love."

This could not be happening. Just *not* happening!

I wracked my mutt brain for any way to win here, any way to manoeuvre Madb into letting them both go. Offering my service for the rest of my life, threatening to bring Odin down on her for putting a mortal he'd favoured at risk of death Bargain with her somehow. Anything …

Nothing would work. The Queen of Shadow wanted to see me hurt, have me suffer for my arrogance and flippant attitude towards her and the title she had bestowed on me. I'd been happy enough to use the Shadow mark, to call on the magic it gave me on more than one occasion … but I hadn't given enough thought to the price I'd owe her. And now she had called me to her, to collect.

In front of her Court, so that all would see the cocky Redcloak humbled.

Fuck.

The Morrigan was no help, siding with her Queen despite the fact we were basically family. This was duty, she'd said. *Learn that there is a time to listen to your blood,* she had told me.

My blood.

My mother, Margaret Black, would have been smarter. She would never have put herself in a position to piss off an Elder like I had. Or if she did, she would have had something to use, a bargaining chip to make sure she didn't suffer the Queen's wrath. I had nothing.

But my blood wasn't just hers.

And I had my answer. Insane, probably going to get me killed along with both Sarah and Bear. But there was a slim, almost minute chance I'd pull it off. And even if I didn't, I'd still be fucking with Madb's plan to have me suffer the loss for the rest of my life … because I wouldn't *be* alive.

The thought of living without either Sarah or Bear? Nope, wasn't happening.

So I shook my head and Changed, letting my wolfen suit settle over me. The cold wound down a notch, as I snarled out my rage, my fury.

"When my spear touches your throat, you'll release them both. And we'll all be free to go, and you won't *ever* threaten anyone close to me again." I growled out the words, keeping my eyes on the Queen, though I meant for everyone to hear what I vowed.

Madb looked at me, obviously unimpressed with my altered form, and smiled that devil smile of hers.

"But Knight," She commented with child-like innocence. "You have no spear."

I just grinned wolfishly, and held out my hand.

And recalled my father's dying words.

"You will have need soon enough. We are of the same blood. The beast is in both of us. Take mine. Use it wisely."

It was like the Lord of the Wyld had known the shit I was going to face, and given me one last gift. Father to son. A chance to win, when facing off against insurmountable odds. The sort of hunt he would have enjoyed.

The Hunter's spear … my spear … dropped into my hand as I called on it. Not magic, nothing mystical. Just a primal link between the weapon and I, forged in blood.

Madb eyed me, then gave one short, sharp nod.

And I attacked.

Throwing myself off the platform, I whirled the spear around and hammered into the first, very surprised Shadow Knight.

Mayhem ensued.

The arena erupted as creatures of the Court howled, bayed and screamed at the top of their lungs or other breathing apparatus. Mostly for my blood, some for other bodily parts I was very attached to, but some actually sang out my name. Supporting me. There are always those that go for the underdog, and here and now, I was the most under dog of them all.

The other Knights of Shadow were a mixed bag of the monstrous and beautiful, the duality of Madb's Court showing even in her choice of armoured murderers. Two ogres loomed over the bunch with twisted faces ruined by battle scars or possibly self-mutilation … you never knew with creatures of the Real. One had a massive jutting tooth that was more a tusk as it erupted from its bottom jaw and almost touched the bottom of the eye of that side. Which was missing, just a gaping hole where an orb should roll. The other looked like it had been slapped in the face by a porcupine, spikes erupting from its skin but pointing outward. Its piggish eyes glared at me from behind the forest of thorns, burning with animalistic hunger to do violence unto me.

Down at my level, three hobgoblins, taller than the ones I'd seen guarding the Lord and Lady of London Lower. These were hulking brutes of their kind, with blue-black skin adorned with tribal tattoos. Possibly related as there was something similar in the markings across their faces.

Two slim fae were dressed in full plate armour of black ice-metal, patterned with swirls of silver and blood. Both wielded massive swords, much like the weapon I'd seen Manisha or her Ivory Knight cadre use, but these bore cruel hooks and jagged edges. Just to make a blow from them all that much more painful.

Three naga completed the small company, their snake bodies clad in intricate mail carefully crafted so it in no way impinged on their fluid movements. Their dragon heads were encased in metal effigies of snarling behemoths, and their wielded long lances with more spiked and hooked points. Their eyes burned ferally in the sockets of their helmets, long tongues flicking out to taste the air as they slid easily across the ice.

Ten Knights, all of whom I had to assume had fought their way to their position unlike me. I could only guess at the barbaric and violent tests Madb would put candidates through to show their worth, but the sense I got from the gathered group was one of barely contained violence. Madness under tight control, but all to easy to snap when insanity would better suit them. *Berserker* rang in my head, the word effortlessly describing the sort of stability I should expect from them in a fight, or even just simply chatting over an iced latte.

So be it.

The spear in my had felt familiar, comfortable. Like I'd always had it, had trained with it all my life. There was life to it, an energy I felt from the ironwood haft, soaking into my skin as I spun and lashed out at the nearest Knight. One of the hobs.

It snarled a laugh, bringing its own weapon round to block the blow. A club fashioned from the massive bone from some long-dead foe, bandied with fae metal and studded with jagged shards of either obsidian or more Shadow-crafted steel. It had been imbued, glowing a dull violet to show it contained more strength than it ought to, and the hob grinned as it went to knock my strike aside and finish me quick.

The grin slipped from its face as my spear carved the weapon into shattered fragments, blowing out past it to pepper its companions with shrapnel. Even as it … and they howled, I twisted the spear and carved a bloody furrow deep into the Knight's lower chest. Herne's weapon, my weapon, had been forged with the singular purpose of being stronger than anything it faced, allowing the Hunter to hunt whatever he so wished.

Silver blood erupted as I disembowelled the hob, ripping the sharpened head free as its armour fragmented from the blow. It squealed, collapsing to the ice in a spreading puddle of gore which froze almost instantly. The injury was survivable for a creature of the Real, but it was out of the fight.

One down, just nine to go.

Howls erupted around the arena, the sight of spilled blood and a first 'kill' driving the Shadow Court into a frenzy. For their part, the other Knights all seemed to realise suddenly this wasn't going to be an easy victory, that the Redcloak wasn't just going to lie down and take his beating.

With grunts, curses and hisses they came at me, weapons swinging.

This was going to *hurt*.

Slipping one hand from the spear, I unsheathed my claws and parried all the blows I could whilst ducking and rolling away from the others. I *could* have summoned my Ivory armour, to let them hammer at that instead of my actual hide but some small part of my brain told me doing that would be a slap in the face that Madb would not ignore. I was in enough trouble as it was, without having her call down the *whole* Court on my furry ass.

I howled a curse as a swordblade slashed along my ribs, blood following a second later. Both ogres wielded massive hammers, the heads of which were easily double the size of my own and capable of crushing bone with even a glancing blow. Those I dodged and threw myself away from, even as I flicked my spear and my claws at the jagged spikes and blades wielded by the other Knights. The naga wove deadly circles with their weapons, snake-like fluidity granted them by their serpentine nature. The surviving hobs just hacked and slashed with fury, seeing one of their own taken down so easily only driving them to foaming fury.

But I had a fury of my own, and I drew on it until my veins burned with fire and my muscles screamed with the need to release, to simply *do*. Blood slicked down my bared, furry chest from sword and spear cuts, my arms were sliced until the skin was tattered and ribboned, but I slashed and hacked back with all my Wyld might, snapping my teeth onto the haft of one naga's spear as it foolishly drew too close.

The snake Knight tried to tug its weapon free, and for its stupidity, I buried my claws into its exposed throat, ripping and hacking through armour and flesh. More gore gouted out, even as I felt another spear point punch through my side, and the wounded naga rattled its agony as it slumped to the floor.

Two down, only eight more to go.

Ignoring my wounds, knowing they would knit together and let me pay them back for the pain later, I hurled myself into the Knight's midst, punching through their knot and smashing one hob and one fae from their feet. One ogre's hammer crunched to the ice an inch from my furry nose and I scrabbled on the slippery floor to stop myself ramming into the weapon, as the other fae darted in to try to bury its sword in my exposed back. Only with an inhuman twist was I able to block the blow, turning it aside so it only carved a fresh furrow in my ribs. For that, I punished the lithe figure by slapping my claws into its nearest foot. Armour bent and buckled then broke, as my four curved points raked through its flesh and bones.

The fae bellowed, hopping back as it dropped its sword, unaccustomed to being the one suffering pain. That left it open for me to ram my spear up into its groin, the sharpened head punching into and through the Knight like a hot knife through butter. Its bellows turned to high pitched shrieks as I ripped the weapon free and it collapsed with its hands clasping the gushing wound I'd left, as I rolled to avoid an ogre's foot intent on smearing me across the ice like jam.

Three down. Seven more.

I was bleeding from multiple cuts, with at least one serious wound in my side, another across my ribs. But I was still breathing, still had my weapons. Still had my rage, and that was all I needed.

Rising to my feet, I darted at the hobs as they grunted and gnashed their hog-like tusks in fury, forcing them to stagger back. But it was a feint, as I dodged back and using the ice as a slide, slipped beneath the long tusked ogre's smashing strike. I grabbed hold of its massively outstretched arm, levering myself up its mail clad body even as I felt one of the still unwounded nagas tear a rip down my leg with its spiked spear. Pushing the blaze of agony aside, I grappled up the ogre as it clumsily swung around, trying to hammer at me … but instead forcing its comrades to duck and shout out in fury as its weapon bludgeoned the space all around them.

Before its comrade could pluck me free, I spun the spear in my free hand and, like a massive dagger, plunged it into the nearest eye socket that I could reach.

The ogre roared, shaking the icy cavern as it staggered and gasped, dropping its hammer ... unfortunately onto one of the naga as the Knight slithered and slipped to try to get out of the way. The snake screamed as bones shattered, its thick tail flattened under the massive maul, even as I swung myself off the ogre's back with my full weight to pull my weapon free.

Blood fountained, gushing over the wounded beast's face and chest, as it tottered around in shock. Striking the ground, I dogged between its tree trunk legs and sliced the backs of its knees, the thick hide not covered by armour and peeling away under the edge of the spear. The ogre crumpled, its massive body falling after its own weapon, crashing down on the still hissing naga. That silenced its screams, the ogre convulsing as the snake Knight's spear punched up through its own guts and out of its back.

Five left.

The last ogre's maul came at me even as I was turning, catching me across the back and hurling me across the ice as my entire body blazed with pain. Definitely some broken bones, ribs grinding against each other, as I rolled. Somehow I kept hold of my spear as I slid to a stop, agony whiting out my sight for a moment. But I wasn't going to let a little pain keep me down, not when Sarah and Bear needed me.

Snarling all the curses I knew, I hauled myself upright, spitting out a mouthful of blood as I realised I'd bitten my tongue as I bounced. The Knights were coming at me, hoping to catch me when I was down, and I jerked aside to dodge one large sword intent on relieving my neck of the strain of bearing my head. The ogre was slowest, still lumbering behind, but the hobs were there with the one fae, and I couldn't get out of the way of their clubs as they smacked them down on already broken ribs. That earned them a scream of fury and pain as I drew on the font of Wyld might like a thirsty man sinking their first drink.

Something was different, the fury and beast inside me somehow stronger, darker. I almost bounced back to my feet with the surge of energy I felt filling me, the wildness driving me to let rip another howl that echoed around the cavern. Ignoring my grating bones and the feeling of blood soaking my back, I smashed into the hobs, ramming the spear into one's guts even as my jaws closed on the other's throat. Hot blood filled my mouth, sweet and flowery, so unlike the blood of anything from the Mortal Realm ... and I say that having dined on many a blue steak and the like ... as I ripped through flesh and tendons.

Both hobs gasped out as my spear ripped and carved its way through its body, and my jaws shredded anything between the last one's shoulders and jaw. They fell back, as I spat out a mouthful of gore, chest heaving as I faced the final three.

Only to snarl, as I saw movement behind them.

More Knights, filing out from where the first lot had appeared. Five, ten, twenty ... another thirty armoured Shadow Court killers. Ogres, fae and hobs, naga but now joined by slim sprites armed with jagged daggers, dour dwarrow cradling lances of fiery death and even a couple of minotaurs with their huge axes held ready to rend my flesh.

Madb's voice echoed over to me.

"It is foolish to enter a fray without setting the terms, of who you must best to win." She instructed me with cold delight. "It seems you to learn more than one lesson this day."

I shook blood out of my eyes, knowing the simple truth of it. The Queen of Shadow was perfectly in her rights to keep throwing Knights at me, since all I'd said was I would put my spear to her throat to win. Not who I had to go through to get to her.

No matter.

Both Sarah and Bear were looking at me from their icy prisons, my trollhound's expression one of frustration that he couldn't be with me, fighting. Sarah's one ... the pain and horror was writ on her face seeing the state I was in, but there was still the glimmer of hope I told myself I could read there, that I'd win through.

And for them both, I'd fucking move mountains, and end worlds.

"Fight!" Madb commanded, and the fresh, unwounded killers joined their comrades. All of them bellowing for my blood.

"Come take it then." I snarled, spear held ready.

Chapter 38

Hunter, call your hounds.

My mother's voice rang in my head, so sharp and sudden that I almost whirled to see if she had appeared behind me. But no, that would be foolish. She was still resting, recovering herself back in the Wyld. And no way would she be stupid enough to step into Madb's domain without serious protection, which I was in no shape to grant her.

Call. Your. Hounds.

She demanded with a no-nonsense bite to the three words, and I felt the spear throb between my fingers. As if it was awakened, stretching and flexing dormant muscles.

Hounds? I only had one and the bugger was chained up and staked out, about to be kebabbed on a bunch of ice spikes. Had she gone mad, coming back from the dead and mistaken me for my own father? *He* was the Hunter, he was the one …

With the spear.

I looked down, ignoring the Knights drawing closer with weapons raised and crazed hunger blazing in their dark eyes. Down at the spear in my hands, looking at it closely.

Along its length, I'd known there were carved markings, animals which I'd always figured were a bestial, Wyld version of him taking selfies with the creatures he'd hunted and slain. A tally.

But as I looked, I saw that they weren't slain creatures. No, they were moving, shifting upon the surface of the spear. And they weren't any old monsters Herne had tracked to their ultimate demise.

These were hounds. Lots of them.

I looked up at the approaching killers, and smiled a bloody grin as realisation struck me.

The spear was mine, and so were those bound to it. Herne had never travelled alone, never gone hunting by himself. He'd always had his pack with him, even none saw them.

And then, I reached down into the spear with the blood I now had flowing inside me. Blended with my own father's, energised and infused from taking his life into me.

And called my pack.

The Knights stilled, weapons held at the ready, as they eyed me uncertainty. There's nothing like a bloody-mouthed lycan grinning at you with his or her wolfshead to instil just a drop of *what the fuck*, and I was grinning like a madman as I stood bleeding from various wounds, my body a patchwork of injury upon injury.

I felt Madb's dark eyes on me, expression stilling as she watched and waited.

And fuck it if I was going to disappoint her.

The weapon didn't come with any instructions, but something in the blood I'd shared with Herne guided me. I pictured those I wanted, and called to them, through my Wyld strength, my right as son and heir to the Hunter's legacy.

And they came.

Boiling off the spear, the hounds transformed even as they settled on to the ice around and before me.

Herne had called and run with hounds to inspire fear in his prey. Whether they were beasts he'd summoned through the spear, or poor foolish lycan and others he'd transformed himself to fit the purpose, they had been hulking four legged monsters of dark fur, blazing bloody eyes and the sort of stamina to outlast an Olympic athlete many times over.

Great crushing jaws, the sort to rip and tear the prey apart when they were run down, exhausted and their time had come.

But I wasn't my father. I was cut from a very different cloth from him.

The shadows leafing off from the spear fell to the ice … and rose up into familiar figures. My pack … Pack.

Jessica. Jacob. Emma. Siobhan. Charlie. Markus. Pippa. All the faces I knew, one after another. They all rose to their feet, grey shaded versions of the lycan I knew and loved. Some now dead, and passed on to run forever in the Wyld, some still alive. None of them really here with me, but they were my Pack and if I was to run with anyone, it would be them.

My hounds all wore their worgen suits, upright with bestial heads and claws unsheathed. They didn't wear any armour, none of the kit the 'real' them would have carried if they were here, but that was of little matter. Soon over a score of Shadow lycan stood with me, facing off against the Knights. Against Madb.

And I grinned, spitting more blood before letting loose a vengeful, furious howl.

Which erupted from all their throats, stilling the entire Shadow Court into frigid silence.

Only then did we attack.

We tore through the Shadow Knights, my hounds hammering into the surprised fae and Real creatures before they could fully come to terms with what had just happened. Any worry I had over seeing creatures with my friends' faces come to harm was washed away by the raw fury I felt, the raging torrent burning up through the Wyld link, through the blood I had shared with Herne. I was different now, and in this moment, I had no place for fear.

Just the need to see this done.

Silver blood gouted into the air as my hounds slashed and ripped into the armoured foe. The scarred ogre had been upfront, and it made too tempting a target so that three swarmed over the large form. Ripping tendons, shattering bone, carving thick slices into the bellowing beast as it toppled over under their weight. One hound bayed in pain as a naga skewered it with its long thin spear, but the hound broke the weapon off in its own body and tore out the serpent Knight's throat as a suitable reply.

I wove through the frenzied combat, slashing and stabbing alongside my pack as we fought the other Knights. I could have left them to it, could have waited until they cleared a path for me, but that wasn't my way. I had summoned them, and hell would freeze over before I let them bleed and die for me. That was a difference between my father and I, one I was happy to stay true to.

Swords carved furrows in my flesh, drawing more blood. Axes nicked me, as I dodged their curved blades hewing at me, and spears dragged across my hide, so that I was awash in gore. Not all my own. But enough. A sprite slammed her dagger into my shoulder as I batted aside a monstrous bull minotaur intent on goring me with its huge horns. I shattered her arm with my claws, forcing her to leave her weapon behind as she staggered back, cradling the limb. Only to fall under the teeth of one of my hounds as it sprang from her blindside. Jessica, my Alpha, grinning a bloodied smile before leaping off back into the fray.

Step by step, I hewed and cut and stabbed my way through the fight, as much as my attention as I could spare to keep me alive focused the small, slim figure standing behind the Knights. Madb, watching the fray with cold eyes. Unwilling to quit the field of battle, standing alone without any protection.

Not that an Elder of her ancient power needed any backup, but I was surprised the Morrigan was not at her side. Her Herald remained where she stood, having quit the platform to which I was summoned but now only watching the mayhem I'd caused with a crooked smile.

Three hobs sought to entangle me in nets as they drove sharpened tridents at me, looking to trap and skewer me like Roman gladiators used to do their foes. But the Jacob and Emma hounds barrelled into them as I slapped the weapons aside and sliced the hulking goblin-kin apart with my spear. Gore was frozen all over the arena floor, as I staggered forward, ducking an axe blow from another bull minotaur and ripping out its throat with the sharpened spearhead as I snarled my rage and pain.

Closer, step by bloody step, I neared my prey. Another sprite sprang at my back, knife slashing a burning line of pain over my shoulder as I punched my own claws into her armoured body, eliciting shrill shrieks of pain until I wrenched her off me and hurled her back into the fray behind me. More blood leaked from the wound, and I was sure she had left the weapon in me by the way the pain felt.

Closer.

A naga slammed its tail into me, forcing me to jump awkwardly to stop it tangling my legs and sending me crashing to the ground. Its snake jaws latched onto my arm, fangs punching in and sending acid-pain through my flesh as its poison tried to leach through me. A mortal would have died from that bite, but lycan are proof against most of the nasty shit the Real can throw at us, so I ignored the agony from its attack, pounding my claws into its helmet until the metal gave and I sank into flesh and bone. Its eyes rolled upwards and its jaws gaped wide, allowing me to unpeel myself and dump the creature onto the ground, blood leaking from the massive holes I'd made.

Closer.

Agony hammered into me as I felt a spear punch into my back, thrown from the fight behind me. I didn't even bother turning to find out the bastard who'd tossed it, just reached back and wrenched it out before tossing it aside to clatter on the ground, soaked in my blood.

As I swung my own spear up, blade dripping with gore. And pressed it to the soft ashen skin of the Queen of Shadow's throat.

"Free them." I snarled, as everything around me quieted. The remaining Knights who could still function staggered back and disengaged, even as my hounds stilled, soaked in the blood of those that they had savaged. Without even looking, I knew five had been lost, their bodies slumped on the ice alongside the creatures they'd fought. But I would mourn their loss later. Maybe. I wasn't even sure they *could* die, or whether they'd come to life after I returned them to my spear. That was for another moment to worry about.

The Queen remained silent, watching me as I loomed over her. Blood soaked me, dripping from so many wounds it wasn't even funny. I could feel things healing, slowly knitting back together again, but I was a Gods-awful sight, even worse than when Morgana had flayed my skin as I tried to stop her from escaping the place of her rebirth. I had to admit, I had a whole new benchmark for pain now, a threshold I reckoned I *never* wanted to try to beat.

"Free. Them." I snarled, and pushed slightly on the spear. Just enough to draw a single bead of silver blood, marking her skin. For all her Court, for all her Knights, for everyone to see. She could call on her powers, have me skewered by ice shards or frozen solid by the water inside me. Shredded, buried, flash-burned by artic temperatures. A hundred ways to make me suffer.

But I'd reached her. I'd set my spear to her throat.

I'd done it.

And she smiled. Despite my pain, despite my rage, that sight *still* filled me with dread.

Chapter 39

The Queen of Shadows carefully, slowly, rested her child hand on the edge of the spear and gently moved it from where I held it.

I snarled, tied muscles bunching to resist and set it right back, but a look from her dark eyes stilled me.

Then she stepped back, and turned to look around the arena, at her Court.

All of whom silently waited, eyes on the spectacle below. On us. On me.

And she laughed.

A sharp, shattering of glass laugh that had no joy or delight in it. Instead, it was the crack of bone, the breaking of promises. The weeping in the darkness, the terror behind the door. A horrible, horrible sound that echoed around the cavern as she slowly clapped her hands together, smiling a wicked smile.

"Look you all, and understand. Hear me." She spoke softly but her words still filled the air, their tone demanding everyone's attention. Even my own. "To those who doubted my choice of Knight. To those who thought me weak for granting one such as he a position of honour, that all others have fought and bled for such. To those who whispered of Queen Madb's madness ... I say, look at what he has wrought. Is this not a true and proper Knight of Shadow? Has he not bled, has he not bested his brother and sister Knights in feats of combat, of martial prowess? Has he not shown his worth, and the simple truth that *I chose well in him?*"

"Let whispers be stilled. Let idle chatter end." She spoke softly, but the hardness of her tone belied the simple words. This was a command. "Morgan Black was, is and remains my Knight of Shadow. Though he has earned titles from our cousins in Ivory, this first and foremost is what is due him."

"And if any speak out again on the matter of my choice," Madb smiled wickedly, the child face wholly at odds with the viciousness that simple curve of her lips displayed. "Know that their tongues shall grace the walls of my bedchamber. And for those who hear such whispers and do not act upon my wishes, their ears shall join them."

She snapped her fingers and the ice around Sarah and Bear immediately melted back, settling them both down upon the cold ground. Sarah held onto the trollhound to stead herself, still suffering from her confinement, and the furry softie walked slowly and carefully across the arena so as not to let her fall as they joined me. He was due an extra-large heap of black pudding sausages when this was all settled.

The Morrigan also moved to join us, as the Shadow Knights … those remaining upright … picked up their fallen kin and dragged them back towards the stands. Leaving frozen trails of silver gore behind them. My hounds seemed to realise the 'fun' was at an end, their shadow-substance thinning and spiralling back to the spear as they returned to where they would rest. Until I next needed them.

I pointedly ignored both Queen and Herald as my loved ones drew near, reaching out to grab hold of Sarah and enfold her in a tight hug. I didn't care as my healing wounds howled, my knitting bones grated, as I held onto her. She was alive. Safe. At least in this moment.

She hugged me back for a long moment, but then pulled away, her eyes wide as she took in my condition.

"Mio dios! You're … god, Morgan, how are you *standing*?" She didn't care that I'd smeared blood over her too, instead searching around for anything she could use to tend to my many wounds. But I just clasped her hands and stilled her, shaking my head with a wolfish smile.

"I'll be fine." I growled, cricking one shoulder as the healing wounds tightened it. "Just a day's work when dealing with these sort of … people."

Many more suitable words had sprung to mind rather than that one, but I figured I'd only just managed to get us out of the mess my smart mouth had landed us in. Best not to drop us *right* back in, right now.

I leant down with only a hiss of pain and ruffled Bear's furry head as his stubby tail banged a steady beat and he chuffed and huffed his pleasure at being free. I also got the sharp whine and growl in his voice as he glanced across at Madb, but I just gripped his chunky head and shook my head again.

"Not this time, bud. We're leaving."

I glanced finally back at Madb.

"Right?"

This had been one huge fucking trick, a play by the Queen simply to kick some malcontents in her Court back into line. Quieten any rumours that she wasn't still the scariest thing walking the shadows, and reassure her supporters she knew exactly what she was doing. And I'd let her use me, giving her all the ammunition she needed to put me where she needed me, to be her fist used to display her strength.

I was furious, raging, but also I had to acknowledge how well she had played me, her own Court … hell, everyone. She might be a bitch, but there was nothing childish about the small Queen's cunning and strategies. Oberon was an arrogant entitled jock, whilst Titania played the winsome seductress far too often, but Madb? She was a stone cold killer, through and through.

The Queen smiled and nodded, reaching up to trace the point at which my spear had pierced her skin. Her slim fingers deftly drew out a bead of silver blood, spinning it as it thinned and lengthened until she held a delicate chain, with an intricate metallic pendant that looked like a bead of metallic blood.

This she held up, offering to Sarah.

"A small thing, to repay your part in this lesson." The fae told the mortal, who looked ready to slap that hand away and give her a piece of a very pissed off Spanish lady's mind. But I gripped her shoulder, grunting a *no*, knowing you did not refuse gifts offered by Elder immortals, especially ones crafted from their very own essence.

You did however check them for booby-traps and strings.

"What is it?" I growled, even as Sarah let the fae spool the chain into her hand.

"Protection. A warding, made of my blood." Madb replied with a smile. Cold and chilling, but still a smile. "It will prevent your beloved ever being … *taken* as was done to her this time, by any creature of this dominion. It will also afford her greater protection against any who wish her ill, and seek to beguile, charm or harm her."

"She may also, once and once only, use it to call on me." She added, and I groaned. Immortals were all alike, and they loved giving their version on the *rub me and make three wishes* trick. It was something no mortal could resist, and usually resulted in mayhem and destruction on an epic scale, no matter what Disney would have you believe. "But only once, and in the direst of needs only."

"Take it." I growled to Sarah, who still weighed the necklace in her hand. "She owes you *big* time for this shit."

Sarah nodded and hesitantly slipped the chain over her head, letting it rest against her chilled skin. Nothing immediately happened … no trick causing her to turn into an ice statue or transformed into a creature of Shadow … but I still caught the increased beat of her heart, as she braced herself for anything bad.

That was how it went with the powerful creatures of the Real. One moment they could be doing their best to end your life in the most painful of ways, the next they would be offering helpful gifts with smiles and charm. Fickle as fuck did not even begin to describe them.

I noted that the cut I'd made had left a small white scar, healed but still visible. Given just what sort of creature Madb was, I was confused as to there being any evidence left that I'd gotten so close to her. With a naked weapon.

"A reminder." The Shadow Queen told me whilst she still faced Sarah, tapping the thin line. She didn't explain for who, and what the reminder was meant to be for, but I decided I didn't need to know right there and then.

"And now, Knight, I believe you are needed elsewhere." Madb instructed, turning back and locking her dark eyes on me. "A matter of punishing those who imprisoned and tortured our cousin the Hunter. And stopping those who seek to bring ruin to our Realms, releasing the Beyond where it ought never be."

"Lessons there were this day. Remember them, and accept the truth of who you are." She instructed and I bit down hard on snarking back at her, thanking her for being such a bloody great teacher. She's only accept it as a compliment, the shortarse psycho. "Herald, return them."

The Morrigan faced me. My grandmother who had stood and watched as I was stabbed, savaged, sliced and mauled without raising a single finger. Not that I had expected any assistance from her, but it still stung.

But in her eyes I finally saw something. Something other than the cold darkness she had shown me as I stood next to her.

Sorrow.

"Though your hand was the one who ended my son, it was his wish you did so. And so you must carry no burden for sending him on his way." She told me matter-of-factly. Just speaking about the weather, or anything unimportant, rather than me killing my own father ... her son. "Turn your energies instead to those who sought his life, the one who ordered him taken in the first place. You may punish the foolish mortals who acted upon those orders, but find who did this. And make them rue the day they ever were born."

There was only thing I could do, no matter how pissed off I was feeling.

"I swear." I growled, nodding once.

The Morrigan smiled thinly, before handing over my Ivory crafted garments that I had taken off when I'd first thought to strike a bargain with the pissed off Shadow Queen. Given how gore-clad I was, I decided to leave them off for now until I could scrub down a little.

Then the Herald struck her spear on the ice beside her.

"Then, Morgan Black, Knight of Shadow. You are released. Begone."

And with that, the cavern around me swirled and bled way in inky strips, the chill that had bitten into my very bones melting away.

Returning me to the troll-hole. And dropping me right back into *another* shitshow.

Chapter 40

"Morgan! What the hell …?" Felix's voice piped up as I drew a breath, settling myself from the transition back to where I'd come from. "Where have you … What *happened* to you?"

And a moment later.

"What's Sarah and Bear doing here?"

Ah, crap.

After the chill of the Shadow Court, the troll-hole felt muggy and humid, with that weird sensation bleeding through the breach from the Beyond making everything just *off*. Like the smell of spoiled milk in the fridge, or something rotting under the floorboards. Just plain wrong.

The next thing I noticed was the shadows. They lay everywhere, thick and roiling like inky clouds. These were different than the ones I'd seen in the Court, somehow infused with malice and intent. The scent I got from them, which was weird since shadows never really had any such thing, reminded me of one thing immediately.

Dr Zarkof Bremmer. These were *his* shadows.

Which meant the fucker had gotten his strength and powers back. Great for him.

Not so great for us.

Looking around the room, I could see things had happened whilst I was entertaining Madb and her Court of lunatics.

Cormac had been released from his bonds, and now sat on an overturned crate. He looked wan, sweat beading his skin and his hair plastered to his head but he managed a simple nod when he caught me looking. That was the equivalent of a firm handshake, maybe even a hug, from the emotionally repressed OPS agent, so I simply accepted with a wolfish smile of my own.

Manisha also sat, with her truncated arm now carefully wrapped. The Ivory Knight smiled at me, raising her remaining hand in greeting even as she took in my wounded state, making her own assessment of what had happened to me before I even opened my mouth to explain. Puck seemed to have taken on the role of nursemaid to the pair, her concern over Cormac telling me volumes of the … *understanding* the pair obviously had. Even though it messed with my head, thinking how the OPS agent might have any sort of relationship, let alone with one of the fae.

You just never knew.

Greg stuck close to Ellie and Felix, the two witches looking to have recovered a little from their captivity. They had been freed from their bonds somehow, the shattered remains of the metal restraints lying on the rock floor, and someone had donated replacement footwear from their packs, given how both were now wearing what looked like Nike trainers. A glaring fashion statement against the rest of their attire, but I wasn't going to start commenting … just yet.

Then I settled on the rest of the company, and knew *bad* things had happened whilst I was away.

Hunter had shifted back to his familiar form, once again kitted out in his own clothing and carrying his sniper rifle and pack. He bore wounds, a long slice down his right thigh and several deep scratches on his arms. A pair of puncture wounds surrounded by smaller holes glittered darkly on his bicep, like something had latched on and tried to rip the muscle free.

Trix and Dix knelt or sat nearby, the two dark haired half fae nervously toying with their unsheathed knives. Neither looked to be injured, but both were rattled, giving off serious *we want out of here* vibes. Mother also seemed unharmed, but her normally pleasant expression had frozen in a set of grim lines, as she tended to the last member of our hired help.

Janus sprawled on the largest crate, his legs braced and his hands clenched on the wooden box beneath him to keep him upright. The reason for this was the mess that was his chest. Bandages cocooned him, layered over and over but the darkening lines I could see told me something or somethings had attempted to hack him apart from his pectorals all the way down to his lower stomach. No one wound, but lots of them criss-crossing. His clothing and body armour had been shredded, and the set of his jaw told me just the level of pain the half-troll was suffering.

But he still looked up as I snarled at his injuries, grinning teeth stained with blood.

"Is nothing. I laugh it off. Hah hah." He joked, wincing as Mother sighed and poked one of his bound ribs to make a point. Hard. "Ok, ok, is something. Nothing some of your delicious *galushki* will not heal. And a drink. A large one. Several large ones. Maybe more."

"What happened?" I leant on Sarah, feeling a little wear myself as my body drew on its energy reserves to heal the clusterfuck of damage I'd done to it. I could see everyone was back to their normal selves, so Greg had stopped using his gift or whatever it was, which was a blessing as I hated to think how I'd be feeling if I'd suddenly become mortal again with all the hurt I'd done to myself … or had done to me.

She hugged me and steered me to another crate, whilst Bear padded at my side. That was a thought … if Bear got hit by Greg's powers, would he suddenly become a mortal dog? Something like a Tibetan Mastiff or the like, maybe. I tried to picture him as a regular mutt, and snarled a laugh at the thought. It just didn't fit.

Settling down on the crate, I Changed, loosing hold of my worgen suit since for the first time in a while it looked like no immediate threat was about to land on us. That shadowy darkness worried me, but it wasn't doing anything more threatening than undulating in a weird-arse way, so I was happy to let someone else handle it for a moment.

"So?" I prompted again, and Ellie cleared her throat.

"After you … well, vanished, things went a little south, you might say." She told me, nodding to her love. "Gregory had to let his talent end or it would begin to sap his own lifeforce, weakening him. When that happened, Dr Bremmer seemed to regain control of himself. The other two members of his staff were too far gone, but he was able to summon his shadows and hounds to attack whilst he made his escape."

I looked over to where two bodies still lay on the ground, clad in their white labcoats. What lay underneath had shrunk and collapsed, puddling into some sort of weird gloop where bones stuck out of the stinking mess. Nothing recognisable as the men … women … creatures they had been before.

"At the same time, those other creatures like him who fled before reappeared and attacked us. Your friend Janus took the brunt of it, hence his present condition." She continued, and I could almost picture the half-troll battling the corrupted scientists, their long claws inflicting the awful damage the bandages only did a half-decent job of hiding. "Thankfully we were able to drive them off, wounding several, when Gregory used one of their own weapons to break our bonds and grant Felix and I a measure of our craft again."

"What the fuck are they, and how did you manage that?" I grunted, given that when I'd been summoned to the Shadow Court, both witches had been effectively benched. Blocked from their talents, effectively just mortals whilst Greg's jinx was in effect as well.

Ellie smiled, nodding towards the slumped, decayed figures.

"What I believe these scientists have become are strzyga. Mortal vampires, if you would." She took on that lecturer-voice of hers that I knew so well, the horrors of what she had recently faced fading away for a moment as she stepped back into a beloved role … that of teacher. "Their morphology matches the descriptions I have researched of such cursed individuals, though most folklore indicates only women can become strzyga. Obviously the sources they are based on are wrong."

I pushed myself up from the crate, shushing Sarah's warning breath before it left her lips. With Bear padding protectively beside me, I staggered over to the hopefully dead bodies and knelt down to inspect them more closely.

I'd met traditional vampires in the Real. Red-eyed cadaverous wraiths with needle sharp teeth that were hollow to allow them to drain their victims. Creatures of darkness, they tended *not* to have anything above borderline animal intellect, despite the stories and lore about *Dracula* and the like. They definitely did not become scientists in the Mortal Realm, or turn into goo when killed. They also could completely ignore holy symbols and tended to shrug off any injury apart from full decapitation … so something did not gel with Ellie's suggestion.

"*Mortal* vampires." The witch reminded me before I even got to speak, somehow reading my mind. "I wrote a thesis on the interactions of mortals and supernatural beings, and the lore and documented outcomes such unions are said to produce."

"Sounds riveting." I snarked, but Ellie just smiled back at me.

"Why thank you, dear. It is a good read. I'll lend you a copy when we are done here." She promised and I bit back a groan, knowing not only would she keep to that promise but expect me to read it fully and be able to comment on any question she put to me on its contents. Me and my mouth.

"Anyway, the short of it is when mortals and supernatural creatures breed together, if the child survives what can be a traumatic birth, we most often get what we call half-breeds. Born of both bloodlines, with a mix of mortal and supernatural." She continued, waving at the mercenaries. "Depending on the parent's age and inherent power, what the child possesses of non-mortal qualities might be to a lesser or greater extent. A slight aversion to silver, causing a rash. Or at the other end of the scale, skin impervious to most mortal weapons like our friend Janus."

"The mortals have long described such unions as unholy, against any number of gods' will. Begetting monsters. The *nephilim* in popular religious lore, for example. Creatures of horror and terror, or sometimes beings of unbelievable beauty whilst possessing a bottomless capacity for evil." Ellie shook her head, her views on such religious 'lore' obvious. It went hand in hand with how certain popular faiths had viewed witchcraft and treated those they accused of being witches throughout the ages. Brutal was not an understatement. "As we are all aware, much of *that* is based purely on the mortals' fear of the unknown, of anything greater than them. Many have suffered from such small, minded thinking."

"This short version?" Janus grunted, earning a hard look from the witch but Greg whispered in her ear, and she sighed.

"Fine, the *shorter short* version." She started again, with a testy bite to her words. "It is different when mortals *consume* matter of supernatural creatures. Mortals eating mortal … well, that is simply cannibalism but can lead in extreme cases to the mortal becoming a wendigo. A cruel beast of bottomless hunger and a savage desire to rend all life."

I remembered fighting the bastards in the Wyld, and was *very* happy we weren't facing them down in this troll hole. Not when Sarah was with me, potentially in harm's way.

"But when a mortal eats the flesh of something from the Real, or drinks its blood then what is happens is a base corruption of that mortal's own form." She gestured to the slumped, gloopy bodies. "Not immediately, and often the mortal simply is poisoned and dies given the toxicity of most creatures of supernatural origin. But if the mortal survives, and continues feeding in this way, they take on characteristics of supernatural beings whilst losing their inherent mortal form. Yet keeping their mortal nature."

"Feeding as these scientists did, on Real creatures, they staved off the curse Morgan's mother placed them under. Making them more resilient, able to resist its effects and also changing their fundamental nature which negated the curse's influence. But not making them immortal." Ellie shook her head. "I believe Dr Bremmer most likely first simply sampled the blood of the creatures he kidnapped, injecting it into his and his colleagues bodies to see its effect on them. Hence their eventual transformation into creatures who imbibe blood first and foremost. Like vampires of legend, yet still mortal."

"In other words, strzyga."

I grunted again, rising up from the dead strzyga and looked across at her.

"Ok, so how did you run them off?" I queried, knowing it would be good to know how to handle the fuckers so that we didn't have to keep tapping Greg to use his gift. The bit about it draining his lifeforce was new to me, and did not sound healthy to the guardian in any way whatsoever. "You said you wounded them?"

She nodded, smiling as she gestured to Felix.

"That was the easy part. Once I figured out what these creatures were, I remembered that folk lore indicates ringing church bells will cause a strzyga to turn into tar. Every piece of legend is based on fact, and so I simply deduced that it is *vibrations* that they were weakened by." The witch clapped her hands together, the sound ringing out oddly with echoing ripples through the air. On the floor, the two bodies shivered and slumped even more into gelatinous goo, spreading out around their bare bones. "Like *Venom* in the comic books, Felicity was quick to remind me. We were able to channel suitable wavelengths to incapacitate these two, and damage the others enough to force them to flee."

"Incapacitate?" I cocked my head, knowing Ellie to be the sort to care about life of all types, shapes and sizes, and whilst not a pacifist, definitely not the type to kill another unless there was simply no other alternative left to her. "These look a little more, well terminal than that."

The witch met my gaze, losing the smile she had worn for Felix. The truth of what it had cost her plain for me to see in her eyes.

"These men and women, they are living off other creatures' lifeforce. Extending their own at so great a cost." She answered me truthfully. "There was no reasoning with them once Gregory's talent no longer bound them, and it was a case of their lives or our own. My Goddess and I … in this matter, we are agreed. They need to be stopped, and the curse your mother laid upon them for their attempt to bind Herne the Hunter granted its due. Their lives, or what little remains of who they were."

Words wouldn't cover what I felt, hearing her admission and knowing the witch well enough to see the pain this still caused her. Instead, I simply stumped over to her and folded her into a brief, tight hug. She leant into me, and rested her head against my chest for a moment.

"Thank you." She whispered for my ears only. "I'm glad you're ok."

"Never better." I told her, earning a quiet chuckle from her.

"Something's bugging me," She told me, voice dropping to make sure I only caught her words. "I heard Dr Bremmer's story. How something from the Beyond told him to start draining life from Real creatures to save him and his colleagues. But that makes no sense … nothing from the Beyond would know this might even work. They're completely different to anything you or I or anyone know. It doesn't work unless …"

"Unless, yeah." I replied, agreeing with the witch. Something was not right with his story. Or maybe the fuckers had been listening in, spying on us and had more information than we knew. But, still …

Releasing Ellie, I stepped back to rejoin Sarah, who laid a hand on my arm and nodded, telling me I needn't worry about explaining anything to her. She got it. Smart mortal that she was.

"Well then, let us move on to the more pressing matter in hand." Puck finally spoke up, stepping away from Cormac's side after looking at Manisha, exchanging one of those *we're speaking without words* expressions. Whatever they discussed, it left the one armed Ivory Knight less than happy, whilst the spy smiled like it was Christmas Day.

"And what's that then?" I knew I was going to regret asking from her expression, but I just couldn't help myself.

"I am surprised you need to ask, Errant." She replied, using my Ivory title. Which only made my worry crank up a notch. "For it is a task for you and Manisha Na Pendragon Cie to perform. One our Lord and Lady both command of you."

The spy gestured and I realised in all the excitement I'd forgotten about the elephant in the room. The black skinned, weird-arse looking elephant who still was strapped into a frame, watching what transpired with bottomless dark orbs.

The Harrowed Queen.

"By order of Lord Oberon, Lord of the Ivory Court and in agreement with the Lords and Ladies of Shadow, Wyld and Twilight, you are commanded to end the abomination known as *the Harrowed Queen*, pretender to a throne in our dominion." The Ivory fae grinned ghoulishly as she spoke the death sentence. "Her life, what passes for it, is forfeit. Knight, Errant. End the threat she poses to all the Realms."

"Kill her now."

Chapter 41

I looked at Manisha, seeing the truth in her pain-fogged eyes.

The Harrowed Queen ... Harry ... she was a truly fucked up mistake, a mess resulting from Morgana's twisted scheme to revenge herself on all the Courts for her age-long imprisonment and torture, and her desire to be finally granted a crown and Court to rule. And my dumb-ass attempts at stopping her, using anything I had to hand without thinking through the repercussions and consequences as any sane mutt would do.

Morgana had seen her own ending in my eyes, filling her with insanity and fear. Pushing her over edge, when I had doubted she was all that sane to begin with. So much so that when I cornered her, turned all her plays back on her and ruined any chance she had at succeeding, she had given her life to the creature bound to her, to birth something of both the Real and the Beyond. Something that should not exist.

An abomination, as Oberon kept calling her.

A mistake that needed solving, according to all the other Court rulers.

And here she was, bound and vulnerable. At our mercy. The condemned prisoner, their sentence given and judgement made, stretched out on the block. Awaiting the headsman's axe.

Or spear, in my case.

But ...

Manisha went to push herself up from where she rested, that big sword of hers appearing at her side. Ready for her to wield, to dispense justice as per her Lord and Lady commanded. Even with one arm missing, I figured she was strong enough to cut Harry's head from her shoulders with ease. One stroke, that was probably all it would take. Or possibly a stab to the heart. Given Harry was made up of an Elder shadow fae's essence, I wasn't entirely sure what it would take to end her.

But I *was* pretty sure the Ivory Knight Captain would find a way. She was one of the most capable women I knew, especially at ending things she wanted over and done with.

So I stopped her, moving over to her side and gently pushing her back.

"I've got this." I told the Knight, settling her back down. It told me a lot of her condition that I was able to push her given the fae normally could probably arm wrestle me easily and toss me aside if I tried to make her do something she less inclined to do.

She looked me in the eye, then nodded once. Settling onto the crate, she let her sword vanish away again to wherever it lurked when she wasn't chopping her enemies to pieces with it.

Squaring my shoulders, I turned and walked back across the cavern, past Sarah and Bear. The trollhound went to follow me, but I simply shook my head, pointing at my love and he got the hint. Keep her safe. That was his job right now.

Ellie, Felix and Greg watched me, the guardian his normal gruff self, resting his hand on his sword hilt and eyes watchful on all the threatening shadows. The older witch had a hand on his shoulder, seemingly unwilling to part company from him now that they had been reunited, showing the bond between them. The strength she drew from him.

For her part, Felix locked her eyes on me, obviously doubting what I was about to do. She knew the truth of me now, had seen me fight all manner of horrors whilst seeking to right a wrong, stop something terrible from happening. Saving her from the madman who had kidnapped and imprisoned her to try to force her to love him being her first exposure to my *Real* self.

But she had never seen me do the dirty work, the behind the scenes acts that meant getting my hands mucky as fuck. Doing things that were morally dubious, where right and wrong were on the same side of the coin. This would be the first time, and the shock on her face told me how well it *didn't* sit with her.

Killing someone tied down and unable to defend themselves was murder, plain and simple. I wasn't going to argue the point but I also knew that sometimes, the only reason you got to draw another breath was because you made bloody sure the other person didn't.

I just kept my expression set, letting the younger witch make up her own mind on what was going to happen. How she would judge me for what I was about to do.

"Errant, do your duty to your Lord and Lady." Puck told me, not a trace of hesitation in her voice. She was utterly convinced of what had to happen, following the orders given her. And I was fairly sure too. Dr Bremmer had said they meant to use Harry as a way to bring some horror from the Beyond into my own backyard, which could only be described with words like *Armageddon, Apocalypse* and so on.

I had to stop that happening, and the simplest option looked to be laid out before me. Just needing me to do one single thing.

And yet …

Simple never ever worked for me. I'd been tripped up that trick so many times, I practically had the word embedded in my forehead, the amount of times I'd fallen flat trying to do that one thing.

Things didn't add up. As I walked towards Harry, feeling her alien eyes come to rest on me, I mulled them over in my head.

Herne had gone after her, leaving everyone but his personal hounds behind. Following orders to hunt her down and kill her, we'd thought. Trying to be a good father, maybe. But instead of killing her, he'd returned to the Wyld with her. Brought her *back*.

Why?

And wasn't it too bloody convenient that a bunch of insane mortals speaking to *something* from the Beyond would have the answer to all their problems practically land in their laps, the perfect tool for a plan to bring down all the Realms there for the taking at the same moment they were ordered to imprison Herne?

And what about Ellie's suspicion, that something from the Beyond would have no clue how to save a mortal from another's curse, when instead they'd come across the one answer that didn't kill the idiots but gave them enough power to cause chaos and confusion on a truly epic level? Could this thing, this tentacled horror from the Cthulhu cult possibly be *that* lucky to have gotten the million to one chance, the golden lottery ticket, when all other answers would have led to the scientists' well-deserved death and none of this being my problem?

Something stank. Worse than the Bung brothers, from where they still glared at me from their prison cell. We needed to something about those prisoners, get them out of here and back where they belonged, as well as saving our own skin.

First things first, Morgan. Don't go getting distracted.

As I approached, Harry shifted in her bonds, head raised and oily locks framing her almost perfect doll's face of shining obsidian. Scars marred her flesh, grey against the black skin, and I tried to read the origins of them as they mapped across her. This was no spear slashes or strikes that Herne might leave, more like lacerations from multiple claws of differing types. Almost like she had been hit in the face by a frenzied pack of animals, not of one type.

"Strike her down, Errant." Puck commanded, the sharpness of her tone typical of fae ordering around lesser creatures. Which in their viewpoint was pretty much everybody else. Definitely a slide away from *well met merry folk*. "Before she can stop you."

"Stop me? How?" I snarked back at her, gesturing at the bound prisoner. "She's literally tied up and unable to twitch. What's she going to do, eyeball me to death?"

"Do not mock what you do not understand, Errant." The spy instructed me tartly. "This being is unlike anything you have hunted, nothing like those you have fought. She carries the seed of destruction for all us, an end to anything of this dominion. Utter ruin is her nature, no matter the face she wears. Strike her down, and let us leave this place."

Puck was right. The Harrowed Queen was something new, something none of us knew much about. And at least part of her, the bits that had nothing to do with Morgana, were built up of something that devoured immortals. Gave them *true* death. Not something any of us wanted floating around our Realms unchecked, ungoverned and able to act on her own whim without any laws like the Accords binding her.

Something had to be done.

I slowly raised my spear, still struggling to understand the right move here, the correct path that wouldn't brand me a murderer but would end Harry's threat to us all.

And she spoke.

One word.

"Sanctuary."

If I was anyone else and not a lycan, I might have doubted my ears and thought I hadn't heard her right. But even in my weakest suit, I was sure I'd caught that word correctly.

But her eyes were not fixed on me now. They were on the spear I held.

My father's spear.

"What is the delay? End her!" Puck instructed, her expression furrowed. I noted her hands had strayed to those long knives I knew she wielded with deadly skill, having witnessed the mess she had made of the chimerians.

"She said *sanctuary*." I replied, and the Ivory fae scowled.

"Ignore her. She's not bound by our laws and cannot claim ..." Puck replied tartly, hands tightening on the hilts. She had definitely lost her friendly edge, and was all business now.

But Harry spoke up.

"Not claim. *Claimed*." The Harrowed Queen replied evenly, despite the fact I was standing over her with a weapon, and her hearing my instructions to kill her. "The Horned One already granted me sanctuary when I agreed to return with him to his Court. Ask him, since you carry his spear."

"Going to be a bit difficult, since he's dead." I replied, and I caught her even stare flicker, just a touch. Fear maybe, sadness even. "Why would my ... would the Horned One grant you safety? He was sworn to hunt you down and kill you, like all the other Lords and Ladies of the Courts."

"Free me, agree to honour his word and keep me from those who seek to harm me, and I will tell you all." Harry replied, as she gently shook her manacled limbs.

"She's lying." Puck snarled, her face thinning with anger. Cormac set one hand on her arm but she brushed him off, only focused on this one thing. This command from her Lord. "And even if she's not, with Herne having died ... by your hand ... any sanctuary is rescinded. Lost. So just kill her and be done with it."

"You killed him?" Harry enquired evenly, but again I caught that spark, that flicker of emotion. Whatever had happened between them, he had obviously made an impression on her. Remembering the almost neolithic, bestial and very primal persona he had worn around me, I didn't get it but I wasn't one to judge.

"He asked me to. He was in pain, dying slowly but suffering." I told her since the truth wasn't at issue here. His promise was. "How do I know you're telling the truth."

Harry eyed me for a long moment, then nodded to the spear.

"You carry his weapon. Mother tells me that means he bestowed it on you, his scion. Your blood is his blood. Ask it if I lie." She instructed me quietly, and I felt a cold chill as she so offhandedly spoke of Morgana, still alive enough to speak to her. "You will know the truth."

Seek the answer inside. Ask.

My own mother's voice whispered in my mind, reminding me that Harry wasn't the only one with extra people hanging around their psyche.

Feeling more than a little foolish, I closed my eyes for a moment, trusting this wasn't a ploy and I was about to be hit over the head or stabbed or anything. I recalled Herne, building an image of him in my mind before uttering the million-dollar question.

Did you grant the Harrowed Queen Sanctuary?

I sent the question out, into our shared blood, into the bond that existed still between us. One that was beyond death.

And I got my answer.

Yes. Protect her.

Bugger.

I didn't hear words, it was nothing that my mother could have faked if she had wanted to. The answer thrummed in my blood, boiling in my veins. A roar that echoed up through me like an earthquake, unstoppable and nothing I could ignore. This was Herne's essence, the last remnants of him he had left in the blood we'd shared, the primal elemental at his core.

I looked back at the group, shaking my head as I lowered my spear.

"It's true." I told them, seeing Puck's scowl deepen into frustrated anger, whilst Felix gave a small sigh of relief. "Herne granted her sanctuary, and since Briar is sitting safely on the Horned Throne far away from this clusterfuck, I'm going to have to wing it and say Harry … the Harrowed Queen is still under the protection of the Wyld. Until I can find out why my father gave her sanctuary, what he was after. Nothing happens to her until then."

The Ivory fae looked ready to argue, until Manisha this time set her remaining hand on the smaller fae's shoulder. Clasping it hard, not saying a word. Just through the touch, she settled the other, who finally shrugged and smiled.

"Let not I be the one to break old Horny Head's word." Puck quipped, making a short bow to me. "As heir to his … well, whatever he granted you, it is your right to stand in his stead. Mark me though, there are others … my Lord for one, who will *strongly* contest your ability to keep that promise."

"Don't I know it." I growled, as I realised what I'd done.

Only set myself in the way of Oberon's command, denying the Lord of Light and the Ivory Court his judgement on Harry. And not just him, but all the other Lords and Ladies of the Courts. All arrayed, opposite little old me, who had … well, I had my friends, my loved ones, my pack.

None of whom I'd drag into this sorry mess.

Instead, just me and a spear.

I really didn't like my odds of winning through on this one, if I was being perfectly honest.

Chapter 42

"So, um, now what?"

Felix spoke up, as ever not comfortable with awkward silences. Still too young to let them just slide on by until someone else did all the work of filling them. Like she had.

"Indeed, Errant, what now?" Puck enquired, smiling far too politely for my ease. She'd given in far too easily, with whatever it was that Manisha had told her calming her anger. Or so she had le us to believe. "The Harrowed Queen is the key to the mortals' plan for bringing the Realms to utter ruin. And you have saved her, and protect her against any who wish to do her harm. As long as she is here, or alive anywhere, she puts us all at risk."

"So. What. Now?"

"Now? We need to get out of here, get everyone out." I nodded to the cells where the prisoners watched us, some still hammering at the walls as a subtle hint they wanted out, others huddling on the floor, broken from whatever it was Dr Bremmer and his brethren had subjected them to. "Since you blew up the controllers, this place is going to come crashing down soon. We can bury the bastards here, and regroup somewhere safe."

Puck shook her head, even as I kicked myself for the baseborn naivety I was showing.

"Except they won't let us leave. Dr Bremmer's got his powers back, and there are the chimerians and other strzyga to deal with as well." I counted our enemies off, looking around the group. Manisha wounded but still able to fight, Janus also damaged but I didn't know how effective he'd be whilst keeping his insides inside. The rest of the company were in reasonable shape, Hunter functional despite his wounds. And we would have the other captives we'd free to support us.

Not the worst situation I'd been in, but not brilliant either. Sarah was here, and as long as she was in harm's way I'd be distracted. Split, trying to keep her safe. And that sort of divided attention usually led to mistakes.

"I have a suggestion that should solve that problem." Ellie spoke up, and I grinned. Leave it to the witch to work out a solution. "It seems to me you're putting too much on … Harry here. Leaving her alive presents an opportunity for the enemy to use her still, yes. But she is not the key to their plans."

"That is." She pointed to the breach as it crackled and hummed with alien intensity. The cage around it was definitely warped now, cracked in places. It wouldn't last for much longer, not under the pressures being exerted on it. And when it broke? Ka-splat for anything close by I presumed.

"It is a breach, a way between dominions." Puck commented dryly, cocking a slim eyebrow. "What do you propose we do?"

"Close it." The witch replied glibly, and smiled.

The Ivory fae shook her head.

"I have not the art for such an endeavour. It is inimical to me, to the Knight Captain. To any of us. If we tried to force that thing shut, we would be consumed." She sounded pretty certain on that fact, but Ellie wasn't giving up.

"No I wasn't thinking of you." She looked across at me, and I got that sinking feeling in my stomach again. "I was talking about Morgan. He can close the breach. And since the strzyga are drawing much of their unnatural energy from it, given how little they would have been able to consume from the Real prisoners they took, would that not also weaken them? A way to even the playing field, as Gregory keeps attempting to teach me when he makes me watch football."

"Uh, me?" I tried not to sound as surprised or as worried as I felt, even as my mind played back Puck's comment. *If we tried, we would be consumed.* That did not sound like fun to me.

"Yes, you dear." Ellie walked over to me and tapped the spear in my hand. "If I am not mistaken, this is a portal key. Tied to the Hunter or any who carries his bloodline and who is recognised as his heir. It should be powerful enough to use as a conduit, and all you need do is the reverse of what I had you do when we forced our way into Twilight. Not hold a way open, but close it."

"He is still of this dominion, as is the spear." Puck challenged even as I tried to formulate the many arguments I had against doing what Ellie proposed. "If he makes this attempt, he risks the same as would we. And you have uncommon knowledge, witch, about things you should not know of. Portal keys, for instance."

I'd winged it when the portal to Twilight was closing, jamming myself physically and somehow magically as well like a wedge, keeping the thing from slamming shut. It had hurt like the buggery, but that had been simple. Get in the way, stop something from shutting.

How the hell was I going to convince the breach *to* shut? Ask it politely? Threaten it?

"I can help."

Harry spoke up, where she still remained, bound to the frame with tubes sticking out of her.

"As I am under father's protection, I can offer assistance to keep him from harm." She continued and I groaned. Not that bloody thing again. "My essence is akin to what you call the breach. I can guide him, and my blood may shield him from the worst possible harm. If you free me."

Sarah looked across at me, and I shook my head vehemently before turning back to Harry.

"I'm going to free you but for fuck's sake stop calling me your father." I growled, seeing more than one surprised expression amongst our group. It would take too long to explain, and I didn't have the patience for the list of questions I could already see queuing up to be voiced. "Call me Morgan. Please."

"If that is what you wish ... Morgan." She answered, smiling slightly. Revealing the sharp fangs hidden in her mouth, so unlike the young woman's body Morgana had had Robert Knox build her for her return to life.

"If we do this, you know Dr Bremmer is going to throw everything at us to stop us." Greg spoke up, nodding to the churning shadows. "I don't know if he can hear us, but I'm betting he can at least watch what we're up to. As soon as Morgan starts messing with the breach, it'll get noisy."

"Good. We'll spend less time hunting for the fucker if he comes here to stop me." I tried false bravado instead of doubt now. If Harry thought she could help, then maybe I had a chance. "Anyone got any idea how I do this shit? Or what I should expect?"

Ellie shook her head, and even Puck shrugged. Great.

"Fine. You know what, I think I'm just going to shove my spear into it and see what happens. If it blows up, it's your fault for thinking I can do this." I told them bluntly, before gesturing to the shadows. "How about you lot get ready to stop anything they throw at us, and get the non-combatants safe. Whilst I free Harry."

Sarah picked up on the fact I wanted her somewhere safe and as far away from me as possible, giving me a hard look but I just shook my head. Bear gave me even more grief, huffing and butting my leg to shove me to one side when I told him to follow her. But I needed them both out of any potential blast radius. Or the immediate reach of anything like tentacles that came out to stop me.

Just in case.

Feeling Puck's eyes on me the whole time, I untethered and loosened the bonds holding Harry to the frame. I had no idea how long she had been stuck there, so gave her a moment to gather her strength before helping her down onto her two hooves. Feet. Whatever they were.

The Harrowed Queen straightened and rolled her shoulders to loosen the muscles after her confinement. She delicately drew out the needles and tubes that bristled from her, the wounds slowly closing to leave more scars to match those she already wore.

"Better?" I asked, and she nodded once, before stepping close and pressing her lips to my cheek in a quick kiss. Her flesh was cool, not unpleasantly so, just not warm like anything living. But I felt the mark she left burn slightly, as if my body reacted to her touch like a nettle rash or the like.

"Thank you … Morgan." She told me, before walking over to the breach.

The merged child of Morgana and the death of immortals then held out one hand, and drew a long talon across the flesh of her palm. Blood sprang forth, a mix of silver and darkest black, entwined and running slowly from her wound.

"This will protect you." She told me, motioning for me to hold out my own hand. When I hesitated, she smiled.

"You have offered me sanctuary, Morgan. I cannot do you harm." Harry told me. *Cannot*, I thought with a wry smile. Not *will not*. A bit of a difference there, if I had to be honest.

But what the fuck. I was out of any other idea. Good or bad.

I let her draw that sharp talon over my skin, seeing the wound open as if she was using a laser scalpel. Blood sprang forth, and she clasped hold of my palm, mixing the essence of her and me.

Dizziness hit me for a moment, a feeling that wasn't *wrong*, just not entirely right. I could feel my lycan self react as if threatened, and bit back on the urge to snarl and lash out. Instead, I shook my head and took a slow breath, calming my heart that had begun to thunder in my chest.

Harry looked at me for a long moment, before releasing my hand.

"Whenever you are ready."

"I would suggest you *place* the spear against the breach, dear. That might be a better plan than stabbing at the thing blindly." Ellie told me as she came to stand beside me. I wanted to tell her to go back to Greg, but I could see the look in her eyes, the simple fact she was where she intended to be. No use arguing. "And I believe you should probably have Harry place her hand on the spear as well, so she can channel her energies through it. It *should* not react as long as you carry it."

"Should. Might. I'm getting a whole lot of confidence here, lady." I snarked, earning one of her crooked smiles. "Ok, everyone else ready? For, well, anything?"

Felix gave me a thumbs up, as I felt her craft spark to life. The air between her hands shivered as she held them before her, roiling in a way that made me think of thunderstorms. I caught the muted throb that began to echo in the chamber, as she built up to unleash a tsunami of vibrations if any strzyga showed their ugly faces.

Hunter and Mother both guarded Janus, as the half-troll levered himself up and settled on his feet. One arm wrapped around his wounds, the other levelling a stolen rifle from the chimerians. Dix had his knives out, held ready, but Trix seemed less keen to ready herself, eyes flitting nervously around but straying to the top level where our exit awaited.

Gregory gave me a nod, warding Felix even though I could tell all he wanted to do was join Ellie and keep her safe. But the younger witch was more at risk, so he stayed put where he was most needed.

That left Puck and Manisha. The wounded Knight was on her foot, sword held in her hand. Her stance balanced to correct for the loss of her other arm, and her expression focused and calm. Whilst Puck simmered, despite her smiles and light tone, I still caught the anger in her eyes.

Thwarted from fulfilling her Lord's order. I was going to need to keep an eye on her, more so now than usual.

Everyone looked to be ready. Time to kick the hornet's nest.

Harry reached over without any prompt, and laid her hand on the spear haft, overlying my own grip with her long fingers. The coolness of her skin felt like ice pressing against me, but I sensed something else as well. The energy she was summoning, channelling, seeping into me and through me to the spear. Alien, unknown … like a taste on my tongue that was somehow both sour, sharp and sweet with acidic tartness. All wrong, but I pushed aside my misgivings and *carefully* raised the spear.

And slid it through the bowed, warped bars of the cage.

To touch the breach.

Chapter 43

Shit hitting the fan was an understatement.

A howl split the air, all too familiar, as Dr Zarkoff Bremmer shrieked.

"No! Get away from that!" The strzyga snarled from somewhere nearby, his voice resounding from every direction. "Worms! Grubs! You are nothing to *his* magnificence. How you dare seek to stop *his* glorious work?"

We'd pissed him off alright, and he reacted as expected.

Viciously, like a cornered beast.

The shadows writhed and exploded as tentacles lashed out at our small company. I instantly remembered how they had smothered and overcome Greg and I with almost casual ease in the room with the clones, and had a moment's doubt … but drew a breath again as I saw things were different this time.

Felix threw out her hands, and ripples of sound blasted out in shivering waves. The shadows hit these and immediately lost all cohesion, disintegrating into black shreds that boiled away under her onslaught. It seemed not only were the strzyga vulnerable to sound waves, to vibrations, but anything they conjured was too.

Good to know.

Dr Bremmer's hounds came bounding out from the open doorways leading off the chamber, circling and darting in to try to force Felix to split her attention. She couldn't cover all sides, what with the lashing tentacles to handle since almost as soon as she shattered them, more formed from the roiling inkiness.

But then, she didn't have to.

Manisha stood steadfast and solid on her feet, her sword a blur as she carved apart the beasts which came close enough for her to strike. Any doubts I had over her martial skill suffering from the loss of one arm were banished as she slew three massive beasts with brutal skill. Puck darted around the chamber, disappearing and reappearing to carve her long knives into any enemy she caught unawares, whilst Janus and Hunter both hammered the dark monsters with gunfire.

Answering shots rang out, acid rounds shattering on the crates the company were using as cover. Chimerians. But they hung back from coming at us directly, obviously still wary of falling foul to Greg's gift. I hadn't got a clue why they weren't using their suit's whammy devices to knock us on our arses, as the bastard with the knife had done outside the Tower of London, but I was not complaining. Maybe they were too far away, maybe it only worked close-up and personal.

Greg hung back, warding Felix from any tentacle that came too close, or any hound that sprang her way. His swordwork was far less elegant than Manisha's, but it got the job done as he knocked anything coming near away with slashes and stabs.

I took all this in with one look, before I felt the spearhead connect with the breach, and Harry's power flood through me. I could *feel* the breach, like acid under my fingers, slowly eating away at the reality in which it hung. A rip, a tear, nothing natural. This was worse than the simple Ways ripped between Realms, instead something that felt like a pulsing wound infected with virulence.

And I had to heal it. Seal it up. Like I was some sort of field medic or surgeon, instead of just a lycan with a bloody big knife on a stick. What could *possibly* go wrong.

I could feel the edges of the wound, ragged and stringy from where the substance of the Beyond had eaten away at this Realm's matter. I didn't have any sort of plaster to stick over the thing this size or this weird, but I did know a thing or to about sticking an open cut together until it could seal itself. Having had one or two of them myself. So I dragged the spearpoint like a huge and unwieldy needle, and tried to get the edges of both sides to knit together, hoping to fuck I was doing the right thing and that this might work.

In my head, hours ticked by but it was probably only seconds, as I worked. The edges were slippery, undoing themselves half the time or disintegrating if I pushed too hard, but I found a rhythm and had a small section of the breach knit together … when *something* noticed.

The breach suddenly flowered open, pulsing with ill energy as the thing on the other side awakened to my presence, to what I was doing. And I felt myself wrenched through that sickening hole, pulling Harry with me.

Or at least part of me went. Somehow I knew I was still standing in the troll hole, spear pressed to the breach. But also … elsewhere.

My mind refused to really make sense of this other place. All it could do was make rough guesses, based on my knowledge and experience. It was like I hung in a cold vacuum, space all around me. No sunlight, no stars. This was the inky depths of a place far beyond the reach of our sun or moon or any source of brightness. Instead, the blackness was etched in a violet-red glow. The same shade as the energy aura of the breach, and of the energy feeding the shadow hounds.

The Beyond.

I floated, sensing that the Harrowed Queen was also with me, but I could not see her. Instead, I got the impression of impossibly huge … *somethings* … vast like planets, but nothing so simple or benign. No, I caught the twisting of humungous tentacles, arms long enough to reach around the Earth several times over with gaping suckers the size of cities. The nearest body rolled, revealing a single eye without a lid, slitted into three barbed lines, glaring out into the bottomless depths. Mouths opened all along the thing's scaled hide, moaning and screaming and whining, a constant barrage of tormented and tortured souls.

This, I realised, was the Cthulhu. The Gods of that monstrous pantheon. Larger than imagination, worse than anything dreamt up in a horror writer's maddest nightmares. Tainted, unnatural and so wrong in every way. The mere existence beat against me, making me want to puke up everything I had ever eaten, soil myself and curl up in a small ball from the wrongness of it all.

"What manner of thing are you?"

It wasn't speech. Not like anything I had ever heard, or even how creatures of the Real often inserted their conversations directly into one's head without bothering the ears. No, these were more … feelings. Somehow a language translated from the pain and sorrows I had felt throughout my life, born of agonies. Derived from everything negative or bad I'd ever felt or suffered.

This was the language of suffering.

I ignored the presence as it pressed on me, like I had to assume those who dived deep under the sea had to ignore the pressure of the sea weighing in on them. An implacable force, trying to crush them. Just like this fucker was doing to me.

Instead, I tried to imagine me still back in the troll hole, knitting the breach together. Sealing the bastard shut, so we could all go home. And not dealing with a tentacled horror from beyond my understanding. Eyeballing me as I floated in deepest darkest space.

"What are you?"

The presence wrenched the deepest agonies from inside me, twisting them so effortlessly that I had no chance to fight it, no way of stopping it. Or ignoring it.

"Fine. I'm Morgan Black, and I'm shutting down this clusterfuck you're trying to pull off." I snarled, throwing the words back at the unimaginably huge being eyeballing me. "Who the fuck are you?"

The creature ... god ... demon ... whatever it was, it remained silent for a moment, before it reached inside me again and played my emotions to reply.

"**The Unspeakable. That which shall not be named. Dweller in the shadows. The Promiser.**" The words formed all around me, booming in the darkness of space, as the hulking monstrosity howled through all its mouths, as that one eye glowed with virulence back at me.

"Right. I think I'll call you ... George." I snarled back, as the pain ran through me, lit like lightning. "So now that we've introduced ourselves, please go fuck yourself, George whilst I finish closing *your* door. The one you opened and started using to tempt fucking stupid mortals to listen to you, to let you in. Goodbye, George."

Silence roiled between us as pain shivered through me, making me want to scream, to convulse and more importantly want to punch something. Anything.

Then more ripples pulsed from the creature, dragging out agonies I'd buried deep down inside me and newer ones too. Fresh ones for my fight in the Shadow Court, all the pain I'd suffered, the fear I'd felt at almost losing Sarah or Bear. Maybe both.

It laughed.

The sound reminded me of Madb, the shivering cruelty of her humour, but so much worse. This sickened me to my core, making my insides roil even though they weren't even present. Like the stench of a charnel pit, the rotting corpses of a hundred thousand dead. The stink of leprosy, the reek of decay. All rolled together, and soaking into me as it 'spoke' again.

"**We do not open doors. We are those that wait. The Watchers.**" It told me with resounding smugness. And absolute truth, no matter how much I wanted to believe it was lying. "**We have no need to open ways to your dominion. We are invited time and time again. Close this door, some other will open another. We only await the** time when we may all fully awaken, when all hope is lost. When all that is left is what we offer. Absolution, through extinction. The end of all. We were *invited*."

Beyond the Old One, I saw numerous other floating hulks, massive behemoths of nightmare and horror. This thing's brethren. The pantheon of Cthulhu. But beyond them, I saw countless scattered worlds, shattered into fragments, the detritus of worlds these things had visited and *blessed* with their gifts.

Extermination.

"I sense the other with you. Something from our dominion. Shielding you with shared blood." It instructed whilst stabs of pain blazed through me. "Ask her, little Morgan Black. She will tell you the truth. We come only when invited."

"Now. Close this door." The Old One gibbered, its mouths screaming and howling in mad laughter. "If you can."

I felt Harry's energy blaze through me, binding to the breach, tendrils of her essence ripping into it as she and I threw everything we had into pulling it closed. Whilst the Old One watched, gibbering and mocking until it grew bored and lashed out with its smallest tentacle. One lash, one stroke.

Harry and I screamed, the agony ripping through us like ten thousand barbs tearing into our insides. Blood filled my mouth, so far away, but I snarled and spat out the hot metallic taste, hurling everything I had into forcing the breach closed. Inch by inch, yanking it shut.

The Harrowed Queen was sobbing, agonised gasps wrenched from her as her essence burned and unravelled under the touch of one of the gods of Cthulhu. But it was teasing, playing with us. Inflicting only enough of its power to terrorise us, not kill us. Or so I had to think, as the vast bulk of it remained at a distance. Watchful.

Just a little more. A little more … I felt the last few inches of the breach start to close, knitting together as my pulse pounded in my ears, every part of me poisoned, burned, sickened and twisted under the other's touch.

"It is done. For now, your dominion is saved." It sang words of pain through me, as that eye focused one last time on me. Alien and so utterly wrong. "But all you have done is postpone the inevitable. We are what is to come. You cannot escape us. Now, begone."

And then I felt the being simply shove me, a slap as one might shrug off a bug. Sending me crashing back into my body, back in the troll hole even as I felt the breach unravel and fold in on itself. Sealing itself shut, its edges knitted together until it shimmered out of sight like a fading electrical storm.

Dr Bremmer's voice howled out in the shadows on all sides.

"What have you done?! What ... I will crush you, worms!" The strzyga shrieked, his tone one of agony, pain ridden and tainted with fear. But it trailed off, disappearing as the shadows unravelled and retreated back into the tunnels. Wounded, running.

"Morgan! Are you ok?" Sarah ran from cover, coming to my side even as I toppled down to my knees. "My god, you're bleeding!"

I felt hot wetness soaking my skin, running from my eyes, my ears and nose. My brief exposure to the Beyond, to the creatures lurking in its depths, had ruptured things inside me. The pain the Old One had twisted from me, it had been physical. Causing me to suffer and bleed profusely.

"Fuck." I snarled, leaning on my mortal love as I levered myself up with the butt of my spear. "That hurt. A lot. Don't ever ask me to do that shit again. Ever."

Harry was down on her hands and knees, her black body smoking as if she had just hurled herself through an inferno. She shivered, but bent her neck to rest her eyes on me and whispered words for my ears only.

"It spoke the truth. They come only when invited." The Harrowed Queen admitted softly, and I felt coldness settle in my gut. "Which means …"

"Someone from *this* side opened the breach, and called them." I finished. "Someone far more bloody powerful than Dr Bremmer and his crew."

Oh shit on a stick.

Chapter 44

Thankfully, I did not have too long to dwell on the latest revelation, as things went from bad to a whole lot worse, very quickly.

Even as I was gathering my strength to check on how everyone was doing, and anything I'd missed whilst closing the breach, a new alarm rang out in the cavern. Loud, abrasive and just the sort of thing to herald a series fuck up.

"What the hell is that?" I growled, shaking my head as the ringing peal made my ears pound. Seriously, did no one think of us poor lycan when they designed discordantly loud alarms these days?

Ellie was still with us, lending a hand to help Harry up whilst Sarah supported me. The witch looked across at me, then up to the massive structure hanging like a pendulum from the hole's ceiling.

Now that I took a moment, I could see energy crawling all over the framework, fingers of red violet lightning jumping from level to level, as the substructure vibrated and shook. Given that the whole thing was like a massive, mega heavy metallic stalactite, it was not all that reassuring seeing it quiver and shake like that.

"I'm only guessing here," She replied after a moment. "But given your friends blew up the relays controlling the power they were able to draw from the Beyond through the breach, and you've now gone and closed that thing off, I'd say the alarm is signalling an imminent shutdown of this entire structure. The bindings holding the troll hole together failing, and a return to its natural state. In other words …"

"We've got to get the fuck out of here, before we're crushed when everything collapses back in on itself." I groaned, wanting to knock my head against the nearest wall. Of course they'd have the whole place rigged and drawing energy from the breach to keep the extra-dimensional space open and usable. And I'd just gone and twisted the tap, shutting it all down.

A warning sign, a label somewhere. Anything to highlight the risk of closing the breach *might* have been handy. Just saying.

"That's it! I've had it!" Trix almost shrieked as she glared across at me. "This job officially sucks. I've been shot at, had to deal with spider monsters shooting webbing at me, been hunted by freaks with acid guns and fucking dogs made of shadows, and then turned *mortal*. And now this whole place is going to crush us all to death? I'm done!"

"Brother, we're out of here!" She darted from cover, and it was only now that I realised that the shooting had stopped. The tentacles had vanished back wherever the strzyga had run to, but it seemed the remaining chimerians had also gotten the memo of impending doom.

Or those that still lived. Looking around, I saw two more bodies crumpled on the ground. Testament to Hunter's sniper skills I had to guess since the bastards had remained at a distance behind what cover they could find. Still hadn't helped them.

"Brother! I said we're leaving!" Trix stamped her foot, but Dix rose to face her, expression set.

"Not without them." He pointed to the prisoners still in the cells, And then back at the rest of us. "Or them. We've all got to get out of here together, sis. Otherwise we're just as bad as the mortals. Like the ones who made fun of us when we were kids. The ones who have been trying to kill us. We're better than them."

"Oh fuck, you and your morals! You *steal* things for a living!" She almost screamed back at him, the rage fuelled by fear. And it was consuming her. "You break into places and nick other peoples' stuff. You can't be a white knight on a shining steed when you do that. So just quit it and come on."

Dix shrugged, and walked slowly over to the first cell.

"Maybe I can't. But I can at least try." He told her, before turning his back on her and bending over the lock, pulling out a set of picks.

"Oh for the love of … !" She fumed, before stomping over to join him. "Leave it alone! You'll take forever and this place is going to kill us long before you open up one bloody lock."

She drew out a tube of powder from her belt and began sprinkling it carefully into the mechanism. It immediately began to hiss and spark, the metal shattering a moment later. With a glare first at Dix and then at me for some reason, she began working her way along the cells, cursing under her breath loudly.

With that in hand, I gestured from the rest of the company to come in close. We didn't have a lot of time, and stuff needed sorting.

"Ok, so anyone got any idea how long this place might last now that I cut the power to the magic holding it together?" I asked, looking across at Ellie as our expert on all things magical.

The witch shrugged, nodding to where the spike from the ceiling was crackling with uncontrolled energy.

"Without knowing the actual details of the crafting, I couldn't give you an exact time it will fail." She answered but smiled as she read my expression. "*But* I would suggest we have maybe an hour, maybe a little more or less. The structure is the key … when that goes, I assume the dimensional differentials will realign back to their normal position. Returning this whole structure back to solid bedrock."

Trix snarled a curse from where she was working, but Dix just shrugged as an apology for his sister's bad mood.

"I can only agree with the sentiment of the … young woman." Ellie added with a small smile. Behind her, the half fae snorted something that I thought best not to tell the witch. About where she could stick her agreement. "This is not anything we can argue with, convince not to happen or prevent. We need to leave."

"Which is why most of you are going to do just that." I nodded to where Trix had finally finished unlocking all the cells, their doors sliding open. The occupants all slowly shuffled, stumped or staggered out, in mixed degrees of health. Around twenty or so Real creatures, including the two Bung brothers. All from differing Courts, some dressed in the rags of Mortal Realm clothing.

All taken from their homes, some battered by traitorous leaders whilst the others stolen away by the chimerians. All bore wounds, some missing body parts, and all looked drained. Bite marks showing on their skin, veins sliced open for the strzyga to feed from.

"You! You to blame!" Tol Bung stumped over. The troll was instantly recognisable as it was the only one I knew who had lost a leg, and kept replacing the missing limb with anything that it could scavenge. Recently it had been a piano leg, but now I saw … yep, the troll must have decided that wasn't classy enough for the furry entrepreneur. Now it now sported the lower limb from some classic piece of furniture. Dragons entwined the limb, flapping their limbs and with jagged fire roaring from their gaping maws.

It was an elegant, masterful piece of woodwork. Spoilt thoroughly by the troll attached to it, and the fact Tol had thought it needed sprucing up, and painted the thing a vile, bilious green.

"Every time am around you, bad things happen!" Tol snarled, even as Bol bundled along behind its brother, trying to quieten the loud troll. "Lost leg, your fault. Lost home, your fault. Lost clients, your fault. Now stolen by mad mortals wanting to drink Bung blood? Your fault."

I tuned out the angry troll's rant, since I really didn't have the time to go into how so many of the things it blamed me for were down to the Bung brothers' actions and baseline stupidity. Instead, I faced Sarah who had heard my last statement and picked out the nuance that I knew she would do. I couldn't fool her.

"You said *most* of us need to leave, *mi lupo*." She stated, not a question but pointing out the fact. "That indicates some are thinking of staying. Which, if I understand Ms McElvy correctly, would mean being caught here when this unnatural place reverts to its natural state. Solid rock."

I shook my head, knowing how it sounded.

"My bad. I meant we're all leaving, but most of you need to get out first." I explained, seeing her brow furrow at the *you* part. "I have to find Dr Bremmer. He has an antidote to something that's killing Jessica. I almost had it, before Madb carted me off to you know where. I can't leave without it."

I didn't mention the other little detail. The fact I wanted to hunt down Dr Bremmer and that bastard chimerian who had almost gutted me, and make sure neither of them found a way to escape. The others too. They needed to be stuck here, when the troll hole collapsed, buried for all time without any chance of survival.

I figured Sarah might feel a little less inclined to go along with my plan, if she figured I was out for blood, revenge and all those good things she morally objected to.

"One question." Greg wiped shadow muck from his sword, the essence of the hounds he had slain clinging like tar. "What makes you think they are still here? We've hurt them badly, taken away the one thing they needed to complete their plan. They have a load of stolen portal keys … they could have fucked off anywhere by now."

Puck interjected before I could answer, reaching to her shoulder and slipping her pack free. It jangled as it hit the floor, and I had to guess it was one of those magical items fae loved to make where you could put anything inside it no matter the size or weight. Bags of holding, like the one I'd gotten from the Bung brothers and used to trick a very nasty Wyld-born demigod.

"*Had.*" She corrected him with a smug smile. "Whilst you were all busy getting captured, I made myself useful and tracked down the stolen items, relieving these creatures of them all. If the fools have retreated to where they stored them, they will find only useless ornaments of a phallic nature in their *secure* safe. I thought it a good swap."

I grunted a laugh, knowing any moment of levity was worth enjoying when we'd had such a crappy run of things.

"There's also the fact I don't think Dr Bremmer is a runner." I added, tapping a finger to my head. "He's arrogant, sure of his own superiority and more than a little fucking nuts. He'll want to beat us, to show he is better than weak little fools like us. Even if it does mean risking his life. Or those of his colleagues. The chimerians are the same. We've killed some of their number, shown them to be vulnerable. We know of their existence. To them, that means they have to stay to finish us off."

And then I pointed to the next level up.

"Plus, there's the fact the bastard is standing out in the open, watching us."

Everyone jerked up to stare at the warped figure of Dr Bremmer as it stood on the walkway. His clothes were in even more disarray, and he glared down at us with his violet and red burning eyes full of hate and pain. Shakes ran through him, and I could read the damage done to him by Greg's gift but also the closing of the breach. But that didn't mean he was done just yet.

"None of you are leaving here! You will all die!" He hissed, even as Hunter fluidly raised his rifle and lined up the shot. The scientist screamed in fury and fled just as the gun barked and round hammered into the rock behind where the strzyga had been standing a moment before.

The shape changer sighed, letting his rifle dip as he turned back to the group.

"Worth a shot." He shrugged, and Janus slapped him on the shoulder.

"Time's ticking." I called everyone's attention back to me, eyeing the sparking column above us. When that went, it all went. "I know I'm going to regret this, but we're splitting up. The main group will head directly up through the way we came in, back through the main facility and out the hole we made in their back door. The prisoners will need protecting, so I'm sending everyone but Hunter and Puck in that group."

I let the expected rebuttals, arguments and general *what the fuck* comments roll over for a moment before clapping my hands together sharply.

"This is not up for discussion. I need enough eyes to keep a watch for ambushes, and enough capable fighters to knock back anything that gets thrown your way. Don't forget, there's a nest of spider goblins between you and freedom too." I pointed out, locking eyes with Manisha. "The Ivory Knight will be in charge, as I trust her to get all of you out alive. It's what she is good at. Scratch that, she's bloody amazing at it. Don't give her any grief."

"You should have one or the both of us along." Ellie told me sharply, as Felix nodded. "We can counter the strzyga, and Gregory is enough of a deterrent to keep them or their hired soldiers from harming the others. You are risking too much, dear."

I shook my head, smiling reassuringly.

"If you're with me, I wouldn't know how to ask Greg to leave you behind again." I nodded to the guardian who nodded once, an unarguable fact. "And I owe it to Danny to get Felix out of here. The more people I have with me, the slower we'll be and the more chance Bremmer or the chimerians will wound one of you to slow me down. Put me on the defensive, make me split my focus. You are both better off helping the prisoners and getting clear. I'll be right behind you."

Then I turned to Sarah, ready to make my argument.

But she just shushed me, placing her fingers over my lips.

"You just said it. You can't have your attention split, and if I'm with you that's what will happen." She told me, reminding me again why I loved this mortal woman. She *got* things. "I would say take Bear with you, but I'll feel safer with him at my side. Just don't hang around. Get your antidote and settle the scores I know you need to. Then come home."

Yeah, Sarah didn't miss a trick. She'd guessed what I hadn't said anyway. It made present shopping for her a *real* pain.

Bear shook his head, obviously not pleased with the plan. But I just knocked heads with him, pressing close for a long moment. He gave a worried *chuff* and leant against me for a moment before padding to settle by Sarah's side. Her protector, until she was in the clear. Then the stubborn bastard would probably come running back inside for me unless I stopped him.

"Ok, that's settled." I caught Manisha's eye, and she motioned with her hand for me to step to one side for a quiet word. Puck was busy settling the stolen portal keys back on her belt, and Hunter was checking his weapons and ammunition, so I left the pair and joined the Knight.

"What's up?" I asked, as she turned her back so that all the group were to her back. Hiding her lips, I had to guess.

"Your plan is simple, and I think it has a good chance of success." She told me with a small smile, as she rubbed the stump where her arm used to be. "I wanted you to know I will watch over your loved ones, and make sure they get to safety. You have my word on that."

"Never doubted it." I reassured her, knowing the Ivory fae to be an exceptional member of her species. One who understood honour and obligation, and actually seemed to have morals. That was rare. "And …?"

The Knight snorted, shaking her head. But the look she shot me was serious. Deadly so.

"Watch you back, Errant." She instructed me without looking around. But I guessed where her eyes would have fallen, if she had. On whom. "I warned you once that Puck is not to be trusted. She is Lord

Oberon's *little knife*. And you have stepped between her and her Lord's wishes, which is never the smartest move for a long and peaceful life. Be careful."

I nodded, knowing she simply spoke the truth. The Ivory spy had proven her worth many times over on this hunt, but that in no way meant I was ready to forget who she was, and who she worked for.

"Hunt well, Errant and I will see you for a drink to celebrate our success when this is done." The Knight told me, resting her hand gently on my shoulder for a moment. Then, she turned and walked off, calling out for the company to fall in with her.

Time to go find a twisted madman and a psychopath, and put an end to their trouble once and for all.

Chapter 45

We headed deeper into the troll hole.

One lycan, Ivory spymaster and shape changer hunter.

Ranged against us, I figured we had the last three surviving chimerians, including the one who had attacked Jessica and I, and Dr Bremmer and his four remaining brethren. Colleagues. Fang-friends. Whatever.

Seven to our three. Not the best odds, especially when three of them could use their suits to knock us on our arses, having a similar effect as Greg's gift. If we gave them enough chance to use that trick. And the other five could command shadows, summon monster dogs and who knew what else was true from all the myths and legends mortals had about vampires.

Luckily, I hated it when the odds were against me, and had a long running habit of cheating to balance the scales. Whatever worked, as long as I was the one who got to walk away in relatively one piece.

That was why I gripped the stun stick that Manisha had given me back at the waystation. *Slightly* modified, thanks to Ellie and Felix's natural talents for messing with magical artefacts and the simple truth that I knew how fae magic worked. The weapon was keyed to me, which meant I had the mystical version of an admin password to it, and could allow someone to tamper with it. Make subtle changes.

Like changing a weapon that emitted a stun effect to disrupt nervous systems and numb muscles, to instead make it convert all that power into sound waves instead. A howler stick, rather than a taser. Perfect for knocking any strzyga down and keeping them there.

For the chimerians, I didn't have any tricks up my sleeve, but instead had simple knowledge. That they needed those bulky backpacks they had fitted to their suits working, to not just power their knockout effect but keep the whole thing functional. And any breach to their armour was a death sentence, if they were exposed to regular air. Which I had to figure was what we were breathing now that the breach had been sealed.

Actually, I had one trick. A present from my father, one I was keeping for the bastard with the knife. Him, and him alone.

Hunter took the lead, his senses as sharp as my own for tracking our enemies. But he had an advantage, having actually *been* one of them, taking their form. It meant he could find them more easily, his senses coded to their scent, their sound. Even the beat of their hearts. It's what made shape changers very efficient hunters and killers.

Creepy, hell yeah, but still efficient.

We'd started at the bottom level of the troll hole even though we'd seen Dr Bremmer one level up, ducking for cover from Hunter's inhumanly accurate pot shots. That didn't explain where the other twisted scientists and chimerians had gone, and the last thing I wanted was to be caught between them in a well planned ambush. The last one of those had almost cost me my alpha, let alone putting me out for almost two days to heal the damage I'd suffered.

So, we went fast but methodically. Level by level. Whilst the clock ticked closer to the troll hole expiring and reducing us all to something thinner than atoms within solid rock.

No rush, then.

The tunnel we chose led off a short distance, but even before we had travelled half its distance we could all tell what awaited us. The smell was unmistakable.

Death.

The chamber we stepped into, with weapons raised and eyes searching for trouble, was large and rough hewn like most of the troll hole. Inelegantly crafted, which fitted with this being something done by mortals. No matter any guidance given them from supernatural beings, they were still limited in how they manipulated the craft compared to any creature of the Real.

Tables were set out in a four by four pattern, with benches set on each side. And atop these lay the bodies of half a dozen Real creatures, limbs splayed in death, eyes glassy and chests stilled. But they did not lie peacefully, their suffering writ in their twisted poses.

These poor victims had been fed on, and I had to guess whilst they still lived. I saw a Wyld fae dryad, her wooden limbs stripped of muscle, strings of tendon falling from the table like wrinkled elastic. Two dwarrow, both bled dry so that their bodies were even whiter than normal, veins opened with surgical precision and clamps attached to stop healing from happening. A pair of hags, stripped and left horribly naked with bite marks crowding their limbs so that it looked like they'd fallen victim to a frenzied attack by a pack of wild beasts, not corrupted mortals. And finally, a lone sylph, her gauze wings broken and bound, fragile body shattered to allow her attackers access to the marrow of her bones.

It was disgusting, not just the way they had been killed and fed on, but the total lack of respect shown to their dead bodies afterwards. Left to rot where they had died, discarded now that they were no longer of use. No animal, no carnivore, would act in such a manner. This was their mortal nature showing through, the arrogance of creatures who saw themselves at the pinnacle of their food chain. No wonder the Mortal Realm was in such a shitty state of pollution and degradation, when mortals crawled all over it with this selfsame lack of care.

We moved amongst the fallen victims, Hunter sweeping under the tables with his gun whilst Puck and I kept topside in case anything dropped from the ceiling or the like. But the place seemed empty, deserted, so I nodded for the shape changer to take the only way out.

With our backs to the grim harvest, I stiffened as something shifted behind us. A groan quivered in the air, a throat struggling to release whatever scream or cry had been trapped in it. And the wet sliding of stiffened muscle and cracked sinew, the rasp of bone grating against bone.

Slowly, we turned, to look back at the tables.

As the six dead creatures dragged and heaved themselves off the tables, wrinkled orbs lit with the same flame as had burned around the breach.

"Zombies. How … quaint." Puck commented dryly, even as the dead lurched upright, hands stiffened to claws and mouths gaping with broken teeth showing.

I'd dealt with the walking dead in Twilight, the draugr of legend. Creatures born of mortals who died after living despicable, selfish lives which twisted them into undead monsters with a burning desire to punish the living and make them suffer. And their stronger, even nastier cousins, the wights who could call on death magic to inflict even more suffering.

These weren't them.

The six creatures shambled on broken limbs, clawing at the air and groaning out their misery. Given their tattered, damaged conditions I was surprised at least half of them were able to remain upright, let alone be any threat to us. But I wasn't going to leave anything like this at my back, not when I had enemies a-plenty lurking nearby.

The howler wouldn't have any effect on these things, so I put it away and instead drew out my sword. Touching the link to Ivory, I ignited it so it burned brightly, spitting sparks and pushing back the shadows. The zombies did not have the feral intellect of their Twilight counterparts, no recognition showing in their shrivelled orbs of what they faced.

Hunter hung back, covering us with his gun as Puck joined me, her long knives unsheathed. She bowed to me, gesturing at the shambling horrors.

"After you, Errant." She gallantly told me, so I ducked under the nearest corpse's slow lunge and hammered my burning back through its neck with a rising blow. There was almost no resistance as the dead dwarrow shuddered, its head toppling off to thump to the floor.

Decapitation. The simplest way of dealing with anything undead. The body slumped to the ground, and I moved on to the next one. Duck, swing, slice and thump. Rinse and repeat.

I left the bodies scattered on the floor, their heads rolling under the tables or into the darkened corners. In my mind, I told them I was giving them peace. Final rest, and an escape from whatever hold Dr Bremmer or whomever of his group had over them that allowed them to raise the victims from the dead. This was the only reprieve I could give them but at least it was final.

"Let's get going. We're done here." I told Puck, killing the flame and wiping the cooled sword on my leg to clear the flaking ash that had been bodily fluids from the toppled dead.

"Ahem. I think not." The Ivory fae told me, nodding back behind me.

It is never that easy.

The bodies were still twitching, gore seeping from them and pooling out on the floor. Spreading ... touching ... merging. Even as I swore, the body parts began to draw together, melting into each other as the dead uttered groaning cries from six separated heads. These were drawn up into the bulk of the thing's carcass, as it slowly rose on trunk-like legs. Tables were pushed apart as the behemoth loomed over us, massive arms crafted from the six's limbs rising as its moans filled the air.

"I believe these are known as hulks." The Ivory fae commented dryly, eyeing the disgusting creation. "It will keep repairing itself until we burn all its remains. Rather a tiresome task, but it will only follow us and inconvenience us otherwise."

And that's when the strzyga attacked.

Two figures hurled themselves from where they had lurked, one with its labcoat discarded, the other still clad in its security clothing, their warped bodies twisting as they barrelled over the tables with talons outstretched. Hunter's gun barked, and the security-clad vampire jerked and tumbled to one side, black blood spurting from its forehead from his shot.

Padded, protective clothing only stops a bullet if the shooter shots you where you are wearing the stuff. Simple, really.

"Take the hulk, I'll handle these two." Puck told me sharply, already moving to confront the strzyga Hunter hadn't shot.

"Oh gee, thanks!" I grunted, sparking up my sword when I'd just been about to sheath it.

The hulk gibbered and swung a fist at me that was a mangled lump of twisted flesh and bone. I slipped under the blow, hewing at the misshapen forearm and searing it with fire so that the undead beast screamed from all its mouths. Charred remains flaked off the limb, revealing gnarled bone, but if I had to carve this thing apart and burn it piece by piece, we'd be here from hours.

Hunter fired again, staggering the vampire he'd already shot as it scrabbled at a table to pull itself up. The wound in its head bled dark gore, but it only gaped its too large mouth wide and hissed in fury, obviously gone past the point where mortal speech was an option. Given it's clothing, and more devolved state and muscular physique, I was betting this was the remains of Jurgen Blass, their security officer.

The shape changer bellowed back at the thing, and shot it through that dagger filled maw. Corrupted flesh and bone blasted out the back of the thing's head, and it convulsed in agony as it crashed back to the floor leaking brains and sticky blood.

I spared a glance at Puck, seeing her batting the other strzyga's claws aside with her knives and darting around its clumsy lunges to slice it again and again. Targeting muscle clusters, nerve junctions, pinpointing each with a delicate stab or cut. Drawing screams from the creature as its limbs flopped, its body jerking and losing any coherent control.

My inattention was punished as the hulk pounded its fists down, smashing one table and sending it crashing into me even as I dodged the massive clenched hands. I flew across the chamber, feeling my healing ribs protest at the mis-treatment of them, and snarled at my own stupidity. Deal with the big ugly fucker first, then gawp at the rest of my party having fun later.

With the burning sword held high and drawing the hulk's attention, I scrabbled at my trousers' many pockets, looking for the thing I needed. Manisha had made sure I was reprovisioned according to the basic Redcloak kit I always had on me, and that included helpful tools for handling situations where an inferno was the only solution.

My fingers brushed a likely flask, quickly finding and checking the braille-like inscriptions we used to identify our gear. We needed to be able to find tools by touch alone and Jessica and drummed the naming practice into us until we could identify one of over several hundred items with a quick brush of our fingers only. It made sense … there were always times we couldn't waste a moment to look at whatever we'd found to check it being right, and there's nothing more embarrassing than going up against a critter who is reactive to mercury but instead of using that, dousing the thing about to chew one's leg off with aloe vera.

Hence, the training.

So when I yanked out the flask, flicking the lid off and tossing the contents all over the moaning hulk, I had no worry I'd used the wrong thing. Plus my nose told me immediately I was spot on.

The reek of gasoline and nail polish remover filled the air as I drenched the undead monster with all of the highly flammable cocktail I carried in the flask. Even as it reared up over me, unable to smell what I'd tossed over it and its brains not processing what I might have done, I rolled over a table and hammered my sword into the broad chest. Where all the screaming, moaning mouths sang their dirge.

Flames roared up, scorching the ceiling as the hulk staggered back and tried to slap at the burning liquid sticking to it. This only spread the flames, as its flesh began to flake away. Bones cracked as the extreme heat ate through them, and the beast sagged on legs unable to support it.

The thing was toast, even as I ran my burning blade over its domed head to make the flames burn brighter, hotter. Its knuckles crunched onto the floor in an effort to support itself, but too much of it had burned away already. Of course, I hadn't thought what setting fire to something its size might do in a confined space, and kicked myself even as I staggered back, coughing.

Thick black smoke that stank of spoiled meat and burned flesh roiled off the creature. The strzyga Hunter had shot was dragging itself across the floor, the gaping hole in the back of its head still oozing thick gore. With most of its brain missing, it didn't seem to understand the danger it approached as it blindly fled the shape changer ... instead crashing into the hulk and catching on fire itself with a despairing shriek. The black blood oozing from its wounds erupted in blue-white flame as it howled and writhed, blackening to dust.

The other strzyga had lost one arm, separated clinically by Puck as she toyed with it like a cat with a mouse. Its legs dragged as it staggered back from the Ivory fae, shooting a hateful look across at the burning hulk which it must have hoped would be our doom. Then it gave a despairing shriek and threw itself *through* the burning pyre of flesh and bone. Puck tried to trap it, her knives carving deep furrows in its body as it fled, but the vampire twisted in a way no mortal body ever could, and its long arms and claws bit into stone, dragging it away.

Hunter shot it as it passed, the bullet shattering into its body and causing the thing to cry out, but before we could halt it's escape it was gone into the darkness of another tunnel.

"Quickly! It's running, and will lead us to the others." Hunter growled, his voice rusty from lack of use. But he spoke true, the creature was hurt, wounded badly. It would flee in desperation to its remaining brethren, an instinct every prey falls victim to and one every good hunter with experience knows well.

A trail of gore led us on, as smoke choked the air behind us. The tunnel the strzyga had fled through led to a stairwell heading up, and we quickly took the stairs, rising to the next level of the troll hole. One tunnel led out onto the walkway surrounding the inner chamber where the breach had hung, but the warped mortal had not gone that way. Instead, it had headed back into the facility, the passage unlit and silent.

Too silent.

"You know it's probably leading us into a trap, right?" I commented as I nodded to the way forward. Dark and quiet, not suspicious *at* all. "Just so we're all clear its about to get nasty?"

Puck grinned, showing her canines in a very feline smile, whilst Hunter simply nodded. He chambered another round, the large calibre bullets he was using only mildly smaller than the shells you see fired by tanks. No mortal could have handled his gun and its recoil, let alone so easily and quickly loaded and reloaded the heavy ammunition.

"Ok, in we go." I growled, sword and howler stick unsheathed and held at the ready. "Don't shoot me in the arse by accident."

Then I hurled myself into the dark tunnel.

Chapter 46

The good news was, I was right.

Probably should have that engraved on my tombstone, if I ever need one.

Gunfire cracked out as I loped forward, following the trail of blood and gore left by the strzyga. Acid splashed on the tunnel sides, eating into the rock as bullets shattered above and around me. I'd gone in low, only my lycan born balance allowing me to keep on my feet in such an awkward position. But whoever was shooting had been aiming high, trying for upper body or a clean headshot, and so missed me.

That was all Hunter needed as he came up behind me, tracking the bullet strikes back to their point of origin. His rifle barked, and something shattered off in the darkness, followed by a gurgling cry and the heavy thump of a body hitting the ground.

Then I felt it ... the suckerpunch slamming into me as a high-pitched whine filled my ears. My strength fled, muscles turning to rubber as I staggered and collapsed to the stone floor. Behind me I heard Hunter snarl, his rifle thudding to the floor as he too was taken out by the chimerian's stun. The bastards had lain in wait, and even though the shape changer had shot one of them, that hadn't stopped them triggering their little zapper and knocking us sideways.

I rolled, testing how fucked I was. Surprisingly, I found the effects less than when I'd been taken out at the Tower. Not totally overpowering. Enough to drop me, but I still managed to drag myself up to my hands and knees ... only to have a boot solidly connect with my ribs, sending my tumbling.

"You bastards shot Evan." The chimerian growled in the near darkness, cloaked by Bremmer's control over the shadows. I didn't know if that meant the twisted fucker was close, but I knew at least one stryzga was. The wounded one. I could hear it gasping and hissing somewhere nearby. The stink of it filled my nose, all manner of wrong in every way.

"Gonna make you suffer before they feed on yer." The soldier snarled, and I could tell this wasn't the one with the knife. It … his accent was less Afrikaans and more East London street. That didn't make him any less dangerous, given he had us at his mercy.

"Another …" I caught the wounded strzyga's hiss, panting out the word with almost all its strength. Movement in the dark told me there was one other, two of them at least. We'd ended one with the hulk, so that left Bremmer and three others. Too many to handle if I was stuck like this.

I inched my fingers toward the howler, even as I growled under my breath and forced myself to get back up.

"Stay down! Wait yer fucking turn." The chimerian slammed his boot behind my knees, folding my legs and sending me crashing back down. "I want the one who shot me mate to suffer first."

Hunter chuckled, a bestial laugh as he staggered upright. Yep, the stun effect was definitely not as bad as before. Maybe it was keyed to the power in this place, so when we'd fucked that up we'd messed it up too. Or maybe it just was worse when more of them used it together … the one with the knife had had his comrade with him when they'd attacked Jessica and me, doubling the weakness caused.

Who the fuck knew. Who cared. I just focused on the fact the idiot had dropped me onto the howler stick, as I gripped the weapon tightly.

"C'mon on then. I didn't just shoot this fuckwit, I shot *all* your mates." Hunter bragged as he raised his fists. "Come make me bleed. If you can."

The chimerian snorted a laugh, and brought its gun round to point its muzzle at the shape changer's face.

"Naah, mate." He drawled. "I reckon they'll bleed you well enough. I'm just gonna spread that pretty face of yours all over the wall. See how smug you'll be then."

There was no way Hunter was going to be able to dodge any bullets fired almost point blank into his face, and no matter his healing abilities that acid was going to ravage him. Badly. I fed Wyld might into my muscles, fire raging through me as it sought to overpower the weakness keeping me down.

"Another!" The strzyga screamed, as the chimerian went to pull the trigger. "There was ... another ... one!"

"So there was." Puck commented out of thin air, as her swords crashed round. Slamming into the back of the soldier and shattering the bulky backpack before driving deep into his body.

The gun went off, but the soldier was already sinking to the ground, spine sliced apart. Acid chewed into the rock by Hunter's feet, as the stunning effect drained away and I pulled myself up.

Puck had her back to where I'd heard the strzyga scream, and one came flying out of the murk, talons scoring the air and jaws gaping wide. It screamed ... but this time as I slammed the howler into its mouth and activated the weapon, sending a stream of vibrations out and through its warped head.

The vampire convulsed, talons scratching sparks from the nearest walls as it writhed as if electrified. It dropped to the stone floor, foaming bursting from its mouth as I hammered another blast of soundwaves into it to keep it down. Even as I turned away from the creature, Hunter staggered over and planted his rifle into its foam-sodden maw, and pulled the trigger. Flesh and gore blasted out, as the skull shattered.

Shadows shredded as they had done before when Felix fought Bremmer's power. Revealed, the wounded strzyga lay slumped against the far wall, its body charred from the burning hulk's flames and broken by Puck's knives. It glared across at me as I raised the howler and pointed at its forehead.

"Where the fuck is Bremmer?" I snarled, Changing and snarling through my worgen jaws. It was a better suit to threaten something as ugly as the strzyga, my jaws close enough to rip its face off if it didn't answer.

The wounded creature … the scientist … hissed and spat, but raised one hand as I pressed the howler into its flesh and let it feel the power build.

"Gone! He's gone. We were just … meant to … delay you." The thing panted, snarling a vicious smile. "One last key, he has gone to the black lake. Petra has … gone to awaken … the others. None of you will live … to leave here."

"Others? What others?" I snarled, images of more of the strzyga lurking in the darkness, hanging upside down like bats and just waiting to be unleashed filling my head. I really do watch far too many horror movies. "There are more fuckers like you?"

"Gnnnh, no." The creature hissed, raising a hand and pointing back where we had come from. "You met … his … pets below. Those were just … his … test subjects. He made … improvements with those you found … above. So many …"

I shot a confused look back at Puck and Hunter. What I'd found above? The only thing Greg and I had found were … and then it hit me. Petra Ingless. Dr Bremmer had said Dr Ingless had perfected the *cloning* process, creating multiple copies of the scientists before they found my mother's curse wasn't cured by them simply jumping into new versions of themselves.

The shattering of glass was loud enough to reach us two levels down, and the sirens were suddenly underscored with a horrible discordant noise. The angry, hungry moans and groans of many things, and I visualised the chamber with the clones. All those glass tanks filled with naked hairless bodies. All suddenly coming alive, clawing their way free of their confinement.

How many more clone banks hadn't we found? By the sound of it, *lots.*

We'd found vampires, so I really shouldn't have been surprised that we had zombies to deal with as well. That's just how my luck runs.

"Your ... friends ... they have no idea what is ... coming for them." The strzyga hissed a laugh, eyes blazing with hateful triumph. "Petra's ... pets will tear them ... apart. And bring our prize ... back to ... us."

Fuck. I clawed out the whisper-stone, knowing Manisha had to be carrying one. Hoping she hadn't given it back to Puck.

"Zombies. He's sending fucking zombies after you. Lots of the bastards. Get the fuck out of there!" I hissed urgently into the lump of rock, feeling it pulse as the message was relayed.

I got no answer back. Fuck!

"They are ... already most ... likely dead." The strzyga glared up at me, licking its sharp teeth. "You are ... next."

"Oh shut the fuck up." I snarled, triggering the howler.

The stick was still firmly planted in the creature's forehead, and the sonic blast ripped into it's skull. The strzyga screamed, its body convulsing as its head bashed against the rock behind it uncontrollably. I let the howler hammer through the thing until grey and black sludge erupted from its ears and bled from its eyes, and the body slumped down with a final wheezing gasp.

Then I looked back at the Ivory spy.

"Why didn't the chimerian's knock out gizmo work on you?" I asked, even as my brain struggled to work out what had happened, how much worse things had just gotten. "It kicked Hunter and I in the nuts, but not you. Why?"

The fae smiled, shrugging.

"I'm not familiar with the science the mortals used to devise their device," She acknowledged. "But I can hazard a guess. Magic, and those creatures like yourself and Hunter, all exist on what the mortals call a frequency, or wavelength. Like light. It travels at a particular speed, and can be measured. Magic does much the same. So if some clever mortal were to build a tool that interrupted that frequency, I can imagine it would work like the grey men's device."

"Why it might not have worked on me, well, that is easy." She added, her smile curving up smugly. "The setting for *simple* creatures like yourselves is most likely fairly standard, quite weak. One that would affect most lower creatures, as I presume they tested on those they captured. Whilst I … being of a much more singular nature and let us admit, a much more refined and powerful personage, well, the frequency they would need to find to target me would be much stronger, much harder to block. They *might* have managed to affect me, if sufficient numbers worked together. A single soldier though? There is little chance of that happening. Or so I surmise."

I grunted, knowing it didn't really matter. We had more pressing things to worry about.

"Let's go kill some dead bastards. Again." I snarled, leaving the slumped chimerians and strzyga on the floor behind us.

We ran, taking the nearest tunnel leading back to the main chamber. Once there, we pounded up the stairways to each level, even as we caught sight of movement far above us. Naked, hairless bodies scrabbling free from tunnel mouths, crouched over like animals, their eyes burning with violet - red fire and those horrible cries bursting from their open mouths. They didn't move like traditional zombies, didn't lurch like the risen dead we'd already faced below. These were feral, scrabbling and jerking with discordant movements, under the control of Dr Petra Ingless and filled with a singular purpose.

To rend and tear. Devour.

Hunter began firing even as we took the final stairwell at speed. His bullets hammered into the nearest creatures, shattering skulls and twisting bodies round under each strike. But more spilled out of the tunnels below and around us, many many more. The bastards must have created a whole fucking army of clones, kept them on ice just in case something like this happened. Or for the great new world Dr Bremmer wanted to fashion with the horrors of Cthulhu. Possibly to serve as obedient slaves, dog soldiers maybe.

As they fell, I saw the same black gunk running from their broken bodies, pooling together like rotten stringy cheese. These began to pull together, flesh melting together as hulks began to rise where the zombies had fallen. Behemoths, making the metal under their misshapen feet groan and bend as they clawed their way upright.

There was no way I had enough oil to burn all this lot.

Igniting my sword, seeing Puck call flames to her own knives as well, we hammered into the zombies as we struck a path to where I hoped the rest of the group were. The entrance to the troll hole. Hunter switched to his stolen chimerian gun, the acid bullets shattering the zombies he shot, eating at their flesh and sending them crashing to the floor. But more came on, too many more.

I hurled bodies off me as they tried to claw and bite at me, weighing me down. Trying to drag me to the floor where they could feed on me as a pack. My sword slashed and carved the clones apart, burning flesh and shattering bone, as I drove inward. The tunnel we needed was wall to wall filled with zombie clones, the bastards climbing up the sides with fingers shredded to bone, scrabbling like disgusting four legged spiders to reach their prey.

"Morgan! Is this your doing? Did you let out a horde of angry undead by some chance?" From down the tunnel, I heard Ellie's strident query, and bit back a snarl of a laugh. Of course I'd get the blame for unleashing a horde of zombified clones on her. Why ever not.

I was interrupted from replying as a groaning roar echoed through the entire chamber behind us. This was vast, shivering the rock and metal on which we stood, carrying a bottomless rage and never-ending hunger in its wake.

A massive hand, as big as a car, slammed down onto the walkway, bending metal so that the railing shrieked and twisted. A second one hammered down, then a third and fourth, as a massive dome of flesh slowly rose like a beaching whale. Multiple eyes glared across at us from a misshapen hillock of skin and bone, its mouth big enough that I could have stood inside it without hunching. Teeth like tombstones glittered with spit as the monstrosity levered itself up. Three of those hands, attached to arms as thick as a bus, anchored the humongous body from the metal spire hanging down from the rock ceiling as it raised its last limb threateningly.

"Now that's something you don't see everyday." I snarled, even as I caught sight of movement on the thing's right shoulder. A strzyga, body bent and twisted, clung to the behemoth and grinned savagely down at us as the other zombies cowered and snarled under the vampire's glare.

"None shall leave this place!" The strzyga, what was left of Petra Ingless, hissed as it pointed directly at me. "Ill begotten get of Margaret Black! Your death shall be one I will savour!"

"I get that a lot!" I snarled back at the warped creature, raising my burning sword. "But I don't care about you. You're just a flunkie. A stooge. I want your boss. Dr Bremmer. So do us all a favour and fuck off somewhere and die painfully. I'll even say *please*."

The strzyga screamed in fury, and the monstrous hulk it rode roared and heaved its arm down, intent on squashing me and my arrogant mouth into a bloody pulp. But I'd counted on the thing being as cumbersome as its smaller cousins, the hulk we'd fought before lacking any quickness or agility. It was pure mass, incredibly strong but so slow, I was able to dart out of the way of the blow.

Puck and Hunter, both inherently quick, dodged the scything limb even as the shape changer snarled a curse at me. Maybe I should have tried to warn them. Oh well.

What didn't get out of the way were the numerous other zombies, still in whatever thrall the strzyga held them under. Bodies were smashed to the metal floor, tossed over the railing side and broken as the hulk drew its arm back, bits of the hairless creatures stuck in its sagging flesh.

"Hunter. The frame. Shoot the fixings." I hissed across at him, whilst Petra Ingless screamed in fury and pounded on the hulk's shoulder, foaming with rage. "Think King Kong."

Hunter was as quick on the uptake as I'd hoped, rising into a crouch and slipping his rife free. He swung it up towards the ceiling of the cavern, and took careful aim.

The crack of his gun rang out sharply as bullets hammered into the metal fastenings keeping the entire spire fixed to the bedrock above us. Normally, I reckon what I was hoping for would never have worked, even with the sizeable bore of the shape changer's ammunition. But I also seriously doubted whoever had crafted the spire and fixed it in place had been told to make sure it bore the weight of a monstrous zombie hulk, swinging from it as it took aim to try to splat me again.

Four shots were all it took, as metal suddenly shrieked in the air. Petra Ingless snarled as it looked up, the hulk beneath it moaning as the spire suddenly lurched … and dropped with a crashing roar.

The strzyga screamed again and threw itself off the zombie's shoulder, twisted fingers clawing to grab the railing and halt its fall … but I'd been watching, and as those digits grabbed at the bent and shattered metal, I snarled into the vampire's wide eyes and swung my burning sword in a short, heavy blow.

Flesh parted, the hand sheared clean from its wrist bone, and the strzyga plummeted after the zombie hulk as it smashed down into the rock below. Not far enough to kill it, I had to figure, but a decent enough drop to do serious damage to the warped bastard.

Its trailing wail triggered something in the clones, those that hadn't been pulped into sodden mulch by the massive hulk. As the strzyga dropped, they swung their hairless heads back to where both had vanished, and with great scrambling leaps, heaved themselves over the edge to follow. Like undead lemmings, hurling themselves into the void after the one who controlled them.

"If you try to say you *knew* that would happen, I'm going to call you a big fat liar." Hunter grunted a laugh as the last clone hurled itself off the edge, vanishing into the void beyond.

Before I could form a suitable reply, Ellie poked her head out of the tunnel, eyes wide.

"Morgan, what did you do?!" She asked sharply, but held up a hand even as I went to answer. "Don't bother dear. This has your handiwork all over it. The spire was the central foci for the crafting controlling the troll hole's stability. Since you've just destroyed it, we need to leave. *Now*."

Ah, fuck! I scrambled away from the walkway's edge, shoving Puck and Hunter before me. We barrelled down the tunnel, where I could see the entrance standing open. Our way out.

The air grew thick and heavy, a solidness that made my ears throb and the blood pound in my head. My legs tried to tell me I was running not through empty space, but something far more solid, dragging at me and trying to pin me down. I snarled breath through my teeth, hurling myself the last few feet, rolling out the portal and crashing down into the open space beyond … as a mighty crunch resounded through the air, and the tunnel, troll hole and all that had existed there vanished forever.

Chapter 47

We'd done it. We were safe.

I should have known it was never that easy. Never that simple.

Even as I groaned and pushed myself up from where I'd crashed, I felt the ground underneath me tremble, and heard a groan that had nothing to do with the walking dead but more to do with rock being *incredibly* unhappy at its treatment. The sort of tearing noise usually heralding a landslide, earthquake or possibly in our case, an imminent collapse.

"I was afraid of this." Ellie spoke up, dusting herself down from where she'd landed herself. "The magic to create dimensional spaces is delicate and very tricky. If it's not unpicked right then it's not just the hole that is affected, but the area around it too."

"I think it's safe to say I didn't *carefully unpick* the bloody thing." I snarled, getting a smile and nod from the witch. "So this place is fucked too?"

"I think it safe to assume we need to leave wherever this place is as soon as possible." She agreed.

Fine. Except I still had one last job to do.

"Ok people!" I shouted to be heard since all of the prisoners we'd freed chose that moment to start to panic. Supernatural creatures might have special powers and be mightier than the average mortal, but they all still flap like maddened geese when frightened. It's one of the things they *don't* tell you in the fairytales. "Listen up if you want to get out of here alive!"

"No trust you." Tol Bung growled from the back, the other Bung brother shushing it with a slap over its wrinkled muzzle.

"Zip it, stumpy." I snarled back, then nodded to the mercenaries. Dix had been helping Janus whilst Trix and Mother had fought off the zombies with knives, guns and some of the less deadly explosives from the half gnome's stash, given that both of them were covered head to foot in gore.

"These lot will get you out of here. Stick close to them and get outside as quickly as you can. Don't hang around in the pipe either." I told them all, then looked over at Ellie and Greg. "Get Felix and Sarah out as well, and move down the hillside. This place could all come crashing down, and I don't want you getting caught up in that, ok?"

"What about you?" Sarah asked calmly, even as Bear butted my head for a scratch.

"Dr Bremmer got out. He still has the antidote." I told her, nodding to the other route from the basement level. The path to the black lake. "If what that strzyga said is true, the bastard's got a portal key and is probably going to try to use it to escape. I need to stop him."

"So why don't we …?" She went to ask, but I stopped her, shaking my head.

"Too many people. And there's the last chimerian with him, I reckon." I told her, nodding to where Trix was already ushering the prisoners towards the stairs. No-one was going to trust the elevators when the power could suddenly go, and leave them trapped in a metal box as the entire facility came crashing down. "I'll take Puck and Hunter again. We dealt with the last lot, so two more shouldn't be a problem."

"Help get them all out. I'll be right behind you." I promised, and she sighed, punching my arm lightly. "Nothing will get in the way, trust me."

"Last time you said that, you let a horde of hungry zombies come between us." She told me tartly, before nodding. "Just … just don't do anything stupid."

I nodded, then shot a look over at Greg, who simply nodded. He would get Sarah and Bear out, with Felix and Ellie. I trusted him, and he'd proved himself enough for me to finally release I needed to let the shit I had against him go. He *deserved* that.

Bear grumbled a hearty growl, but I gave him a shove to get moving.

"Look after Sarah. I owe you *many* sausages when we're home." I promised, and he gave a huff of agreement before padding to the woman's side and letting her grab hold of him.

The sub-basement gave another lurch, and I heard the Real creatures cry out as rock and dust dropped from above us. There wasn't a lot of time, and I needed to finish this.

We ran into the last tunnel, following the metal tracks set for the cargo carts that DOPA had used to transport goods into the facility … and most likely to dispose of the remains of their experiments. Far from anyone's eyes, the evidence of the Accord breaches hidden away, using the standard mortal thinking … *if no-one sees it, it never happened.*

I hurled myself down the passageway, sword and howler held ready, knowing who would be waiting for me. The last chimerian, and the leader of the strzyga. Both had been wounded, damaged by Greg's little gift, but they'd had time to catch their breath, recover some strength. I couldn't let them have too much of a lead, no chance to use that portal key to escape to fuck knows where. Both were dangerous individuals, but Dr Bremmer needed to be stopped permanently if the Realms were to be safe.

I wanted to end that chimerian *badly*. I knew leaving him alive would only give him a chance to get back at me. Probably through those I loved. So it was simple, he had to die.

And I'd be happy to oblige him.

I barrelled out of the tunnel into the huge cavern where the lake lay … and slowed to a standstill at what I found waiting for me. Hunter and Puck were a breath behind me.

Dr Bremmer stood at the foot of the pier leading out over the lake, his twisted tainted body hunched and bent in all the wrong angles. He clasped a silver rod in one hand, and I could taste the magic coming from the thing even at a distance. It was active, the portal key just waiting for its user to start the ritual to open a Way elsewhere.

But he hadn't. He had waited.

Before him, the last chimerian stood, facing me. He had drawn that big knife of his and held it loosely in one hand, but it was the other one that caught my attention. The one holding a bulky contraption. One I recognised from far too many late-night movies, old war films and action series.

A detonator.

"Yeah, that's about far enough thank you." The chimerian spoke calmly, evenly, but his Afrikaans accent still made him sound angry. Then again, I'd helped annihilate the remaining members of his squad, so it was possible he harboured some fury towards me. I knew I had bucketloads for the armoured fucker.

"In case you're wondering, this is a controller for the numerous explosives rigged throughout this complex." He waggled the device in his hand carefully. One finger was held over a red push button, and I had to guess it was a hair-trigger, meaning all he had to do was squeeze it to set off the explosives. Nothing more. "The entire place is wired to go up if I press this trigger, and it'll be a whole lot fucking quicker than it'll take the facility to collapse after you fucked things up so thoroughly. Your mates, the prisoners you set free, all of them will be wiped clean off this fucking planet. Unless you follow some simple instructions."

"And don't think your boy with the rifle can get a shot off quick enough to stop me." The chimerian added, nodding to Hunter. "I've seen him work. He's quick, but not that quick."

Then his domed helmet swung to look at Puck.

"As for your fae friend, well, I've seen her trick. Cute, really." He growled, and nodded to a wide circle of sparkling silver and white grit he had surrounding him. "But I'm betting silver and salted iron will stop her vanishing and appearing behind me like she did to Charlie and Bernard and those nasty knives of hers. So she gets to stay put too."

"What's your plan?" I growled, knowing I had a fine line to walk here. String him along as long as I could to get as much time for the rest of my friends, hired help and prisoners to get clear of any potential blast … whilst knowing the entire facility was coming down around our ears anyway, and needing to get this over with quick. Nothing like conflicting goals …

"Simple, really." The chimerian drawled, bouncing on his armoured heels. "Your mates get to stand there, looking pretty. Whilst Dr Bremmer there opens up a door to someplace nice and safe for us to fuck off to. And you and me are gonna finish what we started outside the Tower of London."

He waggled the detonator, then slapped it to his chest armour where it stuck.

"If you're quick, you can get your mitts on this and maybe stop me killing all your mates. And finish me off, like you did my squad." He snarled, and I could imagine the hate burning in his hidden eyes. "Whilst I'll be busy gutting you and leaving your insides all over the floor. Before I fuck off through that door, leaving the rest of you lot to do whatever you want. We got a deal, mutt?"

I shot a look at Hunter and Puck, nodding over to Dr Bremmer.

"If he looks like he's doing a runner before I'm finished, shoot him in the head." I snarled, seeing the shape changer nod once. Puck just grinned, letting her hands rest of her knife hilts. "I won't be long."

"Cocky bastard. You almost remind me of me." The chimerian laughed, before stepping to the furthest edge of the circle. "Now, drop those fancy weapons of yours. I won't use my knock-down and you won't use any fancy tricks. Just you, me, your claws and my knife. The way it's meant to be."

I shrugged, and slipped my weapons free and piled them on the floor. The howler I left on top, in case the strzyga tried anything and I need to trigger the weapon to stop him. It. Whatever he was now.

Then I stepped into the circle.

"Told you I was gonna finish what I started." The soldier growled at me, rolling his shoulders. I remembered his unnatural strength and had to guess he was a meld of ogre at the very least under his armour. Probably had other gifts from the creatures' body parts bound to him, but I didn't really care.

I was going to end him. For what he'd done to me. What he'd done to Jessica.

I wanted *blood*.

I snicked out my claws, slowing circling the chimerian. He drew his long knife, and I caught the unmistakable stink of a very familiar poison. I snarled, but the soldier just laughed nastily.

"Ok, right. Like I'm gonna face down one of your *sort* without the right tools. Told you I was going to make this hurt." He laughed again, and came at me swinging.

I knew the wolfsbane he had smeared all over his knife was the same vicious variant they'd used on both of us at the Tower. I'd rid myself of the stuff the old fashioned way before, but I somehow doubted the bastard would give me time to throw up any of the poison he got into me. So, I told myself, let's not get stabbed again.

Easier said than done.

The soldier moved fluidly despite his armour, holding the knife professionally. Not like some thug on the street, looking to intimidate more than anything else. Instead the chimerian knew his weapon intimately, and was focused purely on the kill.

My claws caught his first flurry of blows, the strength behind them definitely unnatural and way beyond anything a mortal could possess. His armour leant him bulk to match my own, and we slashed and punched at each other, rocking on our feet but refusing to give even an inch.

I risked a glance over his shoulder to check on Dr Bremmer, finding the strzyga still where we had left him. Inhumanly tall, crooked back and with his warped features making him seem less anything mortal and more an escapee from some twisted madman's nightmare. He watched the fight with eyes burning brightly, but kept glancing past us, back behind me.

A hot burning pain brought me back to the fight, as the chimerian punished my moment's distraction by slashing a deep cut in my upper arm. I felt the sting and sickness of the wolfsbane immediately, but drew on my Wyld strength to weaken it's hold on me. Still, I could almost see the bastard's grin as he held up the knife, coated in my blood.

"Lots more of that to come, mutt." He sneered and I snarled. I didn't have time for this. And I knew his weakness.

Barrelling forward, I let him slash me again with the knife, feeling blood flow and the bite of wolfsbane sting inside me. But I didn't care, smashing my claws and fists into his armour again and again.

The chimerian staggered, blocking with his forearms and cutting me again, but I focused all my attention on one section. One plate of his metal suit. I felt the material creak under the abuse I heaped on it, piling all my rage into the blows and smashing again and again.

He carved his knife into my shoulder, trying to cut me deeply and force me away, but I butted my head into his helmet and hit again. And again.

And felt something go *crack*.

The plate I'd been targeting finally gave, shattering under my repeated strikes. Gases hissed out of the cracks I'd made as bits fell away, and I staggered back even as I spat out a mouthful of blood and poison, snarling with dark joy.

"Now you die, you bastard." I barked at him, even as I saw the soldier stagger, knife lowering and dripping my blood onto the ground.

His body shook, muted sounds coming from inside the helmet. His death throws, I had to hope as I felt the poison coursing through me bite hard and deep. I wasn't going to be on my feet long if I didn't purge myself. And then I'd still be feeling like shit for a while. But it had been worth it …

Only …

The sounds sharpened, and I snarled as I realised what I was hearing.

The bastard was laughing.

Chapter 48

The next moment, the chimerian's armour made a series of loud popping sounds, and metal plates crashed to the floor in the circle.

Revealing the soldier in all his horror.

The man had been tall, well over six feet and heavily muscled from his bone structure and breadth of shoulders and chest. But that was pretty much all that remained of the man he had been.

His skin had the grey cast and stony knobbling of troll-hide, with criss-crossing scarring showing where it had been expertly stitched onto his body. His shoulders were massively malformed, the joints inflamed and bulging where his arms connected … except the tree-trunk limbs were not his, or at least not the ones he'd been born with. No matter the amount of weightlifting and steroids he could have done, no mortal would be able to have such massive limbs except by the most diabolical means possible. They made Arnold Schwarzenegger's ones look puny, even in his prime.

Further down, his thick waist and groin were also horribly deformed, with trunk-like legs attached with massive scarring at each joint. All he wore under the armour was a dirty grey pair of shorts, and these strained to cover the muscles bulging from each calf.

His chest bore even more scarring, bulging out with thicker ribs than any mortal might have and showing that at some point he had been opened up, and Gods knew what the fuck had been put inside of him. More enhancements, making him the monster supreme of any Frankenstein story.

At his thick neck, flaps quivered with each breath. Like gills, but since the bastard wasn't underwater, I had to figure they were from some other creature. Helping him breath the air that was toxic to all the others of his kind. Saving the fucker's life, when I thought I'd ended him.

I finally looked him in the eye, taking in what remained of his face. And that's when I realised what had happened. How he had survived what should have killed him.

The chimerian's skull had warped, starting to show similarities to the strzyga scientists. Not wholly transformed, there being enough of his original features to see the man he had been. Strong jawed, heavy browed. Eyes sunken beneath the bone. But his skin had melted against those bones, and his lips drawn back to show teeth lengthening to fangs.

"You're one of them." I snarled, spitting out more blood and wolfsbane.

"Only a little." He replied, his thinned lips curving in a bloodless smile. "Only enough to make sure I could survive if some sneaky bastard like you tried to end me quick-like by … oh I don't know … breaching my survival suit."

"You fed on *people*." I spat out, as the poison inside me made my stomach churn. I needed to get rid of more of the stuff but didn't want to take my eyes off the chimerian long enough to allow him to do me more damage.

"Ha, no mate. I fed on freaks. Like you." He spat back at me. The mad anger blazing in his eyes. "You're all the same. Fucked up monsters that need to be put down. It's what me and my boys were trained for, and we knew all your little tricks. Just like now."

"That reminds me." The chimerian reached out and yanked out something from the crumpled armour. "Seeing how you don't mind playing dirty …"

The next moment my ears caught the familiar whine of the chimerian's knock down machine and sickening weakness washed over me, driving me to my knees. The chimerian looked up and back at Puck and Hunter, the shape changer starting to raise his rifle as he felt the effects of the machine.

"Uh no you don't, mate." The soldier held up the hand holding the device from the armour, showing that he also held the detonator curled up against it. His hand, large enough to be from a troll or the same ogre as had 'donated' his arms, easily held both. "Back off a few steps and you won't feel so shitty. But point that gun anywhere near me and I'll bring this whole fucking place down on us."

I slumped, the weakness slapping down my rage as it allowed the wolfsbane to surge back through me. Nausea gripped me, and I snarled as I felt myself Change, switching back to my mortal suit as I struggled to fight the effects of the drug coursing through me.

The chimerian laughed, shaking his head.

"Nice mask." He sneered, tapping his own deformed face with his knife. "But I know you look just as ugly as me. Just as nasty. The difference is I don't go trying to hide it. Pretend I'm not a monster. I *know* what I am. And what you are."

He leant down as I pushed myself up, forcing myself not to throw up. Not give him the satisfaction of seeing me so weak, even if it cleared out a load of the wolfsbane.

"What's that then?" I panted, and he smiled cruelly as he levelled the knife, ready to thrust it into me.

"Meat. And I'm going to carve me a nice bloody steak out of you." He snarled.

I brought one arm up, putting all my strength into raising it high enough to thump my closed fist into the flesh below his deformed jaw. Not a powerful punch, not even enough to make his choke, and he laughed as he pressed hard against my hand.

"Is that the best you've got? Fucking pathetic." The chimerian laughed … but I just laughed back at him.

"No. I've got one last thing." I told him, even as I let the pretence of weakness fade, my voice strengthening with the rage I felt as I stared into his mad eyes. "A present. From my father."

And I summoned the spear.

I'd held my hand cocked, the angle just where I wanted it to appear. And the thick haft settled into my palm, fingers gripping it tightly … even as the rest of the weapon drove upwards. Running up directly below the chimerian's chin, spear head splitting flesh and bone as it formed. Inside the fucker's head.

I saw dark blood burst in his widening eyes as his mouth sagged open, revealing the metal head carving up through his jaw and into his brain. His fingers spasmed, and I quickly grabbed the detonator out of his thick fingers just in case the bastard managed to pull one last trick.

The point ripped through the top of his skull, bone and brain fragments exploding out as the weapon fully formed. The chimerian convulsed, spitted on the spear as I glared at him, watching the agony burn through him, then twisted the haft sharply and ripped it free.

Gore flooded down from the gaping wound, the ruined mess I'd left of the soldier's brains spattering to the floor. He dropped to his knees, somehow still alive, still conscious. Unable to speak, unable to do anything but convulse as I slowly rose to my feet.

"I know what you are." I told him quietly, as I gripped the spear with both hands, rolling my shoulders as I drew on my Wyld might and strength.

"You're history. And you should have fucking stayed there." His blood-drenched eyes widened with whatever intelligence still remained in his wrecked brain, as I brought the weapon round in a whistling arc.

The exotic metal slashed through trollskin, flesh and bone, and the chimerian's head went tumbling from his shoulders to thump in a puddle of gore on the stone floor. The body twitched, then collapsed beside it as clotted fluids gushed from the savage wound.

One bastard down, one to go.

With the spear still dripping the gory remains of the chimerian, I strode over to face Dr Bremmer. The strzyga had frozen, eyes flaring as he saw the soldier fall. He and I both knew he had no time to activate the portal key's ritual, no escape as I glared across at him. Shadows writhed around his body, but the damage we'd done him seemed to have weakened him enough that he was no threat.

Just a problem that I needed to be solved.

"Let's try this again." I snarled, raising the spear and pointing it at his face. "Give me the fucking antidote to the shit you poisoned my alpha with. Drop the fucking portal key you stole and I *might* be convinced to leave your head on your shoulders. But do it *now*."

The strzyga hissed and reared up, eyes glaring down at me but I simply thrust the weapon hard to strike at his throat. Not deep enough to do him significant damage, but still enough to draw the black blood that filled the corrupted mortal.

"Don't try me." I told him, knowing I should just kill the fucker and be done with it. But there were still things that needed clearing up. Answers he could provide. And I'd drag his twisted arse out of this tomb to answer them, and then let Cormac find a nice deep hole to drop him in. Possibly lined with spikes. And with rats. Lots of them.

"Here!" He hissed, plucking the glittering vial from his clothes and tossing the precious antidote to me. "Take it! But I never *stole* anything. The portal keys were gifts, gifts from *him*! To be used as *he* commanded! He even told us whom to take, to preserve our lives and gain the strength to usher in *his* judgement on all! Fool!"

I grabbed the antidote with one hand, even as his words bounced around my skull.

"No. That's not right." I snarled back at him, grey cells crashing together. "There's no way some freaking tentacled horror from the

Beyond could've gotten hold of all those keys. They're stored in the Court vaults. Nothing … no-one could have *given* you them."

"Unless …"

Ellie's suspicion that something from the Beyond would have no clue that commanding a mortal to ingest the vital essences of a Real creature could save them from a curse.

The Harrowed Queen's assertion that the Cthulhu or whatever the fuck they were wasn't lying to me when it said they had been invited from *within* the Realms. That they *hadn't* sought out Dr Bremmer and tried to get him to kick-off Armageddon. Someone from the inside had done that.

The fact this whole think had felt hinky from the word go, with vengeful ex colleagues of my mother crawling out of the woodwork just at the same time she was reborn as a Crone of the Wyld. They'd kept themselves secret until then, so why blow their cover by kidnapping Herne and literally lighting the bonfire and waving flag saying *come find us*? And a bunch of special ops world war two assassins coming after Jessica and I just as we started to poke around, revealing their existence stupidly when the insane Frankenstein-monsters were meant to have all been destroyed decades ago?

Facts tumbling around my head, and then clicking together as my father's final warning came back to kick me hard in the backside.

"*Beware. Betrayers … come in … all colours.*"

You always reckoned the backstabbers and evil villains dress in traditional colours. Black, deep reds. Sometimes exotic dark purples and greens for that *cruella* or *poison ivy* look. But traditionally, they're all into their wannabe goth ensemble. Hell, look at Madb and her weird Wednesday Adam vibe.

You never think the ones in white are the bad guys. Till they stab you in the back.

Or the ones in *Ivory*.

I turned to look back at my companions. Hunter had his gun half raised, his expression confused as he muddled through what we'd just been told. What I'd blurted out. But I saw dawning comprehension widen his eyes even as his rifle began to lift again.

And Puck.

Who sighed and shook her head.

"Well, fudge. I guess the cat's out of the bag." She told me with a sweet smile.

Chapter 49

None of us were quick enough to stop her.

As she had done before in the cavern with the breach, the Ivory spy's image flickered and vanished. Only to reappear behind Hunter, her sharp knives already drawn.

The shape changer managed only a sharp cry of surprise, before those sharp blades connected, cutting as easily as my spear had done. His head sagged and toppled as silver blood spilled out over his clothes and he slumped to the ground.

Dead. Very dead.

She vanished again, re-appearing by the gear I'd had to dump whilst fighting the chimerian. Dropping one knife, she snagged up the Howler and pointed it directly at Dr Bremmer. The strzyga snarled and threw up shadows to ward himself ... but these shredded as she activated the weapon. He was picked off his feet, portal key tumbling from his fingers to clatter on the ground as Puck blasted him again and again until he was a convulsing wreck on the stone pier, foaming from his warped mouth and shuddering like he was gripped by the fiercest of fevers.

This had taken two breaths. Maybe three.

I was already raising my spear, drawing a bead on the spy when she dropped the last knife and instead sketched a glyph in the air. One I knew well. The same mark I wore as a brand, the Ivory glyph that allowed me to summon armour and ward myself from harm.

That's not what happened this time.

Instead, I felt the armour form but lock in place, binding me to the floor and constricting around me until I could hardly breath. I couldn't move, not my arms or legs or even my head. The magical armour encased me, freezing me like a statue as I snarled and raged against its grip. I tried to call on my Wyld might to burst free, but found only emptiness … the strength deserting me the moment I needed it. Locked away, out of reach.

I couldn't reach the whisper-stone to summon help, and everyone who might have been of any aid was already hopefully outside the facility. Safe, but no bloody help at all.

She had me.

Puck walked back over to Hunter and nudged the body over, leaning down to check its pulse despite the fact it had no head. Satisfied, she pushed herself back up.

"No witnesses." She commented to me, as she walked past where I was frozen.

The fae reached down and picked up the discarded portal key, slipping it into the bag with the others she had collected. Then she casually sent another blast of angry vibrations into Dr Bremmer, making him shriek and writhe.

"Just making sure he stays put." She explained before slowly walking back to face me. Smiling, relaxed. At ease.

The bitch.

"I bet you are positively *fuming* right now, Errant." She reached up and stroked a finger down my cheek, where the armour left my skin clear. Her touch was light, tender, but I snarled all the same, wanting nothing more than to smash that smug smile of hers from her face. "It's a pity you did not listen to dear one-armed Manisha. She *did* try to warn you not to trust me. Ah well. We live and learn."

She looked back at Hunter, then winked at me.

"Well, some of us do."

"Why?" I growled, finding I could at least talk. If I could keep the fae chatting, there was a chance I'd find a way to break the Ivory-born constraints. Or at least force her to panic if the facility started coming down around our ears. She was too at ease, too relaxed. I wouldn't have a chance of getting free unless I messed up her mood.

"Why what? Why did I kill Hunter?" She mused, tapping the Howler to her lips before shrugging. "As I said, I didn't want any witnesses. I *could* have probably bribed him to keep quiet, but then he would have something on me, and you and I both know shifters are untrustworthy. All too quick to go back on their word, change a deal, anything if it suits them. So, I decided the easiest option was the best."

"For me." The fae added with a smile. "Not for him, I would have to admit."

Then she threw out her hands, encompassing where we stood.

"But I *think* you meant why this? All this messing with mortals and threatening the end of the Realms. Crazy stuff, I have to say." The fae walked slowly around me, poking me with the Howler but not triggering it. I had to figure, like the Ivory glyph, she was able to use anything crafted by her Court even if it was bound to me. Handy to know, if I'd been given bloody a user manual or something.

"It's simple really." She didn't trigger the weapon, just used it to test that I was still frozen stiff, imprisoned and unable to act.

"My Lord, the ruler of the Ivory Court … he desires it. War. Power." She explained and I started to understand just how big a fuck up I'd made, and how deep in the shit I was. And sinking fast.

"The Realms, in his opinion, have stagnated since the Accords and the Lord of Ivory desires a return to a more … primal time." She explained, walking over to the dead chimerian and plucking up the detonation device, tossing it up and down in her free hand. "One where the mortals do not stand as equals as beings such as himself. Or, of course, the other Lords and Ladies of the Courts."

The fae casually slipped the chimerian's device into her belt, close to hand. Probably in case it looked like I was going to get away from her.

That last bit she added far too off-handedly for me to believe. If Oberon was after power, then he only wanted it for himself, not an equal share amongst the rest of the elders.

Puck's next words confirmed my suspicions.

"Of course, my Lord understands that should he succeed, he would be best suited to lead the other Courts back to their glory days and usher in a new and wonderous era for all." Puck managed to recite that with only a faint trace of sarcasm, whilst I snarled at the ego of the immortal. "The other Courts, and their Lords and Ladies, they will learn to accept his way … or face his wrath. As Twilight did once before."

"When Ivory and Shadow betrayed them, and stabbed them in the back?" I spat out, but Puck simply smiled and nodded.

"Exactly. And if a mere lycan can understand the moral of that particular lesson then I shall not worry whether the Lords and Ladies should struggle either." She mocked back at me. "But I digress. We have little time, and you really *should* understand just what sort of mess you've stepped in … and been stepping in for quite some time now."

"The fact is, Errant, you've been getting in the way." Puck stepped up to me and gently tapped me on the cheek as if schooling a naughty child. "Thanks to those wretched Accords, my Lord cannot simply challenge the mortals and their Goddess, and wrestle power that they are so unsuited to wield from them. If he tried, he would have found himself at the mercy of the Furies before they were dealt with. And now, well, all the Courts and the mortals would simply unite against him. Which would not end well, for all parties."

"So he has been busy. Arranging matters, seeking to manipulate events so that his intervention would be unarguable, and something all the other Courts would support." She laid it out for me, the scale of how long Oberon had been planning. Pulling strings. Moving pieces.

The spy started ticking items off her fingers, as I raged and tried to find the crack, the weakness, anything I could exploit to break free. To no avail.

"You did not think the Lady of the Lake *really* came up with so convoluted a plan as to arrange for a mortal weapon to detonate through a Way ripped open from the Mortal Realm, and was simply lucky enough to sway Artur Pendragon with her much faded wiles to grant her access to Excalibur? When, if it had succeeded, would have granted my Lord the excuse to challenge the mortals for the damages wrought, and require from them restitution in the manner of a share of their power?"

"Did you not wonder how Morgana managed to slip her bonds, when her own sister oversaw her imprisonment? Allowing her to escape, and begin spreading chaos throughout all the Realms?" She continued, as all the little lines started to cross over. Like the ones used in detective shows where the hero starts to use string to connect all the seemingly random events, revealing everything had been connected and orchestrated by a single insane genius or certifiable lunatic. Oberon fitted both, to be honest. "How she acquired the services of a mortal capable to building her a new body, breaching numerous Accord laws, and set up the very Furies to be vanquished. Removing them as a threat to my Lord?"

"Or did you think it not odd that Oberon himself would fall victim to Morgana so easily? That he should succumb to the influence of her shade, be persuaded to threaten the very life of his Lady? When my Lord is master of all Ivory itself Nay, even the whole immortal Realm?" She mocked with a sharp smile. "A little nudge here, a pretence of weakness there ... my Lord has worked unceasingly to create events to jeopardise the status quo of the Realms, and grant him the opportunity to seize control."

Puck stopped in front of me, and tapped me on my nose. I wanted to bite those fingers off, the beast in me talking but I was happy to listen right there and then.

"But of course, you kept fudging it all up." She shook her head, adopting a woeful expression. "The proverbial spanner in the works, the bull in the china shop. Wrecking carefully laid plans, breaking delicate strategies and ruining investments lain to rest and mature. And my Lord has had enough."

"One lone lycan. You were just a tool, for the Lady to use and then dispose of. Not a great ask, my Lord thought. But she couldn't even manage to do that simple job. Such a wretched mistake, but one that cost her her immortal life." The fae sighed with great theatre. This wasn't for me, she was performing on some stage in her mind, enjoying the delights of expounding my foolishness to an unseen audience. "You were never meant to vanquish Dagur at the Beltane Tourney, instead he was *meant* to escape and pose a significant threat to the Realms. Enough for my Lord to raise a call to arms and steer the Courts towards the mortals having been to blame for the Twilight fae's evasion."

"One thing after another, wrecking carefully laid plans. Ruining the intricate web my Lord spun."

"You might have wondered why Herne and the Harrowed Queen were chosen, stolen away by these foolish, easily manipulated mortals?" Puck asked, and I snarled at the realisation Herne's taking hadn't been an accident. It was connected, which meant his death lay at Oberon's feet as well. "The Hunter, well, we were all meant to believe he sought out the abomination for your sake. To learn of its links to you, what a father might feel could pose significant danger to his son. But my Lord suspected an ulterior motive, and this was confirmed when the Hunter sought to return to his Court with her alive and unharmed. Having granted her safety."

"And it is why my Lord seeks to silence her before any might talk to her." She shook her head. "He cares not of the part of her that comes from Beyond. The *death of immortals* we know to fear. No. What my Lord wishes to know is what remains of the other … *Morgana*. She who he freed, who he manipulated and led so carefully. He thinks there is a chance a shred of his cousin remains in the abomination, and that shred might know of his … involvement in her plans for freedom and domination. Which he cannot allow any other to learn."

"So, both had to be silenced. The Hunter, sacrificed to further the madness these petty mortals could sow, allow them to breach more Accord laws and so grant him the right to move against them *lawfully*." The fae smiled, as I snarled out my impotent rage. "And the Harrowed Queen ... well, since you failed to finish her off as I had intended, then I believe she will just have to fall to some accident before she reaches the Wyld Court. That would normally fall to one of the lesser members of the Court, but my Lord has commanded that *I* deal with this matter. So once we are finished here ... well, my schedule still seems quite busy."

She reached down and plucked the antidote from my fingers, the armour not allowing me to even stop her doing that. Bloody fae magic! If I survived this, I was done with using their *gifts*. No matter how helpful they had been, they only led to trouble.

"Do not fear. I will deliver this vial to your Alpha in your stead." The fae told me, holding it up and glancing at the shimmering liquid contained inside. "If she still lives, I would that she survives her interaction with these mortals. She was never on my list to deal with, and she and your pack might still prove useful in the coming times. Cleaning up the mess that undoubtedly will occur. That sort of menial task."

She tapped the howler to her lips, eyeing me even as rumbling shivers ran through the cavern and cracks began to inch their way across the concrete.

"Of course, this all should indicate that *you* are not part of my Lord's ongoing plans. A matter I know have to deal with." Puck ticked the vial away into a pocket before drawing one of her very sharp knives.

She idly traced it over my chest, finally letting it settle against my throat.

"My Lord wishes me to kill you. Make sure you are no longer a problem to haunt him. Given the trouble you have caused him, restoring the true Lord of Twilight and providing Sanctuary to the one creature who *might* be able to reveal his involvement in so many troublesome events ... well, you can hardly blame him, can you?"

I growled, throwing all my strength into reconnecting with my Wyld might. Even reaching for the Shadow brand, to see if I could freeze the Ivory fae. Or even myself, maybe shattering the armour constraining me. But it was like neither existed, both robbed from me in this moment. What the fuck was going on?

The Ivory fae peered around me and let the knife fall back as she stepped round to cross to stand by Dr Bremmer. The strzyga was still groaning and foaming from his mouth, twisted body twitching and jerking but he had somehow managed to get to his hands and knees. She looked down on the creature with no pity in her eyes, and rested the howler against the domed skull.

The blast from the weapon knocked the warped mortal back down, body shredding as the vibrations ripped into him. He screamed, neck snapping back and mouth gaping as she lashed him again and again, until his cries were mere hoarse gasps of agony, and his body was a mess of ribboned flesh and black bleeding ichor. The fae casually wiped the tip of the howler against her leg, leaving a line of dark filth, before walking slowly back to face me.

"However, I am a fickle thing." She told me with a hard smile, her eyes glinting mischievously. "And your actions to save your comrades and loved ones cannot be ignored. Simply slaying you whist you stand there, unable to move … well, that sits badly with me."

She slid her knife back into its sheath, and reached to her neck and pulled out a long black key from where it hung on a long chain. The sort you see used in old locks, with an intricate head made up of multiple teeth projecting in every direction.

The fae held this up, so I could taste it's essence. Very strong magic, enough to make my eyes sting and head throb. I hadn't felt anything like it before.

"This is *my* portal key." She told me, tapping it against her chin thoughtfully. "It is unique, there is not another like it in all existence. I had it forged by both Ivory *and* Shadow smiths, neither fully knowing what it was they were creating. And both now long gone to their graves with its secret."

"You see, portal keys can open up gates … Ways … to almost any*where*." She explained, me her captive audience. When she'd told me Oberon wanted her to kill me, and the whole bloody place was falling down around us. She chose to *lecture*, for fuck's sake. "Unless wards block their access, a portal key can allow its user to venture anywhere they are familiar with, and oft times places only glimpsed in dreams. Or nightmares."

"However, the user will find that they will arrive at the same moment they departed their previous location. Portal keys allow passage to any*where* as I said, not any*when*." She smiled like the Bayun Cat as she indicated her key."

"Except this one."

"My key will only allow passage to *one* place. No other." Puck shrugged as this was of no matter. "It is a place I found useful oft times to have a moment to myself. A reprieve from Court intrigue and somewhere I might go where no one may find me. It *also* happens to be a very handy place to send individuals who I want to vanish. Disappear. Never be seen again."

"For without my key, once they are there, they find the place …. Most unpleasant. Inhospitable. Not suitable for long term habitation." She activated the key, the ritual beginning to draw power. As Dr Bremmer should have done the moment we appeared. It felt like cold fingers running over my bones, a weight settling down to press me to the floor. "And without my key, there is no return from this place. A *when* that none have ever appeared back from, except I."

"Yes, I think it a suitable place to send you." The fae laughed brightly, as my guts roiled. This couldn't be it. There had to be some last play, something I was forgetting. Anything. "My Lord will have no knowledge of you, in fact any who scry for you will find you gone. Lost. Beyond all succour, any aid."

"As the mortals say … you will be, to them, deceased as a dead parrot. If they have wit enough to understand the reference."

I grunted, a thought making me smile nastily.

"Won't work. Fine, you'll tell them I'm dead." I replied with as much of a grin as I could manage. Which, to be fair, was not much. Not when I faced imminent translocation to someplace that sounded truly fucked up. "But I'm a lycan. If I die, my spirit will cross over. I'd be found in the Wyld. If I don't show, they'll know something's not right."

Puck thought for a moment, then simply shrugged.

"Then I will lie. Tell them this mortal had one last trick up his sleeve. Powers he was granted from his contact with the abomination, or the creature he called his god from Beyond." She blithely admitted. "In my tale, you heroically saved me from certain death, taking a grievous wound that devoured your utter essence. Allowing me to escape with the antidote for your Alpha, to ensure your friends and loved ones made it to safety. You will die a hero, Errant. That is the least I can do for you."

"The least you can do for me is fall over dead right now." I grunted back, my brief hope flitting away on fairy wings. Puck was renowned as the all time liar of liars. If she spun a tale, I didn't doubt she'd have everyone believing it without too much effort. "You're reneging on what Oberon wants. That's betrayal."

"Only a smidgeon." She replied with a sharp smile. "And if I'm honest, the Lord of Ivory has made some … *questionable* decisions of late. Involving mortals far too much, risking the Realms by opening a breach to the Beyond and allowing them to contact the things that exist there. I am making my decision on what I feel is right, not purely on what I am ordered to do."

"Besides, where I'm sending you, it's only a short step away from immediate death anyhow."

I watched as the key glowed a deep dark virulence, power building in it. So strong, it made the cavern shake. More rocks fell from the ceiling, crashing into the boats lined against the pier and breaking them apart with shattering roars. Puck remained stable on her feet, and I was bound upright. The strzyga screamed as pieces of the cave hammered down on him, further smashing his essence and smearing it over the floor.

"Where the fuck are you throwing me?" I roared over the deep thrum that began to fill the air, as I felt something begin to drag at me. Like gravity, or the depths of the sea. Pulling me, inexorably towards my certain doom.

Sarah. If this was my last moment of conscious life, I wanted to picture her. Smiling, safe. Beside Bear, Felix and all my pack. My friends. This wasn't my time, not right now. Not when there was so much yet to be done …

To be said.

Puck smiled as darkness gathered around me, her eyes shining with pure delight as my own sight began to darken.

"Where, Errant?" She stepped in close, leaning in to whisper in my ear.

"You will soon find out." The fae told me with a smug smile.

As darkness crashed down on me, and I screamed my fury silently into the void.

Chapter 50

Puck remained standing in the cavern as the Way she had opened closed with a snap, the power fading and dying from her portal key. When it was safely at rest once more, the Ivory fae slipped it back in to rest against her skin. Close to her heart, so she knew where it was at all times.

The air shivered, and she drew a breath as the next moment, she was no longer alone in the cave with her strzyga.

"It is done." She told the newcomers, turning to face them where they stood. "I laid things on as thick as I possibly might, so ... well, you can tell your Queen, we shall just have to see."

Dark eyes locked with her own, as the Morrigan leant upon her gnarled staff. Clad in her armour, her raven bodyguards perched upon her shoulders, red eyes glaring out at the Ivory spy.

Beside her, a slim, tall woman stood. Clad in robes of earthen shades, her hood pulled up but long locks of jet black hair tumbling from within. Where her feet rested upon bare rock, even from only a moment's touch, small fungi blossomed up from the hard floor.

Margaret May Black. Black May. Newly anointed Crone of the Wyld.

The final figure was clad in woven grey robes, tall and tattooed with intricate silver wode. Her fae features were solemn, as befitted her station.

Skuld, Norn of Twilight. Sister of the three, she who saw the future.

"My son will surprise us all." Black May told Puck, who shrugged, indicating she might or might not believe that statement. Only time would tell. "*If* you have done as your Lady asked."

The spy smiled wolfishly.

"My Lord instructed that I end your son's life, so that he might pursue his plans without the distraction that particular lycan causes simply by drawing breath." She replied, her posture relaxed, unfazed by facing two very dangerous women. Two very powerful creatures. "However, my *Lady* asked me to assist in your endeavours, and to alter how I met that command in ways that might allow us all a chance of a future. Instead of the utter ruin that Shadow, and now Twilight, have glimpsed. And so I have done."

"As did we." The Morrigan commented dryly, as the crows shuffled for footing and hissed loudly, showing their purple tongues. "When Morgan called upon the Wyld and Shadow to aid him against you, we blocked him. To allow you to succeed in sending him to the only place where he might find what he needs. What we all need."

"What I have Seen." Skuld uttered, her tone cold as bitterest night.

"An answer to Oberon's madness. To the utter ruin he will wreak."

The spy nodded, and then gestured back to where the strzyga lay slumped on the floor.

"Oh, I know we did not agree to exchanges gifts at this meeting, but I feel two of you might approve of what I offer. The creature who brought down the Hunter. Son, and lover. The Errant's father." She smiled as the Morrigan's expression grew cold, and Black May's hands curled into claws. "I can imagine you will find some way to pay him back for his hubris, in such a manner that anything he might have heard is never told. I believe he is due an eternity of pain and suffering, and who better to meet out such a fate?"

Black May nodded once, looking across at the Morrigan.

"I lay claim to him. He took my lover. The father of my son." The Crone snarled, her eyes blazing from within the hood. "I shall find somewhere deep in Wyld where his screams will not be heard, but his death shall last till the end of times."

The Morrigan tapped her staff once on the ground.

"Then I cede my right to oversee his demise. Let him suffer for what he did to my son." She intoned, and the Wyld Crone gestured with her crooked fingers.

Vines erupted around the strzyga, who was still too broken to resist. He could only scream, his warped features stark with fear, as the crawling tendrils encased his tattered and ragged form … then sank back into the bedrock, taking him with them.

"Now, good ladies, I must away." The spy told the pair, holding up the detonation device. "This facility must be thoroughly destroyed, and Morgan's companions told my lies concerning the fate of the Errant. I shall return those he cares for back to their abodes, and then seek out my Lord to give him the … ah joyous news."

"That Morgan Black is dead."

The four women nodded, and three shimmered and vanished. Leaving the spy to take one look around her, before smiling brightly and addressing an invisible audience.

"And so, good night everyone. Show your appreciation by clapping your hands, and I, Robin Goodfellow, will make it up to you in return for your applause."

Laughing, she bowed deeply before turning on her heel, detonator held in her hand, stride taking the fae into the shadows … to vanish.

Chapter 51

I awoke.

That was a surprise, given what Puck had told me before she tossed me into a Way leading to … well, I had no fucking clue where the hell I was. Some place she used to dump people who upset her or her Lord.

Oberon.

That arrogant bastard. I had known most fae were inherently warped and lacking in even the base morality to keep their shit together and act for the common good. Immortality has a way of warping what one thinks of as right and wrong. Good and evil become the same side of a coin.

But to hear how thoroughly the Lord of Ivory had been fucking with things, for so long, simply because he wanted to be the king of the hill, the lord of all and with the most power … the lives he had wasted, the deaths he'd caused without a care. The utter, ignorant, selfish, megalomaniacal *bastard*.

He needed to be stopped.

Now I just had to work out how the fuck I could do that. Wherever the fuck I was.

The darkness receded and I blinked my eyes, tasking ash and smoke that layered grit on my tongue and made me want to hack out a furball. Instead, I tasted the taint in the air, knowing it to be familiar. I had smelt the same when Morgana had made her play and attacked London to distract the mortals from her real goal, to steal the throne of Twilight.

This was the aroma of total destruction.

And as I gazed around me, I realised I knew where I was.

Horribly so.

I stood on broken concrete, slabs that had once been paved as a path. With railings set to ward the idiots and incautious from falling headlong into the fast flowing river known world-wide as the Thames.

But not anymore.

Beyond the blasted, twisted and pitted path, the land dropped away to a dried up and cracked plain of mud, muck and mire. Metal poles, legs from old piers or the rotting remains of boats that had once plied the waters, stuck up like rusted skeletons of beasts long dead. The stink was horrendous, the mud black and viscous, and it contained shapes that my eyes slowly made sense of, disjointed and broken as they were.

Arms. Legs. An upthrust head. Bodies broken and shattered. Tossed to the mud to sink into nothingness.

The Thames had become a charnel pit.

Looking up, I cast around but what greeted my eyes was the same everywhere I looked. Shattered, broken buildings smudged with old smoke or still burning with licks of hungry fire. Where once had been an avenue of trees, only rotten stubs of wood thrust up from the pavement now, withered and blackened.

The building in front of me looked to have been hit repeatedly by something heavy. Possibly a wrecking ball, maybe a bomb. Or several. The top third was a shattered mess, struts sticking out of broken concrete, the odd shard of glass glinting in the gloom. But no matter the ruined state, there was no way I could mistake the place where I had spent so much time. Lived so much of my life.

My home. It was a ruin, hollowed out and broken.

What the fuck had happened?

When the fuck was I?

I cast down river, looking for the familiar sight of Tower Bridge, of the Tower of London lurking behind it. But all I could see was rubble and ruin, the once great spar that had spanned the Thames now a twisted jumble of metal and stone, most of its length broken off and tumbled to the mud far below. And the Tower … that looked to be in even worse state than my home, the towers it was famous for simply gone, its walls collapsed inward. Smoke hung over it, a pall that no wind could shift.

London was dead.

There was nothing living in the air, no scent of another nearby that I could taste. No sound above the quiet howl of a wind that chilled me to the bone, as I stood looking out over the devastation. All I could think of was my friends, my loved ones … where were they in this horror-strewn landscape? Did they still live?

Inexorably, my eyes slowly lifted, as if seeking some solace … some peace from the sky above me. But that was when the true horror of what had happened sparked to life in my numbed brain.

The sky was clear, the smoke wafting away to reveal the expanse of heaven above. And I could see more clearly than ever, as if the stain and pollution the mortals filled their air with had been ripped clean away, leaving nothing behind but the vast unending expanse of empty space.

Except it wasn't.

Hanging high above, huge beyond imagining, a mass of tentacles and claws and eyes hung. Lit against the vast blackness, the behemoth loomed overhead, that massive eye glaring down on the world below. Beyond, deeper into the void, I saw other forms. Equally monstrous, equally huge, impossibly *there*. And I had seen them before.

Cthulhu.

Beyond, I saw the moon … or what was left of it. A broken sphere with fully a third of its mass shattered into lunar lumps, floating away like a blood trail. Its surface no longer shining white, but stained black and grey, mottled as if sickened. And beyond, some visible to my naked eye, I could see other planets equally destroyed. Their celestial bodies shattered, bleeding out their substance into space.

But at the same time, I realised there was something wrong with what I was seeing, as if two images had been superimposed one on top of the other. A flickering graininess that meant everything looked only half there, not entirely real.

Like the Beyond and our own Realms were merging, one into the other. Bleeding into each other, but so inimical one to the other that each was unravelling the other as they met.

And I realised just where Puck had dumped my arse, and just how impossible my task was to try and stop Oberon from fucking things up for everyone.

Because I was standing in the remains of our whole dominion, looking at the proof that *he'd already done it*. Shattered the Realms, broken the fundamental laws separating us from the Beyond. Brought two things together that never were meant to meet.

Destroyed it all.

The Cthulhu hung as if lifeless, and I could see at least one of the monsters was leaking matter from massive holes, rips torn in it's gigantic body. Its eye was grainy and blind, making me think there had been no winners here. No victor standing proud and tall over the field of battle.

This was the end. Of everything.

And I was all alone.

Everyone I had known, loved and cared for. Dead. My enemies, gone beyond any hope of my reaching them. Even the trace taste of magic I had always sensed in the Mortal Realm that told me Terra remained our guardian, lost.

Only me.

Alone.

This was it. The worst situation I had ever found myself, with no clue whatsoever how to even start to un-fuck this mess.

For *real*.

Morgan's story, and that of the Pack, will conclude in Book Ten – Gone To The Dogs.

Coming soon.

About the Author

Born the fourth son of the sprawling Cameron Clan, JP Cameron was introduced to the wonder of words and story-telling with the magical tale of The Hobbit, as one of the first books he remembers.

Taking The Lord of the Rings to primary school as his book for class set his feet firmly on a path, an endless road and a love of the fantastical, strange and magical.

Through school, work and into adult life (what little of that he knows), JP continues to expand his library and scope of writing, exploring other genres and inventing strange new worlds. But his love of fantasy remains at the core of his writing. Living with his wife and their hairy behemoth disguised as a Chow Chow in the green rolling hills of West Sussex, he is often found gazing happily at bookshelves groaning with volumes by Sir Terry Pratchett, Terry Goodkind, Terry Brooks and many, many more authors not called Terry.

Otherwise you may meet him up and down the UK coastline, celebrating a rich and happy history of piracy in fine company.

His published works to date include Tales of the Blade, and The Spire set, and now his debut into dark fantasy – The Lycan Files.

Find him at @JPCAuthor for tweets and questions.